ROMAN

UNPARALLELED OUTRAGE

By

John William McMullen

This book is a work of historical fiction. The people, places, events, and situations in this story are based upon the true story of the Reverend Roman Weinzapfel, O.S.B. (1813-1895).

ISBN: 1-4107-1460-8 (e-book)
ISBN: 1-4107-1461-6 (Paperback)
ISBN: 1-4107-1462-4 (Dust Jacket)

This book is printed on acid free paper.

1stBooks - rev. 04/29/03

Acknowledgments

A word of thanks is in order to the Ohio Township Library of Warrick County, Indiana, Willard Library of Evansville, Saint Meinrad Archabbey Library, Philadelphia Free Library, The Knox County (Indiana) Public Library, and especially to the staff of the Evansville-Vanderburgh County Library for my seemingly endless requests for books and inter-library loans.

The deepest of gratitude is extended to the late Virgil F. Timmermeyer, who completed his Masters Thesis on this infamous case in 1973, entitled, *The Reverend Roman Weinzaepfel: An incident in American Nativism.* (M.A. thesis, Catholic University of America); The Rev. Herman Alerding, for his great work, *The History of the Catholic Church in the Diocese of Vincennes*, (published in Indianapolis 1883); and the *Trial of Romain Weinzoepflen, Catholic Priest at Evansville, Vanderburgh County, Indiana, on a Charge of Rape, preferred by Mrs. Anna Maria Schmoll; held at Princeton, State of Indiana, Gibson Circuit Court, March Term, 1844, on a change of Venue from the Vanderburgh Circuit: Reported by A.E. Drapier, printer, stenographer, &c.,* (Louisville, Kentucky, 1844); *Early Protestant-Catholic Relations in Southern Indiana and the 1842 Case of Roman Weinzaepfel*, an article by C. Walker Gollar, *The Indiana Magazine of History*, September, 1999; *The Journals and Letters of Mother Theodore Guérin*, Edited by Sr. Theodosia Mug, S.P., Saint Mary-of-the-Woods, IN, Providence Press, 1937; *The History of the Sisters of Providence of Saint Mary-of-the-Woods*, by Sr. Mary Borromeo Brown, S.P., New York, Benziger Bros., 1949; *The Catholic Church in the Diocese of Vincennes, 1847-1877*, Sr Mary Carol Schroeder, Washington, Catholic University of America Press, 1946; *The Protestant Crusade, 1800-1860*, by Ray Allen Billington, MacMillan, New York, 1938; and *The History of Saint Meinrad Archabbey, 1854-1954*, by Rev. Albert Kleber, O.S.B., Abbey Press, St. Meinrad, IN, 1954.

The following newspapers containing references to the case were consulted: The Louisville *Catholic Advocate*, The Louisville *Public Advertiser*, The Brookville (IN) *Indiana American*, *The Evansville Journal*, *The Vincennes Gazette*, and *The Vincennes Sun*.

I also thank those members of the Weinzapfel family who graciously offered me assistance in this project by providing me with several of Roman's letters and oral traditions about their "Great Uncle Father Roman," particularly Wilfred Weinzapfel. Also a special thanks goes to Mike and Esther (Weinzapfel) Stofleth, and their daughter, Christan (Stofleth) Shockley, without whose essay I may have never thought to pursue this project.

Thanks to the Evansville attorneys, Tim Klingler, Mary Pulcini, and Stephen Thomas for their legal assistance and research in proofreading the trial scenes. Thanks also to Michael Goelz for providing me the special Kentucky recipe for frying passenger pigeon.

To Rev. Cyprian Davis, O.S.B., Jeanette Knapp, Sr. Gloria Memering, S.P., and Chandler Hagey, and all those, especially those at *Mater Dei*, who read the manuscript, thank you. Mike Whicker and Amy Craig deserve a special debt of gratitude for their editorial advice.

To Rev. Joseph Cox, O.S.B. and Rev. Simeon Daly, O.S.B., of Saint Meinrad Archabbey for their assistance in the Archabbey's Library; Steve Rode, Robert Gatterer, and Mark Heinig for their assistance in German translations; and Joan Vickery for her French translations. And all that either endured my reading aloud the unfinished manuscript or humored me by reviewing bits and pieces of it, your time in Purgatory will be shortened.

To Roger Sills and the art students at Mater Dei who translated my idea for the cover design into a computer graphic.

To my fellow writers, Jean Becker, Doug Bovinet, Al Letcher, Judy Lyden, M.G.B. McMullen, Jim Stone, and Mike Whicker for their constant encouragement and constructive criticism.

To Andrew Martin McMullen and Theodore Guérin McMullen for their patience while their Daddy disappeared into the 1840s.

Lastly, and most importantly, I thank my beloved wife, Mary Grace Bernardin McMullen, without whose faith, hope and love this book would never have been written.

Dedication

To the Benedictine Monks and Oblates of Saint Meinrad Archabbey

&

The Priests and People of the Diocese of Vincennes

—Ut in omnibus glorificetur Deus

That In All Things God May Be Glorified.

Saint Benedict, 480-547

"If you forgive others their transgressions, our heavenly Father will forgive you. But if you do not forgive others, neither will your heavenly Father forgive your transgressions."

Matthew 6.14-15

"Amen, I say to you, whatever you bind on earth shall be bound in heaven, and whatever you loose on earth shall be loosed in heaven."

Matthew 18.18

The Lord is close to the brokenhearted, those whose spirit is crushed He will save.

Psalm 34.19

Even Darkness is not dark for Thee, O Lord.

Psalm 139.12

Chapter 1

Apprehension

6 May 1842

Vanderburgh County, Indiana

Father Roman Weinzoepfel nervously opened the cabinets in the sacristy looking for Mr. and Mrs. Schmolls' marriage agreement before he remembered where he had placed the document. He moved through the doorway to his small bedchamber, opened the top drawer of his dresser, pulled out the paper, folded it, and put it inside his shirt pocket underneath his cassock. Returning to the sacristy, he opened the parish record book, angrily dipped his quill pen and scratched out the Schmolls' marriage validation, letting the black ink bleed over the written date of May first.

Placing his black priestly biretta atop his head, he went around to the rear of the church and saddled his horse, Shadow. Taking the reins in his left hand, the agile twenty-nine year old stepped up on the horse and sat down. Balancing himself in the saddle, he squeezed his legs into the horse's sides, and tugged at the reins. He pressed his heels into Shadow's flank, nudging him forward, cantering up the muddy dung-covered, fly infested street.

As Roman brushed away flies, he reached for his rosary to make sure it was dangling at his right side. Taking the relic into his right hand he fingered each wooden bead, inching his way to the well-worn silver corpus of the crucifix.

Once past *Bulls' Head Tavern* at Eighth and Main, he snapped Shadow's reins and called out, achieving a full gallop. A part of him wanted to ride off into the Illinois prairie and continue as far west as Indian Territory, or he could ride east to Louisville and easily board a boat to New Orleans. Or again, he could take a train from Cincinnati to the Atlantic and set sail for Europe. The thoughts were tempting. *Oh, to be anywhere but Evansville, Indiana. Is this my last day as a free man?*

I am to be hanged.

A few miles north on the Vincennes Road, Roman caught sight of a horse and rider coming in from the country. He made out the face of the man as the figure hastened closer. It was Martin Schmoll.

Roman anxiously pulled the reins of his horse to a stop.

Schmoll spoke first. "I've just come from my father-in-law's."

"I found the agreement." Roman reached in his cassock and produced the document.

"Hold on to it for now." Martin put his hand out as if to stop the priest from handing it to him.

"No, I insist. You wanted it this morning. It's yours." Roman continued to hold it out to Mr. Schmoll. "I regret the trouble that it caused you."

Schmoll grabbed it out of Roman's hand, jerking it away. At once he tore it, scattering the pieces to the wind. He stared at him, squinting in the light. "There. Now where are you going, priest?"

"I'm on my way to see the bishop." Roman's eyes fixed on Schmoll's revolver strapped to his side.

"You'd best stay in Evansville. Wait a few days. Let's not make this into something worse than it already is." Roman sensed that despite what was said the matter was not about to be dropped. Schmoll glared, called out to his caramel colored horse, and snapped the reins causing the beast to whinny and break off in a mad gallop.

I am sure to be hanged.

All his years of penitence and self-denial, even the wearing of a penitential hairshirt, hadn't prevented his coming to this hour. And in his agony, he felt no angel of mercy sent to comfort him. There was no Cyrenian to help him carry his burden up the narrow path to Golgotha.

In his mind, angst violently thundered along with a migraine headache. Approaching the Long farm he thought of his visit there December last when he had prepared Mrs. Long for death. *Anna Maria, I grieved for your mother as if she was my own, yet you mourned her passing by marrying a Protestant, engaging in drunkenness and debauchery.*

He tugged at Shadow's reins as someone else emerged from behind a line of trees along a curve in the path. He recognized the white spotted horse belonging to Anna Maria's father, Louis Long. He braced himself for the worst. The look on Long's face said it all.

He knows.

2

If an arrest warrant was to be issued, then Roman must remain in town. If he fled, then his action would betray guilt.

"Where do you think you're going?" The old man stopped ten feet from him.

"To the Fitzwilliams'." Roman touched his biretta, acknowledging the man. "Their baby was born early this morning. I'm on my way to baptize her."

"You didn't think I'd find out, did you? I should have known what you were up to the night you came to my house. Imagine, dishonoring my daughter while her mother lay dying in the next room. No wonder the girl felt compelled to marry Martin. She's carrying your child!"

The sharpened words pierced him through like a knight-errant's sword.

"Mr. Long, allow me to explain. Surely you don't—"

"No. You listen to me, priest. In my daughter's love for God and the Church she was willing to bear the fruit of your loins to save the Church from scandal! You're an insult to the name of God and all religion. I wish I'd never met you."

"There must be some way to convince you—" He tugged at his collar and pinched the skin about his neck. The heat of the sun felt like a blaze upon his back.

"Just stay away from me. I'm on my way to town to visit my daughter."

"This afternoon I am off to see the bishop in Vincennes concerning your daughter."

"If I were you, I'd hold off telling the bishop anything."

"I'll return on the morrow."

"I'll inform my son-in-law you're leaving town." Long clenched his jaw and secured his hat, spurring his ride away.

Roman struggled to pray the remainder of his rosary, but the thought of Mrs. Schmoll rendered his devotion vapid. Squeezing the rosary with his right hand, he ran the fingers of his left up and down the front of his cassock, pinching and pulling at the buttons, obsessed with the thought of ravishing Anna Maria Schmoll.

He finished the rosary, crossed himself, and kissed the crucifix. The green of the budding trees and the hills' smell of spring were familiar reminders of happier days, but the anguish of the accusations continually jolted him back to reality.

3

When he arrived at the Fitzwilliams' farm he dismounted Shadow and tied him to the hitching post. The midday sun was shining down brightly upon the treeless clearing of farmland and pasture, scorching him in his black cassock as he walked to the house. Mr. Fitzwilliams came out of his barn pushing a wheelbarrow. Dinner wasn't quite ready so Roman said he would pass the time by remaining outside to pray his office. He took the breviary from his saddlebag and opened it, finding his place for the noon hour prayer.

Walking up and down the road he flipped the ribbons, meditating upon the Scripture, attempting to offer his chalice of suffering to God, hoping to unite his anguish to the cross of the Savior. Familiar psalms graced his tongue yet the words remained upon the page far from his heart.

Strangely he heard no birds singing, only the hum of honeybees, the thrum of May beetles, and the whir of flies around the pigsty. *The noonday devil tempts the Christian to abandon resolve and despair of hope.* He knelt in the grass and prayed the *Angelus*.

The stillness of his midday rest was displaced when two armed men on horseback drew near. Roman focused upon his prayer trying to ignore the men even though he was sure they had come for him. Looking up from his breviary again, he saw the two men dismount their rides watching his every move. They were speaking with Mr. Fitzwilliams who had just walked out of his house. Roman clutched his rosary beads as the revelation stabbed his heart. The glint of sunlight reflected off the silver badges upon the men's chests. They were constables, representatives of American law and justice.

As he neared the porch, the two riflemen closed in upon him. Stepping forward, they presented themselves. Only one of them spoke. "Are you the priest, Mr. Roman Weinzoepfel?"

"I am the *Reverend* Roman Weinzoepfel, yes."

"I have a warrant for your arrest." Both of the men moved to grab his arms.

"Arrest? On what charge?"

"For the assault, battery, and rape of Mrs. Martin Schmoll."

"Schmoll! Traitor!" Roman clenched his jaw shut.

As the handcuffs clamped shut around his wrists, the men helped him to his horse. As the constables led him back to Evansville, Roman thought of the events that had led him to this unfortunate moment.

4

Chapter 2

Vincennes

Autumn 1839

On the thirteenth of October *The Republican* had floated into the port of New Orleans, a bulk of splintered driftwood, sagging sails, and fractured paddle wheels, over two and a half months since leaving Strasbourg and setting sail from *Le Havre*, France. After seven days aboard a steamboat traveling north on the Mississippi and Ohio Rivers, Roman finally arrived in Vincennes on the twenty-first of October.

He had expected that the Bishopric city would be more civilized and urbane. However, the first thing he saw was that none of the streets were paved with blocks of stone. *What kind of place is this? The streets are paved with dung!* The others with him asked the same questions and others like them. The stench of manure and sights and sounds of flies and livestock filled the air. The horses and cows grazed wherever they pleased, on the street or in the woods and there were hogs everywhere, possibly numbering in the thousands: sows, boars, and piglets all, scurrying up and down the alleyways and in the yards. It seemed no one had erected a fence. The hogs ran, freely up and down the main roads throughout the village. For this was a village, not a city, and hardly a seat for a diocese. *What kind of a people are these Americans?* The sheer spectacle of squealing and grunting pigs running wild bordered on the absurd.

"Where's the Cathedral," he leaned out and asked the whip.

"There on the left," the whip answered. "Saint Francis Xavier's." Roman kept looking but saw only a simple brick structure. He was anticipating a grand cathedral in the wilderness, expecting to see a glowing gold fleur-de-lis cross towering over the See city. Instead, there was hardly a church and certainly no steeple, save for a small cupola or belfry where a steeple should be. It was so different from the Strasbourg Cathedral.

Monseigneur Hailandière told us things were primitive, but this primitive?

5

****

Once settled in Vincennes, Roman took up residence in the seminary. The dormitory was one long room in the school itself and each bed consisted of narrow planks covered with straw, far different from his former accommodations at the Jesuit Seminary in the heart of Strasbourg. A few short weeks into his new life in America found him joining the ranks of most clerics, who had willingly tucked their cassocks and birettas in their trunks in exchange for civilian work clothes. A pervasive anti-Catholicism had all the seminarians in its grip. It seemed to Roman that fear was the order of the day in the New World.

The days passed swiftly as autumn became winter. Roman passed his first Christmas in America. He discovered that Indiana winters were as extreme in their harsh cold and deep snow as autumn had been in its unseasonable heat and humidity.

One cold February morning in 1840, as he sat at the dining table of the Vincennes seminary, the seminarians began discussing, rather heatedly, Bishop Hailandière and his massive building campaign. It was a plan to erect new schools and churches for the burgeoning number of Catholic immigrants entering the diocese, as well as to build an Episcopal palace for himself and his successors. In the meantime, he would also secure more missionaries to meet the spiritual needs of his flock. Yet many in the diocese, priest and parishioner alike, questioned the ambitious plans for his mansion, claiming it disproportionate to the meager resources available for providing the sacramental needs of the faithful.

"I believe his Lordship is correct in his objective," replied Monseigneur Abbé Augustine Martin, the Vicar General of the diocese, raising a cautious hand. "He is, however, perhaps moving a bit too hastily for some members of the clergy." Roman thought that Abbé Martin's tone conveyed some reservations. "Nonetheless, he is our bishop, and it is not our place to question his judgment. His Lordship's most recent announcement is quite exciting," Abbé Martin continued. "The Congregation of the Holy Cross in France has tentatively promised to establish a college and religious house somewhere in the diocese of Vincennes. It is to be called *Notre Dame*. He also intends to bring the French Sisters of Providence to Terre Haute, Indiana to open a college for girls. Sister Theodore Guérin is to be the Mother Superior. She is a most competent and able woman. She and the bishop knew each other in Rennes."

This news caused much excited talk at the table, but Roman was disengaged from it all. Homesickness and the onslaught of a migraine headache had beset him that morning.

The seminarians rose as Abbé Martin led the after-meal prayer of thanksgiving. Roman excused himself and started toward the dining room door to begin another day of study when the Abbé approached him. "Roman, I must speak with you," he said, tugging at Roman's cassock sleeve with some urgency.

"Yes Abbé. What is it?" he anxiously asked.

"The bishop wishes to meet with you this morning."

"This morning? What does it concern, if I may ask?"

"It concerns your ordination."

"My ordination?"

"Meet me outside his Lordship's study in fifteen minutes."

Abbé Martin hurried out the door before Roman could question him further.

He knew it. He had heard the stories all too often before back in Strasbourg. A seminarian, one or two years away from ordination, called into the rector's office, informed that he had been found an unworthy candidate for priesthood.

****

Roman sat waiting in the west parlor, down the hall from Bishop Celestin Hailandière's study. He recalled another time, just months prior, when he sat waiting on Hailandière in the Archbishop's palace in Strasbourg. There was always anxiety surrounding a meeting with this strange and unpredictable man, but the anxiety was far worse this time. He thought of any possible transgression he might have committed since his arrival in Vincennes. *I haven't missed Mass or Choir. I'm progressing well in my studies.* The questions raced through his mind. What would he do now? Would he return home a failure? Should he stay in America? What possible life was there for him if he did not become a priest? He had really never considered any other options. The Church was his life.

Despite the welcoming fire in the fireplace, Roman shivered. Acknowledging Abbé Martin when he entered the hall, Roman concentrated hard upon presenting the calm exterior for which he was known, lest revealing his anxiety. He rubbed his index finger nervously back and forth across a slightly worn and frayed spot on the arm of the red silk chair upon which he sat. He caught himself and stopped as Abbé Martin glanced over at him, giving him an enigmatic smile. He was unsure whether it was a smile of reassurance or pity.

Roman checked his irritation that was building within. He felt in his pocket for his treasured rosary, the same rosary that had brought him safely through the storm at sea and the first few months in this alien land. He ran his thumb along the smooth and worn silver corpus, allowing the cross to plant into his palm. He stared down at his black, three-ridged biretta dangling in his hands, balancing it with the tips of his fingers as he sat on the edge of his chair.

His Lordship at last entered the room with all the stately pomp of a king. He was clad in his long close-fitting purple cassock with tight sleeves and red buttons from his collar to the floor. The matching purple mozzetta, a short cape, covered his shoulders. His magenta cope of silk about his shoulders nearly reached his feet and was fastened under his chin by the morse. The silk biretta atop his head was crowned with a tassel. Unlike the standard priestly biretta, the bishop's was the traditional magenta colored square cap with four ridges, owing to his doctoral degree of divinity.

Roman, nearly forgetting protocol due to the grandiose presence the bishop exuded in his Episcopal garb, rose to greet His Lordship when he saw that Abbé Martin was already on one knee kissing his ring. Roman genuflected and kissed the large signet ring on Hailandière's extended hand. He stood back up and bowed his head slightly, careful to speak in French. "Your Grace."

Roman dropped his biretta.

"You dropped something." Hailandière cleared his throat.

"*Merci.*" He picked it up off the floor.

"You may be seated." The bishop motioned toward the chairs. Roman and Abbé Martin obediently sat while the Bishop remained standing. The bishop removed his biretta revealing the round magenta zuchetto skullcap covering his matted-down, graying hair. He paced back and forth, as if he was to address them on some monumental subject, fidgeting with his biretta until he placed it on his desk. He stopped amidst his stride, clasped his hands, and intertwined his long, smooth fingers around the bejeweled gold pectoral cross pinned to one of the red cassock buttons at the base of the mozzetta.

"There is a reason I have called you here this morning, Roman." His Lordship paused from caressing his cross and restlessly adjusted the gold signet ring on his left hand. Roman feared to take another breath lest he miss the bishop's words. "Roman Weinzoepfel, you are to be ordained as soon as possible."

Roman's mind reeled and his stomach twisted in a whir of emotion. He was relieved that he was still considered a worthy candidate for priesthood, and that his fears were not to be realized, yet he was still overwhelmed at the sudden announcement.

"Know that our Vicar General, Monseigneur Augustine Martin, was made aware of this decision. He expressed some reservations at first, but after some thought, I am quite sure he has come to see the wisdom of such a decision." Hailandière glared down with commanding authority at his vicar general who refused to look up.

"If it please Your Lordship, I pray I may humbly state my concerns once more," interjected Abbé Martin.

"It does not please me, Augustine," the Bishop straightened his back, still standing. "But then again," he said, regaining his composure with a smile, "you must always feel free to express your opinions to your Lord Bishop."

Roman was struck by the discord between Hailandière and Abbé Martin. The camaraderie between the two evidenced months ago was now gone.

"Your Lordship, you had originally promised to give Roman two years to finish his theological training and acclimate to the customs of the American way of life, becoming proficient in the English language."

"Augustine! He speaks the language well enough. My distinguished English priest, Reverend Michael Edgar Evelyn Shawe has taught him well. Why, Roman speaks English better than I ever will!" Roman knew that the truth of the matter was that His Lordship refused to learn English, let alone speak it.

"But what about his headaches?" The abbé protested.

"Everyone has headaches! Why, I have one now!" He frowned at Abbé Martin.

"But the doctor here in Vincennes has been treating him for headaches."

"There are doctors in—" The bishop stopped and looked at Roman, perhaps not wanting to reveal where he was going to send him. "There are doctors where I am sending him. He will be fine." He glanced at Roman. "Isn't that right, Sub-Deacon Roman?"

"My Lord—" Roman had hardly opened his mouth before the abbé continued.

"These are migraine headaches, Your Grace," the abbé sighed. "They are more severe. During his time here in Vincennes, the doctor has been working on a remedy."

"Roman *will* be ordained this spring. Prepare him accordingly." Hailandière turned to look out the window. Roman was taken aback by the brusqueness of his bishop.

"But the doctor has cautioned that due to his affliction we should wait," the abbé persisted. Roman was uncomfortable as the tension increased. "Besides, I am hesitant to allow it, owing to his need for further theological studies. I am certain that his Lordship wants priests who have a solid understanding of the Church and her teachings."

"He is a sub-deacon. He is close enough!" His Lordship turned back toward the two.

"Precisely my point. He is merely a sub-deacon, not even a deacon yet."

"Inconsequential." The bishop angrily shook his head.

"But your Lordship, he must serve as a deacon before priestly ordination. It is the Church's own rule."

"It's a mere formality for my Canon lawyer, Reverend Shawe, to sort out. I intend to dispense with all that. It has been done before. Roman has the necessary detachment from the world and he has a gifted mind. His professors in Strasbourg noted prudence and prayer as his greatest gifts."

"But must we act in such haste?"

"*I* am the Bishop," Hailandière clenched his teeth and smacked his hands on his desk. His face was red with rage as he leaned towards the two men. "I need priests! How do you propose I serve the multitude of Catholic immigrants that are settling in this area without priests?"

"*Multitude*, your Lordship? Is that not a bit of an overstatement on your part?"

"The Irish are already here and more Germans are arriving everyday. And I can assure you that many more are coming. The unrest in Europe is too great. I want this young man ordained and I want him ordained at once. The matter is settled. Do you understand?"

The argument had escalated to the point where the two could have come to blows. Roman fingered his rosary, silently telling an *Ave*, his eyes closed, his lips mouthing the words.

"Bishop, could I have a few words with you in private." Abbé Martin said after a momentary pause which seemed eternal.

"There are no secrets here. You are the vicar-general. I am the bishop."

"Célestin. Please."

"Very well," he agreed.

Roman moved into the hall as the heavy wooden door closed behind him. He sat in one of the high backed chairs in the hallway and waited. The silence was accompanied by the tick of the swinging pendulum of the grandfather clock that stood at the foot of the stairs at the end of the hall opposite the fireplace. A loud exchange between his Lordship and Abbé Martin suddenly exploded, shattering the silence.

The voices stopped as suddenly as they had erupted and the door swung open, spilling Abbé Martin out into the hallway.

Roman rose at once.

The door slammed shut. Abbé Martin sighed. "Roman, you are to be ordained deacon and priest on the fifth of April this year."

"But Abbé Martin, the Bishop gave me his word that I should have two years to prepare for ordination. Surely he hasn't gone back on his word? Has he?"

Without an acknowledgment or even a quick glance, Abbé Martin turned, disappeared into his study across the hall, and quickly shut the door.

Roman was alone.

****

On the fifth of April 1840, without much ceremony and with only a few parishioners on hand, Roman readied himself to be consecrated as the Reverend Roman Weinzoepfel, a priest forever in the Roman Catholic Rite.

He approached His Lordship Hailandière from the center aisle. The towering tongue shaped éclat-jeweled tiara crowned His Lordship's head as a helmet of salvation. Hailandière, seated upon the throne wearing white gloves in his full-length lavender Episcopal vestments-complete with train, shoulder cape, and champlevé liturgical cope- looked like the pope himself. Reverend Shawe stood at his right wearing a humeral veil, holding His Lordship's pastoral crosier, the symbol of the bishop's authority over his flock.

Roman draped his multiple priestly vestments in which he would be clothed over his left arm and carried a candle in his right hand, trembling as he processed up the steps of the sanctuary to kneel before the successor of the Apostles. Roman glanced up at the altar and saw in a painting the enraptured face of Saint Francis Xavier.

He had his mission.

****

6 April 1840

Roman's first mass was scheduled for Sunday, the seventh of April. That Saturday evening after vespers, he took dinner and went for a walk along the river. About an hour after sunset he entered the darkened cathedral to pray. He planned to make an all night prayer vigil in the cathedral, much like the night he spent in his native Ungersheim in Saint Michael's Church prior to leaving for America. He had resigned himself to the fact that much of the theology he would have learned in the seminary would now have to be learned as a priest.

Smiling, he walked past sawhorses and shovels that littered the front of the sanctuary. Hailandière's idea to create a crypt for the tomb of his predecessor, Bishop Simon Gabriel Bruté, under the sanctuary of the high altar caused a contentious debate in the parish. Hailandière had commissioned out-of-work Irish canal workers for the job. Some of the illustrious French parishioners said that all the Irishmen knew how to do was drink, dig, and weaken the integrity of the church. The double entendre was well understood.

Genuflecting reverently, Roman opened the gate of the communion rail and ascended the steps to the high altar lit only by votive candles. He lifted his arms and prayed aloud. *Let my prayer arise before you like incense, the raising of my hands like an evening oblation.* Afterwards, he knelt down and prostrated himself before the Blessed Sacrament. Lying prostrate in the sanctuary, he heard shifting sounds from under the church. Vibrations followed and then the western wall of the sanctuary began to visibly sag. He scrambled to his feet, catching his cassock on his shoe. He held his breath as suddenly the entire structure began to come down around him, the walls first, followed by the roof, culminating with an explosion of sound, and crowned with a massive cloud of dust.

A few seconds after the crashing rumble of the cave-in, he managed to crawl away and get to his feet. Coughing, he clung to the communion rail. Rubbing the dirt from his hair, he noticed he had lost his biretta.

Within moments of the collapse, Bishop Hailandière made his way into the cathedral. Spotting Roman leaning against some timbers where the altar steps used to be, he rushed over. "Roman! Father Roman, What happened? Are you all right?"

"Yes. A bit dazed, but undamaged, I think. I seem to have lost my biretta though." He bent down and lifted a timber, thinking he saw his missing hat.

"What happened?" His Lordship was now standing in front of him

"I was praying in the church when everything around me began to collapse."

"What did you do?" Hailandière's voice thundered.

"Nothing, bishop. I was praying when the walls began to collapse. I think it was an earthquake." He searched further for his biretta.

"No, it was no earthquake. It was those drunken Irishmen I had working for me! They dug out too much of the foundation and they weakened the whole building!" The bishop was mumbling under his breath as he crept over the mound of debris.

Roman climbed through the dust and joined his bishop in the main aisle of the nave. The apse of the church was completely destroyed and the expanse of the heavens shone down in the roofless sanctuary. The two men stood silently together in the blue moonlight that poured through the open cavity. They surveyed the damage and beheld the great oil painting of Saint Francis Xavier balanced atop a pile of rubble near Saint Joseph's altar. It was unscathed. The bishop's throne was also unharmed and the pillar to which it was attached was still erect.

Hailandière, nearly in tears, climbed the heap where the painting rested. "Am I ever relieved. Do you know this painting was a gift to my family from Napoleon Bonaparte?" He lifted it up, blowing dust off its canvas. "And the Cathedral throne was blessed and installed by Bishop Bruté."

Roman merely nodded. *Never mind the paintings or the building, I could have been killed.* The reality of what had just happened finally struck his conscious mind. "Your Excellency, I could've been killed."

"Well, thank God you were not. That would leave me with one less priest."

By now Abbé Martin, Reverend Shawe, and many of the seminarians had rushed into the collapsed church.

"Well, you had best go to bed, Father." Hailandière motioned to Roman like a father coaxing a child back to bed. "All of you! Just go to bed! I'll get some of the men of the parish to clean up the mess tomorrow."

Roman imagined His Lordship trying to put the church back together in time for morning Mass. The church looked like it had received cannon fire. Then he remembered what was scheduled for the next morning.

"What about my first Mass?"

"You *will* celebrate your first Mass," Hailandière boomed. "We will provide an altar. Have no fear. The people of our diocese can wait no longer for an additional priest." At that His Lordship stepped over some downed beams and broken plaster, and stood in front of the tabernacle. As he went to remove the Blessed Sacrament, he genuflected. But rather than immediately rising he reached down on the ground amidst wood shingles and grabbed something. He stood and turned to Roman. "Here, I believe you were looking for this."

It was his biretta.

"*Merci beaucoup*, My Lord." Roman dusted it off and put it atop his head and returned to his room in the seminary building. He lit a candle and finished praying his breviary. Once he got in his bed, he prayed his rosary. He had not quite finished before falling asleep.

****

The next morning, once the steeple bell rang, he lifted the veiled chalice and paten, and reverently carried it through the nave of the church, and stopped in front of a makeshift altar made of a few wooden crates and an old trunk. The sunlight poured through the eastern windows of the Cathedral as he ascended the steps of the side altar dedicated to Saint Joseph. *I will go to the altar of God, to God, the joy of my youth.* He meditated upon the picture of Saint Francis Xavier, which the bishop had propped up on top of one of the crates.

At the end of the Mass, His Lordship informed Roman that he would be expected to take up the missionary responsibilities of Parochial Vicar in Evansville to minister to the increasing number of German-speaking immigrants in the Ohio River Valley. Roman, not quite twenty-seven years old, was now on his way to the southwestern tip of Indiana.

Chapter 3

Evansville

Spring 1840

When Roman arrived in Evansville, he took up residence in a single room log cabin adjacent to a horse stable, used as a summer kitchen and smoke house. The property belonged to the Heinrichs, a Bavarian Lutheran couple who had converted to Catholicism at the hands of Reverend Antony Deydier, the Pastor of Evansville.

One morning in May, Roman was feeding Shadow when Father Deydier startled him.

"*Bonjour, Abbé.*"

Father Deydier cleared his throat, "As you are well aware, Father Roman, the Catholic families of Evansville now number more than fifty and for that reason I have decided to abandon the log chapel in favor of the second floor above the Lewis Grocery store."

"The Lewis Grocery Store?"

"Yes, you are acquainted with Mr. Lewis?"

"Why yes. He and his wife are daily communicants."

"That they are. Good Catholics and most generous. Mr. Lewis has agreed to lend the four upstairs rooms to us for use as our church. The largest upper room will serve as a Chapel, and the three other rooms will serve as a sacristy, my bedroom, and a classroom." Roman wondered where he would be living, but before he could ask, Deydier continued. "I think it will be all right if you use a corner of the classroom as your sleeping quarters. I thought you would be pleased to know that you no longer have to share a room with ham hocks and sausages. Perhaps you will finally get the smell of smoked meat out of your clothing." Father Deydier laughed at his own joke.

Roman sniffed the sleeve of his cassock. "Perhaps I have become so accustomed to it that I no longer smell it." By now Father Deydier was red in the face from laughter. "There is more to my news. His Lordship, Bishop Hailandière, has purchased two hundred thousand bricks and is sending a thousand dollars authorizing me to purchase the lot at Second and Sycamore Streets for the construction of our *Church of the Assumption.*"

"*The Church of the Assumption*?" Roman paused from brushing Shadow.

"Yes, that is what His Lordship desires for our church to be named."

"When will construction begin?"

"Sometime in early August. To mark the occasion, His Lordship has designated August 5, 1840, the feast of *Our Lady of the Snow*, as the date to lay the cornerstone. The Prince Archbishop of Nancy, France, will be in America on behalf of the Holy Father in Rome and the Propagation of the Missions, so he also plans to travel here and celebrate a High Mass with His Lordship. There are efforts to invite President Van Buren since there is already a campaign trip planned by the Democratic Party."

The fifth of August was just over a year to the day from the time Roman left Europe the year before.

****

On August 5, 1840, the feast of *Our Lady of the Snow*, the Prince Archbishop of Nancy, France, and Papal Ambassador of Pope Gregory XVI, and an assistant Bavarian prelate on visitation to the Americas from the Vatican's Propagation of the Missions, prepared to celebrate the mass.

President Van Buren came from Louisville following a campaign stop. The presidential race for the White House was well underway, with the Whig candidates Harrison and Tyler having visited Evansville the previous December.

The long black cassock Roman wore soaked in the sunlight, inviting the heat, but what made it all the more unbearable was the hair-shirt, made of the coarsest horse hair which he secretly wore across his chest. He had begun wearing the hair shirt shortly after he moved from the Heinrichs' summer kitchen to the room above the grocery store. Feeling that his new dwelling lacked adequate mortification, he hoped that the sacrificial nature of a hair-shirt would bring him closer to God, unite him more intimately to the cross, and enable him to share in the sufferings of Christ. He felt modern comforts made one complacent, and adopting the hair shirt was an effort to mortify himself and drive worldly thoughts and temptations

17

away. The constant scratching against his skin reminded him of his humanity and his lowliness, a perpetual act of humility known to none but himself. He had already adopted a sparse diet, believing that even milk and eggs were a luxury. No worldly pleasure should ever displace the experience of penitential suffering. He believed in offering his suffering to God, especially for the suffering souls in Purgatory. Prayer and penance were the marks of a good priest.

The Catholics of Evansville were awaiting the arrival of their bishop when they learned that Bishop Hailandière would not be making the journey south for the occasion. The French Prince-Archbishop informed the parishioners that Hailandière was prevented from attending the ceremony because of urgent matters.

"His Lordship Hailandière sends his hopes and prayers," the Prince explained to Deydier and Roman. "His Lordship is prevented from attending the ceremony because he wishes to ensure that his new sanctuary and crypt at the Vincennes Cathedral are being constructed properly." Roman could not help but think of the last time he was in the sanctuary of Saint Francis Xavier Cathedral. He only hoped that his bishop had employed more temperate carpenters this time. "The body of Bishop Bruté, his saintly predecessor, is to be disinterred from the Cathedral cemetery and reburied under the high altar."

Roman wondered whether Bishop Hailandière had failed to attend due to his failed efforts to force the unity of the Catholics in Evansville. It was no secret that the small villages of immigrants at Saint Philip, Saint Joseph, and Saint Wendel wanted their own churches, and they resented being expected to come to Evansville for Mass. The bishop had repeatedly refused their requests for churches, not merely for lack of priests, but because he knew that some of the *hard-headed Dutchmen*, as he called them, did not want to come all the way into a Protestant town like Evansville and have to pray with the likes of a bunch of English-speaking shanty Irish. The animosity between the Catholics of different nationalities was to such a degree that the bishop thought he could break down their prejudices if he were to force them to come together into one parish.

Therefore, the weight of the miter took its toll upon the Vincennes bishop in part as a result of his efforts to break down bigotry. Roman had the suspicion that it would take something greater than the call for unity of spirit to bring the Germans and the Irish together, but exactly what that might be he did not know.

****

After the Presidential visit, both Deydier and Roman believed the religious climate in the area to be softening towards Catholics. Nearly all of the Protestant townsfolk of Evansville were friendly with their Catholic neighbors and the laying of the cornerstone for Assumption Church had revealed a growing respect between the different Christian denominations. Of course, there were a few of the bullnecked, hardhearted Whigs who were thoroughly anti-Catholic, but they were, for the most part, a small minority. Roman knew there were elements of the old prejudices, but he planned to prudently proclaim his Catholicism by wearing priestly attire.

Roman, being a horseman for much of his life, and coming from a family of farmers and tree-fellers, was accustomed to manual labor. On the Eighth of September he and a gang of men took to the forest to acquire the lumber for the construction of the church. Much of Indiana was still one great wood, the virgin forests towering as high as a gothic cathedral's spire. He and his team of men felled eight large poplar trees that would be used as the pillars for the church.

Roman worked with the builders whenever he could, helping them plane timbers, cut stone foundation blocks, erect beams, secure the pillars and plaster them with lime and sand. He hammered pegs, drove nails, applied mortar, set bricks in place, and chopped wood shingles.

With the work well underway by October of 1840, the Catholic cabinetmaker, John Karges, drew up the design for a hand-carved, elevated pulpit with stairs that would wrap around the right front pillar. The church sexton and sacristan, Josiah Stahlhofer, supplied the oak timbers from which they eventually fashioned the church pews. Roman knew it would only be a matter of time before Evansville had a fine church and school of its own.

****

One October evening, while Roman was overseeing some of the construction being done on the church, Father Deydier and six women clad in black dresses approached from the river. Roman was leading his horse around the churchyard when Deydier approached. "Father Roman, you must meet our dear Sisters."

One of the sisters spoke French. "*Bon soir, mon Pére.*" Good evening, Father.

"*Bon soir, Sisters.*" Roman removed his straw hat.

"They are the Sisters of Providence from *Ruillé-sur-Loire*, in France," Deydier explained.

The sister who had greeted him bowed her head slightly and continued. "We have been sent here on mission to establish a motherhouse and novitiate in the Diocese of Vincennes. I am Sister Theodore Guérin. I am to be the Superior."

Roman had heard of her expected arrival while he was still in Vincennes. This woman of about forty years of age had an aura about her face, aglow, as that of Moses descending Mount Sinai.

"I am Father Roman Weinzoepfel. There were reports of your appointment to the diocese." He nodded out of respect as she inspected his clothing.

"Father your clothes!"

Roman became acutely aware of his old torn coat and pantaloons that he had patched up himself. He looked down at his ragged shoes, muddy and worn.

"Excuse my appearance, but here in the wilderness one has to make do with what one has."

"Your housekeeper must lack tidiness."

Roman laughed to himself, looking at Deydier. "Sister, a housekeeper would be the last thing we could afford here."

"What? No housekeeper?" She looked at both priests. "Who then does your housework, makes your beds, or prepares your food?"

"Sister, one must have a house before one can employ a housekeeper." Deydier chuckled.

"I cannot believe this. Is *Monseigneur* Hailandière aware of such conditions?"

"*Oui.*" Deydier replied.

"This is an outrage! You are priests of God."

"Christ was born in a stable." Deydier smiled. "Let us remember Saint Francis of Assisi, for today is his feast day. He loved poverty and called us to embrace it."

"Yes, very well. May we visit the church, Father Deydier?" Sister Theodore seemed perturbed.

"Certainly. Here it is. Pardon the breeze inside," The pastor replied, smiling.

"Oh." Sister Theodore Guérin had a look of disbelief. "I thought you were raising a barn."

ROMAN

"Oh, no. This will be our church. The school will be in the basement."

"Our current church is only a temporary chapel," Roman explained.

"Father, everything is temporary. Is the Lord present in the tabernacle?"

"Yes."

"We desire to make a visit to the Blessed Sacrament and say our prayers. Where is this chapel?"

"On the second floor of the grocer's next door."

"Our Lord is residing in a grocery?"

"Sister, in America we are mendicants. We take what we receive. You too will learn this." Deydier led them away to the store.

Sister Theodore turned to Roman. "*Adieu.*"

"Say an *Ave* for us, Sister."

"*Oui.*" Sister Theodore turned to Deydier, "I thought *Monseigneur* was exaggerating the feral conditions in America."

Roman watched them disappear up the stairs. In spite of calloused hands and aching muscles, he enjoyed the task of raising a church in the New World. Such was one of his dreams of becoming a missionary priest fulfilled.

Christmas came and winter thawed.

****

1841

By the end of spring Roman had made Evansville his home. His daily custom of walking through town revealed much about the town and its two thousand inhabitants. They were mostly hard working, industrious American pioneers along with a few hundred immigrants. In spite of the Protestant majority, the small but ever-growing immigrant Catholic population began to make itself known. By the summer of 1841 the new church was standing, though its interior remained stark and unfinished. Nevertheless, the Catholic faith had taken root amid the Presbyterians, Methodists, Episcopalians, Baptists and German Lutherans.

In the same block where Assumption Church stood, between Second and Third Streets on the west side of Main, was *Ansel Wood's Tavern and Inn*. It was a raucous place at night, as were the other taverns and public houses that could be found along Water Street or Main Street. The nighttime babel of the saloons with the clamor of banjos, tin-flutes, fiddles, harmonicas, and the banging of out-of-tune pianos accompanied by the revelry of drunken patrons and barmaids would awaken him at times. On the river, whistles and obscene caterwauling came from floating brothels affectionately called *gunboats* where flatboatmen and other libertines carried out their vice with lewd women. Much to Roman's dismay even some of the immigrant Catholics had found their way to some of these boats. He had heard several confessions naming the sin of adultery and other debaucheries with such women. Life in the New World was a perpetual dance between the sacred and the profane.

The Feast of *Corpus Christi* fell on the fifth of June that year, which was also the feast of the Patron Saint of Germany, Saint Boniface. The interior of the church was far from finished; the walls nothing but crude timbers and stone, but the liturgical rites and prayers would be just as efficacious. Andrew Martin, the Negro bell-ringer for the church, jubilantly called all to prayer as the worshipers ascended the stone steps and entered the narthex.

Deydier arose and held the monstrance aloft, giving Roman a sign that it was time for the procession to begin. The choir began singing the traditional Eucharistic Hymns of *Corpus Christi* while the processional cross, flanked by two candle-bearers, lead the way out of the sanctuary. Roman carried the incense, while Deydier followed with the Blessed Sacrament exposed in the *ostensorium*. While Andrew Martin gleefully pulled the belfry's ropes, the congregation emptied the church pew-by-pew, spilling out into the street, and forming a cavalcade along the thoroughfare as the choir chanted the Litany of the Saints.

The worshipers processed formally, either responding to the litany, singing Eucharistic hymns, or silently praying their beads, behind the tall ceremonial crucifix. The large silver monstrance containing the Blessed Sacrament glistened brilliantly in the midmorning sun as it followed the cross and candles up Main Street to Third, past the newspaper office of the *Evansville Journal*, where its Whig editor, Will Chandler, stood watching expressionless. Past the courthouse and jail, all the way to Eighth Street in front of *Bull's Head Tavern*, and back down Sycamore, past the hardware and liquor stores, then east on Second Street to Locust, the procession continued on, walking by the dry goods and grocery stores, south on Locust to First, between taverns and hotels.

Roman looked at the homes and businesses along the route. Single-storied mud-daubed log houses, two-storied clapboard-sided homes, as well as federal style red brick and whitewashed Greek revival structures dotted the plat of the town.

He studied the faces and dress of the town's people, rich and poor alike. American dandies sporting pompadour hair cuts or felt stove pipe hats, patricians in cotton shirts with ruffled collars and cuffs, black frock coats, with brightly colored scarves around their necks and waists, smoking pipes or cigars, lined the dirt streets. Ladies in calicos with lace bonnets secured under the chin, boys wearing breeches with knee high stockings, and girls in calico dresses similar to their mothers'.

The laboring population—blacksmiths, lumberjacks, coopers, farmers, grooms, millers—all in their denim jeans or long trousers, work shirts, straw hats, and boots stood quietly out of respect or curiously conversing with their fellows in an attempt to understand the Catholic ritual.

There was another group in town, fifty or so roughnecks, made up of *Kaintucks* and *Alligator Horses*, euphemisms for the canal workers, and flatboatmen. They were armed with rifles, pistols, knives, and swords. Some of these rough characters refused to work, preferring to knock passenger pigeons from trees at night, horse thieving, poaching farmers' cattle and sheep, pilfering fruits and vegetables from the grocers, purloining perch from the fishmonger's market, or lifting wallets. Others would work a few hours unloading a flatboat or steamer and spend the rest of the day hunting, which amounted to shooting every creature in sight, only to return bragging about their fearless bravery in killing bear or wildcats.

The sight of these roughs, rowdies, bucks, or bloods, as they were called, tainted the town, and vulgar American slang besmirched with blasphemies flowed from their mouths poisoning the air. Their presence was not easily dismissed. There was something about their eyes, Roman believed. Many of them had the cold, wolf-like stare of a conscience that slept.

They shaved their heads from the back of their necks to the crown, but let their front hair grow, wearing it in longs locks slicked down with bear grease or pig lard left to dangle on the side of their faces.

23

Some braided their hair with bits of rope or tied their locks in a knot under the chin, while others grew a beard, allowing the whiskers to grow long on their necks until they resembled goats. With their soap locks and scraggly beards they looked like cloven hoofed devils, unnerving many of the residents and frightening women and children, especially making sport of the naïve, immigrant families. When drunk, these men could be horrendously cruel, a veritable incarnation of Swift's *Yahoos* straight from the pages of *Gulliver's Travels*.

Standing with their dissolute women in the shadows of the taverns' swinging doors, smoking homemade cigarettes or chewing on a wad of tobacco, shading their eyes with floppy wide brimmed felt hats, or wearing colorful bands of cloth or bright handkerchiefs tied around their head, what an appearance these boys and men made. With half bald heads, barbaric soap locks, ringed ears, goat beards, dangling amulets, unfastened and torn night shirts, dirty and loose fitting denim trousers, filthy bare feet or ankle-high brogan boots, they were *American barbarians*, bearing a close resemblance to the gypsies of France and Germany. His Jesuit professors in Strasbourg had taught him that as a priest he would be sent as a lamb among wolves. *You must be as cunning as a serpent, yet innocent as a dove.* How correct they were.

Their womenfolk were just as rebellious with their unkempt appearance and wild tousled hair, clothed in men's nightshirts and pantaloons or décolletage dresses opened at the top and without corsets. These were moral vagabonds, clinging to their profligate men.

Even in the face of such wanton abandon, Roman knew that his theological studies and reading of the gospels taught him that these boorish, repulsive individuals were his neighbors. *Whatsoever thou dost to the least of these thou hast done unto Me, There is more rejoicing in heaven over one sinner who repents,* and the numerous passages where Christ ate with publicans and sinners had frequented his mind on more than one occasion. To the self-righteous Pharisees Christ had prophesied, *Amen, I assure thee, the publicans and prostitutes shall precede thee into the Reign of God.*

By now the *Corpus Christi* worshipers had returned down Main Street, reassembling inside the church to mark the end of the procession. The Lutherans, Methodists, Baptists, and Episcopalians all took notice of the proud display of their Catholic neighbors.

Roman knew that not all of Evansville was pleased with the Catholic presence, Divine or human.

That evening he took Shadow for a ride along the river and through the wilderness. Upon his return, cantering through the wan, moony night, he saw the serenely lit river town as he approached from the west, the sphere's pallid blue-white surface shimmering in the waves of the Ohio River.

In the ghostly blue moonshine, the temperate night air with a soft northerly breeze tenderly caressed the lushly leafy, vibrant foliage of the quiet earth giving it a silvery tint. By day the grass, shrubs, trees, and fields were of such vivid greens, and the wild flowers of bright yellow and purple, the vigor of life, the very embodiment of *Genesis*. The trees brought forth buds and clusters of white, pink, and purple blooms, the beauty of which was only rivaled by the foothills of his native fertile Alsatian Vosges valleys.

Pulling the horse back to a trot, he tarried on the hill overlooking *La Belle Rivière* and the Pigeon Creek valley. From the distance he could make out the faint outline of the cross and bell atop Assumption Church touching the pale blue sky as flickering lanterns from the front doors of several of the houses beckoned his return. He snapped Shadow's reins and lightly spurred him forward, fording the stream and cantering through the settlement of Lamasco and finally trotting into Evansville from the east side of the creek. Overhead the lesser light followed him to Shadow's stall.

On such nights the silhouette of the cross was a reminder to the world of the presence of God. For the weary traveler or passerby who sought a moment's refuge from the world and to spend it in quiet contemplation of the Lord, it could become a welcome respite. Before the tabernacle again, the unwavering flame of the candlelight glowed ruby red from within its colored glass—a burning sentry beckoning all who entered the nave to bow and bend low. Meanwhile, the votive candles quivered in front of the image of the Blessed Virgin Mary, the *Theotokos*, casting off distorted shadows and shifting apparitions upon the wall above her altar.

****

The New World's newness was waning, the frontier becoming more and more settled as people moved farther west, establishing towns and cities. On the other hand, the flatboatman was his own man, a man of travel and adventure. Many of these men were only known as *Kaintucks*, as the French called them since many of them were from Kentucky and the Ohio River valley. To Roman, these unusual men had been well named, since in the American Indian tongue *Kentucky* meant, *the dark and bloody ground.*

What kind of a world is this? Lord, do you wish for me to spend the rest of my life here?

He looked out at the riverboats on the Ohio River. The environment aboard was raucous, filled with cursing, drinking, fighting, smoking, gambling, and carousing, the mere mention a scandal to many.

It wasn't unusual for a captain of a steamboat to challenge another captain to a boat race. On more than one occasion one of the boilers had exploded, sinking the vessel and killing passengers. These races seem to be symptomatic of the madness, the restlessness in the hearts of these Americans, constantly racing to and fro, going nowhere at best and ending up dead at worst.

Perchance it was the miserable climate that created a foul disposition in so many of the Americans. Summer temperatures were horrid. Stifling air during the day and sultry humidity lingered through the night with no cool breeze. The mosquitoes were monstrous, some of the largest biting insects he'd ever seen. And if it wasn't mosquitoes, then it was fleas, or worse, lice. Malaria had killed many already

Despite all this, he was a missionary priest and he derived great pleasure marveling at the American landscape, the beauty of God's creation. The spectacle of nature at play upon the river filled him with the most wondrous awe. The waterway of the Ohio River was incredibly pure, clear to the bottom of the channel. Large one hundred and fifty-pound Catfish dubbed *Mississippi Muds* lay up and down the banks of the virgin water with countless hosts of other fish.

Ducks, cranes, heron, and other species of waterfowl nestled along the current. The birds reminded Roman of the storks in his own beloved Alsace. Flocks of geese flying in formation hovered overhead, while the skies blackened as swarms of passenger pigeons swept across them, casting great shifting shadows, blocking out the sun. Morning, noon, and evening the skies surrounding Assumption Church were darkened with the signature flock of these birds, *Ectopistes migratorius*, as millions of them would descend into the forest on the banks of the Ohio and all along Pigeon Creek, so named for its birds.

Snakes of all colors and sizes, thousands upon thousands of tortoises sunning themselves upon rocks and logs, symphonies of frogs and toads, and choruses of locusts and crickets filled the nights with delightful sounds.

Buffalo, bears, and other wild animals dwelt at the rivers edge, along with the occasional wildcat or wolf. The virgin forests, with trees fifteen to twenty feet in diameter, hundreds of years old, dominated the land.

In many ways this was like the world in its newness of creation, as it was in the beginning.

Chapter 4

Wayward Lambs

12 December 1841

On a cold and snowy December evening, Roman rode through the falling snow heading towards the northern settlement of Blue Grass, a village five miles north of town near Pigeon Creek. Winter had an early start and by the feast of Saint Nicholas there was already a foot of snow on the ground and more was falling.

Called again to the home of Mr. and Mrs. Louis Long, one of the German families of the parish, Roman feared it might be one of the last times he would visit the sick woman. It had been a quotidian afternoon when Mr. Long rode to town to tell Roman that his wife, Mary, was dying. She had been in bed with a strange ailment called *the black tongue* or *the milk sickness* for some time now, but her condition had been worsening with each passing day. He had brought her communion several times before in November, but now her condition had deteriorated meriting the Last Rites of the Church.

She was not the first to contract the illness. He had seen it all before—the notorious blackened tongue, fever and chills, and night sweats. Prepared to administer the sacrament of Extreme Unction, hear her confession, and give her Viaticum, he packed his crucifix and holy water and oils in one of the saddlebags, carrying the Holy Eucharist in a pyx in his left shirt pocket, close to his heart.

Roman first met the Longs and their seventeen-year-old daughter Caroline one Sunday after Mass in the spring of 1841. The family had first lived in Cincinnati after arriving from Bavaria, but Mr. and Mrs. Long and their youngest daughter had moved to Evansville early in 1841. Since that time he had only seen them at Sunday Mass. They were not sociable as were the other German immigrants. It was only after Mrs. Long had become ill that Roman was invited to visit their home.

Upon arriving at the saltbox farmhouse, he was met by Mr. Long. "Father, we've been waiting for you."

"*Herr Long.*" Roman knocked the snow from his boots before crossing the threshold. Closing the door behind him, he expected to feel immediate relief from the cold December wind, but instead it felt as if the door was still open and the wind blowing. Roman removed his gloves and took off his wraps, placing them on a chair near the hearth. The fire was slow to warm him as was Long's greeting which bore no hospitality.

Roman had no particular reason to be suspicious or harbor misgivings about the family, but he only knew there was an oppressive presence that he'd sensed before in his brief encounters with the Long family. Upon entering the home this evening, he sensed it strongly.

"I'm glad the snow didn't keep you from coming." There was almost a sarcastic bite to his words as if Roman might have used the weather as an excuse to avoid coming.

"Not at all. Has Frau Long's condition improved?"

"After I gave her the medicine that Doctor Trafton prescribed for her," Long explained, "she got worse."

"I see."

"You know, the druggist told me that Doctor Trafton was involved in a scandal a few years back."

Roman smelled whiskey on Long's breath, and refused to engage in the gossip, even though the tale was common knowledge. "There's a good Catholic doctor here in town by the name of McDonald who-"

"I heard that Doctor Trafton took in a nigger woman and her four children," continued Long, "but then after he had earned their trust he put them on a boat for New Orleans so he could sell them as runaway slaves. Some constable figured what he was up to before they got too far down the river. Trafton's wife divorced him over it and she got half of everything." Long seemed to gloat over the telling of this tale. Did the unhappiness of another somehow give him comfort, making it easier to avoid looking honestly at his own unhappiness? Roman's question remained unanswered.

"So," Roman cleared his throat, "Frau Long had a bad night."

"She told me last night that she didn't think she was going to live beyond the week. I don't know why she'd say a thing like that. Caroline cried half the night after I told her what her Mama said." Long laughed, revealing both his decayed and missing teeth. It was a strange laugh, certainly inappropriate given the circumstances. More

29

of a nervous laugh, a man's way of dealing with the difficulty of his wife's serious illness. Roman felt sorry for the man, yet it was pity mingled with revulsion.

"Why would my Mary ever say a thing like that?" Long lost his smile and looked Roman in the face with an accusatory expression. He explained it away knowing this was how some men cope with grief.

"Sometimes, Herr Long, a person has a certain sense before they die."

"Die? Oh no, she can't die! I won't let her! Isn't there something you can do to help?"

"I can pray for her and administer the sacraments. They're efficacious against the worst maladies—diseases of the soul. Let us pray that she'll recover from this terrible black tongue. If not, may the angels lead her into paradise, and may the martyrs come to welcome her."

"So you want her to up and die on me? Is that it, Father? You were here a few days ago. Did she tell you she wants to die? Is that it? She wants to leave me?" Long was red in the face as he shook his fist in the air. "She'd rather float on the clouds with fair-haired angels than stay here with her family? What if I still need her here?" Roman backed away as Long reached for the poker. The man calmed himself, forcing a smile as he carefully poked at a log in the fire. Outside, the wind kept blowing a tree limb against the house, causing it to scratch the windowpane.

"You're a priest. You don't understand. I can't imagine life without my Mary. My sons are in Cincinnati and my daughters are lazy, frivolous girls! I can't expect either of them to run my house. The girls are a disappointment to me." He stared into the fire as he deliberately poked at the same log over and over again. "She's all I have!" Roman had only known Caroline, never meeting the two sons and other daughter.

"I *do* understand. I too have had loved ones die. Both parents and my—"

"Yes, but you've never lost a *wife*," Long interrupted Roman and looked up from the fire. "And you never will." He tossed the poker down in front of the fireplace and collapsed in a chair. "A priest's life is not very complicated, Father. Look, you read your Mass, pray your beads, hear confessions, and say your prayers. You have everything you need, a house, a horse, a housekeeper to feed you and clean up for you. Priests don't know what it is like out here in the frontier." Roman could have offered a rebuttal but he was there on a Sacramental call. He knew he didn't wish to argue with a man whose wife was dying. Neither did he wish to argue with a man who'd been drinking. Besides, there was no arguing with *him.*

"Perhaps I should go to Frau Long's bedside now." Roman started to stand up. He knew the way, through the kitchen, up the back stairwell, in the hallway to the right.

"No," Long snarled back. "She's still sleeping. My youngest will come get us when she awakes. Now you just sit down."

Roman fell back in the chair. The two men sat in silence. Long's unblinking gaze was transfixed upon the fire. Cold and tired, Roman longed for some tea, but the common courtesies of hospitality seemed to have been long forgotten in the home of this sour and silent host. He counted the seconds that ticked away on the wall clock's swinging pendulum, desperately searching his mind for polite small talk that might help the time pass more graciously.

By the look in Long's eyes he sensed there was something else the man wanted to speak about. He decided to inquire about it, honestly and directly. After all, the Germans admire frankness. The sacrament of confession had given him a better knowledge of human nature, and the one thing he could see was the ease with which this gruff and hostile man sitting across from him could intimidate others. He did not know what was behind all this hostility, but he knew one thing, Long was not someone with whom you could hesitate. You have to be confident and unwaveringly bold in stating your mind lest you be knocked over and trod upon.

"Herr Long, what troubles weigh on your mind, besides your wife's illness?" Long's scowling face seemed to be lost somewhere between the licks of flame which darted about between the crackling logs. As he spoke these words, Long's scowl lifted ever so slightly. The square-faced man with his firmly set jaw turned and looked directly into Roman's eyes. It was the first time since he entered the house that Long looked at him with any degree of respect and he felt like a priest, not merely a bug waiting to be crushed under his heel.

Did he have something on his conscience? If so, he needed to free his soul of its burden. He was so unhappy. Taking advantage of their moment alone, he kindly asked, "If it's something you need to confess, know that I hear confessions every morning before Mass. Of course, I am here to hear your wife's, so I could hear yours as well." Roman was shocked at his own boldness. He didn't know where the words came from.

Long's face softened, his nose and cheeks blushed, and his eyes filled with the grief of one about to weep. Roman noticed that his jaw was not clenched tightly shut. He thought he had broken through the hard stone of the man's heart.

Long, however, suddenly clenched his teeth together hard and set his jaw firmly against the world as his large rock-hard fist swiftly came down on his thigh. "I don't have anything on my conscience! Be assured of that, Father. *She does.* She's the one who needs to go to confession!" The pitch of his voice was on the edge of cursing.

"Your wife?" Roman started.

"No! My oldest daughter, Anna Maria. God knows where she is. Probably drinking whiskey up there at the mill with some man she's never laid eyes on before. At least we got her out of that wicked city, Cincinnati, which she was so taken with. Why, she just arrived this very week. She refused to come to Evansville with us when we moved here. We had to write her, pleading for her to come to her mama's deathbed. Mary's been asking for her for weeks. Can you believe the ingratitude, Father?" Long looked at Roman out of the corners of his eyes. "Her poor mother is dying in the next room and she's out drinking whiskey with the boys, and...and...and only the good Lord knows what else." He closed his eyes, sighed noisily, angrily, and stood. "She's a gypsy of a girl. Headstrong. Says she hates me. Told me so herself, in front of her mother, too. Can you imagine? Hates her own father—her own flesh and blood. Says I took her away from her friends in Bavaria. Says I mistreat her because I make her work. Since when is hard work considered mistreatment, Father?" Roman's thoughts anxiously flitted about like a moth around a candle, waiting for him to pause so he could speak, but there were no pauses, not even one sufficient enough for him to take a breath. Long was now standing in front of the fireplace, raving, and Roman knew not what else to do except listen as he studied the face on the brown bear skin rug near the hearth.

"She's godless! Her faith means nothing to her. When it was time for her confirmation, it was like dragging a mule uphill. Took her three years. Said she doubts sometimes whether there's a God or not.

She even told me that she didn't care if she ever married a Catholic boy or not. I told her she wouldn't be getting married at all if she couldn't find a Catholic husband."

"I never knew you had another daughter. How old is she, if you don't mind my asking?" Roman looked up from the bear's head, keeping his voice low and measured, trying to calm the man.

"Nineteen. She's my oldest girl."

"That's a tumultuous time for many youth. Young people often say things to their parents that they don't truly mean. Perhaps you should give her a year or two to—"

"A year or two?" he interrupted. "That should give her plenty of time to lose her faith. No, Father, you don't understand. She's going to obey me—or else!"

"Has she heard Mass recently?"

"No. About the time we left Cincinnati there was a group of Protestant preachers getting everyone riled up about the end of the world. They say that between now and the end of March the world will come to an end. Lots of folks frenzied on account of it. Anna Maria's been led astray I fear."

"Yes, I'm well aware of the fanaticism of some zealous American preachers."

"But that's not the half of it, Father. They say that Catholics have come to America to destroy it."

"Yes, I've heard that too."

"One of my sons back in Cincinnati wrote me telling how Anna Maria stopped going to Mass. The Irish priest at the church also sent my son a copy of her overdue pew rental bill. But the most disturbing thing I've heard concerns how she spent her evenings out on the town, even in taverns with men. I hope not all of it was true."

Just then a young woman of about twenty stood in the doorway. She was wearing a fashionable brown bonnet with white ribbon and plume and a bright yellow dress.

There are two types of silence: The peaceful restful kind that lulls one into a sleep and the disturbing kind that is fraught with fear. It was the latter silence which enveloped the room so completely, and left no doubt in Roman's mind that this young woman in the doorway must be Anna Maria.

Long remained seated. "This is my daughter, Anna Maria." His introduction was without emotion of any kind and Roman didn't know if it was defeat or restraint that he heard in Long's voice.

"*Fräulein.*" Roman rose and acknowledged her with a slight nod.

"*Guten abend.*" It was a slow strange smile she gave him, deliberate and bold, not at all the type of smile one would expect from a nineteen-year-old girl. He tried to interpret the smile, but was distracted by her ocean blue eyes.

The presence of her sister appeared from around the corner. "Mother is awake now," the seventeen-year-old Caroline cautiously spoke as if afraid of interrupting them. Roman noticed how different the two sisters seemed. Caroline was smaller and obviously younger, not just in appearance but in demeanor as well. Soft spoken and timid, she nervously wrung out the dull gray apron about her waist as if it were a wet rag. It appeared that Caroline had learned to calculate her every word and deed lest she rouse her father's wrath.

"Mother says she would like to visit with the priest," the meek voice of Caroline rang through the silent hostility of the cold, gray room.

"Damn! Fire's gone out." Long shouted, poking at the dying embers in the fireplace, apparently oblivious that he had cursed.

Roman watched sparks flare.

"Well, go on, Father." Long turned to Roman. "I suppose she wants to speak with you. Alone."

He acknowledged Long's words with a slight nod and turned to exit the room, relieved to leave.

Anna Maria stepped forward. "I'll show you to my Mother's room, Father—" She stopped and glanced into his eyes, the right first, and then the left.

"Weinzoepfel," he finished the sentence. "Father Weinzoepfel."

"Father Weinzoepfel."

She gave him a look that most young girls reserved for suitors, and certainly not priests, and yet he was strangely drawn to her stare. Her glance called to mind her father's tale of taverns and whiskey and men. He cast his eyes away from her gaze, remembering the admonition never to look a woman directly in the eyes.

"Follow me, Father Weinzoepfel." Anna Maria brushed past Caroline who was anxiously working away at a loose apron thread, giving it all her attention.

"Anna Maria! Long pointed the fireplace poker at her. "You just show the priest to your Mother's room and that's all! Your mother doesn't need you in the way. She wants to speak to him alone. Besides, you and your sister should be in bed. There's work to be done around here tomorrow. Now get to bed!"

"Stop ordering me around, old man." Anna Maria shouted. "I'll go to bed when I like. I'm not a child."

"I shall go to bed now," said Caroline, nervously scurrying out of the room. "If you'll excuse me," she curtsied. "Goodnight Father. Goodnight Father Weinzoepfel."

"Goodnight, Fräulein." Roman bid Caroline goodnight with a slight smile intended to comfort the frightened young girl. He was the only one who bade her goodnight for Long and Anna Maria seemed too preoccupied with their seething fury toward each other to notice she had left the room.

"I treat you like a child because you are a child!" Long snarled back, still holding the poker. "Now do as I say or I'll—I'll—"

"You'll what, Father? Beat me with a switch again or will you use the poker? Well, go ahead, beat me. Beat me till I'm bloody."

If they fought like this with a stranger in their presence—a priest no less—how did they fight when they were alone? Were they restraining themselves because of his presence, or did they simply not care if an outsider observed their every word and deed? There seemed to be no sense of propriety. He believed he had to intervene.

"Fräulein. Please." Roman said firmly. "Address your father with respect."

She looked at the floor shamefacedly.

"Ah, see?" Long shouted at Anna Maria with an air of triumph. "The good Father sees what a disobedient child you are." He tossed the poker in front of the fire and turned to Roman. "Do you see what I'm up against, Father?"

"I see only an ill-tempered father and a rebellious daughter," Roman replied in his own harsh tone. "Both of you seem equally stubborn, thinking only of yourselves and not of your dying wife and mother. If you care about Frau Long, as you say you do, then I suggest you spare her the agony of having to hear the two of you fight during the final hours of her life. Now, if you will excuse me, I'll show myself to her room." He could have said more, but the words he did say hadn't come easily.

Roman exited the room without hesitating long enough to see what reaction he had elicited in Long and his daughter. He strode down the short narrow hallway toward the steep stairs, which he climbed thoughtlessly. The vexation that the man and his daughter had given him surged within him as he ascended the crooked steps with little effort.

Anna Maria was a beautiful woman, possessing the inner potential for sanctity, but she seemed to have an obstinate disposition, resembling her father with her firm set jaw and a fearless manner. Perhaps her father despised her so because she held a mirror up to him that he couldn't bear to look into, and everything he despised about her he despised in himself.

When Roman reached the top of the staircase, he followed the sound of Mary Long's coughing down the narrow hallway to her dimly lit room. It was far colder upstairs and he could see the vapors of his breath appear. The winter wind continued to howl and a cold draft blew through the hall. The hardwood floor squeaked noisily under his feet as he approached Mrs. Long's room. Still perturbed from his encounter downstairs with Long and Anna, he stopped and took a deep breath to settle himself. *I'm about to administer the Sacraments to a dying woman. Lord, be with me.*

He knocked softly on the heavy wooden door causing it to screech.

The sick woman coughed and called out in a hoarse voice. "Father Weinzoepfel, is that you?"

"Yes, Frau Long." His breath appeared in front of him.

"Please come in."

Upon entering the room, sickness and death hung in the stale, cold air like the thick smoke coming from the candle on her bedside table. The floorboards squeaked once again. Roman stepped more cautiously, trying not to make any noise, but the floorboards only squeaked louder. Mrs. Long opened her eyes and looked up at Roman. She wheezed loudly and coughed up phlegm as he neared her bedside.

"Father," her voice rasped, "you don't have to be so quiet around me. I'm well accustomed to noise."

She was lying in a four-posted bed with a faded worn quilt covering her slight frame. Her complexion was a sickly pale, greenish hue. Her hair was damp with sweat and her lips were dried and cracked. Without asking, he walked over to her dresser, picked up the drinking glass and the porcelain pitcher and poured her some water. He took the glass to her bedside, supported her back as she strained to sit up, and then raised the glass to her lips.

"Sip it slowly, Frau Long."

"Thank you." He took the cup away from her mouth and slowly lowered her head back upon the pillow. She closed her eyes.

Roman placed her drinking glass on the bedside table.

Her voice quavered, full of pain. "I know I'm dying, Father." She squinted her eyes open, noisily inhaling air. She exhaled and the warm breath of her mouth was briefly visible in the flickering flame of her bedside candle.

He didn't respond, surprised at her words.

"Will you hear my confession?"

"Yes. That is why I have come. I have also brought you Holy Communion." Pulling his purple stole from his pants pocket under his cassock, he draped it over his shoulders.

"Thank you, Father. I believe I'm ready to confess." She reached up with her right hand and grasped his left. "Don't leave me before I confess."

He clasped her frail, cold hand into his. "I won't leave you."

Painfully, she shut her eyes again.

Tracing the sign of the cross on her forehead, he began. "*In Nomine Patris, et Filii, et Spiritus Sancti. Amen.*"

She whispered the words of the *Confiteor* and began. "Bless me, Father, for I have sinned." Her breath disappeared as quickly as it appeared.

"When was your last confession?"

"Many months." She repeatedly coughed, unable to speak for a few moments, though she was still holding his hand. Wiping her nose and mouth with a handkerchief clutched in her other hand, she continued, "It's been months since my last confession. I don't think I've made a good, honest confession in years." Opening her eyes again, she looked at Roman and squeezed his hand tighter. "Never once did I confess my greatest sin. I hid it from myself, you see. I wasn't even aware of it, until I got sick. Then I had time to think." Her words came out in strained breaths and Roman detected the glint of a tear in her right eye. "I wasn't a good mother. I didn't protect my children from him, especially the girls."

"How so?"

She sputtered out the words between coughs. "I didn't protect them from...from..." She began sobbing and couldn't finish. "I stood by and allowed it. I didn't want to believe it was happening."

"Allowed what?"

She stared at the ceiling for a moment before speaking again. "The beatings. The abuse. The cruel words. The screaming and hollering. I thought myself the innocent one because I wasn't the one doing it. It was Louis. His rage is unbearable. Yet I didn't lift a finger to stop it. I thought it wasn't my place. I told myself the children were unruly and needed a firm hand. Sometimes Anna would look at me and plead with me to make him stop. I never did. I either left the room or acted like nothing was happening. Poor Anna has suffered the most at his hand. That's my sin, Father. Years and years of doing nothing. I was more afraid of someone finding out than I was of what it might be doing to my children." Just then the loud angry voice of Louis Long and a high-pitched scream sounded from downstairs. "They're at it again, Father. All that constant arguing and fighting..." Her words trailed off as she slipped her hand out of his. "Can God ever forgive me? Can the children?"

"It's a sin of omission, but if you're truly repentant, God will forgive you. God already has forgiven you by sending His Son, and with God's grace, your children will forgive you also." He paused and questioned whether he had said what she needed to hear. "Have you anything else to confess?"

"No."

"Are you certain?"

"I think so."

"Then make an act of contrition."

She uttered a traditional German prayer and Roman raised his right hand over her head and pronounced the words of absolution. "*Ego te absolvo...*" Anointing her forehead and palms with the oil of the sick, he administered Extreme Unction and said the prayers of the dying. Bringing the pyx out from his breast pocket, he took out the Eucharistic host and held it up for her to see. "*Corpus Domini nostri Jesu Christi custodiat animam tuam in vitam aeternum. Amen.* May the Body of our Lord Jesus Christ preserve thy soul to life everlasting." She opened her eyes as he tenderly placed the humbled Savior, present in the form of an unleavened wafer of bread, on her outstretched, darkly discolored tongue. He watched as she slowly closed her mouth and allowed the sacrament to dissolve on her tongue. She relaxed, closed her eyes, and began to breathe more easily.

"I'm tired, Father," she wheezed.

"You may sleep now."

"Pray for me, Father," she said, her eyes still closed. "Pray for us all."

"I shall remember your family in all my Masses."

She made no reply, already asleep. He wondered if this would be her eternal rest. So often after a good confession and the Last Rites, death followed. He had seen it happen before. He knew it had happened that way with his own mother.

Mrs. Long reminded him of her. He had never quite forgiven himself for not being at his own mother's bedside when she died. It was four years on the third of November since she had slipped the bonds of earth. He sat for some time in the glowing candle-lit silence of Mrs. Long's room praying for both her and his own mother. Finally, he stood up from kneeling by the bedside and blew out the candle.

He stepped out into the hallway and pulled the door, leaving it slightly ajar. Turning toward the stairs, he bumped into something. Someone.

"Pardon me." Roman started.

The candle she held revealed her face. It was Anna Maria. The bright flame on the candlestick danced under her chin, casting shadows across her face. "Oh, it was my fault, Father."

She was so close to him that the cloud of her warm breath in the cold air rolled up in his face, as did the scent of her perfume. His eyes met hers.

"Thank you so much for coming, Father *Roman*." In her nightgown and robe, her hair was down and she toyed with the drawstrings about her neck.

"*Danke*, but I prefer to be called Father *Weinzoepfel*." Catching himself in her stare, he was irritated that she had called him by his first name. Only the bishop, fellow priests, or other certain souls whom he trusted called him that, not a girl ten years his junior.

"Father Weinzoepfel. How is my Mother?" She brushed the hair from her face.

"She's sleeping." He took note of a stray wisp of her hair that curled down along her right cheek which she began twirling around her index finger.

"I *am* worried about her, you know, but my Father doesn't think so." Her lower lip quivered and she wiped her eyes with her free hand. "I'm sure he told you all about me."

Roman gave an empathetic expression, but did not respond before Anna Maria resumed.

"You do believe me? I do have a heart."

"Why should I doubt you?"

"Because my Father told you what a terrible girl I am, didn't he?"

"I was always taught never to judge a person simply by what others think or say."

"But you saw how we fought." Anna Maria shook her head.

"Christ taught us never to judge by appearances. Saint Peter brandished a sword in the Garden of Gethsemane. One of the Apostles was a zealot and another was a publican. I'm sure they argued. James and John are called the sons of thunder—"

"Does my Mother believe that?" she briefly gave up the hair twirling.

"Believe what?"

"Did Mother say she loved me? We've had our quarrels, you know."

"I know your Mother loves you very much." Roman tried to reassure the girl.

"Sometimes I think no one loves me—not even my mother." Her teary eyes stared down at the floor with the same lost and far away look her father had staring into the fire.

"You must never think that. Even if your mother didn't love you, the Blessed Mother loves you as does our Lord. He came to earth and died out of his love for you. Despair is a sin we must all avoid, my child."

"Do you ever despair, Father?" Her candle flickered in the draft.

"One must never despair," he quickly answered. *"With God all things are possible."*

"Then I shall try not to despair, but sometimes it's so hard." Her eyes met his again and seemed to be pleading for comfort. "You're a priest. Life must be easier for you."

"Not really." Roman said, realizing that Anna had been inching her way closer to him. Feeling closed in upon, he backed away slightly. "I shall pray for you and your family."

"Thank you."

"My own mother suffered an illness several years ago, before she died."

"Where are you from?"

"Originally from Ungersheim, Alsace." Regaining custody of his eyes, he glanced away and hurried ahead of her. "Well, I must go. It's late."

"I'll see that you make it down the steps." She followed behind. "They're too steep."

"That's quite unnecessary. I'll be fine."

"You wear the frock in public." She was at his elbow now insistently continuing the conversation.

"Yes, I believe it to be important as an outward sign of my priesthood—*and vows*."

"How long have you been a priest?" She was once again in front of him, blocking the stairwell.

"A little over a year and a half." He tried to move but couldn't get around her.

She moved her hand through the hair upon her shoulders revealing the base of her neck. "You remind me of a young man I once knew in Bavaria."

"Yes, well, you're tired and I must be going," Roman said firmly as his irritation gained momentum. In his effort to move, he bumped against a small table at the top of the stairs.

"I love my mother, Father *Roman*—Weinzoepfel." She placed the candlestick on the table and put her arms around him.

Roman hesitated for an instant, captivated by the sight of her neck and the flesh of her shoulders, and her rose perfume scent. Smelling her hair, he was vexed within, taken off guard by the temptation, and against his will, he found himself stirred to the depths. He felt the hair shirt scratching against his chest. His instinct was to draw her close but he kept his arms at his sides. *Custody of the eyes. Blessed are the pure in heart.* However brief the moment, the time that he wavered in resolve felt like hours. Finally Roman unloosed his tongue.

"There, there, *You* need to tell *her*, Fräulein." He thought words would never come as he pushed her slowly away and put his right hand up to his collar to make sure it was securely fastened.

"Don't worry, it's buttoned." She tightened her drawstrings, covered herself, and took up the candle again. "You remind me of life back home. I miss the old country."

"Yes, we all do, but *this* is our country now." Roman didn't exactly know how to interpret the girl's words and actions without construing things. He made a move for the stairs.

"Will my mother live?"

"I can't say. We must pray."

"Father thinks I'm a heathen because I haven't heard Mass."

"Then we shall see you in Church."

She glanced away, saying, "I can't sleep. I'm afraid she'll die."

"You must get your rest. An illness takes its toll on a family. You never know what the morning will bring. You and your sister need to be there for your father, no matter how difficult that may be."

"Yes, I must go to bed or else Father will put his switch to my backside. Good night."

Roman turned to see Louis Long standing at the bottom of the stairs.

"What was that noise I heard?" Long squinted, looking up.

Roman couldn't respond quickly enough and wondered how long the old man had been standing there.

"What's going on up there? Anna Maria, you leave him alone! Did you have him in your bedroom?"

"He wasn't in my bedroom, father."

"Go to bed, Anna. Now!"

Roman was sickened that Long would imply any such impropriety. "The noise you heard was me knocking against this table."

Long ignored him, moving back into his kitchen. Anna stepped aside and retired to her room. Roman nervously descended the stairs yet he knew he wasn't guilty of anything.

Emerging into the downstairs room, Roman explained himself. "Herr Long, I met your daughter in the hall after I finished praying with your wife."

"Never mind the girl. How's my Mary?"

"Resting peacefully." Roman was still rethinking the conversation with Anna Maria and Long's insinuation.

"Herr Long, I hope there are no hard feelings."

"For what?"

"For what I said about you and Anna Maria being ill tempered and stubborn."

"Oh." Long nodded and sighed. "Nothing I haven't thought myself."

There was an awkward silence as Long sat down in his chair.

"It's good to have a priest who can minister to us in our mother tongue. Some of the Irish priests in Cincinnati didn't have any time for us Germans."

"Yes, well sometimes we misunderstand each other, but we belong to the same church. Roman remained standing, desiring to leave. "Herr Long, I must be on my way."

"She's forward, you know." Long smirked, looking up into Roman's face.

"Pardon?" He feigned ignorance.

"That girl of mine. Watch yourself around her. I don't trust her. Don't ever believe a word she says, Father."

"I shall remember your entire family in my morning Mass tomorrow."

Roman walked into the front room, lifted his muffler and long black cloak off the chair and draped them about himself. "*Dominus vobiscum.*"

Long didn't give the Latin response.

Roman bowed his head slightly, secured the chinstraps of his parson's hat, replaced his gloves, and opened the door. "*Auf Wiedersehen.*"

"*Auf Wiedersehen,*" Long replied as large wet flakes of snow blew in from the outside.

Roman braced himself against the wind and snow, made his way to the fencerow, mounted Shadow, and cantered down the snow-covered lane to the Vincennes Road.

On his way back to Evansville he assured himself that he had committed neither a sin nor an impropriety. His fleeting temptation had been but a passing thought. *Temptation, yes; sin, no.* He wasn't interested in the woman, or any woman, but the thought had come nonetheless. Surprised by the temptation, he was angry at himself, yet he was also ashamed of himself for not saying anything when he allowed her to get as close to him as she did.

Why did I hesitate? I should have kept walking. Her behavior was inappropriate. Then again, maybe all she wanted was someone to talk to about her dying mother. Am I guilty of turning her away in her hour of need? Did I fail to comfort the sorrowful? I know what it is to lose a mother. Why didn't I say more?

The incident gnawed at him perpetually. *How could I have allowed myself to even look at her? She's one of the souls entrusted to my care, but in my haste to avoid temptation did I neglect the welfare of her soul?* He wrestled with his tormented conscience all the way back to Evansville.

The next day Roman was notified that Mary Long had died during the night.

****

Two days later Roman presided at the funeral rites at the church on the fifteenth of December, just ten days before Christmas. Deydier thought it only fitting since Roman had anointed her the night she died and he was also a German-speaking priest. Anna Maria kept to herself. All during the wake she was distant and acted like she had never met him before. Roman, though in no way attempting to avoid her, didn't approach her knowing that people address grief in their own way. *She may be a wayward lamb, but she is still a member of the fold.* He prayed for her and the entire Long family.

Vested in cassock, white surplice, black stole, and black cope, Roman waited for the funeral procession in the open door of the narthex under a frozen snow-clouded sky. Father Deydier, minus a cope, assisted and stood next to Roman. As the bell ringer repetitiously tolled the steeple bell, Roman stepped out on the snow-covered steps. The death knell slowly pealed fifty times. It reminded him of the funeral mass of his own mother just four years earlier. For a moment he was back in Alsace at St. Michael's Church.

In time, the black horse slowly trotted through the slush in front of the church pulling the funeral hearse that bore Mary Long's remains. The mourning family clothed in black trailed behind in the street's muddy snow as the pallbearers lifted the coffin off the black draped dray and carried it up the steps of the church.

Roman observed the stern-faced Louis Long walking behind the coffin with his two daughters in veiled black bonnets. Caroline's eyes were in tears, while Anna Maria's face was coldly unresponsive. The two sons were the lead pallbearers on either side of the coffin. He recalled visiting the family for the wake and having an opportunity to meet the two sons. Caroline had tried to comfort her father, but his grief only came out in anger. With Mrs. Long's body laid out in the front room, Anna Maria argued with her father about the dress he had chosen for her mother to wear. She had gotten her coat and hat and left the house before Roman had even begun the rosary.

Now here were the Longs all together at the threshold of Assumption Church for the funeral of a wife and mother.

Roman made the sign of the cross and reached for the aspergillum resting in the holy water pail, sprinkling the coffin. The bearers processed in with the bier into the nave in front of the sanctuary, as Deydier intoned the Gregorian chant of the *Miserere*, the fifty-first psalm.

Roman finally stood and moved to the gospel side of the altar, reading from St. John's account of the death of Lazarus. He looked out from the pulpit to see the sullen face of old man Long, the weepy Caroline, the crestfallen brothers, and the unemotional stare of Anna Maria. He noticed that Anna Maria's black bonnet was adorned with fashionable plumage.

He prayed his words had given the Long family some comfort, yet he knew that they would have to grieve just as he had done for his own mother.

Roman and Deydier received the Eucharist and knelt in front of the altar, for it was the Advent Season and no one came to communion. After a period of silent thanksgiving, Josiah appeared from the sacristy to help Roman exchange his chasuble for the mantle of the black cope that Deydier ceremoniously placed upon his shoulders again. Descending the sanctuary steps, Roman stood with the holy water pail and faced the coffin. Deydier was to his immediate right swinging a thurible of incense.

"Eternal light shine upon her, O Lord, with Thy Saints for ever, for Thou art merciful. Eternal rest give to her, O Lord, and let perpetual light shine upon her with Thy Saints."

Roman went around the coffin twice, first sprinkling it with holy water and incensing it with the thurible.

From there, Deydier sung the closing prayer, *In paradisum*. "May the angels lead thee into paradise, may the martyrs receive thee at thy coming, and lead thee into the holy city of Jerusalem. May the choirs of angels receive thee, and mayest thou have eternal rest with Lazarus, who once was poor."

Roman and Deydier left the sanctuary and stood at the head of the coffin, allowing the coffin bearers to return to their place, lifting the corpse. Carrying the processional cross, Josiah Stahlhofer, in an old cassock, led the coffin out of the church while two boys in cassocks carried lit candles on either side of him. Following the body, Deydier carried the smoking thurible while Roman held the large book of prayers and the holy water pail and aspergillum.

The funeral march wound around to the churchyard on the west side of the church. The pallbearers let the coffin down near the freshly dug grave and the pile of dirt mixed with ice and snow. Roman stood before the open tomb and read a passage from St. John's gospel before sprinkling holy water on both the coffin and sepulcher.

Deydier then handed him the incenser. Holding the chain in his left hand, Roman took the thurible in his right, three times swinging it in the form of a cross, allowing the chain to clank against the lid. The words of the *Benedictus* filled the cold, grey air.

Roman concluded with the *Pater Noster*. "May her soul, and the souls of all the faithful departed, through the mercy of God, rest in peace. Amen."

The service was then at an end. He watched as each of the family members walked by the coffin and made their way out of the cemetery. Caroline was the last to leave, kneeling in the muddy snow, leaning on the coffin, sobbing. Her father pried her away and helped her walk to the carriage where Anna and her brothers sat waiting.

Chapter 5

Christmas

24 December 1841

It was a snowy Christmas Eve when Roman and Father Deydier celebrated Midnight Mass at Assumption. The votive candles burned before the altar and manger scene and the voices of the choir singing the Advent hymn *Veni, veni, Emmanuel* warmed the dark, damp stone building.

Gaude! Gaude! Emmanuel,
Nascetur pro te Israel.

Meanwhile, Roman seated himself in the confessional booth to hear confessions. In the midst of Roman's line of penitents, a young woman knelt and began reciting the Confiteor as the choir chanted another hymn.

The penitent wasn't too familiar with the ritual, indicating either infrequent confession or a tepid faith or both. She said her last confession had been during Eastertide.

"Have you made a careful examination of your conscience?"

"As best as I can."

"What are your sins?"

"I took something that wasn't mine."

"Could you be more specific?"

"I needed a new dress and bonnet."

"So you stole a dress and a bonnet?"

"Well, not exactly."

"Well, then, what exactly?"

"I needed the dress and my father had the money..."

"So...you stole the money?"

"Yes, but I deserved a new dress and he refused to buy it for me. I work hard for him and he could have easily given me the money..."

"Are you sorry for what you've done?"

"I'm confessing, am I not?"

"Yes, but your contrition must be sincere and from the soul, not simply on the lips."

There was silence on the other side of the grille as the choir continued singing.

"Is there anything more?"

"Whiskey... Maybe I've had more to drink than I should have."

"Maybe? Please be specific."

"One time, for sure."

"It's important that you try and remember the number of times."

"Well, three or four times. Probably four times. But you know what can happen when a girl's been drinking."

He recognized the voice as belonging to Anna Maria Long. She cleared her throat and paused.

The only voices were those of the choir.

> *O Christ redeemer of our race,*
> *Unfailing hope in sin's dark night,*
> *Thou by the Father's will didst come*
> *To call his fallen children home.*

"What happened?"

"I wasn't alone," she sighed. "I couldn't stop it."

"Stop what?"

"I went to his bed."

"Did you violate the Sixth Commandment?"

"Which one is that?"

"Thou shalt not commit adultery."

"Yes."

"Are you married?"

"No."

"Is the man married?"

"I don't know."

"You knew this man intimately four times and you do not know whether he's married or not?"

"It wasn't with the same man."

"It was with a *different* man each time?"

"Yes."

"And you'd been drinking each time you committed this sin?"

"Yes."

"These are serious violations of God's commandments."

"I know. That's what that old Irish priest told me."

48

"Last Easter?"

"Yes, in Cincinnati."

"So, you've confessed these sins already?"

"No. These are new ones."

"Have you discontinued these relationships?"

"Yes, when I left Cincinnati."

"How did you know these men?"

"I met them in one of the taverns there. I'd have a drink or two and—"

"Have you done anything like this here in Evansville?"

"I haven't met too many men since moving here. My father keeps a close eye on me, so I haven't been to any of the taverns."

"I see." Roman thumbed his rosary beads. "You need to avoid the near occasion of sin."

"I know."

"You're not planning on going to any taverns, are you?"

"No, Father *Roman*."

Again he was uncomfortable the way she said his name so freely, but he didn't say anything. "Are you truly sorry for these sins?"

"I'll say that I am, but then I'm liable to go out and do the same thing over again."

"But are you resolved to amend your life and avoid these sins in the future?"

"I hope."

"You must decide in your mind that you're not going to do them again."

"I know."

"Do you know why we need to be sorry for our sins?"

"If I'm not, then I'll go to hell."

Roman knew that her sorrow was imperfect contrition, but it was contrition nonetheless. "This is true, but we ought to love God so much that the sorrow we express is out of a fear of the loss of heaven. When we sin, we offend against his eternal love and act contrary to his will. Our disobedience grieves the Sacred Heart of Christ, thus depriving us of heaven and condemning us to hell."

"My father says I'll go to hell."

"No one should ever say a thing like that. It is not the will of our *Heavenly* Father that anyone should perish into the everlasting flames."

"Well, living with *my* father is hell, the way he orders me around. He beats me and my sister. He used to do more—when we were younger. My mother died of a broken heart. She couldn't take it any longer."

The choir raised the strains of *Adeste, Fidelis*.

"Have you done penance?" He continued the examen.

"What's the use? My father says I'll probably just go out and do it again."

"With God's grace, all things are possible—including self control."

"I'm bad, Father *Roman*. God's probably given up on me."

"No one is beyond hope, my child. No sin is too great for God's mercy. Perhaps you've been too quick to give up on God. One must never despair of God's mercy."

"I heard a preacher in Cincinnati who said there was no use in doing penance. He said the Catholic Church is wrong to make people go to confession."

"You don't believe that, do you?" He resented the thought knowing the history of the Sacrament of Confession.

"The only reason I came in here was because my father made me."

"I'm not so sure of that. I think you know what you have to do. Now, I'll ask you again, are you truly sorry for your sins?"

"Yes, Father. And I don't want to ever have to confess these sins again."

"Is there anything else you wish to confess?"

"No."

"As part of your penance, you must return the money you stole from your Father. And as for drinking...that's not wise, now is it?"

"No."

"You need to avoid any occasion where you might be exposed to drinking around men. In other words, avoid the taverns. As for the sins of the flesh, I'd like for you to pray the rosary every day, asking the Blessed Mother to give you the grace of chastity and self-control."

"That's easy for you to say. You've always been good. You don't know what it's like. Haven't you ever been tempted?"

"Fräulein, you're the one confessing, not I." He knew his temptations and sins, but they were reserved for his confessor—not her.

50

Andrew rang the church bells loudly as the choir sang the Christmas hymn, their voices raised in four part harmonies.

> *Venite, adoremus,*
> *Venite, adoremus,*
> *Venite, adoremus Dominum.*

"How difficult it can be for a Catholic to live in the midst of Americans who believe in satisfying their every desire. As for these new dresses and bonnets you so desire, one must learn that he can never fulfill his heart's deepest longing with earthly goods. Only in God will our souls ever be at rest. Pray God give you patience and strength in the face of such temptations."

Roman recalled how she had conducted herself in his presence the night her mother died, so he added another admonition. "Immodesty can also lead to mortal sin. Be careful, *Anna Maria.*"

It was only after he said the words did he realize he had called her by name. "Now make a good act of contrition."

She stumbled through the prayer, but Roman entrusted her to God's mercy. He assigned her the penance of a rosary each day and reminded her of her obligation to hear Mass every Sunday and Holy Day. "Don't forget to return your father's money. And avoid the taverns."

Taking her at her word, he then absolved her of her sins. "May our Lord Jesus Christ absolve thee; and I by his authority, absolve thee from every bond of excommunication and interdict so far as I can, and thou needest. Then I absolve thee from thy sins in the name of the Father, and of the Son, and of the Holy Ghost. Amen.

"May the Passion of our Lord Jesus Christ, the merits of the Blessed Virgin Mary, and of the Saints, whatsoever good thou mayest have done or evil undergone, avail thee for the remission of sins, increase of grace, and reward of eternal life. Amen."

As she stood from the kneeler and disappeared from the other side of the grille, Roman feared he had said all the wrong things. He wanted to save souls for Christ. That was his sole reason for becoming a priest. Through the Sacrament of Confession he had the ability of reconciling her to God, setting her free from bondage to sin, and returning her to the good graces of the Church.

He recalled the passage from Luke, *There is more rejoicing in heaven over one sinner who repents than over ninety-nine righteous who have no need for repentance.* He closed the confessional grille and opened the other side, turning to his next penitent.

There was none. Midnight Mass was ready to begin.

After communion, Roman knelt before the manger scene in front of Mary's altar while the choir sang *Stille Nacht.* The figures of St. Joseph and a noseless Virgin Mary, a donkey with only one ear, an ox with chipped horns, a shepherd and two sheep, and an angel tied to the roof of the small cattle stall surrounded a badly broken baby Jesus. Josiah took great pride in his work for the Church, but Roman remembered how mortified the man was the day before when he had dropped the statue of the infant and broke off both its hands and left foot.

Now as the choir chanted the *Alma, Redemptoris Mater,* Roman meditated upon the Mother of Christ—missing her olfactory sense—beholding a broken Son and Savior. *How will she ever smell the frankincense on the Feast of Epiphany?* He laughed to himself.

Josiah would have no idea that Roman planned to use the broken Jesus image as part of his sermon on Christmas morning. Teresa of Avila had prayed, *Lord, save us from sad faced saints. What would she say this happy Christmas morning in light of Josiah's accident? Lord, save us from broken saints?*

6 January 1842

It was a piercingly cold and heavily frosted January morning on the feast of the Epiphany. When Roman entered Assumption Church his warm breath turned into a visible mist Dipping his hand in the holy water font, his fingers cracked through the layer of ice that had formed overnight. Preparing for morning mass, he knelt before the tabernacle praying his breviary when suddenly the church doors thrust open. It was old man Long.

"Father Weinzoepfel," he said, walking through the church, "you must help me. I've lost Anna Maria."

"What do you mean?"

"She married outside of the Church!"

"When?"

"On New Years' Eve she ran off and eloped with a Protestant. She went down to the Justice of the Peace and he married them."

"Whom did she marry?"

"That wealthy fellow, Martin Schmoll. She met him down at the mill two days before Christmas and by week's end she married him."

"I think I know the man. In his mid-thirties? I think his wife died last summer."

"That's him. He just lives down the street. He's a lonely widower—made his money on steamboats and the canal project—and he didn't even ask for her hand! The worst of it, he's Protestant!"

"A disobedient, disrespectful girl I raised. First I lose my Mary, now I lose her. You'd think she'd have some respect for her dead mother. She didn't even mourn her passing. I wouldn't be a bit surprised if she's out there in the churchyard dancing on her grave."

"Have you talked to her?"

"Only to let her know that I refuse to recognize a secret marriage."

"Have you talked to Father Deydier?"

"Two days ago, but that was before I found out she was with Schmoll. Father Deydier said he would talk to her if he saw her at mass, but she never went. And now this!"

Roman could have challenged Long as to why he failed to attend Mass regularly, but he didn't, knowing the man was still mourning the loss of his wife. "Father Deydier will be back by week's end. He's giving a retreat to the Sisters at St. Mary-of-the-Woods."

"You should talk to Anna Maria. Maybe she'll listen to you."

"I believe the pastor should be the one to speak to her."

"I thought you could do it. She mentioned you a few times after my Mary died. She said you're the best priest she ever met. You must have made some kind of an impression upon the girl when you told her she couldn't go to the taverns."

Roman couldn't comment because that was information given under the sacramental seal of the confessional.

"Just tell her the marriage is null and void," Long demanded.

"It's not that simple."

"What do you mean? Sure you can. Schmoll's a Lutheran. That makes him a heretic."

"Yes, but if Mr. Schmoll is a baptized Christian, then the marriage may very well be sacramental."

53

"That can't be! My Anna's Catholic! Schmoll and that preacher are Protestants!"

"Reverend Wheeler is not only the Justice of the Peace but he's also a Methodist minister authorized to perform marriages. I'll have to ask Father Deydier to make sure I'm right." Roman was bothered that he was unclear about the marital dilemma, but it was one of those things he would have learned in the seminary had he been allowed to finish his training as planned.

****

Later that week Roman informed Deydier about the conversation with Louis Long concerning the Schmoll marriage.

"I believe the Catholic Church recognizes Protestant marriage as a valid Sacrament even though the Protestants don't regard marriage as such." Roman said.

"You may be correct," Deydier explained. "Nevertheless, I'll take up the matter of the marriage with the bishop when I'm in Vincennes this week. I'm unsure about the validity of the marriage."

This was much to Roman's relief for he didn't particularly relish the prospect of mediating a conflict among Louis Long and Anna Maria and Martin Schmoll.

****

In the meantime, Anna had moved into Schmoll's home no more than a block from Assumption Church. She never came to church but Roman would see her nearly everyday.

Returning from his meeting with Bishop Hailandière, Deydier discussed the matter with Roman. "Every marriage between a baptized Catholic and Protestant is *ipso facto* a sacrament, even if the Protestant party does not regard marriage as a sacrament. So, Mr. and Mrs. Schmoll *are* married in the eyes of the Church, for Christian marriage enjoys the favor of the law. However, before the marriage can be recognized as licit and valid, Mr. Schmoll must sign an agreement promising that he will do nothing to prevent Anna Maria from practicing her faith and he must also agree that any children born from their union must be reared as Catholics."

Roman was pleased that he had been correct in his assessment of the marriage.

Chapter 6

Revelations

In March of 1842 a traveling preacher appeared in Evansville, distributing anti-Catholic literature and pamphlets. Such ministers were making regular stops in the area, lecturing upon the evils of Rome, fanning into flame latent embers of anti-Catholicism.

The traveling preachers staked their tent on the east side of Evansville on the same spot where the circus tents had been erected the summer before. Some of the parishioners had told Deydier that the preacher was setting people at liberty by the Word, so after nearly a week of non-stop revival, Deydier asked Roman to attend the last meeting. Reluctantly he agreed.

Entering the rear of the tent wearing his biretta and soutane, he cautiously looked around at the crowd of over one hundred people singing the Lutheran hymn, *Ein' Feste Burg*, A Mighty Fortress is our God.

In the crowd he saw the editor of *The Evansville Journal*, Will Chandler, and the Reverend Isaiah Baker seated up near the pulpit. The Justice of the Peace, Reverend Joseph Wheeler, was there as well, though he was sitting on the other side of the tent. Roman preferred to keep hidden in the shadow of the tent poles and ropes.

His attention focused upon the preacher.

"Thank you, brothers and sisters of the choir for leading us in worship and song." The preacher led those gathered in applause. "We all know who the man of sin is, don't we? We all know who that old satanic foe is, don't we? We know the hordes of devils, who threaten to devour us on all sides, don't we?"

Many in the congregation answered with 'yes, sir,' and 'amen' before he continued.

"It's the Catholic Church and her Anti-Christ Pope with his legion of Irish and German lackeys!" He held a large bible in his left hand and motioned upward with his right. "The Whore of Babylon plans to take control of America and the Anti-Christ, who is called Pope, will rule over us." The man pounded the pulpit.

Roman removed his biretta and wished he wasn't wearing his soutane.

"Catholicism is the worst enemy to your faith as well as to your freedom! A foreign tide is poised to wash ashore and render our beloved Republic no more! For love of God and country, we must rid ourselves of these papist pagans and their Roman religion! Give popery any more ground and the Bible will be no more for Protestants in America!" The preacher was working up a sweat in his denouncements, swinging the open bible through the air, its pages fluttering back and forth.

"We thought this disease known as Romanism had been overthrown by the great Reformers, but now this pope, the anti-Christ of Satan, is poisoning our land with the gangrenous doctrines, once again enslaving Americans who thought they and their descendants would never have to face the monster, who thought they had freed themselves from the fetters of the Old World. The shadow of Catholicism once before eclipsed the light of truth for a thousand years, keeping it hidden from all believers, until Luther and Calvin set it at liberty, but now the pope and his minions threaten to drown the God-fearing American Christian in *hocus pocus* and Irish liquor!" He pointed to the top of the tent and dramatically closed his bible, putting it down on the pulpit. Amens sounded forth from the congregation all around the tent.

Roman was beginning to fear that the man might work the crowd to a frenzy and wondered what might happen if someone were to see him.

"Oh, the tyranny of Rome! These priests and their abominations! How long will Protestant husbands and fathers be duped into allowing their wives and daughters to be the victims of these fiendish demons! Rogues, knaves, lechers all! The priests even threaten their own nuns with their lechery and depravities, and then condemn them to the silence of the cloister!" Saliva erupted from the preacher's mouth as he leaned out over the pulpit, increasing the rapidity of his speech.

"How dare that Whore of Rome to condemn Freemasonry for its secret rituals and carefully worded oaths meanwhile their own are taught they must go through a priest or Mary to secure God's grace! Their rituals, graven images, vestments, and incense, are full of superstition and pagan religion! Oh, the folly of it all! Hocus-pocus of a confessional and pagan altar!

"We know of the lecherous priests abusing girls and women in convents and Catholic schools, infants and children being strangled to death by priests and nuns to hide their villainy! The convent schools are to be the method by which to indoctrinate young Protestant children and turn them into Catholics. Then Catholicism will overtake Protestantism and our beloved Republic will fall to Rome! If you send your daughters to those schools, you risk her virtue and your country's future!" The preacher angrily curled up his face and pointed his finger at the assemblage. "The Bishop of Vincennes brought a group of French nuns back with him to open Catholic Schools throughout Indiana and Illinois. If you know what's good for you, you'll put a stop to these meddlesome women. Their Mother Superior is particularly villainous."

Roman was about to leave when a man in the front of the tent stood and exclaimed, "Stop this madness!" Everyone turned towards him. "I'm a Methodist, and John Wesley would've never approved of a service such as this!"

"Who are you?" The preacher looked up, regaining his composure.

"I'm Reverend Joseph Wheeler, and Sir, I believe you're the one spreading poison doctrine." Roman was surprised at Wheeler's boldness.

"He's a friend to the Catholics—" the Reverend Isaiah Baker stood.

"And Protestants alike." Wheeler finished Baker's sentence.

"Joe, why don't you just sit down and shut up? You might learn something. Why, I hear tell that you're soft on Catholics."

"I'm certainly no Catholic, but I ask, have you never read Wesley? He said that 'hatred on the part of Protestants destroys brotherly love! For God is the Father of us all, Protestant *and* Catholic alike. The Son of God purchased each of us with his own blood. A true Protestant must love his neighbor as himself, as Christ laid down his life for each of us, so we must lay down our lives for our neighbors, friend or foe.' Are we to hate our enemies and only love our friends? I believe the scripture reads, '*Do unto others as you would have them do unto thee.*'"

"Thank you for your interest, Reverend Wheeler," the visiting preacher continued, "but I don't believe you speak for the majority of Protestants in America. These popish Catholic immigrants have no business coming to America! If we don't stop the flow of these idle, criminal immigrants, the decent, law-abiding American citizen will become a minority in his own land. The true patriots of this nation must unite and resist these enemies to the Republic."

"But these *enemies* are our neighbors!" Reverend Wheeler pleaded with him, turning around to the gathered congregation in an attempt to gain support. "Nearly two hundred of our neighbors, men, women, and children, who happen to be Catholic, are not our enemies."

"That's what you think. It's a good thing the Whigs won the election." The preacher looked around for a laugh. "I don't want foreigners outvoting the Americans. And I resent them bringing in languages that I cain't understand. And if memory serves me correctly, I don't recall any of us Americans inviting any of these immigrants here. Reverend Baker here tells me that just five years ago there were only twenty Catholic families here. With that many immigrants, in five years the Catholics will outnumber American Protestants. It's criminal!"

"Are you Christian?" Wheeler asked emphatically. "What then of the Golden Rule? What of *Love thy neighbor*? Did Christ say we could pick and choose which neighbors to love and which to hate? These *criminal* immigrants you speak of are fleeing the oppression or conditions much like our own fathers did, why then will you not welcome them as your own ancestors were once welcomed here?"

"Our ancestors weren't Catholics!"

"Being a Catholic shouldn't be a curse. This is a disgrace to a nation that prides itself as being founded upon the principle of equality for all! These poor souls have come to the land of promise seeking life, liberty, and the pursuit of happiness. Why then must we close the door in their face?"

"America is for Americans."

At that Reverend Wheeler darted out of the tent. Roman, for his part ducked behind the tent folds and exited himself but not before catching a glimpse of Martin Schmoll and Anna Maria seated among those in attendance. He emerged from the revival and stood in the shadow of the moon.

The next day, Roman related his experience to his pastor.

"I even saw Martin and Anna Maria Schmoll."

"Pray for them, they know not what they do. We must love as God loves."

That was so like Deydier, he thought. *Short, subtle answers, full of deep, theological insight.*

****

March 28, 1842

The new parish church had been built, but not paid for. Lent was over and on Easter Monday Pastor Deydier had arranged to leave for the eastern states to solicit funds for the Catholic missions in the Diocese of Vincennes. Lord Hailandière's vast Diocese of Vincennes included all of Indiana and the eastern half of Illinois, extending even to the town of Chicago.

For the last week of March, it was piercingly cold despite the beautiful sunrise and the calendar indicating spring. After celebrating the Liturgy of morning Mass, Deydier sat on the steps of the altar playing his guitar, strumming out an American hymn.

> *Forgive, O Lord, our severing ways,*
> *The rival altars that we raise,*
> *The wrangling tongues that mar thy praise.*
> *Thy grace impart; in time to be*
> *Shall one great temple rise to thee,*
> *One church for all humanity.*
>
> *A sweeter song shall then be heard,*
> *Confessing in a world's accord,*
> *The inward Christ, the living Word.*
> *That song shall swell from shore to shore,*
> *One hope, one faith, one love restore*
> *The seamless robe that Jesus wore.*

"Do you believe that?" Roman asked, as Deydier packed up his instrument.

"What? That one day we shall once again be one?" Deydier genuflected and led Roman out of the church. "Without a doubt.

Christ himself prayed for it. The Reformation was a bitter divorce. The Church won't be whole until the body is reconciled."

Roman picked up Deydier's valise on the front step of church and thought about how he would miss Father Deydier.

"I can get that," Deydier said as Roman picked up his valise.

"No," he waved him off. "I insist."

"Thank you." Deydier paused before speaking again. "Some of the boatmen said it snowed last night," Deydier said as he and Roman left the church for the wharf.

"I'd say. My fingers are numb," Roman placed his left hand under his arm to protect it from the bitter wind.

"Ah, 'cold and chill, bless the Lord, frost and chill, bless the Lord, ice and snow, bless the Lord,'" Deydier quoted holy writ as he pointed to the heavy frost glistening upon the grass and budding trees.

"It's spring, Abbé." He could see his breath.

"Yes, very well, but we're in Indiana," Deydier explained. "The seasons here sometimes change places. Just two years ago we had two feet of snow on the third of April and the year before that I broke a sweat on Christmas. Don't be surprised by the weather, the American climate is fickle."

"Like her citizens." Roman smiled.

"I plan to begin the fund-raising campaign in Maryland," Deydier returned to Church affairs. "From there I shall go to New York. I have some old friends at the school of music who promise to be generous with money and supplies so we can plaster the walls and I can begin building the pipe organ. From there I may go on to Massachusetts." Deydier, with the guitar case swung over his back like an Indian's quiver and bow, stood along the wharfage under thick, milk colored clouds. "But first I have to take the steamboat to Madison and from there I'll take the railway to Baltimore."

"Railway? What about Pope Gregory's condemnation of them?" Roman pulled his coat tighter around his shoulders and pushed his biretta down on his head to keep it from blowing away.

"The pope has condemned railways in the Papal States, not the United States. However, railways will be the future means of transportation, mark me. Besides, there is hardly a difference between a river steamboat and the railway steam engine. I'm taking the train. Again, I do not exactly relish the idea of all that travel, but our new church still has construction debts and I shall not rest until they are paid, right down to the last penny."

"I understand, Father. It's a necessary journey. God's blessings go with you."

"And you as well, my son."

"So when do you plan to return?" A puff of breath became visible as he spoke, but it vanished just as quickly into the arctic spring air.

"I shall be home by the feast of St. Boniface."

"I see." Roman cleared his throat in an attempt to hide his dismay. "Today is Easter Monday."

"I'll return in a little over two months from now in time for the German holyday. I'm sure all will go well for you, Father Roman. I've prayed for you." Deydier gave him a fatherly smile. "Do not fear. Remember you're in God's hands. He shall take care of you."

"I'm not afraid, Father," he said, trying to convince himself. "Whatever gave you that idea?"

"I've lived with you nearly two years. I believe I know you by now. Besides, you have every reason to be anxious. A young priest under the age of thirty, all alone, placed in charge of the Evansville congregation and surrounding mission territory. It is a daunting responsibility. Who wouldn't have reservations? I wish there was some other way, but with the lack of missionary priests, we simply have no choice but to leave you on your own."

"*We?*"

"Yes, Monseigneur Abbé Martin and I spoke with his Lordship about the matter. Not that we have any doubts in your abilities, it's just that we did not wish to place such a burden on your shoulders. Nevertheless, his Lordship has the utmost confidence in you and it was ultimately his decision." Roman handed Deydier's valise to one of the stewards.

His Lordship. Again. Roman's thoughts were displaced by the whistle of the steamboat.

He looked at the pink and orange morning sky reflecting on the river water as it lapped against the shore, harmonized by the sound of birds singing their morning paeans. He wished he could enjoy all this beauty as he once had, but his self-doubt and anxiety assailed him, leaving no space in his soul for a moment of joy. Of course, he managed to keep the inner fears hidden from his superior.

The dock creaked and rocked, bobbing in the shallow water.

"This is where we bid one another farewell, Father Roman." Deydier stepped up on board his vessel and placed his hand on Roman's shoulder. "His Lordship is not the only one who has great confidence in you, my son. I do as well."

"Thank you, Father. I won't disappoint you."

Deydier stepped away, but then turned around as if he had forgotten something. "Oh, and there's one more thing: the Schmolls marriage. There's a chance that Mr. Schmoll might agree to sign the agreement while I'm away. In case he should, then I trust that you will handle things."

"*Mais oui.*" Of course. He didn't relish the thought.

"You have my complete trust."

The two men embraced and bade their adieus, one to the other. Roman watched in silence as Father Deydier took his seat on the boat. He stayed long enough to watch the boat depart as a series of thick, low clouds moved in from the west. A strong wind blew in from the west against his back as a flurry of snow descended and quickly became blizzard-like. The rising sun on the eastern horizon was now a wan, glowing white orb shining down through the clouds like a galactic Eucharistic host held aloft by the Heavenly Father himself, the clouds verily concealing the fingers of God.

Roman returned to the church. Fingering his rosary and keeping his eyes focused on the cross atop the church steeple, he grasped for God in the wintry spring morning.

****

Chapter 7

P's & Q's

21 April 1842

On the twenty-first of April, Roman went to the print shop of *The Evansville Journal*. William Chandler was busily working with one of his apprentice printers when he entered.

"How many times have I told you devils to watch your p's and q's?" Chandler asked the youngest apprentice. "I suppose I'll have to go through the upper and lower case and put all the letters back where they belong. Do you think you can remember the alphabet in order?"

Chandler walked over to Roman. "Yes, what do you need?"

"I have a story for your newspaper. I hope that you have room in the *Journal*."

Chandler didn't look up from his work, but labored over the imposing stone, framing the composing stick, eyeing each letter as he carefully placed them in the rectangular iron chase.

"Freedom of the press. Isn't it a wonderful thing?" Chandler smiled, finally looking up from his work.

Roman hoped it was only a rhetorical question, but if not, he had a ready reply. *It depends on whether the editor is responsible. Pen and ink have slain far more than the sword.*

"So, what is this *story* you think so newsworthy?" Chandler's eyes returned to his work.

"It concerns our celebration of Ascension Thursday here in Evansville. It falls on the fifth of May this year marking the fifth anniversary of Catholicism in Evansville."

Chandler took the mallet and tapped a small splint of wood along the edge of the chase locking the letters in the frame.

"Mr. Chandler," the young apprentice called out from the back of the room. "I'm ready."

Chandler left Roman momentarily and walked over to the boy at the wash trough. "Now wash the letters and frame with water and lye, and don't leave another mess to clean up or I won't even give you gruel for lunch!"

Chandler walked back toward Roman. "Now, what exactly is it you want, Mister—My mistake. Rev'rend Weinzoepfel?"

"Father Deydier has been pastor of Evansville since the fifth of May 1837 and—"

"Where *is* your pastor?"

"He's traveling in the east."

"Five years? It seems longer than that. So, what do you need me for?"

"I hoped that you could place an article in your journal to inform your readers of our planned celebration. You wouldn't even have to write the article, I would do that."

"You would, would you?"

"I'd prefer to write it."

"Is that right?" Chandler smiled, but Roman could feel the resentment behind the facade. "So, what are your plans?"

"A German *musikfest* and parade, May Crowning of Mary and Forty Hours devotion."

"I don't think I can get it in. I've got stories for the next two weeks."

"But the Catholic population in Evansville—"

"Is negligible. There's only a few more of you than the nigger population."

"There are over fifty families," Roman answered, "not including the Catholic communities north and west of here."

"Don't remind me. But there's absolutely no room for the story. Sometime next month I *might* report it if I judge that the activities merit mention."

Roman looked up at the newly printed papers hanging on the drying racks and silently prayed an *Ave*.

"If that's all the business you have today, Rev'rend, I need to get back to work. So if you will excuse me," Chandler returned to his workbench, "I've got to put this news to bed." He picked up the composing stick and chase, walked it over to the press, and handed it to the older apprentice. "Now make sure you have the paper ready and the letters inked before you put the galley on the table. C'mon, we don't have all day! Today's Wednesday and the paper goes out tomorrow! Hurry it up!"

Roman walked out of the office, angry. *Freedom of the press. Only for Americans.*

64

****

On the twenty-ninth of April Roman picked up a copy of *The Evansville Journal* and perused its four pages of news to see what could possibly be deemed more newsworthy than the Evansville Catholic celebration. He paged through the paper only to find two news articles, one entitled, *President Tyler—The Greatest Democrat The Whigs Ever Elected—is a traitor to the Whig party and the American Republic...* the other article lamented dismal economic prospects: *America Still Reaping The Harvest Of Democratic Seeds.*

All sorts of notices, and advertisements filled the rest of the pages. Roman put the paper down when he saw an advertisement for a new cast iron stove. He shook his head. *Chandler was right. There doesn't seem to be room for Catholicism in America—or Christianity for that matter.*

April was at an end and a month had passed since his pastor had left him in charge of the Evansville flock. Roman entered the darkened brick church and softly closed the door behind him to pray before his morning Mass. He genuflected and dipped his hand in the holy water font, but before he could even finish crossing himself, the door opened, light rushed in, and the door slammed shut. Turning around, he recognized the grey thick hair, the broad shoulders, and worn coat. It was Louis Long. His first instinct was to keep walking and ignore the man.

Although other parishioners came to Roman or Deydier with their problems, it seemed always to be more complicated with the Long family. The presence of Louis Long signaled turmoil of some kind, especially with the stormy relationship with his daughter, Anna Maria, and his Protestant son-in-law, Martin Schmoll. His encounters with Long left him fatigued.

He had spoken with Deydier about the matter before and they both agreed that the Longs were of a certain type of people who expected someone else to fix their problems for them, never taking responsibility themselves. They seemed to create their own problems only to lay them at the feet of others. One of those others was usually Deydier. Now with the pastor away, that responsibility fell to Roman. He prepared for an explosion of rage.

He had already done penance for the resentment he felt for the poor man and his family. After all, the old man was a recent widower and Anna Maria had brought him great grief. Priests aren't supposed to turn anyone away, especially those who are in most need. Weren't the Longs, after all, the kind of sinners most in need of Christ's love? He knew this in his head but his gut knotted with disdain at the sight of the man.

Then again, he reconsidered. Maybe he had come to go to confession. *Come to me all you who are weary and I will give you rest.* His thoughts turned to prayer as Long eyed him.

Deydier had been dealing with what old man Long called Anna Maria's *secret marriage* to Martin Schmoll since January, despite that it had only been a secret for the first day or so. Now that Deydier was gone, there was no way Roman could get away from the Schmolls and Mr. Long. It was up to Roman to resolve the marriage impediment between Anna Maria and Martin Schmoll if the opportunity presented itself. He prayed it wouldn't, but something said that old man Long's unexpected visit was related to the issue.

Long's voice broke the silence. "There you are!" He spoke in his Bavarian German. "I've been looking for you." Long approached.

"*Guten Morgen.*" Roman was cordial.

"Tomorrow." Long smelled of whiskey as before.

"Excuse me?"

"This Sunday at four o'clock. Martin will sign the marriage certificate."

"The agreement?"

"Whatever. Just be at Martin Schmoll's place by four o'clock tomorrow for dinner."

"Are you sure he's ready to sign it?"

"Yes, I'm sure he'll sign."

"Have you talked to him recently about it?"

"Yes, yes. Last night at his house."

"What did Mrs. Schmoll say about it?"

"Who?"

"I was speaking of your daughter, Anna Maria." Roman remained polite. "What has she said?"

"Who knows? Who cares? My son-in-law makes more sense than she ever did."

"Four o'clock?"

"Yes, four o'clock tomorrow, the first of May. Well, I have to go now. I have to see a man about some of my cows." He turned and was about to leave the church when he wheeled about in the aisle. "Oh, I nearly forgot. Anna Maria is with child." Long exited the church and slammed the door.

As Roman vested for mass, sacristan Josiah Stahlhofer busily lighted the candles on the altar. Roman glanced at his breviary and prayed the final psalm of Lauds.

He ascended the altar and began the Liturgy. Praying over the sacrificial gifts of bread and wine, he contemplated his own sacrificial nature as priest, offering himself upon the paten to the Lord. The priesthood, in its giving and renunciation, was to continue the Incarnation of Christ, allowing the Word of God to become flesh again in his own person. *In persona Christi.*

He prayed for the same zeal of the Apostles and Saints, a transfiguring fire within, not only transforming bread and wine into the Body and Blood of Christ, but transforming the souls of men into souls for Christ, bringing souls from the City of Man into the City of God, begetting new life through the regenerative power of the Word and Sacrament.

Lifting the chalice at consecration, he knew that every morning his hands held the very body of his Lord, he who bled and died to set him, and every human being, free. *Every morning I consume his flesh as food and his precious blood as drink.*

Genuflecting before the Sacrament of the Altar prior to his communion, he prayed. *If only I could have a fraction of Thy passion and thirst for saving souls!* He thought of all the souls—both devout Protestants and fallen away Catholics—who were sacramentally malnourished, famished from want of the Eucharist, unreconciled by the confessional, or deprived of unction and Viaticum. He prayed for all the living that they might turn back to the true faith and he remembered all the poor souls in Purgatory suffering the pain of expiation. For those whose condition was infinitely worse in the very flames of hell, there were no prayers.

After praying in the sanctuary after Mass, he went around the back of the church and saddled Shadow for a brief ride. Snapping the reins, he rode along the river, pondering his spiritual fatherhood of the Catholics in Evansville. He knew that his chastity had begotten new life in Christ through the Sacraments. He knew that the indelible mark that his priestly ordination had left upon his soul was permanent. Nothing could ever change that.

His thoughts on marriage were those of the Church. *Whoever denigrates the glory of virginity, chastity, or celibacy, also denigrates marriage.* Perfect continence, a gift of divine grace, gave him the will to be devoted to God with undivided heart and helped him as a priest to be more fervent in his love for God and man. Such graces of the consecrated life allowed him to give of himself totally, conforming himself to the obedient Christ who laid down his life for all. It was the same Spirit that had enabled the Apostle Paul to become all things to all men. The words of Christ were clear: *Blessed are the pure of heart, they shall see God.*

He knew of Religious who struggled to keep their vows. He also knew that he must trust in the Lord's mercy, recognizing his more excellent state of consecrated virginity. He practiced mortification, and custody of the senses, especially the eyes, knowing that a man covets what he sees long before he acts upon the desire. He touched the front of his cassock, causing the hairshirt to scratch his chest. He knew that his chastity was best securely preserved by living the communal life, such as he had during his years in Strasbourg, and had for the six short months in Vincennes, but being a secular, missionary priest in a Protestant town in a Protestant country had taken away all of the close-knit associations and familiar trappings of the European priesthood.

He pulled Shadow's reins and watched two redheaded Sandhill Cranes feeding along the water's edge. When the birds took wing, Roman's eyes followed their flight until they were well out of view. He clicked a signal to Shadow and started back toward town.

He had renounced the companionship of marriage for the sake of the kingdom of heaven, in order to better witness the future resurrection of the dead. He knew that celibacy anticipated the beatific vision of everlasting life and he had always felt called to the priesthood, even when he delayed his entrance into the seminary by two years. And even though he was ever reminded that his piety outshone that of his fellow seminarians such an honor grated on his desire to remain humble.

No matter how happy he was or had ever been, there was a longing in his heart. It was an emptiness that he knew could only be filled by prayer and contemplation. His mother had taught him to pray the rosary at night to help him go to sleep, for he was always the last to fall asleep, lying awake, thinking and imagining a hundred, if not a thousand, things—things such as becoming a priest.

The memory of one girl in his life, one whom he once loved, stirred in him as never before. Even so, the day he left for the Strasbourg seminary, he put all those feelings behind him. Or so he thought. *Colette was a beautiful girl. She'd be a woman by now. Colette.* She was from the village of Ungersheim and she had attracted his eyes at the parish fair two years before he left for the seminary. Only now could he admit in the silence of his heart that she was part of the reason he had delayed his vocation.

She wanted to marry but the desire wasn't mutual. At least not then. For the first time since his entrance into orders, old feelings stirred within him. *Now that I've taken my vows, I shouldn't have these feelings. What if I would have married her?* He could scarcely believe he was allowing himself to ask such a question. *From where do such fleeting thoughts originate? From a lack of prayer and penance, Abbé Martin might say. My brother Franz said I was running away from women when I enrolled in the seminary at Strasbourg, but my vows were made upon the altar of God*, he assured himself, *witnessed to by hundreds.* Yet even his hairshirt seemed ridiculous now, inadequate to quell such thoughts.

Perhaps it was the beginning of a migraine headache. He hoped that he wouldn't have any more migraines while the pastor was still absent, and he prayed God would continually grant him relief as in the past few weeks.

Meanwhile Shadow trotted in front of the church and Roman dismounted him. Freeing his right foot from the stirrup and swinging his leg over the saddle, he slid down Shadow's left side, descending to the ground. He led him to the hitching posts of the stable just behind the church. Removing Shadow's saddle and bridle, he took a handful of hay and rubbed the horse down. Then taking a pail, he lowered it into the cistern, filling it with water for the animal.

He thought about the responsibilities that his Lordship had given to him. It seemed almost too much for a priest his age. He was sure there were some members of the parish who thought so. Maybe even some of the non-Catholics as well.

Taking the currycomb, he rubbed Shadow, moving the brush in small circles, stimulating the blood circulation, careful to comb the hair in its direction of growth. Finishing the body of the horse, he

69

combed the stiff dandy-brush through the mane and the tail, removing loose hair and mud. He cleaned his feet as well, examining the shoes. "I'll have to take you down to the smithy, Andrew Martin, my friend. Your shoes are wearing again." He stroked Shadow's face and body with a soft brush, polishing him smoothly. After such tender care and massage, he draped a blanket over his back and walked him around in the open until the horse dried off. "Why can't people be more like you, Shadow?" He bade the horse adieu and attended to some other chores.

Roman took up his axe and began chopping firewood from a downed tree, a victim to a lightning strike during a spring cyclone the week before. He removed his thick white collar and unbuttoned his cassock, shedding the clerical garb for the more practical shirtsleeves and trousers, preferring to swing the axe unencumbered. As he swung the axe he thought about his brothers Franz and Michael and how many days in Alsace they had felled trees and chopped wood together. Oh, how he longed for some of the old conversations with his family. He was disheartened that the mail was so slow and undependable. He had only received a handful of letters from Michael and Franz and his sisters in the two years he had been in America.

His concentration upon the angle of the blade and his preoccupation with his family in Europe was broken when he happened to glance over to see Anna Maria Schmoll standing at the gate of her white-washed picket fence not quite half a block away. He wondered how long she had been watching him. When he saw her he fastened his open shirt. She immediately turned away and went back inside her house.

She hadn't been to church since Christmas. Placing Shadow back in his stall, he gave him two quarts of grain and more water before returning to the church.

He knelt and fervently prayed. *O Lord, in thy house I am a passing guest, a sojourner, nothing more than a pilgrim. O good and gentle Jesus, Thou promised that anyone who had given up home and brothers and sisters or father or mother or wife or children or lands for Thy sake would receive a hundred times more and inherit eternal life. Sustain me with this hope. Help me to live Thy words, losing my life for Thee so that I might take it up in eternity. I know that all things work together for good to those who trust in Thee. Help me to believe this, O Lord. Convince me, O Jesus, that nothing, neither*

70

death, nor life, nor the present or future trials, nor height, nor depth, nor loneliness or imprisonment, can separate me from Thy love.

He reflected a few minutes and prayed again.

Dear Lord, Anna Maria Schmoll is my neighbor. Help me to love her as Thou would have me love her. For as long as there is a sinner still held bound by her sins, then I shall willingly suffer with her and for her. If she will not do penance, then I will do it for her. O Lord, may I atone for her sins by my continued prayer.

****

The combination of the heat from the sunlight bearing down upon the iron handcuffs about Roman's wrists and laughter coming from a crowd of men gathered at the mill on Pigeon Creek brought him back to the present reality of his arrest and impending arraignment.

Chapter 8

The Agreement

The constables paused at Pigeon Creek Bridge to give the horses a drink. Roman observed those gathered near the mill and acknowledged the pain of his headache enveloping his skull like a crown of thorns being crushed down upon it. The spectacle of a Catholic priest in chains provided the rumor mill with an ample measure of grist. He likened the passersby humiliating scoffing and laughter to that of a merciless public scourging.

All during the burdensome ride back to town, he recounted again and again exactly what had actually happened while hearing her confession. *Would she abuse the seal of confession to betray me?*

The sharp pain of his migraine jabbed him above and behind his right eye. He winced but the ache only increased. The bright sun and blue sky were displaced by tall thunderclouds moving in from the southeast. He fixed his eyes on the chains between the iron manacles that locked his wrists. He was too tired and too confused to think anymore. He swayed in the saddle as he involuntarily rubbed his thumb over the cross on the front of his breviary, again and again, his mind ever absorbed with the charges pending against him.

Voices soon interrupted his dismal reverie and he realized that he was arriving in Evansville. The officers paraded him down a crowded Main Street, past the jail, past the courthouse, past the scaffold and pillory, down to Second Street in front of Assumption Church. At least twenty Catholic parishioners stood on the steps with either tears in their eyes or horrified countenances. The officer then turned his horse around and Shadow followed up Main Street to the Courthouse lawn where Roman was sure an entourage of Protestants eagerly awaited his arrival.

As Roman came down off his horse and the officers conducted him into the courthouse, he was led past Messrs. Long and Schmoll who were standing on the front steps. Across the street in front of the *The Evansville Journal's* office stood its editor, Will Chandler, smoking a cigar and wearing his signature speckled felt top hat, red

neck scarf and gray topcoat. He only smiled as Roman was led into
the two-story log house that served as a courthouse.

*What a fool I was to think that I left all the political and religious
turmoil of Europe behind.*

Roman was told that it would be a few hours before Judge
Wheeler would have time to call his case, so the sheriff escorted him
across the street to the two-story log house which was the county jail.
It was very small—four rooms on each floor. The sheriff led him
down a wooden ladder and placed him in the basement dungeon-like
cell. A small window, level to the ground, looked across the street to
the courthouse lawn. The scaffold and pillory loomed large.

Observing the frayed rope on the scaffold in the public square,
Roman recalled a March execution of a convicted murderer. The
memory of the sound of the trap door falling away and the taut rope
snapping the man's neck jerking his body to a stop jolted him.
Brooding over his own prospect of such a grim end, the haunting
image of the man's limp body swaying upon the gibbet, and the
gathered spectators cheering and applauding as if exacting justice
from his life's blood assuaged the guilt of the crime and the grief of
the victim's family, continued in his mind. Roman feared he would be
the hangman's next victim.

The specter conjured his memory of other infamous horror stories
he had heard growing up of how the guillotine in France had yielded
human blood at the height of the *Revolution* and the *Reign of Terror*.
He questioned whether hanging a man provided solace in the face of
an injustice or merely gave the jaded world a means of amusement.
No, the thirsty noose only quickened the desire for more blood and
the Americans were obsessed with letting blood, as if bleeding the
human race would improve it. Roman believed that the only time a
man's lifeblood had ever wrought release was when Christ had
mounted the gibbet of the Cross.

As the number of people gathering increased outside the jail and
courthouse, he heard some of the talk.

*When the cat's away, the mice will play. He dispensed with his
vows and helped himself to Schmoll's wife. How long has he known
her? I saw him give her the sheep's eye a time or two. I heard she had
a spark for him. She's carrying his child.*

Meanwhile he requested a writing tablet and pen and ink. The
jailer reluctantly obliged.

Dear Bishop Hailandière, I write to you from the Vanderburgh County Jail. I have been arrested and am being held on a charge of assault and rape upon Mrs. Martin Schmoll. You may recall that in January you and Abbé Deydier had discussed her illicit union with the Lutheran, Martin Schmoll. This past week he finally agreed to sign the marriage promises. I doubted his sincerity then, and now, unfortunately, my doubts have been confirmed. There is to be a formal arraignment on the charges today and the trial will probably begin tomorrow. Apparently, I am to be given no time to prepare even a hurried defense. Hopefully you will receive this letter in time to send some worthy counselor to argue my case before the court and defend me, your unworthy priest.

To my despair, the judge who will preside is the same judge who married the Schmolls. I believe you have just cause to fear the worst. Mrs. Schmoll has claimed I attacked her while in the confessional. Anything I may say will ruin me as a priest. I cannot violate the sacred seal of the sacrament. Greater misfortune, I fear, is yet impending. What injury have I brought down upon the Church? It is true my conscience does not reproach me with the horrible accusation that has been brought against me since I entertained not a thought, or spoke a single word, or acted otherwise, than duty before God obliged me to think, speak, or act. But how will it be possible to repudiate the foul and scurrilous charge now before the court?

Unless God, in His goodness, will through some extraordinary intervention, avert my condemnation, may Your Grace have the kindness to forgive me for bringing disgrace upon the fair brow of the Church. May it please the Lord, that this unhappy visitation of evil upon His Church, prove somehow beneficial and one day serve the greater honor and glory due His Name.

Your humble servant, R. Weinzoepfel

He folded the letter and placed it in the pocket of his shirt inside his soutane. Praying through his anger, he knelt against the cool, damp, basement wall of the cell and opened his breviary.

O God, guide me in your justice because of my foes, for there is no truth in their mouths; their hearts are corrupt, teeming with treacheries. Their throats are open graves, on their tongues are subtle lies, all honey their speech. Declare them guilty, O God; let them fail in their own designs.

O Lord, hear a cause that is just, pay heed to my cry for nothing more than justice; turn Thy ear to my prayer spoken without guile, for no deceit is on my lips, no malice in my heart. O God, plead my cause, lying witnesses arise and accuse me of things of which I do not know. Yet well I know, O Lord, the just man has no fear of evil news, with a firm heart he trusts in Thee. With a steadfast heart, therefore, I will not fear, I shall see the downfall of my foes. I will hope in Thee, hold firm, and take heart. I shall hope in the Lord.

The thought of the marriage agreement displaced the psalms and before he realized it, he had put his breviary aside. The first of May filled his thoughts as he stared at the clouds through the bars of his cell's window.

****

May 1, 1842

Roman had no intention of being late for his meeting with Martin and Anna Maria Schmoll. Why Schmoll had waited until Deydier was out of town to sign the marriage agreement was beyond him. At least the union would be recognized in the eyes of the Church once Martin Schmoll's signature was on the marital agreement. The old man, Louis Long, had been pushing his son-in-law on the issue since January, but Roman hoped Martin hadn't simply agreed to sign in order to placate his father-in-law.

Roman stepped up on the porch and was just about to knock when he heard Martin Schmoll's voice.

"Your old man... doesn't go..."

He knocked, not wanting to eavesdrop.

Schmoll continued, getting closer to the door. *"That priest—"*

Roman knocked harder this time.

"I still don't know what business they have in telling me how I'm to raise my children."

He could hear Anna Maria's voice, but he didn't know what she said.

"No, by God!" Martin's voice returned with the sound of a stomp to the floor. "I swore I'd never forget how those German Catholics treated my mother and father."

The rest was inaudible, but Martin's voice was enough to bring on a migraine.

Anna Maria again said something. Then silence.

Roman knocked long and hard on the door for a third time.

"It's *the priest*." Martin said *the priest* like a worn-out epithet.

A pang of nausea squeezed Roman's stomach.

When Anna opened the door, Martin was sitting by the fireplace in the front room with his right leg propped up on a small stool with a bottle of whiskey to his left. He stared at Roman who was standing in the doorway.

"*Guten Tag*, Mrs. Schmoll. Mr. Schmoll."

"*Guten Tag*, Father Roman," Anna Maria replied weakly. "Won't you come in?" She looked at him sadly with her blue eyes.

Upon seeing Martin, Roman's nausea intensified. Martin didn't rise to welcome him. Anna Maria motioned Roman to take a seat by the fireplace opposite her husband before she went into the kitchen.

Martin finally acknowledged him with an odd grin and a nod of the head. Martin was older than Anna Maria, every year of thirty-five to her twenty. *Was she desperate to marry, simply to get away from the tyranny of her father?* Roman wondered. *Though a Lutheran, Schmoll was the son of immigrant Germans.*

"Where is Herr Long?" Roman asked Martin.

"He'll be here..." his voice trailed off as he looked at the fire, leaning to one side.

The temperature was cool for May and already at four in the evening there was a chill in the air.

"It's been a cool spring this year." Roman cleared his throat, adjusting his collar.

"Don't worry, it'll heat up," Schmoll said, his eyes unblinking. "The wind is blowing from the south."

The conversation that Roman hoped would come from an innocuous exchange concerning the ever changing climate of southern Indiana was fruitless.

He was already uncomfortable becoming involved in the marital agreement and had rehearsed his lines that morning, preparing a response should Martin lecture him that the Church has no business placing restrictions on marriages between Protestants and Catholics. Putting his hand to his chest, he felt the parchment of the agreement under his cassock. He also felt the hairshirt scratch his chest.

Before your union can be recognized by the Catholic Church as licit, the Protestant party must sign this agreement ensuring that you will allow your wife to practice her Catholic faith, and vow that any children born of your union must be raised as Catholics.

Again, he recalled that Deydier had presented these facts to the Schmolls on several occasions, yet Martin had refused to sign the contract. Deydier said that Martin was simply being obstinate. Roman also questioned Martin's sincerity in wanting to sign the agreement.

Martin stood up, placed his right foot on a chair, and worked to tie his boot. Looking down at Roman, he squinted his left eye.

"I was told that you're prepared to sign the marriage contract." Roman said.

Martin sat again and reached to his left to grab his bottle of whiskey. He poured a glass, emptying the bottle. "The old man told you, didn't he?"

"Herr Long."

"They tell me you're the smartest young man in town."

"Oh, I wouldn't say that."

Martin sneered and crossed his arms.

Roman cleared his throat again. "I understand that Mrs. Schmoll is with child."

"My wife's condition is of no concern to you."

"Mr. Schmoll, I didn't come here to be argumentative. If you would like more time to consider the agreement, then I shall be happy to leave."

"Are you accusing me of not being a man of my word?"

"No. I just want to be sure you don't feel like you're being told to do this. You can't be coerced—"

"No one tells Martin Schmoll to do anything he doesn't want to do."

Roman's nausea intensified.

Just then Anna Maria reappeared from the kitchen. "Are you two getting acquainted?"

Before either of them could answer, there came a knock at the door. Roman looked up and saw Louis Long and his daughter, Caroline, outside at the door.

In a way, Roman was relieved to see Long. This was a first. Opening the door, Long acknowledged him. "Father Weinzoepfel."

He stood as Long entered but refrained from saying anything. He folded his hands and watched a shifting log in the fire scatter sparks up the chimney. Martin looked up from the fire and glared at Roman, inhaling hard through his nasal cavities. He snorted out through his mouth and spat upon the glowing embers. He laughed and took another drink of whiskey. Roman, still standing out of respect, wondered whether he should leave.

"Well, Son-in-law, have you signed the paper yet?" Long spoke to Martin.

"No." Martin turned to Long.

"Why not?"

"Because Anna's still working on dinner. I'll sign it when Father's ready."

"I just arrived, Herr Long." Roman explained, hoping to ease the tension.

Caroline went into the kitchen.

"He *will* sign the paper, Father," Long's timing was poor. "Right, son-in-law?"

Martin put the glass to his lips, swallowed the rest of his whiskey slowly, and looked at his father-in-law over the rim of the glass.

"Mr. Schmoll will be the one to decide that," Roman replied, looking over at Martin.

"I appreciate the permission to speak for myself," Schmoll said.

"My son-in-law takes a while to warm up," Long interrupted.

"I've been sitting near the fire, old man, and it's May, so I'm mighty warm as it is!" He slammed his fist down on the arm of his chair.

Long walked in front of Martin in order to shake Roman's hand. "Father, a neighbor said he saw you up near my farm today."

"Oh, yes. I made communion calls this morning. Patrick Fitzwilliams' wife is with child."

"Speaking of mothers-to-be, where is that oldest daughter of mine?" Long looked to the kitchen.

Caroline reentered the room and set the table. "Anna Maria thinks she just felt the baby kick!"

"Even more reason to sign the agreement, Martin. Right, Father?"

Roman squirmed in his chair.

Martin fumbled with his empty tumbler and got up. He moved towards a small table and opened another bottle of whiskey. "Old man, you could care less about your daughter." He poured himself another glass, and turned back to Roman. "The only reason he's here is for me to sign that paper. That's it, isn't it, old man?"

Anna Maria entered the room again and embraced Martin allowing the question to go unanswered.

"Why don't you help your sister," Long snapped. "Caroline's doing all the housework and you haven't once offered to help her since she arrived!"

Caroline glanced up at her father. Anna Maria glared at her sister, clenched her jaw and pursed her lips.

"Yes, Anna, why don't you listen to father?" Caroline smiled at Martin who returned a grin.

"Where's that lawyer friend of yours, Martin?" Old man Long interrupted.

"Lawyer friend?" Caroline turned around.

"You know, Jay Davis," Martin explained, "I thought he could be one of the witnesses to my signing of the marriage agreement, him being a lawyer and all. I suppose it *is* a legal document, isn't it?"

"Mr. Davis is wealthy, Papa," Caroline Long interjected with enthusiasm.

Roman knew he had heard the name of Davis somewhere, but he didn't know where. However, he was certain he was not a member of Assumption Church.

"Where's Peter?" Anna Maria asked her father. "I thought he was coming for dinner."

"No," Long hastily answered, "your brother's off in Cincinnati taking care of some of your—"

"Unfinished family business," Caroline coughed out the words loudly, finishing her father's sentence, as if to prevent him from completing his own thoughts or saying something else. She shot a look at Anna Maria.

Long stared hard at Anna Maria, his eyes two mere slits above either side of his nose.

Anna Maria refused to look at either her father or her sister.

"Excuse me," Roman spoke up, addressing all in the room, "but I don't recall a parishioner by the name of Davis registered as a member of Assumption Church."

"Davis isn't a member of your church," Martin snapped. "He's not even Catholic."

"On behalf of the Church, I must object." Roman stood despite the fear that his concern might be interpreted as dogmatic arrogance. "For the agreement to be authenticated by the bishop, Canon Law—Church Law—requires that both witnesses be practicing Catholics."

Martin leaned forward towards Roman in front of the fire. "Well, is that so?" he said, moving in his chair.

Roman was unnerved, but tried to appear calm.

"Don't worry about that Martin, I'll witness it," Long said. "Right Father?"

"Not quite. I've already made arrangements with two of our parishioners to witness the agreement. In Father Deydier's notes on your marriage, he preferred the witnesses not be family members. It makes the agreement more objective."

"You invited two strangers to my house?" Martin asked with an edge of anger in his voice.

"Not exactly—"

"Who are they? Do I know them?"

"The grocer, William Heinrich, and our church sexton, Josiah Stahlhofer. They should be out on your porch sometime sooner or later."

"You told *your* friends to make themselves at home on *my* porch, did you?"

"They'll wait until you're ready to sign the agreement." Roman answered.

"Will they, now? Well, that's mighty white of them. Heinrich's a convert, isn't he?"

"Yes, he and his wife both."

"You know, he was a Lutheran when he first came to Evansville."

"Yes."

"You seem to have things in order, *Father Roman*." Martin said his words coolly, deliberately, looking Roman in each eye, back and forth, back and forth.

Just then there was a knock on the door. A young American dandy with knee-high brogan boots, tailored grey breeches with matching cut-away coat, white spotted cravat, and tall, narrow stove pipe hat opened the door. Upon entering, he removed his hat to reveal a pompadour cut.

"Father Weinzoepfel, that's the attorney, Jay Davis." Long took it upon himself to introduce him.

Martin and Davis exchanged a sneer.

Caroline looked as if she was about to swoon over the visitation of Davis as she took a large wooden spoon to a pan. "Dinner's ready! Come and get it before it gets cold."

Martin took Davis aside near the fire, speaking with him privately before they came to the dinner table.

"Let Father pray," said old man Long.

Roman was hoping that Martin Schmoll would have led the prayers. *Now I can't even pray in my own home*, Martin might say.

"I'm the host here," Martin grunted, "but if he wants to pray, let him."

"Oh, no. It's your home, Mr. Schmoll—"

"No, go ahead. If the old man wants you to pray, then you pray."

Roman acquiesced and said a short traditional meal prayer before everyone sat down.

He listened to Long ramble on about corn, cows, the late spring rains, and the new *John Deere Plowshare*. Martin talked about land speculation, the canal projects, hunting passenger pigeons and bear, and investing more money in steamboat operations at the Howard Shipyards at Jeffersonville. The young lawyer, Davis, was preoccupied with the alleged unlawful actions of another lawyer, James Jones, and two other men who were smuggling fugitive slaves through Indiana.

It seemed they were all talking at the same time, none of them listening to the other. *Deydier's right,* he thought. *The American dream must be to kill every bird and beast with a shooting iron, chop every tree down with an axe, and till every acre of soil with a newfangled plow.*

81

For his share, Roman would have greatly preferred discussing Moral Theology, a Mozart Mass, or a Shakespeare play. Instead of Mozart's tranquil *Ave, verum corpus*, the feeling in his stomach reverberated like that of the fiery cacophony unleashed in a Beethoven Overture. He sat there, picking at the meal of pig brains and sliced potatoes, stoically offering up his suffering, saying nothing. Such conversation was a penance far beyond the irritation of a hairshirt.

At the end of the meal Caroline cleared the table and Roman looked out on the porch and saw that Messrs. Heinrich and Stahlhofer had already arrived. The men were talking with some of Schmoll's boarders when he stepped out on the porch. He returned in the company of the two and everyone gathered around the large dinner table. Martin and Anna Maria Schmoll sat across the table from Roman as he revealed the document from his pocket, unfolding it in front of them. The two Catholic gentlemen sat on either side of the couple to witness the signing.

Roman began the scrutiny, his hands shaking slightly. "Mr. Martin Schmoll, are you prepared to sign this marital agreement in good faith and of your own free-will?"

"Yes." Martin looked down at the table and spread his wide hands with their turgid veins and bristly-haired bouldery knuckles.

"And do you promise to never afflict through word or deed your wife's Catholic conscience?"

"Yes." He flexed his fingers back and forth, kneading his palms.

"Mr. Schmoll, as a Protestant, you are promising that you will not interfere with your wife's Catholic religion. You further promise that all children resulting from your union will be reared as Catholics."

Martin again answered in the affirmative. "Just give me the quill and let me be done with it!" He knotted his left hand into a dominant fist while his right hand reached for the pinion.

"You mustn't feel coerced into this decision, Mr. Schmoll."

"No one coerces me to do anything I don't want to do, Mr. Weinzoepfel."

Schmoll took the quill, dipped it in the mixture of linseed oil and soot, and scrawled his name across the paper. Roman felt that the way he signed the document spoke loudly of his resentment for everyone in the room, even Anna Maria. It was as if he had just compromised his Protestantism.

Even before the ink soaked into the paper, Roman began to rethink his decision to go to their home. He questioned everyone's motives, including his own. In Roman's haste to secure the parchment from the tabletop, he didn't realize that Martin still had hold of it and pulled it from his hand. Examining the document, Roman discovered that Schmoll's signature had smeared.

"You got what you came for." Schmoll stared at Roman eye to eye and spoke with a cool deliberate resolve.

"There, now that wasn't so bad, was it, Martin?" Long patted his son-in-law on the back. "You've made an honest woman of my daughter."

"What was I before?" Anna Maria glared at her father.

The old man set his jaw and looked at her through the slits of his eyes but said nothing.

Martin walked back to the front room with Jay Davis by his side and poured two more shots of whiskey. The two men were laughing. Roman couldn't help but feel intimidated.

Messrs. Heinrich and Stahlhofer looked at Roman as if they had overstayed their welcome. Neither man was the kind to risk taxing Schmoll's hospitality any further. As they left, Roman took the hint and stood to leave. Anna Maria saw him to the door and accompanied him out on the porch. He awkwardly handled his biretta and deferred eye contact.

"Mrs. Schmoll, I hope you will fulfill your obligations and attend Sunday Mass from now on. You live so close. Now that Mr. Schmoll has signed the agreement, there's no excuse."

"You *can* call me Anna Maria, Father *Roman*."

"Yes, well, you're a married woman now, Mrs. Schmoll—"

"You're not angry with me, are you?"

"Why on earth would I be angry?"

"I haven't been to Church since Christmas."

"Ascension Thursday is this week." He lifted his head and looked her in the face, briefly making eye contact. "And if you have yet to fulfill your Easter duty, this is the time to do it." He broke away from the momentary glance and retained his discipline.

"Yes, *Father*." She sighed.

"Woman!" The voice of Schmoll came from the opening door. "Get in the house."

"I was telling Father Roman goodbye," she said with the same sad look on her face that Roman had first seen earlier in the afternoon when she had answered the door. She turned away and hurried into the house.

****

Roman's memories of her pitiful look faded into the wet stonewall of his basement jail cell. He fell upon the rigid bunk, still exhausted from the migraine the night before and extremely weak from being deprived of nourishment all day. Even when the jailer brought him a few morsels for dinner, he didn't feel like eating.

That evening his eyes moistened the pages of his breviary.

Chapter 9

Easter Duty

7 May 1842

The next morning, Roman awakened surprised at how well he had slept. He had neither an appetite nor a migraine. The robins were singing and the sunlight revealed a cloudless blue sky. Had he not awakened in the forsaken dungeon he would have thought the previous day an eerie manifestation of evil. His only visitor had been the jailer who brought him a breakfast consisting of stale biscuits and a tepid cup of coffee—or, at least, that's what the jailer called it.

By nine a.m. a crowd noisily began to gather as Officer Curl and the Sheriff had returned to take him to the first floor courthouse office of the judge, the Reverend Joseph Wheeler. Due to the size of the crowd pushing in to see what was happening, the judge moved the appearance to the upstairs courtroom. The crowd became an angry mob, chanting and snarling murderous threats against Roman. He felt like a lowly exhibit in a traveling circus. *The enemies of the Church have turned the priesthood into a sideshow.*

One of the parishioners made his way through the crowd of what must have been over two hundred people. "Father Roman, shall I inform Bishop Hailandière of your arrest?"

"That would be a great kindness. Ask the bishop to bring with him the Reverend Shawe. Both the bishop and Father Shawe practiced law before taking Holy Orders." Shawe was also a Canon Lawyer, so that could serve as an additional benefit.

Roman nearly forgot the letter he had written to the bishop. "Please see that His Lordship gets this." He removed it from his shirt and handed it to the man. As the man disappeared in the restless crowd, Roman hoped the man would make it safely to Vincennes considering the angry array. As Roman stood at the bar under guard by the constable, Officer Curl, a slight framed, black-haired, bearded man approached him in the midst of the confusion.

"Reverend Weinzoepfel?"

"Yes?"

"It appears that you are up to the hub in trouble. James Jones, attorney at law, at your service." He held out his hand.

"Excuse me?"

"My brother and I should like to defend you." James and his brother, Wilbur, were partners in their practice of law.

Roman maneuvered his manacled hand and placed it in James'. "Is this bravery or a public stunt?"

"Neither. An accused man needs representation and we are available."

"But—" Roman stammered.

"We would like to serve as your defense counsel."

"I have no money."

"Payment is not an issue. We seek justice. My brother, Wilbur, is speaking to Judge Wheeler now."

"Are you certain you want to do this? Neither of you is *Catholic.*"

"And *you* are not a *Protestant.*" James grinned from behind his mustache and beard. "All the more reason we should defend you."

Roman had the faint beginnings of a smile, but it faded quickly.

The clean-shaven Wilbur offered Roman his hand as he came away from the judge's bench. "Wheeler said that he saw no conflict with our defending you if you'd have us."

By now the Chandler brothers had worked their way to the front of the courtroom. They looked eager to hear Roman's conversation with the Jones brothers. John Chandler, the attorney, approached. "Now, suppose I should wish to defend him, Mr. Jones?"

"Be my guest, but I believe your offer is insincere." James replied.

"Of course it is. But what if I truly desired to defend him?" He looked at Roman. "Priest, who would you rather have plead your case, the best lawyer in Evansville or Jones and Jones, a sorry pair of law school failures?"

Roman refused to answer him.

The County Prosecutor, James Lockhart, suddenly stood in front of them all and laughed at his fellow attorney. "John, *I* am the best lawyer in Evansville. Don't be taking on any new clients for me." He turned to Roman. "Especially the likes of him."

Roman looked down, humiliated.

Will Chandler stepped up near James Jones' face. "Have you taken leave of your senses, man?" He shot a look at Wilbur and

86

pointed at Roman. "How can you two even think of defending such a knave?"

"It's very simple," James answered. "We believe him to be innocent."

"If you defend him," John replied, "neither of you will ever argue another case in this city or state. It will ruin both of your careers, and in short order. This *priest* is guilty beyond a doubt."

"I believe we should let a judge and jury determine that," Wilbur said. "After all, does not our Constitution provide for a presumption of innocence?"

Roman felt some solace in the law of the land.

"You two aren't even Catholic." Will's voice raised.

"True, but irrelevant." James looked at Will eye to eye.

"And I suppose you'd defend a nigger, too." Will said.

Roman knew that the Joneses had assisted runaway slaves in the past and had even allowed them to sleep in their own homes.

"Why, I'm surprised at you, Will," Wilbur laughed. "I thought all Whigs were abolitionists."

"And I thought all Democrats favored slavery." Will added.

Neither brother spoke.

"Listen, if you go forward with this misguided scheme to defend that priest," Will pointed at them both, "as a journalist I will print your names for the entire world to see. Both of you will be finished as lawyers, just as surely as Roman Weinzoepfel is finished as a priest."

The words sliced Roman's soul.

"We shall see." Wilbur smiled. "I always thought that the difference between American justice and a lynch mob was the protections of the Constitution and a sense of fundamental fairness."

"Don't lecture us on the law." Will Chandler's face was red. "Just let me say one more thing before you both go off and ruin yourselves. What do you think you can possibly gain by defending this lecherous whoremonger?"

Roman felt his face growing warmer as the beating of his heart increased.

"We will have defended the poor and oppressed." James Jones didn't flinch. "And we will have been true to the Oath of Attorneys which we swore before God to observe. Can you say the same?"

"Mrs. Schmoll is the victim in this case!" John shouted. "You have everything to lose and nothing to gain. Case closed." He began to walk away. "Come on, Will. They've been infected by the Democrats and their immigrant lackeys." The two left the room.

Roman managed to remain silent during the entire exchange. He knew the Joneses were friends with most of the Catholics in Evansville, and he had seen the Jones brothers and their wives visiting with the Heinrichs and the Lincks.

As the Joneses returned to the judge's bench and spoke with the Reverend Wheeler, Roman was still ired that Wheeler had married Martin Schmoll to Anna Maria just five months prior. Now he had even more reason to resent the man for issuing the warrant for his arrest. He couldn't even look at the man.

"I am not desirous of presiding over the trial of this priest," Wheeler explained to the Joneses. "I have become privy to some disturbing things about both Mr. and Mrs. Schmoll, things I'm not at liberty to divulge." Roman was surprised at his words.

"Well, then could we postpone the arraignment until Monday morning?" James asked.

"I don't see why not." Wheeler answered, looking at Roman. "The only thing you will have to do this evening is post bail if you want to avoid spending another night in jail."

"How much is his bail?" James asked calmly.

"The bail is two thousand dollars."

"Where am I to obtain such an ambitious sum of money?" Roman asked calmly and looked up for the first time.

"Father, you don't have to worry about that." Francis Xavier Linck, Senior, stepped forward, producing a large bundle of bills. "We took up a collection from the parish and came up with your bail." Roman had a feeling that Linck had probably supplied the largest portion himself. Linck was a Catholic and also the owner of *The Mansion House Hotel*.

"Oh, but I can't accept that. I'll spend the night in jail."

Linck leaned in close and whispered to Roman and the lawyers. "There are plans afoot to storm the jail tonight and lynch you. Accept the bail and stay at my house tonight. Reverend Shawe has sent word that he'll arrive by nightfall."

Roman asked whether the bishop was coming, but Shawe had made reservations only for himself and a Vincennes attorney. He was humbled at the outpouring of generosity from both his parishioners, and the Joneses' willingness to defend a Catholic in a Protestant town.

Roman explained to the Joneses that he would need to consult with the diocesan Canon lawyer before committing them to his case. He also inquired with them about a change of venue to a more Catholic friendly county for his trial.

James Jones asked Wheeler, "Reverend Weinzoepfel might petition the Court for a change of venue."

"On what grounds?"

"There is a concern that the religion of the defendant might preclude a fair hearing."

"Allow me to be generous, gentlemen. I'm not a prejudiced man, Reverend Weinzoepfel. I realize we have our differences, but I harbor no ill will for you. If the truth be known, this morning I made arrangements to transfer this case to the Honorable Nathan Rowley." Wheeler looked at the attorneys, and said in a lowered voice. "I do not desire to preside over the destruction of this man."

Roman was taken that this Protestant minister, rather than being vindictive, had instead shown mercy and granted his lawyers' requests. Now he regretted his own prejudice and recounted Wheeler's willingness to clash with the preachers at the tent revival.

"However, as for transferring the trial to a neighboring county," Wheeler continued, adjusting his cravat and judge's robe, "I wouldn't hazard a guess on the chances of that happening. You might have better luck betting on a blizzard in July rather than Rowley allowing for a change of venue."

Once Roman had made bail and was set at liberty, he exchanged his soutane for work clothes. In the company of his defense team and for reasons of personal security, he traveled incognito as a groom to the church and packed a few personal items and returned to the Linck's *Mansion House* for the night. He spent the evening in anxious prayer fearful that some of Schmoll's friends might burn the church down or discover his whereabouts and break in *The Mansion House* and kill him in his sleep or abduct him only to lynch him under cover of darkness.

In his sleeplessness, his mind returned to the previous Wednesday, Ascension Eve.

John William McMullen

4 May 1842

The difference between Sunday, the first of May and Wednesday the fourth was forty degrees. By Tuesday morning the heat of summer had gripped May by the throat—the clear, blue sky and cool, crisp breeze was usurped by a cloudless, colorless haze and stifling, suffocating airlessness. It rained Wednesday morning, but rather than having a cooling effect, it only added to the sweltering conditions, the rising sun turning the precipitation into a miserable steam. The thermometer had reached ninety degrees by mid-morning and by Wednesday evening it had only cooled to the upper eighties, still with an oppressive humidity.

That evening was the vigil to the Feast of Ascension and Roman entered the church to hear confessions. Before morning mass he had posted a notice on the church door indicating that confessions would be heard from five to six o'clock. The morrow was the Holy Day and the next day would be the last day for the faithful to fulfill the Easter Duty obligation so as to receive Holy Communion during the Easter Season.

He entered the church and saw four parishioners waiting to confess. Stepping into the confessional box, he draped the violet and fringed stole around his neck, sat, and slid open the wooden screen. He prayed the beads of his rosary as he waited for the first penitent.

In his experience in the confessional, he strove to bring his theological training to bear upon the sinner, but he wasn't exactly sure he was getting anywhere with many of the Catholics. Some of the penitents nearly demanded absolution as soon as they knelt on the other side of the screen while others cringed to learn that the priest has the obligation to examine and judge whether to loose or bind them from their sins. He remembered his conversation with Abbé Martin.

The confessor who would withhold absolution runs the risk of being disdained by some in the congregation. Even so, Christ said to expect persecution. All sinners who enter the confessional expect absolution. If it is withheld, there must be good reason. Abbé Martin's words were still fresh in his memory. *The penitent may despair or reject the sacrament altogether.*

As one of his pastoral responsibilities, Roman viewed his time in the confessional as a labor of love, knowing that sooner or later, every Catholic would have to confess, and as a physician of souls, he would be there to prescribe the spiritual remedy, binding up the wounds of sin through the healing salve of the sacrament.

He prayed that he would always be a conscientious confessor. Some priests only *heard* confessions, granting absolution to all, failing to intervene in men's sinful habits, and neglecting to offer them proper spiritual medicines for diseased souls. The role of confessor was a grave responsibility and he believed many penitents failed to recognize the seriousness of sin.

The Sacrament of Confession is a direct confrontation with Satan as the priest frees the sinner from bondage to sin and gives him back to God. A man's redemption is contingent upon his willingness to conform his rebellious will to the will of Christ. "What you bind on earth is bound in heaven, what you loose on earth is loosed in heaven." Christ's words clearly trumped any human claim.

The sound of someone entering the box interrupted his thoughts as he opened his eyes. The outline of the face and familiar voice whispering the *Confiteor* belonged to Mr. Heinrich. He had seen him and his wife kneeling in a front pew upon entering the church. He didn't notice who the others were, but then he wasn't interested who they were—the confessional was confidential. Nevertheless, the Heinrichs were weekly penitents of the confessional and he expected them.

Patiently, Roman heard Wilhelm's sins, number and kind. The man was jealous of another Protestant storeowner in town who dealt in dry goods; the man had more customers, it seemed, because he was Protestant. And he had also lusted for one of the young girls in town while she browsed in his store. "I caught myself thinking, 'what if I was younger?'"

Then his confession turned to a dilemma. "Was it wrong for me to lie to the sheriff when he came to the store asking if I knew where the abolitionists were keeping the niggers?"

"The pope has condemned the slave trade. The Bishop of New York and the Vicar General of Bardstown have come down hard in their condemnation of those bounty hunters who are pursuing fugitive slaves. Saint Peter said in the Acts of the Apostles that if a law is unjust, meaning that a civil law is contrary to the law of God, that it is far *better to obey God rather than obey Man.*

"Therefore," Roman continued, "I would consider it a venial sin. Say one *Pater Noster* and an *Ave*. And do be careful in hiding these fugitives. It can be dangerous, you know. The bounty hunters pursuing these Negroes carry guns and they aren't afraid to use them."

No sooner had he departed with his penance did the voice of Mrs. Heinrich sound from the other side of the grille.

She confessed her sin of repeating a rumor about Doctor Trafton and told how she occasionally skipped her evening prayers or started some days immediately without saying her morning prayers or rosary, and failed to keep up with her domestic chores, as she should. "I was late getting my husband's dinner on the table. I got angry with him. He always wants dinner on time. I don't see him cooking. He doesn't understand what it's like."

She was also guilty of looking at herself in the mirror too often. The American infection of *being better off* was a hindrance to a Catholic's efforts in *being better*, in Roman's opinion.

Mrs. Heinrich continued, confessing that she had listened to gossip about the Schmolls and hadn't said anything in their defense. "There are rumors about her pregnancy, whether it's Martin's or not." She admitted that she was judgmental towards the Schmolls, coveting their new horse and carriage, and begrudging Anna Maria's clothing. "She buys her clothing from New York and Cincinnati already manufactured, rather than buying material and making her own clothes like the rest of us."

Roman took her to task for listening to such calumny and for her envy.

She then confessed to lying to the sheriff when he came to the store looking for Negroes. "I helped the lawyers, Messrs. Jones and Messrs. McCutchan and Carpenter. We helped them with five nigger boys. They'd been beaten up pretty bad by their masters, so my husband and I hid them in the store. We took two of them in the back while the other three we hid under a load of clothes that we'd unloaded off one of the boats. We carted them up the hill and out of town, waiting till dark to send them up the canal's tow path."

Roman cautioned her of the moral dilemma she faced, the illegality of her actions contrasted with the immorality of chaining a man like an animal. "Don't go getting yourself killed, Mrs. Heinrich. Slave-owners consider fugitive slaves their property."

Running slaves isn't something a woman ought to get involved in, he thought. He assigned Mrs. Heinrich her penance and pronounced the words of absolution.

Before she left the confessional, she said through the grille. "Father Roman, don't forget to join us for dinner."

"Yes. *Danke.*" He wasn't too comfortable with Mrs. Heinrich's personal comments, but all the same he was hungry.

Roman already had suspicions that other parishioners were helping the Protestant abolitionists. Now Mr. and Mrs. Heinrich had both confessed that they were accomplices. Why should he be surprised? Deydier himself was in on it as well, learning his tactics from the French underground during the round ups of Catholics during the *Reign of Terror*. On more than one occasion his pastor had brought black men and women to Evansville freed with his own money, including the bell ringer, Andrew Martin. Unfortunately, too many Catholics in the North, as in the South, were ambivalent towards the question of slavery.

Another penitent followed and after dismissing him with the blessing, Roman was feeling rather cramped in the box, hoping he could step out for some fresh air and stretch his legs. He waited in the hot box for a minute, fingering his rosary, making a selfish plea for his task to be complete.

He opened the confessional's door thinking that the last penitent had finished making his act of contrition and praying the prayer of penance. As he stepped out of the confessional box and reached to his shoulders to lift the priestly stole from around his neck, he looked around to see if there was anyone left in church. Something drew his attention and as he turned around he saw the curtain of the confessional move. Someone had just entered the booth. He looked down and saw the shoed feet of a woman dangling over the kneeler as the drawn mantle swayed over them.

He carefully replaced the stole, reentered the booth, shut the door, and sat. A female voice stammered through the familiar Latin *Confiteor* and began her confession in German. "Bless me, Father, for I have sinned..."

When was your last confession?"

"Christmas. Don't you remember, Father Roman?" The woman gave off a perfumed scent—an aroma of rose petals, a worldly superfluity for someone with expensive tastes. *Anna Maria Schmoll.*

"What are your sins?"

"I don't know where to begin."

"Have you examined your conscience?"

"Yes."

"Then what sin brings you to the confessional?"

"You...You told me to come. It's my religious duty, Father *Roman*."

Roman resented the way she intentionally called him by his first name.

"What sins have you come to confess?"

"I haven't been to Mass since Christmas."

"Why?"

"Because my husband wouldn't let me. He doesn't love me. He drinks. He hits me. He has guns, you know. He pointed his rifle at me the other night. I didn't know what to do."

"Have you provoked him?"

"No. He calls me a whore."

"Did you imagine things would be like this when you married him? You had only known him for less than a week. And he was a Protestant."

She sighed..

"How happy did you think you would be married to Mr. Schmoll?"

"I don't know. He says that I'm unfaithful to him. He accuses me of committing adultery."

"Have you?"

"Yes."

"How many times?"

"How should I know? I don't count my men."

"Mrs. Schmoll. We've been down this path before."

"Lately I only know I've tried more often than I've succeeded."

"Now stop playing games and be serious."

"I *am* serious."

"Are you sorry for these sins?"

There was no answer.

"Are you remorseful for violating your marriage vows to your husband?"

"I thought you said my marriage to a Lutheran wasn't a true marriage."

"I have never said that! What I said was your marriage would be recognized once your husband allowed you to practice your faith and raise your children Catholic—"

"He never meant to keep his promise to that agreement," she sighed.

He believed her. "Are you confident that your marriage is legal and, as you say, true?"

"Yes, Martin and his lawyer friends have told me it is."

"Regardless of opinion, it *is* a legal union, a sacramental bond recognized in the eyes of God and the Church."

"Well, you're right about that, but Martin beats me, you know."

"I am sorry for you." So much of her life was tragic and he could have said much more, but he kept his comments to a minimum.

"Is that all you can say? Don't you care about me? Martin comes home after drinking all day at one of the taverns here or over at Lamasco and then makes me go to bed with him."

"He forces you to have conjugal relations?" The thought angered him.

"What?"

"He forces himself upon you?"

"Yes, he has his way with me despite my condition. You do realize I'm with child?"

"Yes." He paused. "How often does he demand relations?"

"Often enough, twice or three times a week. Why should you want to know?"

"I'm taken aback by his cruelty."

"Now he even questions whether it's his child or not. He got drunk last night with that Will Chandler and the two of them talked about *you* half the night. He wasn't going to let me come to confession this evening, but I reminded him of the agreement, so he let me. He says you and my father forced him into signing."

"I did no such thing."

"I told him at least you had a heart and then he hit me in the face. He thinks I was already pregnant before I married him. He says I knew my father would disown me and that I wanted the child to have a father. Then he said he wouldn't be surprised if the child is *yours*."

"Mine?! Mrs. Schmoll, don't be absurd! It *is* his, isn't it?"

"Of course it's *his*."

"Mrs. Schmoll, I am an ambassador of Christ concerned for the welfare of your immortal soul, whether you will spend your eternity in heaven or in the flames of hell."

"Hell couldn't possibly be worse than the life I've been given. And to think I used to think that life with my father was bad. With Martin it's worse!"

"Then why did you marry?"

"He had money. He bought me things. He told me things no man had ever told me. I thought he loved me."

"So you entered into marriage without properly discerning the dignity of the married state?"

"I thought we were in love. He took me to his bed."

"And now you have to live with your decision."

"You have no idea of what I'm talking about, do you? You've probably never been in love. Haven't you ever wanted something so badly, but when you finally got it you regretted ever wanting it?"

"I don't believe I've ever wanted something that badly."

"Isn't there something you want so much that if you can't have it, then you don't want anyone to enjoy it?"

"You're not that covetous, are you? One ought to desire to lose that which is most dear to him in the whole world, rather than offend the Almighty by even one sin. One must be willing to sacrifice all— even his own life—rather than commit one sin."

"Those are fine words, but can anyone do it? Would you be willing to do that?"

"With God all things are possible. I would hope and pray that God give me the grace to give my life for him if I were ever faced with such a choice. I pray I'm spared of ever such a quandary. I'm not ready for martyrdom, if that's what you want to know."

"You mean you chose to be a priest? It wasn't decided for you by your father or mother?"

"No more than your father arranged for you to marry Mr. Schmoll."

"Why would you want to become a priest?"

"I believed God was calling me to be a priest."

"I knew a boy back home—you remind me of him. He was the youngest son, so his parents decided he was to be a priest and they took him to a monastery and made him become a monk. It wasn't right. He ran away one night and came home. His father disowned him. Later that week he jumped off a bridge and drowned himself. What do you think of that?"

"If what you say is true, then it was truly a tragedy. The young man obviously didn't have a vocation."

"Some priest you are! How can you be so cold?"

"I am sorry for his despair. Now, you were telling me why you married..."

"I was with my father at the mill the first time I saw Martin. I went back the next day and saw him again. He gave me a horse ride and took me to *Wood's Tavern* where we drank. He told me he loved me so I slept with him. Maybe I was just lonely."

"There was no reflection on your part in regard to the Sacrament of Holy Matrimony?"

"No, not really."

"Now that you're married and with child, you have again committed adultery. Are you resolved to avoid this sin in the future?"

"What does it matter now? I've done it so many times."

"I cannot grant you absolution unless you are truly sorry for your sins."

She sighed from behind the grille.

"When you confessed last Christmas I thought you promised yourself and me—and God—that you would avoid this sin."

"Yes, I did. But I'd sleep with any man who'd have me—*even you.*"

Roman felt like sliding the wooden screen shut then and there, but here was a sinner in most dire need of God's grace and mercy, a soiled lamb alone on a rocky cliff.

"I'm sorry..." She broke off in tears. "Won't you forgive me?"

"Yes..." He patiently waited with the thought that she was about to express true contrition and sorrow.

"I'm sorry I married him and not you. Roman, I should've married you!"

"Mrs. Schmoll, I am a priest."

"So? You're a *man* and I'm a *woman.*"

"Madam, there are some things best left unsaid. Now, if you wish to receive the sacrament, you must confess your sins, express sorrow for those sins, and make a good act of contrition—"

Before he could finish speaking, she sighed again, this time loudly.

"Father, I feel faint."

"It's quite warm—"

"Yes, it's my condition."

"Then perhaps you should step out of the confessional for some air."

She departed the kneeler but she cried out once in the nave of the church, "Help me, Father Roman!"

Instinctively, he quickly opened the door of the confessional and met her in the aisle. "What?"

She was slow to move and wiped her brow with her hand. "I think I shall pass out."

He stepped next to her and she began to waver.

"Then you *do* care for me?"

"You're a member of Assumption Church. Your soul has been entrusted to my care."

She turned around, gazed into his eyes, and reached for him. "Are you blind? The first time I met you, I wanted you. I practically threw myself at you the night my mother died. You act like you don't notice, but I know you do. You wear your quaint little three-cornered hat and hide under the cassock and live in your perfect world."

"Why have you come to church, Mrs. Schmoll?"

"I came to see you because my life with Martin is so unhappy. Of all people, I thought, I was hoping you could—"

"Anna Maria, you're still grieving the death of your mother."

"I want you, Roman."

The memory of the last time she touched him filled his thoughts.

"I think about you all the time."

"Mrs. Schmoll, what are you doing? We're not in a tavern; we're in the house of God! I am a *priest*. You are a *married woman with child*. I am vowed to Christ and his Church and you to your husband and child. *I* know who *I* am. Can you say as much?"

She stood opposite him as if ready to embrace him. "Have you never loved a woman?"

He hesitated for a moment.

"Roman, I love you."

"Don't tell me that."

"Kiss me."

"Don't say these things."

It was his last memory before falling asleep.

8 May 1842

On Sunday morning, Roman awoke to the stark reality of the charges. The English priest and Canon lawyer, Reverend Michael Edgar Evelyn Shawe had arrived in Evansville with the Vincennes attorney, Benjamin Thomas. Shawe explained to Roman that Bishop Hailandière had received word of the allegations on Friday evening while he was returning from a visit with Bishop Flagét in Louisville. The story was quickly spreading everywhere. His Lordship had sent the attorney Benjamin Thomas to aid Shawe in Roman's defense. Thomas was originally from Philadelphia and had moved to Indiana where he found himself defending immigrants and indentured servants. He was a recent convert to Catholicism, baptized at the hands of the bishop himself. The two ministers of justice had arrived on horseback late Saturday night and were lodged at *The Mansion House*.

Roman, wearing his priestly soutane, led the Reverend Shawe to the church that Sunday morning. The distinguished Englishman informed Roman that the bishop wanted him to be encouraged by this persecution.

"Father Roman, I regret I must inform you that His Excellency has decided that you should not be allowed to hear any confessions—save an emergency. Rest assured, this does not mean that your faculties have been removed, and it does not mean that His Lordship believes the woman's calumnious charges. It is merely a precaution against further allegations. I am sure you can understand His Lordship's concerns."

Roman put on a white surplice and said nothing as he knelt upon a prie-dieu, absorbing himself in prayer, his face in his hands. Shawe departed the sacristy for the confessional. Roman glanced up to contemplate the crucifix. He had no words.

A few minutes later, Reverend Shawe reentered the sacristy.

"Father Roman?" The English voice cleared the air. "Since today is a High Mass, I wish for you to preside as the main celebrant and I shall function in the role of deacon."

"No, it should be the other way around. I shouldn't be the main celebrant. Not after what I have brought upon the Catholics of the diocese. My imprudence could affect the entire Church." Roman hadn't even intended to vest, fearing that some of the parishioners believed the accusations.

"Father Roman. Where is your faith?"

He gave no response.

Reverend Shawe began to put on the different liturgical garments. "The Vicar-General, Abbé Augustine Martin, speaks highly of you. And I know your dear pastor, Father Deydier, cannot say enough good about you and all that you have done for the diocese." His head poked through the surplice as he looked at Roman.

"It is not due to anything I have done, Father," Roman huffed at the praise. "Give the Glory to God. Humility is not one of my better virtues." He rose from the prayer bench.

"The bishop himself wanted you to say Mass..." Shawe's words trailed off as if he was about to say something else.

He completed the sentence in his own head. *The bishop wants you to say Mass one last time.* Slumping deeper into sadness as he walked over to the wardrobe, he stared inside at his liturgical robes. "Perhaps this *will* be my last Mass."

"Pardon?" Shawe asked.

"Nothing." Roman closed his eyes.

Andrew Martin pulled the belfry rope and called worshipers to prayer while Josiah Stahlhofer worked to light every candle upon the high altar. Roman heard people speaking in the church and peered out of the sacristy to see if there were a goodly number of parishioners. He had feared no one would show, especially after the charges leveled against him had been made known. He was surprised, troubled, overjoyed and fearful all at the same time when he saw that the church was filled to capacity with only standing room.

"Reverend Shawe, why didn't you tell me the church is overflowing with people?"

"Why should that upset you?"

"They can't all be Catholics, can they?"

Josiah entered the conversation. "Many of them are, Father. There are people from Saint Philip, Saint Wendel, Saint Joseph, and even a few from Kentucky."

"It is true," Shawe nodded. "I even saw some from Illinois, Vincennes, and Jasper."

Roman looked out again and saw some familiar faces. He was overcome with emotion. He turned away from the doorway and fell upon the prie-dieu again. Shawe remained silent. Josiah clanked around, preparing the censer, placing two hot coals in it. An acrid odor filled Roman's nostrils.

Reverend Shawe interrupted Roman's contemplation. "You must get vested, Father. Mass must start on time. There's no devotion in delay."

"Yes, Father." Roman worked to put on the garments. What had at one time been such a joy, now felt like lifting a cross up the hill of Calvary. He remembered his ordination and how he had celebrated his first Mass upon a makeshift altar due to the collapse of the Cathedral the night before. He hoped that the weight of all the worshipers this morning would not bring this church down to its timbers.

He prayed the familiar vesting prayers and reverently kissed his stole, the sacramental sign of his dignity as a priest. It was the same stole he had kissed prior to hearing confessions on Wednesday. *Will I ever hear another confession? What if I am convicted of the charges? I am ruined as a priest! This is all I have ever really wanted in life. This is all I have known. Where will I go? What will I do? If I flee, I will be hanged. If the court finds me guilty, I will be hanged. They will kill me either way.* Darkness descended upon him.

Shawe read the epistle of Peter. *"Have a constant mutual charity for all since charity covers a multitude of sins."* The words of Saint Peter ascended, echoing off the apse, deigning to challenge Roman.

Oblivious to Shawe's sermon, he was lost in prayer, penetrating the meaning of that day's Gospel, a passage from Saint John. *Behold, the hour is coming, and has arrived, that whosoever kills thee will think that he is doing a service to God. And these things will they do to thee, because they have not known the Father, or Me. But these things I tell thee so that when the hour shall come, thou may remember that I told thee of them.*

This gospel was prescribed for that particular Sunday. Had he not known otherwise, he might have thought Shawe had read it on his account. *God's grace is boundless. He leaves nothing to chance. There is a reason for everything.* He tried to believe what his faith taught.

Moving to the altar, Roman prepared to offer the gifts of bread and wine. He took the paten with the Eucharistic bread upon it and lifted it to heaven.

Reverend Shawe then approached him, holding a censer. Shawe handed Roman a small bowl of incense and raised the lid of the censer, exposing the glowing red coals. Scooping a small spoonful of incense grains from the bowl, Roman poured them upon one of the live coals. He returned the spoon to the bowl and handed it to Shawe. A sweet cloud of smoke enveloped Roman's face, the aroma filling his nose and mouth. He stood at the altar, his back to the congregation, hands aloft in prayer, beseeching the blessings of God in the mother tongue of the Church.

A terrifying thought introduced itself. *What if Martin Schmoll is in the congregation and is about to stand up and shoot me in the back?* He refocused upon the Latin prayercards.

Before long, he was lifting the host, uttering the words of consecration, *"Hoc est enim corpus meum,"* this is my body. The host between his fingers, he knelt, adored, and rose to his feet, elevating the host above his head so that all behind in the pews might behold their savior's flesh. Returning the host to its paten, he reverently genuflected again.

In a whisper, he voiced the prayer over the chalice of wine, *"Hic est enim calix sanguinis,"* this is the chalice of my blood. Taking the chalice into his hands, he knelt again, and rose to elevate the chalice on high, but suddenly, as if an attack of the devil himself, he grew weak and thought he was about to collapse, utterly crushed under the weight of the chalice. His lip quavered and his vision became obscured and blurred. An audible gasp came from a member of the congregation. Roman swayed off balance and he saw Shawe flinch for a second or two as if to spring forward and catch the falling chalice. He somehow regained his equilibrium, carefully placed the chalice upon the altar, and knelt in genuflection. He remained in that position longer than was usual.

"Are you all right?" Shawe whispered.

"Yes. Give me a moment." The thought of being killed confounded him. He had always known that the blood of the martyrs was the seed of the Church, but he had never considered that it might actually be the blood from his own veins that would water the seeds

102

of the gospel. Reaching into his sleeve and pulling out a handkerchief, he wiped his eyes and nose. The salty taste of a tear was on his lips.

Roman stood and prayed the remainder of the Canon.

Forgive us our trespasses as we forgive those who trespass against us. The words of the *Pater Noster* stuck in his throat like a fish bone. *Forgive? Forgive the Schmolls? How?*

"Lord, I am not worthy that you should come under my roof, but only say the word and my soul shall be healed." He placed the sacred host upon his tongue and drank the precious blood. He hesitated before turning around to distribute communion to the congregation. He recognized some of the people kneeling at the altar rail ready to receive the sacrament, but didn't know them to be Catholic. Some were kneeling for their Easter duty and certainly there were others there at Mass who had come solely out of curiosity to see a reprobate priest celebrate the sacred mysteries of the Catholic religion one last time before being carted off to be hanged from the gallows. Nevertheless, delicately placing Holy Communion upon the tongues of the different members of several of his flocks filled him with purpose. Many of the Catholic faithful openly wept at the rail and it was difficult for him to continue holding back his own emotion.

At the end of Mass, he knelt in thanksgiving and tried not to think of Anna Maria Schmoll.

He felt that he was not only strengthened by the sacrament, but also encouraged by the prayers of the Catholic community. He remained at the prie-dieu until there was no one left in the church save Reverend Shawe.

He retired to *The Mansion House* and met with Reverend Shawe, Benjamin Thomas, and James and Wilbur Jones to prepare himself for the trial. He was troubled by the absence of His Lordship. Roman asked Shawe why Bishop Hailandière hadn't come, knowing he was a lawyer before becoming a priest. Shawe explained that His Lordship was consumed with spiritual affairs.

Roman was convinced that *his* predicament was a spiritual affair for the entire diocese and his bishop should be there to support him.

Chapter 10

Under Oath

May 9, 1842

Monday morning in Evansville, Roman saw crowds of people, horses, wagons, coaches and carriages swelling the streets. His initial feeling was that many of the visitors had traveled to see a contemporary passion play. By noon the throng was trying to get into the courthouse.

Reverend Shawe tried to delicately explain the furor to Roman. "Father Roman, Benjamin and I want to prepare you for what you are about to undergo." The Jones brothers were already in the courtroom.

"I have been praying all morning."

"Good." The corpulent, mustached Benjamin Thomas wore a high collared white cotton shirt with blue cravat, a blue top coat and matching breeches with white socks from his kneecaps down to his black leather, golden buckled shoes. "We will definitely rely upon prayer."

Shawe explained that within the past three days, news of the charges against Roman and his forthcoming trial had gone forth in all directions. "There are a lot of people in town. The sheriff told us that there may be as many as five hundred visitors to the city for your trial."

"Wonderful," Roman gave a quirky smile. "I'm sure the merchants will thank me later."

"Many of them are Schmoll's supporters, mostly Americans." Shawe frowned.

"In other words, *Protestants*." Roman closed his eyes.

"Yes, and many of them have filled the courtroom." Thomas snorted. "They're in an excited state, like the crowd at a Roman circus."

"Is that why I feel like the lone Christian about to be thrown to the lions?" Roman winced. "All we need are the gladiators."

Thomas rubbed his chin. "It does seem that you are on trial for being a priest."

"Yes, when I had Schmoll to sign the marriage promises, it reopened Old World wounds. Alas, I lacked prudence in the matter. It was foolish to dwell upon the irregularity of their marriage. I should have told them to wait until Father Deydier returned."

"Do not be so hard on yourself, Father," Shawe put his arm on his back. "There are also a large number of Catholics here, even more than were at Mass yesterday—Irish and German Catholic immigrants out in force to support a Catholic priest."

Benjamin Thomas spoke. "The attorney Jay Davis is lead prosecutor for this case. Do you know this man?"

"We've met. He's an American through and through. A real dandy."

"It appears that Judge Lockhart, the regular prosecutor, is conveniently detained with another case." Thomas explained.

"How convenient—and predictable," snapped Roman, pacing the floor. "Any other case Lockhart would be scrambling to argue. Why not this case?"

"The Jones brothers are going to request that Judge Lockhart replace Davis as prosecutor." Shawe cleared his throat and shook his head slowly. "From what the lawyers in Vincennes say, this Jay Davis is a shyster lawyer."

"He has a terrible reputation." Thomas thundered.

"It is a prearranged conspiracy," Roman interjected. "I am certain of it. This Davis was present when Martin signed the promises."

"In Vincennes I have helped many of the immigrants there get their legal affairs in order," Thomas continued, "enabling them to vote and such. As a result some of the Whigs have painted me up to be a villain. One of those Whigs was Jay Davis."

Just then the doors opened and the Jones brothers stepped through. "It's time to go, Father Roman. Judge Rowley is ready."

He braced himself for what he feared would be the worst day of his life. As he walked through the open door and entered the courtroom, he adjusted his collar and biretta. The sound of boos, catcalls, whistles, and howls rang his ears and throbbed his head. The smoke of pipes and cigars stung in his nostrils while the smell of whiskey perfumed the room, permeating the thick, humid, insalubrious air making it hard to breathe. He placed his right hand to his chest and the hair-shirt scratched his flesh.

His head hurt too, but it was more than a migraine, it was his mind. He was mentally exhausted and emotionally drained, and so nervous that his hands and legs tingled and trembled. Sitting in the front of the court, he felt like a wounded hound dog helplessly caught in a bear trap. He, the priest and minister of the sacrament of confession, regarded by Protestants as a cancerous tumor, was about to be surgically removed from the Body of Christ. Fidgeting in his seat, his right leg restlessly bounced up and down. He dreaded that at any moment one of the angry Protestants would explode, ushering in mayhem or murder. With each swing of the pendulum, he prayed the trial would get under way and move ahead. Waiting was unbearable.

Several officers mingled with the crowd and maintained the peace, despite the rustling, restlessness of the crowd, shuffling and tromping feet on the wooden floors, and a constant din of whispering and murmuring. The floor shook and Roman wasn't sure whether or not the throng of angry men was about to spring upon his person, strangling him to death to placate their appetites for justice. Even before Anna Maria Schmoll had been sworn in, a mêlée seemed to be breaking out between the Irish boys and Schmolls' supporters in the seats behind him. The constables had already given several warnings to all by the time the proceedings were to begin.

"The crowd is too large, Your Honor," one of the constables said to the judge. "The walls of the building are starting to sway. It's too much weight." Roman thought he had been experiencing motion, but he had attributed it to acute apprehension.

"Thank you, bailiff, but we will proceed. This structure is sound, and I fear the consequences of removing certain observers while allowing others to remain. Now, if you will excuse me, I must step out for a moment. Please see if you could get the prosecution into the courtroom."

No sooner had the judge left the room did the bailiff return, escorting Anna Maria in from a side door opposite Roman. The attorneys John Chandler and Jay Davis followed her while Martin Schmoll brought up the rear.

Mr. Schmoll glowered at Roman from beneath his furrowed eyebrows. Then he turned to the anxious crowd and several men shouted out support for his wife and their desires on Roman. Other cries proclaiming Roman's innocence pierced the air. Meanwhile, Anna Maria and her lawyers and her husband, Martin Schmoll, took their seats at the front of the chamber. Martin Schmoll shot another glance at Roman, leaning over the end of the prosecution's bench. Roman lowered his eyes, yet he knew that hundreds of eyes were upon him. More cries displaced the decorum of the courtroom.

This is your day, Martin! That bitch is a whore! Your wife's honor will be restored by nightfall. Martin Schmoll should be on trial! The mongrel priest will pay for his crimes! The Whigs of this place have politically motivated these charges! Weinzoepfel will die tonight!

Other voices, both for and against him, blended into confusion.

The judge hurriedly reentered the courtroom accompanied by the sheriff. The sound of hundreds of shoes coming down on the floor at once as everyone stood made a noise like that of thunder. Hammering his gavel loudly over a dozen times, he cried out several times, "Order, order in this court." He pounded his gavel until silence reigned. "You may be seated." The crowd took its seat. The judge cleared his throat and began the proceedings. "This is a forum for justice, not vengeance. Now, if the sheriff would please step forward and call the names of those jurors impaneled for this proceeding." The procedure was confusing to Roman as he held his breviary in his left hand and his rosary in his right. The judge presided as the lawyers asked each potential juror questions about their ability to be objective about the case. Roman was numb from the prospective jurors staring at him while the prosecutors alluded to the charges.

More than an hour passed. Finally, after the jury had been seated, the judge turned to the prosecutor's table. "If the prosecutor representing the State of Indiana would please rise and read the indictment."

Jay Davis stood. "If it would please the Court, Your Honor, distinguished guests." He turned and looked around the cramped gallery. "The grand jurors duly sworn to make inquiry for the State of Indiana in this county of Vanderburgh, upon their oath allege that the defendant, Mr. Roman Weinzoepfel, of Evansville, on the fourth day of May, in the year of our Lord, Eighteen hundred and forty-two, with force and arms, upon Anna Maria Schmoll, the wife of one Martin Schmoll, also of Vanderburgh County, did then and there violently and feloniously make an assault at and against the person of Anna Maria Schmoll, and then and there did feloniously ravish and carnally know the said Anna Maria Schmoll, by force and against her will, contrary to the form of the statutes in such cases made and provided, and against the peace and dignity of the State of Indiana. The Second count of the indictment charges that Roman Weinzoepflen did, in a rude, insolent, and angry manner, touch, strike, beat, wound, and ill-treat, with intent, the said Anna Maria Schmoll. The third count of the indictment charges that Roman Weinzoepflen did make an assault, with intent upon Anna Maria Schmoll, to feloniously ravish and carnally know the said Anna Maria Schmoll, by force, and against her will.' In short, for the benefit of the jury, he is charged with assault and battery, and rape."

Roman slumped in his chair and looked at the jurors. Benjamin Thomas sat to his left and Shawe was to his right. Both men placed a hand on his back. He fumbled with the red and violet ribbons of his breviary, which now sat on the table in front of him as he squeezed his rosary beads. Pressing his crucifix close to his pounding chest, his heart felt as if about to burst.

The judge turned to the defense. "Does the defense have any questions or comments to make to the jury regarding the charges lodged against the defendant at the bar?"

"None, Your Honor." James Jones stood. "Except that upon all three counts the accused is not guilty." An eruption of noise vibrated an already quivering structure, forcing the judge to pummel his gavel.

"He's innocent! This is Protestant clap-trap!" An Irish tongue with a hearty brogue sounded forth in the midst of the uproar.

"He's guilty! Hang him, hang him!" A chorus of Americans cried out.

After a minute of such shouts and others like them, and plenty of gavel pounding, order was finally restored.

"The court will not tolerate another outburst like that! There will be no more disruptions of these proceedings!" By now the judge was on his feet, enraged at the rumpus. "Otherwise, I can *and will* dispatch the sheriff and his constables to remove those who are responsible, *incarcerating them* if necessary!"

Roman, so embarrassed to be at the center of this controversy, remained still, his gaze cast down.

The judge was panting. "If the prosecution would please proceed."

"Thank you, Your Honor. The State wishes to call Mrs. Martin Schmoll to the stand." Davis wasted no time. "Due to the victim's poor command of the English language, the prosecution begs the Court's indulgence to enlist the aid of an interpreter."

"The court does not have an interpreter on hand. Besides, this issue should have been the subject of a pre-trial motion, counselor." The judge was still trying to catch his breath.

"The prosecution has secured one," Davis answered, explaining that a Lutheran man from town had volunteered his services.

"The Court is inclined to permit the intervention of an interpreter, if the defense has no proper objection. The judge looked to Roman's defense team.

"No objections your honor," James replied, "but since our client, the accused, does speak German, we will reserve the right to object to any interpretations that are less than literal."

"Your point is well-taken, counsel," the judge nodded, turning to John Chandler. "The prosecution may proceed."

"Present the Holy Bible so that the witnesses may be sworn in."

James Jones came to his feet. "Will the court please hear a request from the defense before the chief witness is sworn in?"

"Certainly, if the prosecution will please yield."

Davis shrugged his shoulders to the judge.

"You may proceed, Mr. Jones."

"Since the victim of the alleged crimes is new to the country, perhaps it would be best if she were sworn in according to the norms of her native Bavaria."

"I shall remind counsel that this proceeding is not being conducted in Bavaria." The judge tilted his head. "Pray thee, what is the norm there?"

"According to the Catholics here, and given that Mrs. Schmoll *is* a Catholic, in the Catholic land from whence she came, in a court of law, to secure a truthful testimony from a witness, a crucifix is placed on a table between two lighted candles as the witness swears upon the Catholic bible." It was the hope of his defense that the Bavarian custom would incite Anna Maria to retract the accusation.

"Granted, this is a Christian Nation, but it is not a Catholic Country—not yet, at least—" This little aside apparently pleased a majority of those in the gallery who were troubled by the ever-increasing numbers of immigrants to Indiana. "However, notwithstanding the irregularity of your request, and if the prosecution does not object, the Court will grant your request."

"Thank you, your honor," James Jones nodded to Judge Rowley.

"Does the prosecution object?" The judge looked at Davis.

"In light of the fact that the accused is a priest of the Catholic religion, it will only serve to make the testimony of our witness more credible in the face of the charges. No objections."

"If the bailiff will do the honor of taking my candlesticks, but who will secure for us a crucifix and a Catholic bible. I seem to be lacking both." Laughter filled the courtroom.

Wilbur Jones addressed the Court. "May I approach the witness, your Honor?" With an approving nod from Rowley, Wilbur stepped up to the judge's bench with a cloth bag with a drawstring. "Here, your honor. The Reverend Shawe has secured a bible and the crucifix from the tabernacle of Assumption Church."

"Very well," he exclaimed pulling a large silver crucifix out of the bag and holding it up high for all to see. "Bailiff, if you please." Handing it off to the court official, he then passed it on to the attorney Jay Davis. In like manner he did the same for the bible.

"This is heavy," Davis remarked, handling the crucifix affixed to a stand. "Real silver, no doubt. Probably quite expensive. Nice." Davis gave a slight smirk as he gazed upon the contorted figure of the Savior. Under his breath he muttered something to Martin Schmoll. "Do they not realize Christ is raised?"

"No, they're Catholics." Schmoll whispered back, leaning forward in his seat and looking to his left towards Roman. Only those in the first few rows heard the exchange, but there was a wave of whispers that moved from the front to the back of the courtroom. Roman heard the snide remarks, and could clearly see Martin Schmoll out of the corner of his eye, but refused to be intimidated by such juvenile antics, especially in a court of law where his life and reputation were at stake. Davis placed the cross down upon its base as the bailiff went to light the two candles on either side of it.

Thomas leaned next to Roman. "Say a prayer that she'll come to her senses and abandon the conspiracy. Certainly she will not commit perjury, realizing the seriousness of the oath and the nature of the charges she has placed against you."

Roman clasped his hands together in prayer, still clutching the crucifix of his rosary. "I wish I could be so sure."

The judge tapped his gavel twice. "The witness will come forward to be sworn in and take the stand."

As Anna Maria stepped forward, Roman took note that she intentionally made eye contact with him. Upon a small table in front

110

of the prosecution's table, the candles burnt and the silver cross glistened in the morning sun streaming through the open windows. Particles of dust as numerous as the stars of heaven danced in a beam of hazy yellow sunlight. It was a momentary reverie for Roman as he basked in the light of the goodness of God's creation. He thought back to an earlier time in his life when his parents and older siblings were still alive.

The judge's gavel knocked him back into the present. The bailiff gave the oath and the interpreter spoke it to her in German. "Do you solemnly swear to tell the truth, the whole truth, and nothing but the truth, so help you God?"

All eyes were upon her as she paused, looked at her husband, and slowly placed her left hand on the Catholic bible, raised her right hand, and swore in the affirmative.

"And now, Mr. Schmoll, if you would come forward, please." Judge Rowley motioned him to approach the bench.

Martin sauntered his way up to the front as if this was one of the proudest moments of his life. He leaned over the small table where the crucifix was standing and blew out the candles. "I won't need any of that." There was more snickering from Schmoll's supporters.

"Will Mr. Schmoll require the aid of an interpreter?" asked the judge.

"No." He retorted. "Despite my German ancestry, I am an American and as such I will answer in the language of this country."

"Very well. Proceed."

Martin raised his right arm half way and stopped. "Get that Catholic bible out of my sight."

The bailiff held out the King James Bible and Martin stretched his massive hand across its cover.

"Martin Schmoll, do you solemnly swear to tell the truth, the whole truth, and nothing but the truth, so help you, God?"

"So help me, God!"

"The response to the oath is, 'I do,'" the judge reminded.

"Then, I do. I swear to God! There." As Schmoll lowered his hand and took his hand off the bible, Roman thought the man's oath sounded more like a curse.

"You may take a seat," the judge said.

"The state wishes to call Mrs. Schmoll as its first witness." Davis said as he came forward.

"Point of law, your Honor." James Jones was on his feet again.

"Objection, your honor," Davis replied. "The case is with the State."

"Objection overruled," Rowley tapped his gavel. "Mr. Jones what is your point?"

"We are wondering why the Vanderburgh County prosecutor is not trying this case for the State. We find it highly unusual that the prosecutor is absent from such a notorious case."

The judge answered. "Judge Lockhart is occupied with a property case in Circuit Court at this time."

"But should not this case take precedence? Is not human life more precious than a dispute over property?"

"That is a philosophical question, my good sir. I deal with practicalities. The other case was filed weeks ago."

"I request a sidebar, Your Honor."

"Granted."

As the attorneys for both sides came forward, the crowd murmured.

"Mr. Davis is a friend of the Schmolls." James explained to the judge.

"So?" the judge leaned over his bench. "Your point?"

"We believe there to be a conflict of interest." James continued.

Jay Davis' face grew red with anger.

"Overruled." The judge shook his head. "This is pure conjecture on your part."

"There is at least the appearance of impropriety." Jones persisted.

"Not as I see it. And I am the judge."

"Then allow us to request that Mr. Schmoll be put out of the courtroom while his wife gives her testimony," James argued.

"To what purpose?" Davis asked.

"Owing to the inflammatory nature of the charges and the fact that her testimony will be of such a personal nature, and subsequently rather emotional for her, he may become too emotionally involved and excited as to commit violence." Jones stroked his beard with his left hand while his right hand methodically caressed the pages of a law book in his hand.

"Point well taken, Mr. Jones." The judge scribbled something to himself. "I will grant the request put to the bench by the defense."

Jay Davis returned to Martin Schmoll and explained to him why it would be best for him to leave during Anna Maria's testimony. Schmoll reluctantly acquiesced, and allowed himself to be escorted away by the sheriff. He exited the courtroom peaceably but not without glaring at Roman on his way out. Just before Schmoll left the room, Roman saw him turn and nod at Davis.

Anna Maria Schmoll took the stand.

Davis, speaking for the State, began the questioning. "Would you please give the court your full name?"

The witness answered without aid of the interpreter. "Anna Maria Schmoll."

"Where were you born?"

"In Bavaria."

"Did you receive an education?"

"Yes," she continued at this point through the interpreter. "I was educated at a convent school until I was confirmed. After that my father told me I didn't need to go to school."

"How long have you lived in the United States?"

"Nearly two years."

"Where have you lived?"

"In Cincinnati, and here in Vanderburgh County at Blue Grass."

"Where do you live now?" Davis turned to face Anna Maria.

"Here in Evansville."

"Are you married?"

"Yes."

"What is your husband's name?"

"Martin Schmoll."

"When were you married?"

"On the evening of the thirty-first of December, Eighteen Hundred and Forty-One."

"Is it true that you are with child?"

"Yes." Anna Maria hesitated before continuing. "I am past my fourth month."

"Where do you and your husband live?"

"Between First and Second Street off of Sycamore."

"And how far do you live from the Catholic Church of this fair city?"

"About four hundred feet, according to my husband," she smiled. "I am terrible at gauging distances."

"In relation to recent events that have nefariously transpired within the walls of that church, reportedly a sacred place of worship for Catholics—" Davis' coughed.

"Objection, Your Honor!" James was on his feet. "I object to counsel's editorial comments during his examination."

"Granted." the judge nodded, with a smirk on his face aimed at Davis. "Counsel, please confine your comments to the facts of the case."

"Mrs. Schmoll," Davis continued without acknowledging either the judge or defense counsel, "could you please enlighten this distinguished jury, and give to the court your account of the events of Wednesday, the fourth of May, including the deed that was committed upon your person by the accused?"

"Yes..." She took out handkerchief and blotted her eyes. "It being the eve of the holy day, I went to church to make my confession."

"What time of day was this?"

"Between five and six o'clock in the evening."

"Were you the only one in the church at the time."

"No. When I first arrived there was a person kneeling in the confessional box."

"What was he doing?"

"Confessing to the priest, I suppose."

"How long did you have to wait before you entered his confessional?"

"Upwards of nearly three quarters of an hour."

"Is that normal for a priest to have a penitent detained for that long?"

"I am unsure since I don't go that often."

"Was this other penitent also a woman?"

"Yes, I believe so."

"Objection, your honor." James Jones came to his feet. "The prosecution is attempting to imply that there have been other incidents of wrongdoing by the accused."

"Sustained."

"Who was the other person?" Davis resumed.

"I don't know. By then it was getting dark, and I was kneeling in prayer, so I cannot be for sure."

"When this other person was finished, what did you do?"

"I looked around to see if it was my turn."

"And..."

"And I entered the box and crossed myself."

"Then what?"

"The confessional door banged just as I knelt down, and when I looked into the priest's compartment through the wooden lattice screen he was not there. Just before I got up to leave, presuming him to have finished with confessions that day, he returned to his chair."

"You saw this?" Davis winced.

"Yes. Through the lattice."

"Where had he gone?"

"I don't know."

"What did he do then?"

"He sat back down, and made the sign of the cross."

"Then what happened?"

"I began with the usual prayers and I confessed my sins."

"Explain what followed."

"He asked me a question."

"What was the question?"

"He asked if I was confident that my marriage performed by the Justice of the Peace was legally binding and to be considered a true Christian marriage."

"How did you answer?"

"Yes, relying upon what my husband had told me." Laughter filled the courtroom.

"Order!" The smack of the judge's gavel stopped the buffoonery.

"Then what did the priest say?"

"He answered, 'yes, such a marriage is a legal union, recognized by the Church.' Then he asked me about my relationship with God and I told him I wouldn't miss Mass anymore..." She paused.

"Was that all?" Davis persisted.

"No..." The interpreter indicated that Mrs. Schmoll was a bit distraught and needed a few moments to collect her thoughts regarding the remainder of the encounter in the confessional. "Give me a little time." She wiped her eyes with the handkerchief.

There was silence in the courtroom as Anna Maria put her handkerchief up to her face and nodded to Davis.

"Whenever you're ready." Davis reached in his pocket and looked at his watch.

Anna Maria started to open her mouth, but paused again, as if to swallow grief. Looking over at her lawyers and looking into the jury box, she began. "He asked me how often my husband and I had relations."

"What kind of relations?"

"Sexual relations. Conjugal intercourse is what he called it."

"What was his question, how did he word it?"

"He wanted to know how often I obliged my husband."

"How did you reply?"

"That I was unsure. He then pressed me for an answer, having me estimate, so I told him 'twice or three times a week.'"

"Was there something else?"

"He was surprised that I would oblige my husband given my womanly situation of being with child. Then I think he asked me if my husband cared for me, if he loved me."

"And your reply?"

"I did not answer him."

"Why did he ask such things?"

"Objection," James Jones called out, coming to his feet. "The question calls for speculation on the part of the witness."

Roman clamped his hands down on the armrests of his chair, firmly setting his fingernails in the grain of the wood.

"I will rephrase, your Honor. Mrs. Schmoll, what did the defendant say to you?"

"He said he was concerned for me. He said that I would be unhappy in a marriage with a Lutheran. He thought I had entered my marriage without properly reflecting upon the sacrament of Holy Matrimony and he also reprimanded me for violating my father's wishes that I not marry. He said I would reap a whirlwind of sorrows from what I had sown. He didn't know how I could be at peace married to my husband. Then he said he wished *he* had married me."

"Repeat the defendant's words for the court." Davis clutched his right hand over his heart.

"He said he wished he had married me."

Roman tensed and the soles of his shoes scratched the gritty floor

"Based upon your experience, is this normal?"

"I don't believe so."

"Are these types of questions and judgments commonplace within the confessional of your Church?"

"Again, I'm not certain. He told me that there were some things best left unsaid and informed me that the questions he had asked were not part of my confession."

"Who was the priest?"

She turned towards the defense table, and pointed directly at Roman. "Father Roman Weinzoepfel." Roman's head dropped as he braced himself for what would surely come next.

"Was your confession at a conclusion?"

"No. He then asked if I had confessed all my sins. After I replied that I had he gave me my penance."

"Please explain to this august body gathered here what transpired next."

"As is our custom, I was preparing to read my prayers from my prayer book when suddenly, the priest came out of his compartment, and, grabbing me by the right arm, pulled me up from my kneeling position, and placing both hands about my waist, he dragged me across the floor, and flipped me over on my back. I bumped my head very hard on the ground—and—"

"And..." Davis leaned over her with his arms outstretched.

"And...he...he ravished me." Tears were in her eyes as her lip quivered.

A roar engulfed the courthouse that shook the building.

Roman had listened intently to her testimony but he had heard enough. He wanted to stand up and recount his version of events, but he knew that any utterance on his part regarding a penitent's confession would be grounds for his removal as a priest and his excommunication as a member of the Church itself.

Moans and groans came from the left side of the courtroom which was filled with Catholic supporters while on the side of the prosecution came cheers and sighs of relief from the Schmoll crowd, pleased that the victim herself had finally revealed the priest's horrible crime. The shouts of victory and anger drowned out the judge and his gavel. The constables regained order after a minute or so of hissing and fist shaking between the Irish and German Catholics and the Americans.

"My patience is at an end," the judge barked, standing at the bench. "This is a court of law, not a circus!" He slowly sat down, pointing to a group of Irish ruffians. "If the prosecution could please continue with the testimony of the witness...." He called the sheriff over to the bench privately.

"He ravished you...in what manner?" Davis looked directly at Roman.

Her voice almost now in a whisper, she continued her testimony. "I had passed out after hitting my head. After he was finished, he pulled me up and carried me over to the front pew whereupon he splashed holy water in my face."

"Did he say anything to you at that time?"

"No."

"What did you do?"

"I cried out, 'O God, what have you done with me?!'" She stopped and looked at Roman.

"And?" Davis raised his eyebrows, leaning towards Anna Maria again.

"He stared at me and asked me if I could remember my penance. When I could not, he gave me another and made me say it aloud to him. Then he reminded me that anything said in the confessional was not to be revealed owing to the secrecy of the sacrament. Then he strictly forbade me from telling my husband about the questions regarding the marriage relationship."

"He did not forbid you from revealing the fact that he had ravished you?" Davis laughed out loud himself.

Anna Maria put her head down. "He acted as if nothing had happened."

Roman sighed, adjusted his priestly collar, and ran his fingers down the buttons of his soutane.

"What was your next course of action?"

"I retrieved my bonnet from the floor and left."

"Now could you describe what happened when you returned home?"

"I felt sick and I nearly fainted as I staggered home, but halfway home I felt refreshed in the open air."

"Did anyone see you leaving the church?" Davis stood tall, straightening his tie.

"My husband, Martin. He was leaning on our picket fence waiting for me to come home and start supper."

"Did he say anything to you or see your distress or notice anything different about you?"

"Yes. He asked me why I had stayed so long in the church."

"And..."

"I did not know what to say so I ran inside the house and started the fire for our supper."

"Did he follow you inside?"

"Yes."

"And..."

"He began to ask me over and over again if I was sick." Anna Maria looked away.

"How did you respond?" Davis spoke softly.

"I was afraid to answer."

"Why?"

"I feared that if I told him any of the details about what had happened to me, he would do injury."

"Injury to whom?"

"To himself or to the priest."

"What did you do then?"

"I managed to prepare supper, but I cried for the rest of the night. At first my husband was worried that I had lost the baby, but then he asked me if my grief had something to do with my confession."

"What did you tell your husband?"

"Nothing, but my silence betrayed me."

"When did you first tell your husband about the outrage?"

"On Thursday morning I told him some of the details, but I told him that I wanted to first go to Mass and partake of the Sacrament of the altar so as to fulfill my Easter duty."

"And what is the 'Easter duty'?" Davis scrunched his eyebrows.

"Catholics are obliged to receive communion at least once a year during the Easter Season," Anna Maria explained. "I had not been to Mass since Christmas, and the feast of the Ascension is the last day of Easter. So I had to go."

"Did you see the accused at church that morning?"

"Yes."

"Did he say anything to you?"

"No. He gave me communion. That is all. Then I returned home."

"Then did you disclose the entire matter to your husband?"

"Yes, immediately following breakfast."

"What was his response?"

119

"He was outraged! He went for his pistol and threatened to walk down to the churchyard and kill the priest."

"Why did he not make good on his threat?"

"I begged him not to do it for fear he would be hanged upon the gallows. I made him promise that he would not do anything rash. 'He's a priest,' I said. 'You can't just kill him.'" Anna Maria glanced at Roman.

"Did your husband ever speak to the accused?"

"After supper on Thursday evening he said he was rational and wanted to talk to him then, but I convinced him that he should wait until morning to visit him. There were prayers or something going on in the church."

"And did your husband go see the accused the next morning?"

"Yes, he was out the door at sunrise."

"That was when Mr. Schmoll confronted the accused with the details of your rape?"

"Yes."

"Thank you Mrs. Schmoll." Davis nodded. "That is all Your Honor."

The judge cleared his throat and turned to Roman and his legal team. "Defense counsel, your witness."

"Your Honor," James Jones stood, "we will require a few minutes for consultation before we begin the cross-examination."

At that, attorney Jay Davis stepped forward to the judge's bench. "Your Honor, the witness is exhausted and seeks leave from the Court. Her pregnant condition and the heat have taken their toll upon her."

The judge acknowledged that what Davis had said was probably true, but encouraged him to have her stay for the cross-examination by the defense. She agreed to stay, but Davis was visibly angered at her willingness to continue.

James Jones walked over to the witness box. "Good morning, Mrs. Schmoll. Could you repeat the date of your marriage?"

"Objection, your Honor. The question has been asked and answered!" Davis stamped his foot.

"Overruled," the judge said. "The witness must answer the question."

Davis sat.

"New Year's eve, eighteen hundred, forty-one."

"And when did you meet your husband?"

"Three days after Christmas."

"Of eighteen forty-one?"

"Yes."

"How long have you been with child?"

"Since January."

"Is the child your husband's?"

"Objection!" Davis called out coming to his feet. "Mr. Jones is attempting to put the witness on trial."

"Sustained. Lawyers for the accused will limit themselves to questions pertaining to the charges."

"Mrs. Schmoll," James Jones cleared his throat, "you said it was dark in the church when you saw the priest and yet you said you were reading from your prayer book in an even darker confessional. How can this be?"

"I admit it was difficult."

"We are told that one does not read a penance in the confessional."

"I was referring to the prayer of repentance."

"We have also learned that on the Thursday morning following the alleged attack, you came to Mass in the company of another young woman and a young man."

"Yes, my sister, Caroline, and my brother, Peter."

"And how old is your sister?"

"Seventeen years."

"The witnesses claim that your sister went to confession on that Thursday morning to the same Roman Weinzoepfel, the same priest whom you accuse of ravishing you not less than twelve hours earlier. And they further state that both you and your sister received communion from him at the same service." James squinted his eyes and leaned in towards Anna Maria. "Mrs. Schmoll, are we to believe that you entrusted your younger sister, only seventeen, into the care of a rapist?"

"Objection!" Davis cried out from his seat. "The question is argumentative."

"Overruled. If the prosecution, please," the judge rolled his eyes. "I want to hear this."

The interpreter spoke. "The witness says she doesn't understand the last question."

"Why did you allow your sister to place herself in the very same confessional booth with the same priest you claim ravished you the night before," James rephrased the question, "and then allow that same sister to also receive communion from the very hands of the same priest?"

"She was required to by the laws of the Church. Besides that, I had yet to reveal the outrage to her."

"Then are we to believe that on the same day you would happily return to the same priest who forced himself upon you in the same church the night before, to receive Holy Communion from his tainted hands?"

She began to break down in tears. "It was my religious duty to do so."

"Objection, Defense is heckling the witness, tormenting the victim." Davis stood and stomped.

"Sustained." Judge Rowley tapped his gavel. "The defense will adhere to proper protocol."

"Mrs. Schmoll," James asked, moving toward the center of the gallery, "Did you, in fact, wear the same dress to Thursday morning Mass that you had worn the night before?"

"Yes. It was my best dress."

"Yet you indicate that you were thrown to the floor prior to the alleged rape," Jones walked over to Anna again. "Now we have visited the church and the floor is quite dusty and dirty—no offense to the kind sacristan who is in charge of keeping the floor swept. I find it hard to imagine that you would wear to church a dress that had been dragged across a dusty floor, let alone a dress that you were wearing while being assaulted in the vilest of manner." Jones paused. "Was the dress dirty?"

"Yes."

"Then did your husband take notice of how mussed your dress was?"

"No, I had dusted it off."

"What about your bonnet? Was it damaged during the assault?"

"Yes."

"Then why did your sister wear it to church that Thursday morning?"

"She did not." Anna shook her head.

122

"Oh," Jones shook his head, "but we have witnesses who claim that she was wearing your bonnet, the same bonnet you wore to confession on Wednesday evening, May the fourth, the night of the alleged crime."

"Maybe she wore it without my knowledge."

"At the time of the alleged crime, why did you not call at once for the constable?"

"I wasn't thinking. I was so overwhelmed that my priest would do such a thing that I didn't even entertain the thought of calling for help."

"Were you conscious during the entire ordeal?"

"I cannot recall."

"If you were unconscious, then how could you have known that he had raped you?" Jones raised his voice.

"Objection, your Honor!" Davis stood and yelled. "They're turning this trial into a witch hunt! This is not the inquisition! I believe that if the defense had their way, they would rather we conduct a trial by water to determine if our witness was a witch. Well, why not? Let's all go down to the Ohio and throw Mrs. Schmoll in! Bind her hands and feet, and if she sinks, she's innocent. Of course she'll also drown, but at least we'll know she was telling the truth. If she floats, the Irishmen here could gather the kindling wood and we'll strike a fire and burn her at the stake!"

"If the State would kindly refrain from histrionics, it would be greatly appreciated." The judge shook his head.

The comic relief gave the crowd a momentary respite from the tension.

Benjamin Thomas leaned over to Father Roman. "It's as if she'd poorly rehearsed her lines for a pathetic stage play." Roman did not respond, traumatized by the whole ordeal, lost in thought as to what really took place that Wednesday evening.

"Is it not true that you and your husband live close to the church, perhaps less than four hundred feet away?" James Jones kept pacing in front of the witness stand.

"Yes."

"Do you think the accused ever thought that by committing such a heinous crime in his own sanctuary, during a time that had been published as the time for hearing confessions, he ran the risk of being discovered?"

"I was his last penitent."

"Yes, but the mere fact that at any moment, at any time, another person—even your own husband—could have freely entered the church and happened upon the outrage and apprehended the accused in the very commission of the crime, raises questions. And as for your husband...." James came closer to Anna. "Is your husband in the habit of threatening to kill others, thereby taking justice into his own hands?"

"Objection, the defense is badgering the witness." Davis was on his feet yet again, nearly in a fit of rage.

The commotion of stamping feet and a slamming door displaced the murmur of the crowd. A shout erupted from the rear of the chamber giving cause for everyone to turn around. "I don't know," the male voice angrily shouted, "but is this priest in the habit of raping young women, taking the wife of another into his own arms?"

It was Martin Schmoll. He was rapidly moving towards the front of the courtroom. The assemblage of people stood as one man.

"How dare you interrogate my wife like that? She's been through enough hell already! She doesn't need any shyster Philadelphia lawyers or grand inquisitors holding her against her will! Let her go!"

"She is *not* being held against her will." The judge calmly said, tapping his gavel.

"Don't lie to me! I might just have to kill me some Catholics!" Pulling back his coat, he reached in his holster and brandished his revolver in the air. "All right, goddamnit, who wants to be the first son of a bitch to take a bullet for abusing the patience of my good wife?"

"Sheriff!" the judge called out. "Maintain order! Get that gun out of his hand! Mr. Schmoll, you're in contempt! You're violating my order to remain outside the courtroom during the questioning of the State's lead witness!"

"Oh, is that so? That lead witness happens to be my wife! And what about all these Catholic peasants—German riff-raff, and Irish Micks? These bastard ragamuffins violate the decency of our town and country." He spat on the floor in disgust. Some of the Irish began to move towards him.

"Mr. Schmoll, you're a German yourself."

"I'm an *American* and a *Protestant!*" Schmoll emphasized the terms. "I swear no allegiance to any flag but that of the United States of America."

Cries came forth from the uproar. *Take her home, Martin! Schmoll, shoot the bastard while you have the chance! She is with child! It's too hot in here for her! Lynch the goddamned priest!*

Roman was afraid to breathe, not sure whether this was to be his last moment on earth as his eyes darted about, following the short barrel of the revolver that Schmoll was handily waving only feet from him.

"Why the hell do they get to stay and I have to leave?" Schmoll lowered his gun.

"Sheriff, remove Mr. Schmoll!" the judge was adamant. Schmoll started to stagger, making Roman wonder if he was drunk.

Some of the more decent onlookers had the good sense to abandon the cause, and began to work their way to the door. The more volatile of the two factions rose and threatened each other, cursing each other into tarnation. Schmoll waved to a few of his supporters who in turn began pushing and shoving some of the Catholics, while a few of the Irish and Germans went to defend Roman. One thing led to another and soon both groups were exchanging fists and kicks.

The judge sought protection as the sheriff pushed him down under the bench. In the midst of the chaos, Roman happened to see Anna Maria, still seated upon the witness stand, looking pale and incoherent. Whether from the extreme heat, a lack of fresh air, pregnancy, or the agitation caused by her husband, or all four in combination, her head began to droop. As the scene turned riotous, Roman looked at Anna Maria. She looked dejected in that all the attention was suddenly upon her husband and not her. He watched her collapse in the chair and fall to the floor with a moan and the sound of a dull thud.

A cry of concern went forth from some of the Schmoll supporters once they observed that Mrs. Schmoll had passed out.

In the midst of all the confusion, and at the same time Anna Maria Schmoll had collapsed to the floor, a stranger briskly pushed Roman out of the courtroom. He wasn't sure why he allowed the man to guide him out of the courtroom, for he could have been one of Schmoll's cronies armed with a dagger or pistol, sent to finish him off. He felt his chest for signs of blood or the instrument of death, but found nothing. Before he could thank the man who may have saved his life, the angel of mercy had disappeared from the door, and he was safe in the judge's private chamber, a small room off the main courtroom.

Meanwhile, Martin Schmoll had been tackled by the sheriff and taken out of the courtroom while Anna Maria had been placed on a bench.

Benjamin Thomas shouted to the judge who was slowly emerging out from under his bench. "We refuse to continue with this charade of justice!"

"What charade?" Davis cracked, lighting up a cigar.

At that the county prosecutor, James Lockhart, entered the room from an antechamber. "What happened?" He winked at Davis as if he was perfectly aware of the tumultuous proceedings.

"What happened?" asked an exasperated Thomas. "As if I have to tell you? Look at this courtroom!" Chairs were askew, upside down, and three were broken. Everyone remaining in the courtroom was on his feet.

"Where's Father Weinzoepfel?" James Jones quickly looked about.

"The prisoner's escaped!" John Chandler shouted. "Did your Irish rabble smuggle him out so he could flee from justice like all the Irish criminals?"

"Here I am." Father Roman walked out from the judge's chamber where the stranger had placed him.

"What's he doing in there?" Jay Davis asked.

"I don't know." The judge shook his head.

"A Good Samaritan placed me there," Roman answered. "I don't know who he was."

"Judge, don't tell me you're going to give in to this pathetic legal team representing a contaminated priest."

Looking at the prosecution team, the judge spoke. "Gentlemen, I am on the side of justice. I thought we all were."

"We have had enough for one day." Benjamin Thomas said.

"So have I," the judge pounded his gavel. "Order! Order in the Court!" He waited until it grew quiet to speak "I am postponing this entire trial."

"Until tomorrow?" Jay Davis anxiously asked.

126

"No! Until *September*! The chaos in this courthouse, nay, in this town, incurred by this case has rendered it, in my opinion, nearly impossible for this priest to receive a fair and impartial trial. Hopefully by then the emotions will cool enough so that an impartial jury can be found and these factions will be governed by reason! As for the accused, I will announce his bail at three o'clock. Court adjourned!"

Chapter 11

Hoosier Justice

From noon onward, Roman could hear the angry mob growing in size, filling the streets near the jail and courthouse. From the sounds of their banter and language, many of the malcontents must have found their way to the taverns where they had gotten drunk awaiting the three o'clock hour.

The Jones brothers tried to allay Roman's fears, telling him that many of the leading Protestants were horrified at the ill-treatment of his good name and the hatred displayed by those in the courtroom. His lawyers principle concern was that there be no subsequent exhibitions like had occurred that morning; otherwise it threatened to turn Roman's case into a mockery of justice.

At the three o'clock hour, the throng was filling Main and Third Streets, spilling into an already crowded courthouse lawn, clamoring to see if Roman would make bail. Roman, still in his soutane and biretta, shackled and handcuffed, was taken from the jail by the sheriff and ten other armed men, and hailed forth in front of the gathered crowds. The carnival atmosphere soon gave way to a shouting match between Schmoll supporters and the Catholics.

Martin Schmoll himself was in the midst of those gathering. "I swear to God, I'll shoot anyone fool enough to go the bail for that black-robed bastard! You'll never see your money again. He plans to flee the country and return to Europe." Despite Schmoll's protestations, the idea of an immigrant returning to Europe was welcome news for some of the Americans.

Other voices joined in. *Keep that priest behind bars! The judge better protect the women and children from this libertine! Polluted priest! If the judge frees him, we'll burn every Catholic home until we find him!*

Roman stood with Benjamin Thomas, Reverend Shawe, and James and Wilbur Jones.

"Gentlemen, I ask that you allow me to remain in jail. I do not desire that the good people of this community who provide me with bail to be threatened with violence."

"I'm not sure we can allow for that, Father," James said. "One of the Lutheran gentlemen here in town has sent me word that one of the constables purposely left your jail cell key at *Wood's Tavern*. Who knows where it is now."

"You're in danger, Father Roman." Shawe said. "I think they want to kill you."

"You *think*? I know. I've been trying to tell you that for three days now." Thomas said, rolling his eyes at Shawe.

"We must alert the sheriff." Roman said.

"I already know." The sheriff said, standing behind the defense counsel.

The judge, cloaked in his robes of office, opened the courthouse doors and stood before the tumultuous multitude.

"I am releasing the prisoner, Mr. Weinzoepfel. His bond was raised to four thousand dollars and it has been paid by several of our respectable Protestant citizens. I trust that his passage back to his parish church will be unimpeded." The judge nodded to the sheriff and he removed the handcuffs and shackles from Roman's wrists and ankles.

The sheriff turned to James Jones. "To guarantee his safe conduct, I'm supposed to escort him back to his church."

The ten armed men formed a circle around Roman and his lawyers in the street. The distance was not more than the length of two city blocks, yet for Roman it seemed like his journey across the sea. Though no violence came to his person, some of the ruffians taunted him with their threats and curses, tossing lumps of horse manure and rocks in his path.

Once the constables had safely accompanied Roman to his church, he entered the nave and fell on his knees in front of the tabernacle. He watched Reverend Shawe open the felt bag and carefully replace the silver crucifix upon the high altar.

The lawyers had told him that a few vocal drunks would probably come looking for him at sunset. "The wicked never move during the day," Benjamin Thomas said, "but Will Chandler, Jay Davis, and Martin Schmoll move all the time." Roman took a few of his belongings with him as he returned to *The Mansion House* under the sheriff's guard. Shawe and Thomas set off for Vincennes at once to inform the bishop of all that had transpired.

****

By sunset, the excitement had not worn off and even some of the law-abiding citizens turned into angry vigilantes. Francis Linck, Jr. and some of the other young men from the parish promised Roman they would stand watch over the church to make sure it wasn't broken into or burnt. Roman learned that a posse was prepared to lynch him before sunrise. Josiah Stahlhofer insisted that he leave *The Mansion House* for the night and stay at his house for sanctuary. The fears were realized when the maddening mob began riding through the streets, hurling brickbats and rocks and a barrage of sticks and stones and verbal assaults terrifying the Catholics, promising to burn their property if they were concealing *that priest*. Glowing torchlights lit the evening and rifle barrels glistening in the moonlight menaced the defenseless immigrant residents. The Irish canal workers who had been in town since noon and the Germans citizenry marshaled themselves around the Catholic homes to protect the innocent from the dangers of the legion.

Serpentine, a cortege of men astride horses as well as those on foot waving torchlights wove their way through the constricted streets like a band of barbarians ready to loot, pillage, and burn. Roman watched out the front windows of the Stahlhofer's home as the hand flames lit up the night sky. The angry mob was threatening to torch the Catholic Church and every Catholic immigrant's home unless he was surrendered to them. Stones and bricks began pelting the home, breaking one of the windows. Then a gun was fired.

Roman fervently prayed his breviary, twisting the ribbons between his thumb and index finger. *O Lord, Thy right arm saves those who seek refuge from their foes, deliver me from their violence. My ravenous enemies press upon me. Their hearts are tightly shut, their mouths proudly roar. They advance against me, and their steps encircle me even now. Their eyes are watching closely to strike me to the ground like lions ready to claw, eagerly lurking for prey.*

"Wife," Josiah called out, "blow all the candles out. Make it look like we're asleep for the night!" Josiah for his part pushed an oak table in front of the door.

"Father Roman, we'd best hide you under the stairwell closet." Josiah pulled the door open and pushed him inside. Grabbing a heavy quilt from one of the shelves, Josiah threw it over the top of Roman. "Don't come out until I say."

Roman pulled the quilt off and fumbled under his cassock for his rosary. He prayed intently as the horde of ruffians continued their reign of terror. *Pater noster, qui es in caelis... Our Father, who art in heaven...*

"When this is all over, bring me my horse, Shadow." Roman spoke through the thick blanket. "I'll ride to Vincennes tonight." *Ave, Maria, gratia plena, Hail, Mary, full of grace...*

"I'm sorry, Father Roman, but I have something to tell you."

"Yes?"

"Shadow was missing from his stall this morning."

"No! Not my baby?"

"Don't you worry; ol' Doc McDonald said that he and the Irish boys would find him for you."

Roman held his head in his hands and rubbed the whiskers of his unshaven face. *Why? O Lord.* He heard the thundering of horse hooves roar by the Stahlhofer home as he prayed the beads under the quilt, beseeching the Blessed Mother's intercession. He couldn't help but think of his very own dear mother and her words, which now seemed prophetic, *Roman, when you become a priest I fear that a particular cross awaits you. Your faith will be greatly tested, but the Lord himself shall be your strength and under his wings you shall bear the cross. A mother knows these things. Pray to Saint Francis Xavier. He shall inspire you. I believe your mission in life will take you far from our homeland and us.*

How could Mother have ever known that I would be asked to go to America? I was ordained in a Cathedral dedicated to Saint Francis Xavier? One of the first men to welcome me to Evansville was Francis Xavier Linck. Coincidence or Providence?

Roman then heard the footfall of a hundred men, like that of soldiers in the street marching off to battle. At first he thought he was imagining things, but after a few times of repeatedly hearing the cry chanted as a refrain he was more frightened than ever. *Whiskey on the death of that priest! Whiskey on the death of that priest! Whiskey on the death of that priest!* One man's voice towered over the rest, leading the chant while the mob repeated the frightful phrase over and over again. *Whiskey on the death of that priest!*

Roman heard the familiar voice of another man trying to shout down the mob. "My God, man, you've already had enough whiskey to kill a horse!"

"Who the blazes are you?" an angry man asked.

"Doctor McDonald. Correct me if I am wrong, but you boys aren't from around here, are you?"

"That's none of your damned business, Mick. This is a free country."

"What brings you here to Evansville?"

"Nothing particular, I suppose. We just heard there was some excitement in this here one-horse town, and we thought we'd come and see for ourselves."

"Is that right? Well I do believe the excitement didn't start until you all arrived this morning. Now why don't you go back where you came from."

"We're looking for that mongrel priest. The damn Kraut debauched one of the young flowers here in town and we hear tell he's done it to others."

The priest must die! The words of the mob crushed his spirit.

Ave, Maria, gratia plena, Dominus tecum, Hail, Mary, full of grace, the Lord is with Thee...

"Are you hiding him in this house? Over here!" His voice became a cry. "I think we found him!"

"He's not there," Doc MacDonald argued.

"Out of our way, *That priest* must pay for his crimes!"

"There are courts of law for that!" MacDonald shouted. "And they meet during the daylight hours when men are not blinded by liquor or the dark side of the moon!"

Benedicta tu in mulieribus, et benedicta fructus ventris tui, Jesu, Blessed art Thou among women, and blest is the fruit of thy womb, Jesus.

"Who lives here?" the man demanded.

"I don't know."

"He's a liar." Another man spoke up. It was the voice of Jay Davis. "That's Doc McDonald. One of our *dear* Catholic brethren. Go ahead and tell the gentlemen who lives here, Doctor."

"They wouldn't know him."

"Mr. Josiah Stahlhofer—" Davis answered, but was cut off.

"Is a kind man," McDonald completed the sentence. "Look, not a lamp's burning. The man and his wife are in bed."

Sancta Maria, Mater Dei, ora pro nobis peccatoribus, Holy Mary, Mother of God, pray for us sinners...

"Stahlhofer is a German Catholic immigrant. He's also the sexton for the Catholic Church here in town. He seems to always know where the priest is or he knows where one might find him. Why, I believe that if we were to wake Mr. Stahlhofer and ask the whereabouts of our dear Reverend Roman Weinzoepfel, I do believe he could tell us," Davis gloated. "Why, I believe that the good priest is being given sanctuary inside Mr. Stahlhofer's home even as I speak."

An unintelligible cry went up from the mob as they crowded on the Stahlhofer porch. Roman had heard every word of the exchange from underneath the stairs and prepared to die. Josiah's wife cried as she kept telling her husband how the number of torches was increasing as the sound of the mob grew louder just outside their front door.

"Come out, you Kraut! Open your house before we burn it to the ground! We're going to bring this priest to justice, dead or alive! If he is not in there, why won't you open the doors?"

"Husband, what are you doing?" Mrs. Stahlhofer called to her husband.

From inside the closet Roman could hear the table being dragged across the floor and see the increased glow from the candles shining through the cracks in the woodwork and doorframe.

Sancta Maria, ora pro nobis, nunc Holy Mary, pray for us, now—

"The man has a point," Josiah whispered loudly. "If we do open the doors they're likely to move on to another house. Just pray that these drunks don't think I'm that smart. Father Roman, pray as you've never prayed before!"

He heard the front door being opened and the roar of the thugs flooded the hallway.

"Let us in." It was Davis. "We've already been to the Heinrich's, so it's your turn."

"Don't burn our home. Please!" Mrs. Stahlhofer cried.

"We were about to turn in for the night." Josiah explained.

"Dressed like that?" Davis laughed. "You weren't in bed, old man. You're hiding *the priest*, aren't you?"

Ora pro nobis peccatoribus, nunc et in hora mortis nostrae, Pray for us now and at the hour of our death.

"No."

"Silence, barbarian! We'll search your home and *then* we'll burn it!"

The sound of feet upon the floor and an increase of light came under the door.

Nunc et in hora mortis nostrae. Amen.

Suddenly several shots of gunfire erupted in the street. Whoever had entered the Stahlhofer home ran outside at the sound.

"They say he's at *the Sherwood Hotel!*"

The pounding hooves and stomping feet quickly departed and the sound of confusion filled the streets following another round of a half dozen shots.

Josiah opened the stairwell door. "Father Roman, we've got to get you out of town."

"Has someone been shot?" Roman flung the blanket aside.

"Whatever happened," Josiah answered, "God forbid that someone got shot, but it may have prevented you from being killed."

In the chaos of stampeding horses and more guns being fired outside, one of the Irish parishioners, Mr. John O'Connell came to the front door.

Roman stayed under the stairs as Josiah opened the front door.

"Josiah, is Father Roman here? Please tell me he is."

"John, are you alone?" Josiah whispered.

"Yeah."

"Get in here."

O'Connell darted through the opening. Josiah closed the door quickly and bolted it shut.

"Is he here?"

"Yes. He's safe."

"Did ye hear what happened? Doc MacDonald and that nigger bell ringer from church saved the day. They was going to search your house, but Doc got the Irish to untie all the horses from the hitching posts along Water Street and up Main. Just when you opened your door, letting them in, that nigger boy took to firing his shooting iron causing the horses to stampede. They scattered through the streets and broke down fences and crashed through a couple of storefronts. I don't know where the other shots came from, but the nigger boy told them Father Roman was down at *the Sherwood*. That's when they commenced shooting."

Roman emerged from the stairwell. "They'll soon discover that I'm not there. I must leave town at once."

"Oh, Father, it's so good to see ye alive, but there'll be no way ye can leave town dressed like that! You've got to get rid of your cassock."

Roman felt his head and realized his biretta was still under the stairs. He pulled the quilt out and the three cornered hat fell out from one of its folds.

"The biretta too, Father."

John conferred with Josiah, whispering in the hallway.

"We've got it, Father Roman," Josiah spoke, "we'll smuggle you out of town in a disguise."

Josiah whispered something to his wife and she left the room.

"You should be proud of Reverend Joseph Wheeler," John said.

"Why? He was the one who married the Schmoll's in the first place."

"Yes. It was poor judgment on his part. He realizes that now."

"How do you know?"

"He said he wouldn't be a party to such a travesty of justice and he called Davis and Schmoll vultures. Then he came down and stood with Francis Linck, Jr. and helped guard the church from being torched like a haystack."

"How could he come to do a thing like that?"

"He was preaching up a storm, mad as a wet hen at the Protestants toting brickbats and carrying torches. He called them hypocrites, saying they were no better than the crusaders they say they hate. He stood in the breach betwixt the church and the rabble and said that the gospel of Christ didn't allow for Christians to duel or attack each other. But they didn't listen to him and they commenced hurling bricks. After that he said he was ashamed that any of them would claim to be Christian, threatening to burn their Catholic neighbors' homes, and then he accused them of conducting a Protestant Inquisition. That didn't sit too well with them, so they turned on him and threw rocks at him."

Roman pondered the man's words and realized that he had been too quick to judge his neighbor.

"Seriously, Father, lots of the decent Protestants in town told us how sorry they was that things got out of hand." John wiped his brow.

"That's good to know." He still wasn't certain of all Protestants even though some of them had made his bail.

"Both Francis Linck Junior and Senior are to be commended, along with some of the Kentucky Irish, for fending off the madness."

"Kentucky Irish?"

"Yeah, must've been fifty of 'em come up from Henderson. One of the Irish boys took quite a beating"

"Will he live?"

"Oh, yeah. Don't you worry; he got in a few good licks before he fell. Filthy Protestant. He'll remember that Mick for a long time." John smiled.

"Please, Mr. O'Connell, don't talk like that. I'm sick at heart for all the tragedy I've caused you and the good people of Evansville."

Mrs. Stahlhofer returned with some folded clothes in her hand. She handed them to her husband and sighed.

"Here, Father," Josiah unfolded the clothing. "Put this on."

Roman took the garment from Josiah and held it out. "Sir!" Roman's back straightened and his eyes widened.

"What?" Josiah laughed.

"This is a *dress*!"

"Yes. I know what it is."

"I will *not* wear a dress." Roman adamantly shook his head.

"If you want to get out of town alive, you will."

"If you step out of this house with that frock on," John interrupted, "they'll be drawing and quartering you before you can say Donnybrook Fair. Either that or we'll find you decorating a cottonwood in the morning. Now go on and get that dress on, Fräulein Weinzoepfel." The man laughed while Mrs. Stahlhofer left the room.

Roman dropped his head and closed his eyes.

"You can dress in the front parlor." Josiah directed him to the room.

He removed his priestly garb, neatly folding the soutane placing the biretta on top. He stepped into the dress, but was having difficulty securing it in the rear. Reluctantly, he had to call for assistance.

Josiah went into the room and blushed at the sight of a priest dressed in women's clothes.

"You know somewhere in one of Paul's letters it's written that a man is forbidden from wearing women's clothes." Roman adjusted the dress around his hips.

"And somewhere else in the good book it's forbidden to murder a man." Josiah replied, securing the last of the buttons in the back of the dress. "So I'd say we're saving a Protestant soul by making it more difficult for him to find you and kill you."

Roman's attention was directed outside where the sound of music and singing could be heard. The melody bore the mark of the Irish with pipes, mandolins, and fiddles.

Grabbed up a bag and put on a hat, left all me friends and family, and crossed the Atlantic for Americay. We're a long ways from home, but don't tell us to leave, 'cause if ye don't like us then ye can go to...well,

The whiskey-moon shined for many a year, we spent all our savins' on whiskey and beer. Oh, thousands of miles from the emerald Isle, we're fightin' and drinkin' all the while. A hundred shillelaghs like Donnybrook Fair, with the beer and the boxin' we haven't a care. We drink when we're fightin' and we drink when we're not, and if fightin' don't kill us, we'll drink till we drop. And when we're dead and the sod upon our graves good and even, make a toast and pray that we're drinkin' in heaven!

The chorus continued as the Irishmen surrounded the house, smacking their shillelaghs in the palm of their hands as if eager for more confrontations with Protestants.

At that, John O'Connell returned to the room accompanied by Doc McDonald.

"You're safe for now, Father Roman." Doc smiled. "We're in good company. The Irish minstrels and troops have arrived with the blessings of the Church."

"You sure are a pretty, lass, Father." John laughed, looking at Roman.

Roman, completely humiliated, found no humor in the frolic of the Irishmen.

"Good work letting those horses go." Josiah chuckled, patting McDonald on the back. "It was chaos out there."

"It was hilarious. You should've heard them hollering, 'Here he is! There he is!' The drunken mob was chasing after whatever was moving!"

"If you consume bottle after bottle of whiskey," Roman sighed, "then you'll chase anything, whether it's moving or not."

The men laughed.

"Your bell ringer boy sho' was good with a gun!" Doc said.

"Is Andrew all right?" Roman asked.

"Yes, yes. He's back at his place between the blacksmith's shop and Igleheart's Mill."

"Are the Heinrich's safe?" Roman anxiously asked. "We heard that their home was searched. Please tell me that their home wasn't burned."

"No, they made out all right, except ol' Wilhelm took a brickbat in the head, that's all."

"Was he badly hurt?"

"No. I took care of him. Put a bandage on his head. He'll be all right. He's sorer over the broken windows than anything."

"Have you found my horse?"

"Not yet, but we're working on it. Not to worry, not to worry."

"In the seminary we never learned how to prepare for any of these circumstances."

"Neither did I." The deep voice of a stranger sounded in the house. Roman turned to see a leathery skinned giant of a pioneer, dressed in a dark brown frock coat and a wide-brimmed hat with a large soft crown. Mrs. Stalhhofer led him in. "Father Weinzoepfel, we've never met, but I feel like I know you." The strange man extended his hand in friendship. "M'name's Elisha J. Durbin. I'm the priest from Kentucky."

He knew him by his reputation as the Patriarch of Kentucky. "Father. I apologize for my dress."

"Jesus, Mary, and Joseph, don't worry about that. Word got to Henderson that you were in trouble so I sent the Irish boys up here. Of course, the Irish are too poor to own horses, so they crossed the river on foot."

"But you—"

"Don't you worry none. I wasn't raised in the woods to be scared by no owl."

"What?"

"Never mind, just an expression we have around these parts. I was born and raised in these woods as was my daddy and granddaddy. No Durbin's afraid of bear or wolves or wildcats, and we sure as Sam

138

Hill ain't afraid of no lilly-livered Protestants who go about threatening women and children with their torches and pistols and shooting irons. No sir, you don't have nothing to worry about tonight or the next, or the night after that, 'cause ain't nobody going to burn down your church or any of your Catholic folks' homes. Not as long as the Irish is in town. The boys are here to save your hide and to defend our fellow Catholics."

Roman wasn't quite sure how to take this priest, if he really was a priest, for he seemed so American.

"Just thank Saint Patrick and Saint Brigid...and a few well handled shillelaghs." He broke off with a hearty laugh.

"Shillelaghs?"

"Used to bludgeon one's enemy into tarnation." Durbin answered somberly.

"They weren't trying to kill anyone, were they?"

"They only used them in self-defense, Father." Durbin smiled.

Roman closed his eyes.

Just then Josiah put one of his wife's bonnets on Roman's head. "All set to go, Sister Mary Roman." Durbin and the two Irishmen laughed.

"How can you people laugh at a time like this?"

"Father...we're Irish," Durbin smiled. "We learned a long time ago that if you don't die laughing, you'll die crying."

He sighed. "You know I told everyone I would gladly remain in jail."

"Father," Durbin reasoned with Roman, "some of your *friends* here in town swore to a pact that they were going to *gladly* storm that shack of a jailhouse and *gladly* pluck you out of your cell and *gladly* hang you."

"And one of the jailers purposely misplaced one of the keys to your jail cell." Doc MacDonald said.

"So I've learned. You've made your point." Roman hung his head.

"I think you'd best get moving," Durbin said. "You have a long road ahead of you. Your attorneys, the Jones brothers, and I have done business before."

"You have?"

"Yes. They've received some of my packages from the south, sending them on if you get my meaning."

Roman knew he was referring to the Joneses' involvement with giving passage to fugitive slaves. "So, we've arranged for you to be put on the same route. You can be in Vincennes by tomorrow or the next day. All you have to do is follow the canal's towpath north about fifteen or twenty miles. There's a farmhouse and barn on the right. The barn has a large red X painted on its door. And there's enough moonlight tonight, so you won't miss it. If it's late when you get there just go on in the barn. The lady will meet you in the morning. John will lead you out of town to one of the houses along the route. Are you ready?"

"I need something in which to carry my cassock, biretta, and breviary." Roman said.

"I have an old handbag you can use," Mrs. Stahlhofer said as she returned to the room. "No lady is without a handbag."

"Good," said Durbin, "you'll need the bag, but give me your clothes and the book."

"No, they were gifts from the bishop of Strasbourg."

"I don't care if they were from Pope Gregory himself, if some hotheads stop you and open the bag, you're a dead man."

Roman surrendered the goods to his brother priest but clutched tightly to his rosary.

"You can't carry those beads either."

"I'm not giving *this* up. My mother and father gave me this rosary for my Confirmation."

"I'll carry your rosary." John held out his hand.

"Danke."

"I believe I have an idea for your cassock and biretta." Durbin smiled.

"But I can't meet my bishop looking like this," Roman argued.

"Would you rather him find you wearing a shroud? Never mind. You can lose the dress once you get out of town. There are folks up the route who'll give you some clothes. Your bishop can give you a new soutane and biretta when you arrive in Vincennes. I'll keep your breviary for you. *Dominus vobiscum.*" Durbin raised his hand and gave the blessing.

"*Et cum Spiritu tuo.*"

"*Deo Gratias.*"

Mrs. Stahlhofer handed Roman one of her handbags as he made his way out the door led by John O'Connell.

John accompanied Roman to the east side of town but two Americans on horses stopped them just as they neared the towpath of the canal out of Evansville.

"A little late for you, Paddy, wouldn't you say?" asked an old bearded rider wearing a fur hat and riding a white horse.

"Who's your lady friend?" A younger rough spoke with soap-locks dangling at his cheeks, a large floppy hat pressed down over his brow, nearly in his eyes.

"This is my wife, Mary," John lied.

"A homely wench, she is." The older man laughed hard, seated upon his white horse. "Are you sure she's your wife, and not one of the Irish bitches?"

"She ain't this man's wife, for sure. He's holding her hand! I hear that you Cat'lickers only hold hands with your whores." The younger man drank a swig of whiskey from a bottle he pulled from his pocket. "Get your slut the hell out of here, you dirty Mick!"

"Looks like that's where they're heading. He's taking her back to the swamp where the fishmonger came from, up there at the Irish shanty town along the canal." The older man took the bottle from his cohort and drank down the last.

"Yeah, at least the Irish *womenfolk* work for an honest wage!" the young rough laughed.

"What the hell's with these cowards? They won't speak. They must be dumb papists!" The two men laughed again, making faces at the unlikely twosome.

John O'Connell whispered to Roman, "I'm a going to slug them to kingdom come!"

"Steady, my friend. Steady." He repeated the phrase like a prayer of exorcism over a possessed man.

"Listen, you don't mind if we ride her for a while, do you? Don't keep her all to yourself. We enjoy a good wenching once in a while."

Roman shivered as if in winter, silently telling an *Ave*.

"Yeah," said the young rough, starting to get off his horse, "Let me see if she'd be worth the time to get my pants down."

Roman suddenly heard a horse galloping their way. The rider was calling out to the two men. "Eli! Jake! Quick, get back to town!"

"Why?" The young rough remounted his ride. Just then half a dozen shots rang out in town.

"What's happening?" The older rider repositioned his fur hat.

"I think we found him," The rider was out of breath. "Whoa, hoss, whoa."

"Where?" the older man asked.

"They found his priest robe and hat down at the river's edge." He brought his horse to a stop. "Damn fool's jumped in the river."

"Let's go!" The young rough cried. "We got to get back to town and find us that priest. There's going be a hanging!"

The three men spurred their rides away.

Roman sighed. At least he knew now why Father Durbin had wanted his soutane and biretta.

John O'Connell took him as far as the home of a Catholic farming family who lived three miles east of town. He was given work clothes and a straw hat in place of the dress and he took supper, the first full meal he'd eaten in nearly four days. Once he renewed his strength, he set off north on the towpath despite the family's protestations, maintaining that no Catholic family was safe from terror as long as he was at large. Still incognito, he followed the canal path on foot through the woods with the hope that those still searching for him had fallen for Durbin's trick and believed him traveling south. Thankfully, his rosary was once again on his person.

Laboring for breath, his body covered in sweat, the taste of salt upon his lips, he marched on through the dark with the prurient charges following his every thought. His mind was filled with nightmarish phantoms of the angry mob descending upon him. All his hopes and dreams for the Catholics of southern Indiana burnt like so much chaff thrown into the furnace. He feared that by the time he would arrive in Vincennes, provided he would, his reputation would be rent asunder, torn to shreds by the malicious tongues of Protestant and Catholic alike, eager to believe every report. He knew that whispering tongues had slain far more souls than the sword. The gloom of despair hung overhead like a readied guillotine blade prepared to dispatch its victim.

The thought of eluding the authorities returned. Rife with temptation to flee from justice, he wanted to return to the solitude of the Strasbourg seminary. *Why didn't I become a monk? Now I'm to be defrocked and I've wrought havoc upon the Church.* He regretted not showing more prudence in his dealings with Mrs. Schmoll. He kicked the dirt in his path.

Aided by moonlight alone, he braved the dangers of traveling through the forest at night, he heard the ravenous howling of wolves and only imagined their insatiable hunger which would make him a prey to their teeth. He prayed the rosary over and over, holding no fear for the wolves who cried out to be recognized, or the bears that might be silently stalking him, venturing the belief that since almighty God in his mercy had rescued him from the drunken fury of a frenzied horde, then certainly the beasts of the forest and field held no threat for him.

Well into the early morning hours, when monks and nuns through the world were rising to chant *Matins*, he was in the middle of an Indiana forest praying his beads. Trusting God in the silence of darkness was difficult, yet *the light shines in the darkness*, wrote Saint John. He recalled the many mornings in Strasbourg when he would process from the seminary under a starlit heaven into the oratory to chant the psalms and canticles, praying for the whole world. He entrusted himself to the unbroken monastic prayers to ensure his safe passage to Vincennes.

As Roman made his way through the wilderness, his thoughts returned to the events that followed Anna Maria's confession on Ascension eve, the fourth of May.

Chapter 12

The Worst Man in All the World

4 May 1842

After he had heard confessions that evening and fed his horse, Roman had taken his supper with the Heinrichs. Afterwards he sat upon their porch and watched the sun go down.

"Father Roman." Josiah Stahlhofer called out to him from the street.

"Yes, Josiah." He adjusted his biretta and leaned forward in the wicker chair.

"I had something to tell you," he said as he approached the porch, "but for the life of me I've forgotten what it was."

"Then it must not have been all that important."

"I'm not for sure." He wrinkled his face and sighed. "I can't remember."

"Did it have something to do with church?"

"Yes, I think that was it."

"I locked up if you were wondering."

"Oh, *danke, danke.*"

"If you remember what it was, you know where you can find me."

"All right. I'm going home now. See you in the morning."

"Mass is later because of the Holy Day. Nine o'clock."

"I remembered." Josiah walked down the street to his home.

Roman's thoughts quickly returned to Mrs. Schmoll.

He and Heinrich sat on the porch after dinner until sunset while the slow crawling migraine descended upon him like the gathering clouds and heat lightning coming in from the west across the Ohio River. The feelings he was experiencing frightened him, welling up within like the approaching spring thunderstorm.

It was times such as this when he knew he should pray. He excused himself from the Heinrich's porch and returned to his room in the rear of the church where he lit his candle and prayed from his breviary. It wasn't the most focused prayer, his mind racing to and fro thinking about the next day's mass, picnic, parade, May Crowning, and Solemn Vespers and Benediction and yet all the while the thought of Anna Maria Schmoll continually crept in.

After praying, he lay down on his bed with his bible, paper, and quill to put the finishing touches on his Ascension Day sermon. With his candle still burning, he fell asleep surrounded by his *ora et labora*, prayer and work.

The next day was Ascension Thursday. Roman felt refreshed from the night's sleep. The episode with Mrs.Schmoll in the confessional hounded him, but once he prayed and ascended the altar steps for mass, his focus turned towards God. Standing behind the oak pulpit, he began preaching his prepared sermon.

"The seed of Catholic doctrine has fallen on the path of commerce, withered for lack of the sacraments, or been choked off by the thorns of temptation. The anxieties, riches, and pleasures of this life thwart a mature faith, a faith borne through suffering and trials.

"Some of our numbers have neglected their duties as Catholics in favor of vulgar pursuits of wealth, seeking to strike a bargain at every turn rather than storing up treasure in heaven where neither moth nor rust destroys. We live in the midst of a society infected with inexorable immorality and an unbridled lust for power and material goods. For too many the allure of secular attractions and fashions and the American emphasis upon industry and mechanical progress and human achievement has caused them to neglect or completely abandon their Catholic faith! All such passing distractions and temporal things turn man's mind and heart from his obligations to Christ, his Church, and his neighbor. As it is, today's feast calls us to ascend with Christ to heaven. We must transcend the whirlwinds of worldly affairs, commerce and trade.

"One does this in his daily practice of prayer, the rosary, daily mass and meditations, and the pious custom of frequent confession. Confession must not be only performed once a year begrudgingly as Easter duty. If we could see a soul in the state of mortal sin, we would be horrified at the sight.

"So when the winds of temptation come we are not washed away in the sea of chaos or found wandering down the path of perdition. The American way tells us that stores, shoppes, or saloons will supply our every need. I ask you, though, seriously, how many passenger pigeons can a man eat in a week? If the Americans do not restrain their insatiable appetites for these birds, the birds will be hunted to extinction!

"How then shall we prepare for that last day? Day by day keep death before your mind's eye. Hour by hour keep careful watch over all that you do, aware that God's gaze is upon you, wherever you may be."

He took the opportunity to look out into the congregation. He saw Anna Maria Schmoll dressed in a light blue dress wearing a white bonnet with matching feather.

At the most solemn part of the Liturgy, he reverently elevated the Eucharistic Lord while Josiah thrice rang the sanctuary bells. An awed silence followed the moment of consecration and Roman devoutly lowered the host and genuflected in front of the altar. He tarried a few moments before continuing with the consecration of the chalice as the sweet smelling incense smoke lingered, suspended in the humid air above the altar.

At the appointed time, he descended the three altar steps and moved towards the communion rail, distributing the sacred species upon the outstretched tongues of the devout. Halfway across the epistle side of the sanctuary, he looked down at the face of the next communicant. It was Anna Maria Schmoll, her hands pressed together in prayer, eyes closed, and tongue extended. Her sister Caroline was next to her. He knew he rightly should deny her communion, but then would he be guilty of judging her as damned if he passed her by? The thought of them together in the church scorched his mind. As he approached her kneeling at the railm he thought, *if I refuse her, it could create scandal, publicly humiliating her. If I single her out as a public sinner, it will make the situation even worse than it already is.*

The words of Christ echoed in his heart: *Judge not lest ye be judged.* And did not Christ give the morsel of his body to his betrayer at that Last Supper?

It felt as if a quarter hour had passed since first seeing Anna Maria bowed down at the communion rail and even though he knew it was but a pause of a few seconds, his hesitation seemed purgatorial if not absolutely infernal.

The young boy serving as his acolyte mirrored his movements and slowly lowered the paten under her chin. Roman now stood directly in front of her in total silence. His fingers trembled slightly in the golden ciborium as he grasped one of the consecrated hosts between his right thumb and index finger. Lifting it gently, he held it before her. *"Corpus Christi..."* He placed the Sacramental Lord upon her tongue. As she closed her mouth, she opened her eyes and looked at him without expression. He stepped aside, giving communion to her sister and the rest of those kneeling on the altar steps.

He returned to the altar and knelt in silence before rising to pray. After mass, he genuflected to the altar and knelt upon the prie-dieu at the side of the altar steps. The entire congregation was silent. He watched the tall, steady fulgent flame atop the large paschal candle. The church was so quiet that he could hear the tongue of fire licking at the beeswax as the heat from the candle distorted his view of the stained glass window above the church doors. The murmur of a lonely whistle and bell of a steamboat far off in the distance penetrated the silence of the brick church, reminding him of the glorious ranks of the pipe organ and the steeple bells of the Strasbourg Cathedral. The sweet memory dissolved as he felt his sacristan tap upon his shoulder. Josiah held out the long candlesnuffer for him to begin the ritual of officially marking the end of the Easter Season by extinguishing the flame symbolizing Christ's Ascension into heaven.

He rose from prayer and moved towards the oversized taper mounted high upon its tall wooden base. Lifting the instrument up to the candle's glowing orange and blue wick, he unwittingly clanked the metal snuffer against the brass follower atop the candle before lowering the bell shaped brass cup upon the burning wick. Covering the flame for nearly five seconds, he removed the snuffer unveiling a thick white trail of smoke that soared up from the wick. The chalk-white smoke ascended halfway to the ceiling and then began folding over upon itself, a wispy serpent of smoke recoiling itself, levitating above the sanctuary.

As he returned the snuffer to Josiah and knelt at the prie-dieu again, the final thin vapors rose off the top of the candela. He saw that many of the parishioners were mesmerized by the sight of the extinguished flame and ascending smoke.

He made his thanksgiving after Mass, tugging on the red and yellow ribbons of his breviary's spine, meditating upon the psalms, whispering the words. He finished his office by drawing his rosary out from around his sash telling the *Aves*. All the time he tried to focus upon his prayer but was ever distracted with his thoughts of Mrs. Schmoll, doubting his judgments in dealing with her from their very first meeting at her father's house to the way he had handled her marriage agreement, his encounter with her in the confessional, and now to the point of dispensing the sacred host to her that very morning.

After a half hour upon the kneeler he arose from prayer and exited the church through the sacristy door. As he stepped around the back of the church to give some water to his horse, Josiah startled him.

"Oh, there you are, Father."

"Yes, Josiah?"

"During Mass this morning I remembered what I had to tell you last night."

"And...it was...?"

He paused with a hollowed look about his face. "I forgot again."

Roman smiled. "Should you remember again, Josiah, you might want to write it down."

"Oh, yes. Certainly."

"I'm sure it couldn't have been too important."

"Oh, no, it was important."

"Then I'm sure you'll think of it."

"Oh, I think I remember...No, that's not it."

"Is lunch nearly ready?"

"*Javoll!*"

"*Bon appetit.*"

The fifty families of the parish had now grown to nearly seventy and there were so many men, women, and children to meet that he completely forgot about Anna Maria Schmoll. The good night's rest the night before and the beautiful festivities of Ascension Thursday gave him a new perspective. Catholicism in Evansville was here to stay. The faithful of the parish were devout. One sinful member of such a parish was not going to ruin the fifth anniversary of the Church in Evansville.

Following lunch, the band of horns and drums led a parade through downtown. Josiah carried the cross, Andrew Martin rang the church bell, Roman bore the Blessed Sacrament in its monstrance, and the Irishmen, Doctor MacDonald and John O'Connell carried the statue of the Virgin Mary.

Once back at the church, Roman led the congregation in Solemn Vespers and ended with Benediction of the Blessed Sacrament. The evening then concluded with the *musikfest* on the spacious lawn of the Linck's *Mansion House* at First and Locust.

Finally alone for the night, he lit his candle and read from St. John's gospel. *This I command you: love one another. If the world hates you, realize that it hated me first. If you belonged to the world, the world would love its own; but because you do not belong to the world, and I have chosen you out of the world, the world hates you... If they persecuted me, they will also persecute you...And they will do all these things to you on account of my name, because they do not know Him who sent me.*

The hour is coming when everyone who kills you will think he is offering worship to God. I have told you this so that when their hour comes you may remember that I told you... In the world you will have trouble, but take courage, I have conquered the world.

Finishing *Compline*, he closed his breviary and had time to think. The silence of the night was welcome when compared to the excitement of the day. But the thought of Anna Maria Schmoll kept coming to mind.

Exhausted from the day's events, he wanted to sleep. But now he was restless. *Why didn't she attend any of the parish festivities?*

Outside, another thunderstorm was approaching, the third of the week. Through his open window, the flash of lightning eerily painted the trees and buildings a ghostly blue while the echo of thunder reverberated off the river and the church.

Was it an ominous foreshadowing of a heavy cross that would be lowered upon his shoulders as a result of what had occurred in the church Wednesday evening? He dismissed the thought.

The wenching songs of the flat-boatmen along the wharf and up and down the Ohio in the gun-boats continued despite the wrath of the storm. As soon as the rains came, so did his migraine. Torrential rain and pain. He was in such misery that he couldn't even lift himself up to close the window. He didn't even feel like having a shot of peach brandy.

Not another migraine. Please, Lord. Not tonight.

6 May 1842

By early Friday morning, at half past four the horrendous headache had rendered Roman nauseous. He flopped on the straw

149

mattress like a perch out of water as he tried to distract himself from the migraine and the thought of Anna Maria Schmoll.

He wished he had someone with whom to talk. He wiped his eyes as he thought of his brothers and sisters in Alsace. His letters had been mailed weeks before and still no reply. He also longed for the guidance and company of his pastor, Deydier, who had now been absent from the community since late March.

Roman's circuit riding tour of the Vincennes Diocese, celebrating the sacred mysteries of the Holy Sacrifice of the Mass, hearing confessions, and offering the hope of religion throughout the *Catholic Pocket* of southern Indiana was his one consolation. He hoped to visit the Utopian commune of Sainte Marie, Illinois, forty miles northwest of Vincennes, for it was largely composed of families from Strasbourg and Alsace.

He felt so free riding horseback to the missions dedicated to Saint Philip, Saint Wendel, Saint Joseph, and Saint James. It brought him great joy celebrating Mass in a farmhouse, at the edge of a cornrow, out in the open air in a wood or near a stream, or even in a blacksmith's shop, nourishing the fledgling faith of Catholic America.

Tossing about on the bed, his thoughts returned to the Schmolls. *Lord, did I do the right thing? Why was I so intent upon ensuring that the contract was signed? Will Martin Schmoll keep his promise?*

Will Anna Maria betray me?

His thoughts faded into a fitful sleep. Drifting in and out of consciousness, in that state of mind between night ruminations and bizarre dreams, he dreamt of the church door repeatedly opening and closing while he sat in the confessional. Someone kept pulling on the curtain of the confessional. The wooden screen was drawn shut. A despairing female voice cried in German, beseeching him, "Bless me, Father, for I have sinned... Bless me, Father, for I have sinned." The words echoed over and over again in his head as he kept waking from the beginnings of sleep.

Through the night the sound of the boatmen's ridiculous American melodies clanged about in his head. He could hear *Turkey in the Straw* and *Yankee Doodle* and other mindless songs being sung to the strumming of banjos along the wharf. The strains of the flat-boatmen's songs, and the revelry of their wenching, dancing, and drinking along the river turned his thoughts to the confessional. He blew his nose, cleared his throat, and propped his pillow.

He had always prayed that he would be a conscientious confessor. Now he wasn't so sure. Was he now guilty of a worse transgression?

The few times he had refused to grant absolution was only to let the penitent know the seriousness of his sinful condition. *What you bind on earth is bound in heaven, what you loose on earth is loosed in heaven.*

Finally, the migraine began to subside as the first streaks of dawn penetrated his window curtains. He realized that he had to be up soon for mass. He tried to fight off his long awaited slumber as he mused on the words and harmony of the *Gloria* from the Ascension Mass. Despite his efforts, he began to drift off into a refreshing sleep. The feeling was euphoric in comparison to the skull crushing pain.

No sooner had his eyes closed when a loud apocalyptic banging on his door startled him. Though he could barely move, the disturbance roused him from the silent shadow of slumber. The door sounded as if it was being kicked down. At first he thought he had overslept, missing morning Mass, and one of the parishioners was trying to wake him. The heavy pounding upon the door was more a nightmare than reality. The pounding jarred him again. He fell out of bed and bumped his head on the dirt floor. He rubbed his forehead and picked himself up only to trip over his chamber pot.

"Yes? Who is it?" He pulled the drapery away from the door's window pane and shielded his eyes until they adjusted to the light.

"It's Martin Schmoll!" His voice was full of anger, but he looked as if he was about to laugh.

"Sir, how may I help you?" Speaking through the unopened door, he quickly worked to get his cassock on and find his shoes.

"Priest! I demand that you give me that marriage agreement! I want it nullified at once!" Schmoll violently smashed the door again either with a fist or boot. "Neither my wife nor I will have anything more to do with you or your anti-Christ church! Hurry up and get out here!"

"I'm coming. Please be patient!" He began to feverishly rummage around in one of the cabinets where he thought he had placed the written agreement. He paged through the baptismal and marriage record books looking for the certificate but his hands shook so badly he could hardly turn the pages.

"Weinzoepfel, get out here in the alley before I come in after you!" His voice became a belligerent growl.

Roman momentarily abandoned his search for the document and worked to make himself presentable. Looking at himself in his small shaving mirror over his washbowl, he secured the last of his cassock buttons. He put on his biretta and opened the door. "Quiet down, Mr. Schmoll. The neighbors are still asleep. What's this all about?"

"Rogue!" Schmoll gritted his teeth and shook his fist at him. "Don't you tell me to be quiet! I want that promise I signed last Sunday evening canceled! As far as I'm concerned, I'll never allow my wife to have anything more to do with the Catholic Church."

"Pardon me?" Roman stepped outside into the morning fog.

"You reprobate!"

"What have I done to merit such abuse?"

"Your lecherous attack upon my wife."

"What attack?" Roman felt his heart beat in his jugular veins. *Certainly she didn't—?*

"Ah, the villain claims innocence in the matter!" Schmoll turned halfway round, as if to speak for the benefit of other hearers. His voice echoed up and down the alleyway onto Second street. "Don't pretend I don't know!"

Roman nervously looked down the alleyway for passersby. "I am at a complete loss, Mr. Schmoll. What did I do?"

"*What* did you *do*? I know what you did to my wife!"

"For God's sake, man, not so loud!" Roman smelled cigar smoke in the alley.

"Do you fear that the truth will be known?"

"I don't know what you're talking about."

"Well, I do. Ever since my Anna went to you for confession two days ago, she hasn't been the same! And we both know why, don't we?!"

"What are you saying, Mr. Schmoll?"

"My Anna Maria is lying sick at home because of your treachery! I had half a mind to kill you last night. I loaded my revolver and I was on my way to shoot you, but she stopped me. I was awake half the night. At daybreak I couldn't wait any longer." Schmoll reached around his waistcoat and revealed the handle of the revolver. He put his hand upon it as if to draw it out and fire. "I still have a mind to kill you right here."

Roman looked down the other end of the alley and in the corner of his eye he thought he saw someone lurking in the shadows of the church, but he wasn't sure. He'd feared that on one of his journeys he might meet up with some Kaintucks who would beat, rob, and leave him for dead, or have an accident while riding his horse. Never in a hundred years did he think that the husband of one of his own parishioners would threaten him. Roman's immediate thought was that Martin was drunk, but then he saw the fire in his eyes and sensed something even worse.

"I demand that you destroy my marriage agreement. In addition, I require that you pay me five hundred dollars for the damages and the insult you've committed upon my wife, and, who knows, I might forget the entire matter. I know that you're not the first knave to have her."

"What?"

"Stop playing games! I know you raped my wife." He got closer to Roman. "Tell me, though, did she enjoy it?" Martin's voice was softer now with a smirk scrawled across his face.

"My good God, Mr. Schmoll, what are you saying?"

"Don't act ignorant, priest. I know how she can seduce a man."

Roman didn't blink his eyes as his jaw hung slightly open.

"You didn't think I'd find out, did you? Swearing my wife to secrecy was a good move on your part, but you should have known it wouldn't work. A husband sleeps with his wife *every* night. Blood is thicker than holy water."

"Swear her to secrecy?"

"Yes, within the confessional." Martin's voice was intense with anger and his breath reeked of whiskey.

"The confessional is under a sacred seal."

"Then what a miserable wretch you are!"

"Are you accusing me of violating the sacrament?"

"You've violated my wife!"

Roman felt his blood rush to his face and his nausea returned making him even dizzier with the headache.

"What do you have to say for yourself, now, priest?"

"What can I say? I have nothing to say." He wiped beads of sweat from his upper lip and forehead as his migraine viciously returned.

"If you're innocent, then why are you sweating and shaking?"

"Who wouldn't tremble at such accusations?"

"Then you do not deny the charge that you ravished my beloved Anna Maria?"

153

"I *do* deny it, and if I had ever done such a thing, then I am the worst man in the world!"

"You are that man."

"Mr. Schmoll, in the Name of God, do you realize what you are saying?"

"*Yes,* I *do.*"

"Why are you saying this? If your wife came to confession and any priest were to have done the thing you claim I did, then that priest would be guilty of sacrilege and be rendered an excommunicate."

"If? If? Shouldn't you say, when? Don't attempt to confuse things. She was with you on Wednesday. I saw her go in the church and come out within the hour. Look, I haven't liked you ever since we first met. There are others who've hated you ever since you came to town. Who do you think you are telling my wife that she didn't have to sleep with me, saying that we had a bad marriage? She said you pulled her out of the confessional, threw her on the floor, and had your way with her!"

"That's a lie!" Roman's face reddened, his teeth clenched.

"Are you calling me a liar? Why don't we just go and ask my wife? Then we'll see who's a liar."

"If she is asked, she won't have the courage to repeat such a shameless charge. As God as my witness, there must be some misunderstanding!" Roman touched his neck and fidgeted with his collar.

"Then let's go ask her." Schmoll calmed himself.

"I agree." Roman swallowed nervously. His head throbbed, joints ached, and his stomach stabbed with even more pain.

He followed Mr. Schmoll to his home. It was not far, a little less than four hundred yards from the church yard on the opposite corner near Second on Sycamore. Roman fumbled with his rosary, but his thoughts could only recall the words of accusation from Martin Schmoll. In the meantime, Martin's tirade had created quite a stir, awakening other people, while others who were already up had gathered in the street between the church and the Schmoll home. The two exchanged nary a word as they walked along together through the rain drenched muddy street.

When the men arrived at the house, Anna Maria was lying in bed, whimpering. She was facing the wall and did not turn around when Roman and Martin entered the bedroom.

154

"Anna Maria, *the good priest*, Father Roman is here and would like to ask you something."

She didn't move, but instead remained in a child-like position, clutching her blankets about herself.

"Anna Maria, he wants to ask you about what you told me yesterday." She buried her head in her pillow.

"Mrs. Schmoll, your husband came to church this morning and presented me with a terrible accusation that I hurt you, physically, in some way. Please tell your husband that it's not true."

She said nothing, crumpled in her blanket.

Roman paused, thinking of something else to say. Meanwhile she had yet to make a response.

"Your husband says I…. Your husband says I violated you." He closed his eyes and continued. "He says I forced myself upon you." The words were repugnant, and he could barely utter them aloud, let alone think what they implied. "Please tell him that it is not true." A long, loud, uncomfortable silence filled the room until it gave way to the humming drone of a fly in one of the windows, caught in a spider's web, feverishly beating its wings, buzzing annoyingly. Roman diverted his attention to the fly's predicament.

"Dear," Martin sweetly addressed his wife, breaking both the silence and Roman's concern for the fly's quandary. "Is it true? Did he drag you from the confessional and force himself upon you? Answer 'yes' or 'no.'"

"Yes." Her voice was barely audible, no more than a whisper.

"Mrs. Schmoll, if ever I had done such a thing, then I would be the worst man in the world!"

Still facing the wall, she said nothing more, but covered her head with the blankets, and curled into a ball underneath.

Roman continued, "Mrs. Schmoll, the confessional is under a sacred seal, but in the Name of God, please tell the truth."

There was a long pause. Roman spoke up, with great emotion. "I could not—would not—even think of such a thing. And if I ever did, then you may rightly consign me to the very fires of Hell."

Her whimpering returned, but only louder.

"Again, he does not deny the charge." Mr. Schmoll gloated.

"Oh, but I *do* deny it." Roman raised his voice and looked at Martin.

155

"I suggest you get your affairs in order, Mr. Weinzoepfel." Schmoll's monotone stung. "By sundown, there will no longer be a Catholic priest in this town."

"I am innocent of these charges! The fact that she refuses to look me in the eyes should be proof enough." *The eyes are the windows to the soul*. How he wanted to look searchingly into hers. He knew there was no way she could possibly look into his eyes and accuse him of rape.

"She respects your priesthood more than you do. If I recall, a priest isn't allowed to look at women."

Roman seethed, not knowing what to say or do.

"As you can see, she's sick on your account," Schmoll continued. "I must be compensated by you and your bishop for the mistreatment she received at your hands. A young woman, ten years younger than you, and with child, mind you, and you ravished her. And yet now you insist on denying the facts. Now I'm more convinced than ever of the other charges. You're a horrible man."

"*Other* charges? What other charges?"

"That you left Alsace after doing this to other girls in your home village. Admit it, you didn't volunteer to become a missionary, did you? No, you had to leave Europe. That's the reason they sent you here. Just another European criminal sent to the American west."

"Who told you that?"

"I heard it down at *Wood's Tavern. The Bull's Head* and *Lamasco Inn* as well."

"What kind of a man are you to utter such vile, malicious gossip?" Roman raised his voice.

"What kind of a man are you to dare wear that collar?"

"Let's summon a doctor to Mrs. Schmoll's bedside and ascertain if she, in fact, has been violated," Roman suggested. "Certainly a medical man could determine the extent of her injuries."

"Yes, I am sure that Doctor Trafton would be more than happy to attend to things."

"I was thinking of Doctor McDonald. He is also quite capable."

"Then I'm not so sure about a doctor." Schmoll's countenance and tone of voice suddenly changed. "In fact, I'm not so sure of the charges myself."

"Excuse me?" Roman was stupefied by the sudden shift. "I'll go and bring both Doctor McDonald and Doctor Trafton back at once."

"Actually, I don't think any of that necessary. Perhaps my wife will take time to reflect upon the accusation and retract it. What do you say?"

Mrs. Schmoll shifted in her bed.

Roman was very suspicious, thinking that Martin's change of heart was too quick for a man who had just stated that he was on the point of revenge and murder. He grew more suspicious. "How am I to respond? The allegations you've made against me are criminal and will be hard to recant, let alone ignore. I must report the whole matter to my bishop in person immediately."

"Do you deny that you ravished my wife?"

"Yes, and I will swear an oath against the charge."

Martin Schmoll suddenly led him to the door of his house. "I'm sorry I took up your morning."

Roman's stomach moiled with a pain worse than any of his headaches as he stood trembling on the Schmoll porch with three of the Protestant neighbors looking on. He prepared to make his way back to the sanctuary of the church. However, on the streets and through the town of Evansville, he was sure the rumors were about to fly far and wide. He heard the pealing of the church bell calling the Catholics to morning Mass as he bounced down the wooden steps of the Schmoll porch and made his way down the plank way. He had nearly forgotten the time of day, never mind what day it was.

I will be hanged. He was lost in fear, trepidation, disbelief, and anger. *Why did I ever become a missionary?* He thumbed the corpus on his rosary's crucifix. As he got to the front of the church, he caught sight of the faithful Andrew Martin, happily tugging on the rope, clanging the bell, signaling all to prayer.

It had been Andrew who informed him about Doctor Trafton and his attempt to kidnap and sell the former slave and her four children before being discovered. Deydier had given Andrew his job as bell ringer as soon as the bell was installed in the steeple. Andrew was a man of simple, child-like faith, and served as an example of what Christ spoke of concerning gaining entry into the kingdom.

"Beautiful morning Rev'rend." Andrew exclaimed, tipping his straw hat to Roman as he climbed the stairs. Meanwhile, bystanders stared at Roman as he entered the church.

"Yes, yes, Andrew, it is."

Roman watched the yellows and pinks of the rising sun displace the purple hues of the western sky as cloudy vapors from the river climbed the steps of church. Glancing down at Andrew's wrists where the chain of slavery had left its mark, he recalled coming face to face with the grim reality of slavery when he arrived in America. The slave marts of New Orleans were conducted with great ceremony, trading in human beings as if they were mere chattel. He couldn't erase from his mind the image of these beautiful, black-skinned, African people; men, women, and children, all experiencing the whole cruel fate of slavery, their humanity forgotten.

He wondered then whether he might be fitted with handcuffs and shackles by nightfall. His thoughts turned to all the strange foreshadowings which now seemed to point to this very hour: His voyage aboard *The Republican,* nearly being swallowed in an Atlantic hurricane, and the collapse of the Vincennes Cathedral upon the eve of his first Mass.

He ambled through the doors of the empty church, looked upon the crucifix, and found himself face to face with a silent God. Numb and sickened with what he had been accused, he ran his hand through the holy water font, crossed himself, and collapsed upon a prie-dieu in the sanctuary. *O God, come to my assistance; O Lord, make haste to deliver me.* He wept thinking of all that he had sacrificed in order to come to America only to be assaulted with this salacious accusation.

Roman meditated upon one of the fragile, flickering flames of a candle upon the high altar that Josiah Stahlhofer had already lit in anticipation for Mass. The quiet of the church gave him space for clear thinking. The words of his brother Franz haunted his memory. *Do you realize what you are getting into? Red sky in the morning, sailors take warning... Why America?... There is no room for Catholics... Are you prepared to endure the trials and tribulations that await you there?*

He recalled the bishop's words of caution. *The old hatreds for the Church have found their way into the thick forests of the New World.*

The words of Abbé Augustine Martin were still fresh. *Roman, if you ever expect to be a parish priest, then you cannot hold the average member of your congregation to the same strict demands that you apply to yourself.*

He prayed, *My God, why do you stand afar off?* The words of the Psalms found new meaning. *O Lord, I am bowed down and brought low; my heart is in tumult, my strength has failed me and my eyes are dimmed with sorrow. I am weighed down, overwhelmed with grief. O Lord, deliver me from those who plot evil...they sharpen their tongues like serpents, venom is upon their lips.*

He questioned himself and searched his heart. He kept rethinking his encounter with Anna Maria during confession. Over and over again he recounted her words and his questions. He remembered placing her upon the pew, stroking her cheek and her looking at him with her beautiful but sad blue eyes.

My God, why did I even touch her?

Was it the heat and humidity or the stress and strain of the responsibilities of a missionary, or both? He was all alone. She was young. He questioned whether his mind had come unhinged? Had his headaches finally taken their toll? Her father had warned that she was forward.

As he removed his biretta and ran his hands through his thick, black hair, he glanced up and beheld about nine people in the church kneeling in prayer. Mass was to have already begun. Roman rose and vested, dressing himself in the alb and amice. Tying the cincture about his waist, he mouthed the vesting prayers. He hesitated upon the words, *Gird me, O Lord, with the cincture of purity and extinguish in my loins the fire of lust, so that, the virtue of continence and chastity may ever abide within me.* He paused, acknowledging his promise of celibacy.

Once the steeple bell rang again, he lifted the veiled chalice and paten, and walked out of the sacristy into the sanctuary. He looked out into the nave before genuflecting before the altar. Sunlight poured through the eastern windows of the apse as he ascended the steps to the high altar. *I shall go unto the altar of God, to God, the joy of my youth.*

"*Kyrie eléison, Christe eléison, Kyrie eléison.*" He found it most difficult to focus on the words of the altar cards as he prayed the liturgy. So preoccupied was he with the accusation that the mass was devoid of meaning. All he could think of was the pounding door and Mr. Schmoll demanding restitution for the crime of rape.

During the moment of consecration, he could barely concentrate. "*Santus, Sanctus, Sanctus...*" He lifted the paten with his left hand, the host with his right, breathing the words, "*Hoc Est Enim Corpus Meum.*" For this is my body. After kneeling in homage, he elevated the chalice. "*Hic Est Enim Calix Sanguinis Mei, Novi Et Aeterni Testamenti...in mei memoriam facietis.*" This is the cup of my blood, the new and everlasting covenant. Do this in memory of me.

Beholding the Eucharistic elements at the *Agnus Dei* he questioned his faith. *Will this be my last mass?*

Drinking from the chalice, he trembled so badly that he feared he might spill the Precious Blood. He gripped the chalice tightly to hide his shaking hands. As he turned to give the benediction to the familiar faces kneeling in the pews he saw nothing but holiness, reverence, and charity in their eyes. Raising his right hand in benediction, he tried hard to stop the tremor in his hand. Tracing the sign of the cross in the air, he could see from the parishioners' demeanor that they had yet to learn of the malediction pronounced upon him by the Schmolls. He knelt on the prie-dieu to the side of the high altar and joined the others in making a thanksgiving.

Perhaps his fears were exaggerated, he thought, but no sooner had this thought crossed his mind did the horrible and outrageous accusation fill him with anger again. He was now sweating yet he also felt an icy tingling in his hands and fingers. They were numb. He resolved to see the bishop before the end of the day.

He rose from prayer as Josiah Stahlhofer snuffed out the last of the candles. Stepping into the sacristy, Roman tried to imagine how he might tell Josiah of the nightmarish charges.

Josiah entered the room. "Father Roman?"

"Yes?"

"You look like you didn't sleep well? And I thought I saw you shaking. Are you all right?"

"Yes, Josiah." He lied as best he could.

"Oh, yesterday afternoon I filled in the grave of that Irish canal worker and inscribed his cross."

"Oh, thank you. Good work."

"Oh, and I hear that more of the workers on the ditch have the ague."

"Yes. Do pray." Roman removed his vestments, not giving attention to what he was doing.

"Oh, and Father Roman, there is something else."

"Yes, Josiah?"

"It's the sanctuary lamp. I can't get it to light. I've tried everything."

"That's odd." He remembered noticing that the lamp wasn't lit, but the accusation made it seem inconsequential.

"Oh, Father," Josiah's eyes opened wide as if he had a revelation. "I'm so sorry!"

"What is it, Josiah?"

"I finally remembered what I needed to tell you Wednesday night."

"Yes, what was it?"

"It happened right before you went in to hear confessions Wednesday night. One of the women waiting to go to confession said something which irritated me, and to be honest, it worried me."

"What woman?"

"Louis Long's girl, Anna Maria."

"What did she say?"

"She swore revenge on you if you refused to grant her absolution. What do you make of that?"

Roman felt like a horse had just kicked him in the head. *So, there it is.* Nausea undulated within him.

"Josiah, why didn't you tell me Wednesday night?" he angrily asked

"I forgot," Josiah started at Roman's anger. "Remember? I'm sorry."

"Have you told anyone else what you just told me?"

"No."

"Then I ask that you not repeat it to anyone, not now at least."

"Certainly."

"Have you been anywhere this morning besides here?"

"No."

"Before you got here this morning," he pressed the man, "did you talk to anyone or see anyone?"

"No, but there was a commotion down at the office of the *The Journal*, but when I inquired everyone stopped talking and told me it didn't concern me."

"Of course. I knew it!" Roman could only imagine the editor of *The Evansville Journal*, Will Chandler, busily working on the Schmolls' story in hopes of distributing it to other Whig Party publications throughout the country.

"Knew what, Father?"

"Josiah, I have something very disturbing to tell you."

"Yes? You look like you've got the weight of the world on your shoulders. Your hands are shaking. What's wrong?"

Roman clasped his hands together, stopping them. "I have been accused of assaulting Mrs. Schmoll."

"What? When?"

"Wednesday evening during confessions."

"But there were others in church. I was around back. I saw the Heinrichs too."

"Mr. Schmoll came here this morning and informed me of the details. He had a mind to kill me."

"Martin Schmoll's a drunken man. Mrs. Schmoll won't repeat such calumny."

"I only wish that were so. After Mr. Schmoll informed me of the accusation, we went to their home..."

"And?"

"And when I asked her, well, she would not speak to me, but she confirmed the nature of the charges."

"Charges? Are there charges?"

"Not as of yet, but I am sure that her husband won't let the matter go."

"What can I do?"

"Nothing for now. Just be prepared to protect yourself and the church. Who knows what irate Americans are capable of doing once Schmoll or one of his friends repeats the story?"

"This is terrible."

"I've thought of nothing else."

"Martin Schmoll is a monster."

"Why do you say that?"

"When his first wife died, he got drunk at *Wood's Tavern* and beat a man to the point of death. I've also heard that he forced himself upon another man's wife in the alley behind the *Bull's Head*. Last year he started a fight down at the wharf and everyone got arrested except him. He's never charged with anything because he has money."

Roman stared out into the sanctuary at the crucifix hanging upon the apse wall. "I'll not be a party to the assassination of a man's character based on hearsay."

"I believe we should inform Messrs. Heinrich and Francis Linck, Sr. of the slander against you," Josiah suggested as he put the chalice and paten away and closed the cabinet door.

"Yes, I believe you're right."

A knock on the sacristy door startled Roman. He turned to see a man entering the church. His face was familiar.

"Father Roman, me baby came during the night." The man spoke English with an Irish brogue.

"Mr. Fitzwilliams. Thank God it's you."

"Are ye all right? Ye look like ye just seen Saint Patrick hisself."

"Yes, yes. I'm fine. I'm happy for you. Congratulations on your baby."

"Well, aren't ye going to ask if it's a boy or a girl?"

"I'm sorry. Is it a boy or a girl?"

"A little girl. We've named her Sarah Jane."

"And your wife? Is she well?"

"Me wife's ready for our next one. She was up with the other child'ern fixing them breakfast when I left this morning. All me family's at me home, and we hoped you could come for dinner around noon. Afterwards you could baptize the wee one."

Josiah spoke in German. "It will do you some good, Father Roman."

"Very well, Mr. Fitzwilliams," Roman addressed the Irishman. "You may set a place for me. I will arrive before noon."

"Thank ye, Father." Fitzwilliams exited the sacristy.

Roman turned towards Josiah with a flash of thought. "I must leave for Vincennes at once. I will take lunch at Blue Grass with the Fitzwilliams, but then after the baptism I'll be off to report this incident to Bishop Hailandière. I should arrive in Vincennes by the vesper hour. Please secure the church this evening and if any of the parishioners need a priest, send word to Henderson. There is a Father Durbin that visits there from time to time. I don't know the man but I'm sure that he wouldn't consider a trip across the river too great a sacrifice to administer the sacraments."

"God be with you, Father Roman."

****

The Howling of wolves in the thicket of the forest snapped Roman's attention back to his present task of escaping Evansville and its environs. He continued northward following the path of fugitive slaves and prayed that the lynch mob was not in pursuit.

Chapter 13

Vincennes, Again

10 May 1842

By the middle of the morning hours Roman made it to the farmhouse with the large red X on the barn door. He went in and collapsed upon a haystack. The sound of a horse neighing gave him the idea of stealing it, the devil working his imagination. He couldn't fall asleep. Could he trust a Protestant? Mr. Jones, yes. But a stranger in a Protestant community? In his fear and exhaustion he entrusted himself to Providence.

The next morning he woke to the voice of someone singing.

Go down, Moses, way down in Egypt land. Tell ol' Pharaoh, let my people go! Go down, Moses, way down in Egypt land. Tell ol' Pharaoh, let my people go!

The deep bass voice belonged to a solid, bare-chested Negro man.

"G' morning. You awake, Sir?"

"Yes. Good morning."

"My name's Jeremiah."

"I'm Roman." He stared at the wounds around Jeremiah's wrists and ankles where the chains had rubbed the flesh raw. The lacerations received from the lash marked the man up and down his back, across his chest, and over his arms and legs.

The Protestant lady who owned the farm appeared in the doorway, inviting them up to her house for breakfast. "You're the Reverend everyone's looking for."

"I am."

"Don't worry, you're safe. The Jones boys sent you, didn't they?"

"Yes."

Roman followed her and Jeremiah to her house where she fed them. Even though he was assured she was an active abolitionist he worked to find the courage to trust her as he sat at her table.

"You ain't dressed like no rev'rend? Why you hiding from the law?" asked Jeremiah, between bites of buttered bread. "You didn't kill nobody, did ye?"

"No, I've been accused of a crime."

"Did you escape from jail?"

"In a way."

"Then you're a fugitive from the law, like me?"

"Not exactly." He thought for a moment, realizing that they were both fleeing injustice. "We're both fugitives from the law, but we're both innocent."

"The good book say, 'pray for them that spitefully use you.' So that's what I be doing. I figure if I hate thems as much as they hates me, I ain't no better. What good's all that hate? Only thing it's good fo' is making you meaner than a big ol' brown bear."

"Where are you from?" Roman asked, taking some tea.

"Kentucky. Rev'rend Durbin hid me in a wagon headed for Evansville, so he got me as far as the river. Massa Carpenter smuggled me through town. They put me up at the Joneses place and that afternoon they sent me on my way. Good Christian mens, they is."

"Yes. I know them. They're a courageous lot. The Joneses befriended me in my darkest hour."

"Honor'ble men, honor'ble men," Jeremiah nodded gaily, "but the Catholics in the south has slaves, Rev'rend."

"The Pope has condemned slavery," Roman said, looking at the man's scars and recalling his own chains.

After eating, the woman tended to Jeremiah's scabbed back while he told how he had passed through Evansville the day before unnoticed.

"You know much about us slaves, Rev'rend?" Jeremiah asked.

"Some, but now I know firsthand the weight of a chain." Until then Roman had looked upon slavery as an unfortunate institution, but now he realized that he could no longer remain a detached observer.

Jeremiah continued with another one of his songs.

In Christ there is no East or West, In Him no South or North, but one great fellowship of love throughout the whole wide earth. Join hands, then brothers of the faith, whate'er your race may be! Who serves my Father as a son is surely kin to me.

The two men got on the cart and hid under old clothes and rags as the woman manned the reins and sang her prayers.

Through all the tumult and the strife, I hear that music ringing; it sounds and echoes in my soul; how can I keep from singing? No storm can shake my inmost calm, whilst to that rock I'm clinging. Since Love is Lord of heaven and earth, how can I keep from singing?

Roman was on the sentry for bounty hunters and roughs, carefully covering himself at the sight of every horse, carriage, cart, or wagon, while Jeremiah sang along with the woman.

By that afternoon they had changed horses a couple of times and had made it to Princeton at the home of another woman conductor who was to smuggle them north over the swollen White River and into Knox County of which Vincennes was the county seat. They climbed into her covered wagon and hid in the shadows.

Jeremiah sang out upon the straw, praising God for his new freedom in a slow, heartfelt hymn.

What wondrous love is this, O my soul, O my soul? What wondrous love is this, O my soul? What wondrous love is this that caused the Lord of Bliss to bear the dreadful curse for my soul, for my soul; to bear the dreadful curse for my soul?

He continued with his prayer and song as Roman found himself strangely attracted to the haunting, soulful melodies and sentiments, alien from the Gregorian chant and traditional northern European hymns.

Jesus walked this lonesome valley; He had to walk it by himself. O, nobody else could walk it for him; He had to walk it by himself.

We must walk this lonesome valley; we have to walk it by ourselves. O, nobody else can walk it for us; we have to walk it by ourselves.

You must go and stand your trial; you have to stand it by your self. O nobody else can stand it for you; you have to stand it by yourself.

Roman pondered the words. Jeremiah had no idea of the significance of the verses. As the cart approached the White River, he looked out at the swirling current. Once across the river, they veered off the Vincennes Road westward toward St. Francisville, Illinois, along the Wabash River. Once past the ferry crossing, Roman got out of the cart and walked the rest of the way to Vincennes. As the horse and cart went off into the distance, Roman could still hear Jeremiah and the woman singing.

There's a balm in Gilead to make the wounded whole, there's a balm in Gilead to heal the sin sick soul. Sometimes I feel discouraged

*and think my work's in vain, but then the Holy Ghost revives my soul
again.*

Roman followed the muddy levee to Vincennes and at the vesper
hour the clouds opened up. By nightfall he had reached Vincennes,
cold and wet, his clothes drenched in sweat and rain. As he neared the
Cathedral, his hope for sanctuary, he heard the footfall of a horse
behind him. When he turned there was no one there. He stepped up to
the chancery door, reached for the rope to the bell, and pulled.
Standing before the darkened chancery, he anxiously looked around.
He still thought he was being followed.

"Yes?" Finally, a voice came from behind the large wooden door.
"Who's there?" He recognized the voice as that of Abbé Martin.

"Abbé, it's Father Roman Weinzoepfel."

"Who?!" Before Roman could answer again, the abbé had pulled
open the door.

"My God, man, you're alive! Am I ever relieved to see you. It's
been nearly two days since you left Evansville." He ushered him in
the foyer and closed the door behind him, bolting it shut.

"I'm sorry to have awakened you, but I have no where else to go."

"No worry. News travels quickly in America."

"So you have heard of my predicament."

"Little else these past few days. There were fears that the
drunkards had killed you."

"There were moments I feared they would accomplish their task."

"You were not followed, were you?"

"I'm not for certain." Roman then remembered that Abbé Martin
had been stationed in Logansport. "Monseigneur Martin, what are you
doing in Vincennes?"

"That's a long story." He explained how he had been in Terre
Haute visiting the Sisters of Providence when he first heard of
Roman's dilemma. "While I was there two diocesan priests were
attacked north of Terre Haute while riding in their carriage. They're
fairly unhurt, but with such things afoot, His Lordship has
reappointed me rector of the Cathedral."

"Where is his Excellency?"

"When he received word that your trial had ended in a wanton
uproar, he set off at once for Evansville in order to investigate the
matter. He should be at *The Mansion House* with the Reverend Shawe
and Benjamin Thomas by now."

"I fear I have made a mess of things for him, for you, for all my brother priests, indeed for the whole Church."

"Father Roman, I have not, for one moment, entertained the thought that you could have even thought of doing what that woman accuses you of doing."

"Thank you, Father, but I doubt that you will be called for jury duty. My fear is what the bishop thinks."

"I believe that his opinion will mirror mine. I have given him a full account of your seminary records and as vicar-general, I vouch for your innocence."

"I pray that I am not to be hanged for this crime."

"At least they do not utilize the guillotine here."

"No, it is something worse. The press. And once the Whig presses get this story, all Catholics will be at risk. We thought the contrived tale of *Maria Monk* was bad, now they have an actual priest in his collar and cassock who is accused. What is more, I shall never be able to take the stand since she accuses me of committing the outrage while hearing her confession. The seal of the sacrament is inviolable."

"*Oui.* It does present a singular problem." He paused, looking at Roman's gaunt unshaven face. "Have you eaten?"

"I'm not hungry. All I ask for is a little time in the church before the Blessed Sacrament-and a new soutane, biretta, and breviary. I won't bore you with the details, but in my escape from Evansville, I surrendered them to the Kentucky priest, Elisha Durbin."

"I see...there are extra breviaries in the sanctuary prie-dieus. You may have one of them."

"*Merci.*"

"I will prepare the upstairs guest room for you."

"*Merci.* I shall not be long in the church. Good night."

"*Dominus vobiscum.*"

"*Et cum Spiritu tuo.*"

Roman quietly walked out of the rectory and through the garden path. Upon entering the church, he prepared to pray. The glow of votive candles gave off an ethereal luminosity as he dipped his first two fingers and thumb into the holy water font, blessing himself. Once in the sanctuary, he dropped face first in front of the high altar.

My God, My God, why? Why hast Thou forsaken me? Lord I believe; help my unbelief. Yes, Lord, I know that all those who desire to live in Christ Jesus will suffer persecution. If possible, let this cup pass me by, but not my will, Thine be done.

He stood and draped himself over one of the prie-dieus in the sanctuary. He looked up at the crucifix, the twisted figure of Christ sagging upon the gibbet. It was a hand-carved crucifix that Bishop Bruté brought over from France. Roman found a breviary under the prie-dieu and prayed from it in the flickering candlelight.

To all my foes I am a thing of scorn, to my neighbors, a dreaded sight, and a horror to my friends. Those who see me, run far from me. I am like a dead man, forgotten. I am like a shattered dish...I hear the whispering of the crowd; terrors and calumny are all around me. They are conspiring against me; plotting together as to how they will take my life. Even though I walk through the valley of darkness and the shadow of death, I fear no evil for Thou are at my side.

He rose from his prayer, returned to the rectory with the new breviary, and readied himself for bed. Upon entering the candle-lit guest quarters, he saw a new biretta and perfectly folded soutane lying upon a wicker-backed chair at the foot of the bed. Exchanging his soiled wet clothes for the clean bedclothes spread across the end of the bed, he laid his troubled head upon the pillow, allowing his weary mind to rest.

Sleep came at once.

For the next few days, Roman secluded himself in the rectory of the cathedral and refused visitors, except the rector, Abbé Martin.

****

May 14, 1842

By weeks end, the bishop had yet to return from Evansville. On that Friday, Roman was kneeling in prayer in the cathedral, praying his office, but more so contemplating his fate. His thoughts drifted to his native Alsatian hills, thinking of his brothers and sisters, fearing that they would soon learn that their brother had committed an ungodly outrage, ruined the family name, and desecrated the name of Holy Mother Church. His thoughts returned to his ordination. It had all happened so fast. Too fast. He looked around at the empty prie-dieus in the cathedral sanctuary and thought of his days in the seminary. He glanced up over the altar and saw the painting of the patron of the cathedral, the enraptured face of Saint Francis Xavier.

The church was devoid of worshipers and the only sound was that of his breathing and his rosary beads tapping against the wooden prie-dieu. His eyes focused upon one of the angels at the right side of the tabernacle that was standing guard over the sanctuary. As his eyes returned to the face of Saint Francis Xavier, he heard a door close. Someone was entering the sanctuary from the sacristy.

"Father? Father Roman?" The voice was familiar for the words were spoken in French.

Roman quickly stood and straightened his cassock. He supposed it was the sacristan or the gardener by the man's attire.

"Father Roman." A blue-tinted feline curled around the man's legs.

"Your Excellency! Bishop, I did not know it was you." His Lordship was wearing work clothes, overalls and trousers. Roman knelt before him and kissed his pontifical ring. "I did not recognize you." Roman stood.

"I have avoided wearing the frock in public. It has become a risk, you know." The bishop took him by the arm. "I see you appreciate art. That painting was a gift to me from Cardinal Fesch. His uncle, Napoleon Bonaparte, had given it to him. It dates back to the Renaissance and was painted by—" Hailandière looked into Roman's eyes. "I apologize, Father. I interrupted your prayers."

"No, I was nearly finished."

"Then walk with me, my son." He led him through the sacristy. "How *did* you make it out of Evansville alive."

"It was most unseemly, my Lord."

"Unseemly?"

"Yes. My disguise."

"*Disguise?*"

"I was dressed as a woman, Bishop."

"A *woman?*" He bent down, scooping up the cat, Simon, in his right arm.

"Yes. A woman. Then I followed the route of fugitive slaves and was assisted by abolitionists."

Silence reigned as they descended the sacristy stairs out into the cathedral flower garden in the courtyard.

"Father Roman, do you remember the evening before your first Mass?"

"How could I forget? It was the night the walls collapsed." His mind returned to that night. In his recollection of the events the evening prior to his first mass, he suddenly realized that Hailandière had stopped walking and had turned towards him.

His Lordship cleared his throat and continued. "Perhaps I should have given you more time before ordaining you, but I still feel the same way about you that I did over two years ago. You are a good priest. Never forget that."

"So you don't believe the charges?"

"Of all my priests, you would be the last I would ever suspect of such a thing. I am convinced of your innocence. Nothing but your confession to the contrary would convince me otherwise." He stroked the slate blue fur of Simon's back causing the cat to purr.

"*Merci beaucoup*, my Lord." He was relieved beyond measure, fearing he was to be defrocked.

"I have just arrived from Evansville. Over the past few days I have consulted with your attorneys James and Wilbur Jones and Benjamin Thomas and our own Reverend Michael Edgar Evelyn Shawe, and not only them, but the faithful of your congregation. They all attest to your holiness and integrity, but are filled with grief over your situation. Many of the parents are at a loss as to explain your absence to their children. I have also met with some of the Protestant population. There are many who refuse to repeat the calumny and I believe that they will become your ally in this ordeal. It seems the editor of *The Evansville Journal*, William Chandler, is the guilty party. According to talk in the taverns, on the day of your trial he and his brother the attorney and some other men bought drinks for all who would mount their rides to hunt you down. These Chandler brothers intend to make sport of you—and me—in the pages of the press. But I would be curious to hear your side of the story for myself."

"Certainly. As you know the accusations stem from the evening before the Feast of the Ascension of our Lord. Mrs. Schmoll came to the church that evening to make her confession and during her confession she claimed she felt sick. Then she told me—"

"Father Roman?" the bishop interrupted him.

"Yes, bishop?"

"You have said nothing of this to your attorneys, have you?"

"No, it took place in confession."

"Do you realize that you can *never* tell anyone what you have just told me?"

Roman looked unblinkingly into the bishop's gaze.

"Even me. The seal of the confessional precludes you from even saying who your penitents were. You cannot even say that she *came* to you for confession, otherwise you have broken the seal. But now that you know," the bishop smiled softly. "Please continue."

He felt as if he had just fallen from a horse. "*Merci.*" He paused and recounted the evening. "Afterwards, I took off my stole and surplice, locked the church, fed my horse and went to the Heinrich's for supper. The next day, which was the Holy Day, Mrs. Schmoll, along with her sister and brother, came to Mass. The entire day went by without the least mention of a problem. I have a feeling that Mr. and Mrs. Schmoll and their cronies were busily arranging the details of their diabolical plot."

"Let us be careful and not give the devil too much credit."

"Agreed. It was on the following Friday morning that Schmoll pounded upon the door at the rear end of the church. When I answered, he demanded restitution for the honor of his wife and leveled the accusation at me—"

"Yes, I am well aware of the rest, I believe. I have also learned that the Whig presses in this country are not going to ignore the potential this has to taint the American mind concerning Catholic immigrants and Catholicism in general. Our friend Will Chandler of *The Evansville Journal* will see to that thoroughly." The bishop continued to stroke the cat in his arms.

"Freedom of the press," Roman lamented. "Mr. Thomas said as much. Of course, that is a relative statement, considering who has control of the presses."

"I will spare no expense in defending your honor and the honor of the Church. I can only pray that should the hideous serpent of calumny ever coil itself about another one of our brother priests, or one of the faithful for that matter, in whatever disguise or masquerade, inflicting him with venom, whoever the victim may be, I pray that the sweet odor of sanctity and the virtues of integrity may be so venerable that I will be able to solemnly deny the charges against him as willingly as I deny the charges against you." The bishop had stopped in front of one of the benches in the garden.

"I pray the judge and jury are as merciful." Roman stopped.

"Of that I am not so certain." Bishop Hailandière motioned for Roman to sit down on the bench as he released Simon, allowing the cat to land on all fours.

"How will it be possible to repudiate the foul charge before the court, when Schmoll and his party use violence to interfere with the legal investigation, and threaten those who could testify to the truth?" Roman sat.

"I do not know. If one priest is said to have fallen, therefore all priests have fallen. If you take the stand and speak the truth, you exonerate yourself, but at the same time you betray your trust, condemn the sinner, and excommunicate yourself. If you refuse to take the stand, your silence will likely be interpreted as evidence of guilt, and you will be hanged or condemned to a life sentence of hard labor."

Roman was wordless.

"As you can see, Father, we must pray for a miracle." The bishop paused, closed his eyes, and lowering his head, he continued. "Speaking of threats, Father, I must inform you of certain threats against your life. I have received word that there is a faction who desires your blood. So I have made arrangements for you to remain here in Vincennes where you should be safe. There is the possibility I could send you to *Colonie de Freres* at *Sainte Marie*, Illinois, or to eastern Indiana as well. The congregations of New Alsace and the missions in Dearborn, Ripley, and Franklin counties have been deprived of the Sacraments for far too long. Perhaps by September the tempers in Evansville will cool."

The cat, Simon, sat in front of them, licked his front paws, and rubbed his face clean.

"Meanwhile, I have a diocese to govern." He stared down at Simon.

"The diocese has grown under your leadership."

"Don't patronize me, man." The bishop looked toward the Wabash River. "The diocesan debt is the only thing that has grown since I arrived. Now there are rumors that I am to be removed." He turned from the cat and again looked Roman in the eyes. "So, have you heard the rumors?"

"No, not actually, my Lord."

174

"You know how widely I am despised in the diocese. Yet I assure you, I will *not* be removed. I would resign before being humiliated by my removal."

"Resign?"

"Yes. Resign. Do you know what it's like to know that your mother is dying, but the apostolic charge requires that you dutifully remain at your post?"

"Yes. My father and mother died while I was in the seminary. Father died unexpectedly, but mother had been ill. I could have approached my superiors and asked for a leave when my Mother was dying, but it was late October and we were in the thick of Thomas Aquinas' *Summa*."

"Yes, I recall your superiors at the seminary and the bishop of Strasbourg telling me. How many children did your mother and father have?"

"Twelve in all, but only six of us are left. Several of my younger brothers and sisters died as infants."

"So you have known your share of suffering and hardship. It is obvious that you have taken up the mantle of our Savior's cross. When I first met you I believed you had the constitution required of a missionary. And just as I believed in you then, I believe in you now."

Roman looked at the bishop in gratitude.

"My mother died this past March." The bishop said sadly and glanced away.

"I didn't know. My prayers are with you."

"I didn't make it public. Some of my enemies may have accused me of using my mother's death to gain sympathy for my failed administration of the diocese. You wouldn't have thought that, would you, Father?"

"No."

"What have you learned from all this—your predicament and all?"

"Much about human nature and the great evil each of us is capable of committing."

"I have known others who upon becoming bishops have changed and brought harm upon the Church." The bishop turned to Roman again. "Am I worthy to be your bishop?" Before Roman could answer, the bishop stood and turned to face the cemetery. Hailandière put his hands on his hips and spoke angrily. "Don't you ever think for one moment that I have regretted my decision to come to Indiana! I *am* the Bishop of Vincennes and will forever be remembered as such!"

Roman stood, shook his head in the affirmative, and clutched at his rosary beads.

"I tell you these things, my son, because you also have been given a particular cross, and I grieve for you. I pray that you may persevere in your mission." He walked along a little further and stopped again. "You knew the risks when you agreed to come to America. Of course, you have known adversity in your life before, so now, as before, you must offer this cup of suffering to the Lord."

"Yes. I shall, Bishop."

The bishop looked around for the cat that had walked away. "Simon! Come here." He paused as if about to speak again. At that, the bishop bowed his head slightly. "You will not fail me, will you Roman?"

"No, my Lord."

"And if you were the only priest left in the diocese, would you remain faithful to me?"

"My Lord, there are others more faithful than I."

"You're too kind. I think you may be the only priest who still regards me worthy of my office." The bishop was still looking down.

"Oh, but you're mistaken, my Lord—"

"Don't argue with me." He bent down, and grabbed Simon in his arms. As he rose, he eyed Roman closely. "I am your superior and you have vowed obedience to me."

"Yes, my Lord."

"You keep everything inside. That is not good, my son." He paused as Simon climbed on his shoulders. "How long do you think a man can hold a grudge, Father Roman?"

"I don't know. Perhaps forever?"

"Christ taught us to forgive," Hailandière reminded him. "Seven times seven, no?"

"Yes." Roman thought of the Schmolls and their Protestant agitators.

"Our Lord's command of mercy and forgiveness extends even to Protestants, my son." He held the cat in his arms. "If we fail to forgive, then we remain unforgiven." He turned to face the river.

"But if these Protestants claim they know scripture," Roman rhetorically asked, "then what has become of 'love thy enemies,' or 'forgive as thou hast been forgiven'?"

"They are Protestant, Father Roman. They interpret scripture as they please." With a shake of his head and a long sigh, His Lordship looked back at Roman. "I can only tell you that a grudge is the heaviest thing you can ever carry. Eventually you must abandon it. *Dominus vobiscum.*" He dropped the cat. Again Simon landed on all four paws.

"*Et cum spiritu tuo.*" Roman bowed slightly.

Raising his hand to Roman's face, he gave the blessing, making the sign of the cross over him. "*Benicat vos omnipotens Deus, Pater, Filius, et Spiritus Sanctus.*" He veered around, and abruptly took leave, returning to the rectory with Simon the feline following close upon his heels.

Chapter 14

Unparalleled Outrage

Reverend Michael Edgar Evelyn Shawe and attorney Benjamin Thomas found Roman in the midst of the cathedral's courtyard garden praying his breviary.

Thomas held out a copy of *The Evansville Journal* issued on the twelfth of May. "Father Roman, look at this front page." Thomas held the paper up for him to read the bold print headline of the article. *Unparalleled Outrage: Great Excitement in Evansville.* Roman nearly collapsed under a wave of nausea and his all too familiar headache returned. He began reading.

> **Unparalleled Outrage: Great Excitement in Evansville**
> **We feel it our unpleasant duty to give the public the particulars-so far as we may with proper decorum-of an outrage alleged to have been committed in our town last week, certainly of the most revolting character that can be conceived of by the mind of man. We have often, and who has not, read of the similar corrupt outrages and dark and fiendish tales charged against the highest members of the Catholic Church throughout its long and sordid history, and we have believed them to be largely exaggerated and highly colored, prompted in many instances, perhaps, by jealousy or reformers. But in this instance our good faith has been taken by storm at the evidence produced and upon examination compels us to the conviction of the entire truth of the charge.**
> **Late on Friday the sixth of May our citizens were astounded with the intelligence that the Catholic priest, the Reverend Roman Weinzoepfel, resident priest here, had been arrested upon the charge of committing an act of violence of the most revolting character upon a female penitent, the wife of Mr. Martin Schmoll, a highly respected German citizen, and herself of a good family and well respected—young, beautiful, but recently married—while at the confessional for the purpose of obtaining absolution for her sins.**
> **The news spread like a conflagration, and immediately upon the prisoner appearing at the Magistrate's office in the Court House the building was besieged by such a con-course of people that it was soon found incapable of containing the highly excited and volatile crowd that**

poured into it. Nothing however was done with the case on this evening; the counsel for the defendant moving for a postponement until morning. The case was adjourned until 9 o'clock the next morning, where the Magistrate required bail in the sum of two thousand dollars.

On the following Monday, the ninth, the crowd was greater than ever, having been swelled by numbers of Irish and German Catholic immigrants and others from the country. Indeed was such the press into the Court House that fears were entertained that the weight would crush its walls, and a number of our more prudent citizens on this account withdrew. A more highly excited state of feeling was also plainly visible, although perfect order was maintained at that time. The prisoner appeared attended by his counsel, Messrs. Jones of this place and Benjamin Thomas, a member of the Bar and of the Catholic Church from Vincennes. The Rev. Mr. Shawe, a Catholic priest from Vincennes was also in attendance.

The only witnesses produced by the prosecution were the lady upon whom the outrage was committed and her husband, and upon motion of the defendant's counsel, the court ordered that all the witnesses on either side should withdraw from the room except the one who should be under examination. The Prisoner's counsel also requested that the female witness might be sworn according to the forms of the Catholic Church as used in the country from which she comes, to which request the lady promptly acceded, stating through her counsel that she had no wish to be sworn in any other way. A crucifix (the one used at the church we believe) was consequently brought in, and placed between two lighted candles, and the lady standing in this presence was (through an interpreter) sworn to speak "the truth, the whole truth, and nothing but the truth."

We took full notes of the testimony, but as it was delivered through an interpreter it is necessarily too prolix (besides being otherwise objectionable) for our column; we shall therefore not attempt to give it either in the language or order in which it fell from the witnesses. Her simple story was in substance and as near as we can give her language as follows: She is a native of Rhinish Bavaria, where she lived until she was about 19 when she removed to the United States, with her father and the rest of her family. She will be 21 years old on the 14th of June next. Her parents as well as her brothers and sister are all Roman Catholics, and as such she was christened and educated—all the Catholic education she ever received having been in a Catholic School, to which she went three years to prepare herself for her confirmation. She was married to Mr. Schmoll on last New Year's day, eight days before which time she had gone to confession and did not go again until Wednesday the 4th of May when, having previously informed her husband of her intention, she went to get her sins forgiven.

When she entered the church between five and six o'clock in the evening, some other person was in the confessional, and she waited till that person went away, perhaps, three quarters of an hour, when, there being no other person in the church, she went into the confessional. (This as the witness described it, is a sort of box, open at the side, and divided into two compartments, each large enough to contain only one person, in one the priest sits, and in the other the penitent kneels upon a stool, the communication between them being through a window of lattice work in the partition.) Having confessed her sins to the priest, he imposed a penance upon her, before she undertook which she wanted to pray, as is the custom of her country, but she could not pray. The priest then asked if she believed in being married by a Squire or Justice of the Peace and followed this question with others of the most lewd and indecent nature relative to her conjugal intercourse. (At this time it was so dark she could scarcely see to read her prayer.) These questions she for some time refused to answer, but the priest insisted upon them in such a rude manner that she became frightened and at length did answer them. He then told her that these questions did not belong to her confession, but that she must not tell her husband.

While she was thus kneeling before him attempting to repeat the prayer which he had set before her as a penance, the priest came out of his box and seizing her by the right arm, dragged her out of the confessional, and then taking hold of her with both arms around her waist threw her upon the floor. The witness then described the liberties which the priest took with her while on the ground. Her testimony excludes all doubt as to the fiendish desire to violate her person. After he had accomplished his horrible purpose, he raised her up, placed her on a bench, and sprinkled her face with holy water.

The examination had progressed thus far when Mrs. Schmoll began to feel very much exhausted, and would be glad to retire. During a large part of this painful recital she wept bitterly and was now tremulous and agitated to a high degree. The court expressed a hope that she would be able to remain a short time longer unless she felt too unwell to do so. The examination was then resumed, but had not proceeded far when Mr. Schmoll appeared at the bar, apparently highly excited, and stated that he was informed that his wife had complained of being unwell and had asked the Court for leave to retire, which had been refused, and that he would not permit the Court to

ROMAN

detain her in such a condition against her will. This was like applying a torch to gunpowder.

In a moment all was uproar and confusion. The friends of Schmoll cried to him to go ahead, that they would back him, and several Irish Catholics brandished their shillelaghs, and joined in the war cry. For a moment or two we thought we were about to have a real 'Donnybrook Fair,' and it was with much difficulty that the influential men of both sides arrested the affray. When order having at length been partially restored, we turned our eyes to the witness stand and we found that the innocent cause of all this confusion had fainted, and was being borne insensible from the room.

This unfortunate turn of affairs here brought the examination to an abrupt close. At 3 o'clock the prisoner's bail was set. He was set free after his bond had been posted, but it was feared that the prisoner would be seized by the mob, and dealt with as their passions might dictate. A throng of irresponsible men had been assembling in the streets since the court had adjourned prematurely earlier in the day. He was however brought out under the protection of the officers and conducted up the street, the entire crowd following at his heels. It is said that the priest passed immediately through the house, and made his escape from town in a wagon previously provided for the occasion. It was fortunate for all the parties that he did so. Had he fallen into the hands of the mob the most fearful consequence must have ensued. And that he was not seized is a fact, in our opinion, highly credible to those of our citizens who busied themselves in efforts to keep down the excitement and prevent violence.

Other charges and serious complaints we understand, have been made against Mr. Weinzoepfel, the man alluded to above, but with these other allegations we have nothing to do. Such an horrendous outrage, committed by a father confessor of the Catholic Church within the very walls of his sanctuary, upon a weak and confiding penitent kneeling before him, could not be increased by any additional charges. It may not be proper for us, and we shall not attempt to express the indignation we feel in common with the whole community. The charge will undergo a judicial investigation, and we should not as journalists attempt to prejudice public opinion in advance. Our only objective shall be to give a fair and impartial statement of the case and the evidence so far as it went, already public in our own community.

Fears have been expressed that the bail is not sufficient to secure the appearance of the accused to answer the charge, (even some of our best citizens share the same fear), but we trust that these apprehensions are groundless. Although it might be difficult to collect

181

the whole amount of the bond in case of default, yet we have every confidence, that it is honestly the determination of the leading members of the Catholic Church, that the accused shall not escape just judgment of the law if guilty. They are men of too much character, and have too high respect for themselves and their church, to lay themselves and it liable to the vengeance of justice. We believe that the Church will make it its business to see that he is forthcoming on the day of trial.

Roman reread a portion of the account. "What's a 'Donnybrook Fair'?"

"It is an annual fair outside of Dublin, Ireland," Reverend Shawe answered. "It is known for its fistfights and drunken brawls."

"Yes, the editor has a way with words in his description of the Irish," Benjamin Thomas replied, obviously angry, "but I understand that there were just as many Americans in the streets engaged in fisticuffs, exchanging blows with their sticks, clubs, and brickbats."

During that first week in Vincennes, Father Roman penned a letter to his pastor who was in New York. *Dearest Father Deydier: Before these lines reach you, you will have learned through the press what great misfortune has lately befallen your congregation and the whole Catholic Church. Mr. Schmoll has made good the scandal of his clandestine marriage to Louis Long's daughter, Anna Maria.*

Mrs. Schmoll has indicated that on the evening before the feast of the Ascension, that she came to the church to make her confession. He then explained in great detail all the events of that Friday morning, the sixth of May, how Schmoll had wakened him and accused him of raping his wife, and how Mrs. Schmoll had confirmed the accusation. *I was on the point of leaving for Vincennes to obtain Bishop Hailandière's advice in this grave matter when I was arrested. My enemies interpreted my journey as an attempt to flee from justice.*

He finished his letter with how the trial ended in a riot and how he narrowly escaped Evansville in an unlikely disguise and had secretly made it to Vincennes.

Reverend Father, I fear, as I have told our bishop, greater misfortune may be in store for the church.

Your faithful servant,

Father Roman Weinzoepfel

****

The following week Vicar General Abbé Martin called Roman into his office and read aloud a letter to the editor of *the Vincennes Gazette.*

> Concerning the priest Roman Weinzoepfel and the unfortunate chaos resulting from his hearing, I believe the good Catholics of our state must hear from their Protestant brothers and sisters. I, as a Protestant minister, will attempt to convey my grief at the display of hatred and intolerance shown at Evansville on this past ninth of May. The Gospel of Christ does not give us the freedom to violently attack our brothers and sisters. If you are sincere about bringing Catholics to the truth we must lovingly convert them, not browbeat them! Oh, the indignation I feel! Have we come to this? Throwing brickbats and threatening to torch homes and churches all in the name of Christ? Did Christ teach us to kill thy neighbor? If this is contained anywhere in the Gospel, then I must have misread Christ's words of the Sermon upon the Mount. Has this become a Protestant Inquisition? For some of you it appears to be so. I pray God that all of those responsible for this blemish upon the white robes of the saints bathed in the blood of the Lamb may find it in their hearts from now on to love thy neighbor.
>
> Signed, Reverend Joseph Wheeler, Justice of the Peace, Pigeon Township.

"So, you see, Father Roman, things are not nearly as bad as they may seem." Abbé Martin went on to say that Reverend Shawe was confident that there would be a quick end to these false charges. Roman wasn't as optimistic or hopeful. "The Church of Rome has weathered storms like this before. Think about it. The testimony of twelve unlettered men with no worldly influence save that of their love for Christ succeeded in defeating the Roman Empire with their word—"

"And their martyrdom."

"Not Saint John."

"No. He only died in exile."

"Don't be so discouraged, Father Roman," Monseigneur continued. "Look at Joseph, the son of Jacob. He was the unlikely son of Israel that saved the nation. His own brothers despised him and plotted to kill him, but settled for selling him into Egyptian slavery for twenty pieces of silver. He was also falsely accused of rape and thrown into prison. Many years later when all of Israel was suffering from famine it was Joseph, by the hand of God, then the second in command of all Egypt, who from his post was able to save all of Israel. Had his brothers not sold him, they may have all perished. God makes all things possible. Consider yourself like Joseph, betrayed by fellow Bavarians—"

"I am an Alsatian."

"Yes, I realize that, but you know what I am trying to say. Besides, we're Americans now. And so are the Schmolls. Consider that there could be a higher purpose in all of this. What we sometimes consider a curse might actually become a blessing."

Roman found some solace in both the letter and Monseigneur's words and decided to spend some time in prayer. He entered the Cathedral and prayed before the picture of Saint Francis Xavier.

The Lord ransoms the souls of his servants; those who trust in him shall not be condemned. O Lord, my God, I take refuge in Thee; from all my pursuers save me and rescue me, lest they maul me like lions, tearing me to pieces and drag me away never to be seen again. O Lord, if I have done wrong, if I am at fault in this matter, if there is guilt on my soul, if I have repaid good with evil, or hated without cause, then let my foes pursue me and seize me; let them trample my life to the ground, leaving me dishonored in the dust, abandoning my soul to the dead.

O Lord, Thou art my light and my help, whom shall I fear? The Lord is the stronghold of my life, before whom shall I shrink? Do not abandon me to the will of my foes, for malicious and lying witnesses have risen against me, breathing out fury. Yet I am sure I shall see Thy goodness, O my Lord, in the land of the living. I shall hope in Thee, hold firm, and take heart. I shall hope in Thy Holy Name.

Meditating upon the face of Saint Francis Xavier, all at once Roman recognized the face of the man in the painting. It was the face belonging to the man who had prevented him from being killed in the courtroom. At least it seemed he had the same face as the man in the painting. The stress related to the charges and impending trial was causing him to imagine things.

Later that day he decided to compose a letter of his own to the editor of *The Evansville Journal*. It was published a week later with Will Chandler's editorial alongside.

Dear Editor Chandler, I have read the article of which I am the subject, in your journal of the twelfth, which in a painful sense, that

great, though I hope unintended, injustice, has been done me by your remarks. Without asking why you have done so much to prejudge my case, for I heartily forgive everything that has been said or done in the heat of excitement by all concerned, permit me to beg you to abstain from all expression of opinion upon the case, and to observe your admirable proposition and claim that as journalists you do not attempt to prejudice public opinion in advance.

It is no doubt quite natural that a charge, such as is alleged against me, should produce such excitement. However, it seems, that in the midst of the furor, the rights of the accused, for the moment, have been forgotten. Is it not the benefit of law in this country that a person accused of a crime is entitled the benefit of the doubt until the proper tribunals of justice have determined his innocence or guilt? And is it not an injustice if an individual is found guilty before he can defend himself in an instituted court of law?

As to the assertion, or insinuation, of my guilt in the matter, or that there are other and more serious complaints against me, I am innocent and I am completely unaware of these other incidents. Therefore, to counterbalance your foregone conclusion, I beg to assert and appeal to the fact, that my entire congregation, not to mention those who are not Catholic, who know me best and have had better opportunities than yourselves of learning all the circumstances upon which depends the result of this great affair, are unanimous in their belief in my innocence. The Catholics for their part could never tolerate a wolf in sheep's clothing.

As to the fears entertained of my appearance at your court, I beg to assure all who may doubt that I shall be there, and pray that the excitement will be sufficiently appeased to prevent a repetition of the multifarious wrongs which I suffered at the first hearing on the ninth of May. Here I would inform your readers that the violent circumstances attending the hearing entirely deprived me of the individual rights that are enjoyed by other individuals in this country who are accused of misdeeds before the law. It was at the point when my counsel was conducting the cross-examination when a mob, led by Mr. Martin Schmoll, broke up a peaceful tribunal and took justice into its own hands, thereby preventing all further investigation. Then the brigands attempted to apprehend me to do with me as they pleased. Thanks to a kind stranger I was shielded from the tempest. The tumult could not be quieted and even the judge sought protection.

My friends, manifesting their strong conviction of my innocence by providing my bail, enabled me to escape the madness, not in a wagon or by horse, but on foot, and in a disguise most unseemly, in order to preserve my life and the peace and safety of the town. Thus a most important judicial investigation, from the uncontrollable fury of a mob, ended in a riot and in the most flagrant denial of justice and unfortunate abuse of an individual. I should have been afforded the protection of law, but instead I was hounded into exile.

The time will arrive, I hope, when a fair trial will proceed and until then will not all good citizens and unprejudiced lovers of truth suspend their judgments, and regard me innocent until proven otherwise, as does the rule of law, which the people of America have themselves ordained? I feel assured that you and the editor will concede to me the same right which I understand to be established beyond question in this country, namely, that the accused is innocent until proven guilty.

Editors Note: William Chandler
I am surprised that a man of Mr. Weinzoepfel's intelligence should have thought to promote his cause by asking the publication of a statement so utterly false in a community where he is probably to stand his trial. Certainly he must be aware of his guilt and hundreds would swear to it. The reason he writes this untruth is because he and his counsel have no defense.

Chandler went on to discount the mention of violence by anyone associated with the trial in Evansville and denied that Roman had been deprived of his constitutional rights.

****

6 August 1842

During the summer of 1842, His Lordship Hailandière had asked Roman to minister to the German speaking Catholics in Vincennes. He also rode to the mission chapels in the southeastern part of the state whenever he was asked since two more priests had left the diocese in protest of the bishop.

In a way he was glad to be out of Vincennes. It helped him put the incident with the Schmolls out of mind. Nevertheless, he knew that September would soon be in the air and with it his forsaken trial.

Before Roman's scheduled return to Evansville, Martin Schmoll made his presence known again, this time with the publication of a pamphlet which appeared throughout Southern Indiana and Northern Kentucky. Benjamin Thomas showed him a copy.

Oh, Right Reverend, Monsignor Celestin Lawrence de la Hailandière, Roman Catholic Bishop of Vincennes, how shall we come before thy unblemished and vestal presence. Oh, thou who but has to utter a whisper to be obeyed! You give a nod of thy head and poor, ignorant, deluded flock fall down and worship thee! And thy priest, who has sullied my wife and filled this land with his debaucheries! The anger of God has been enkindled against thee, and judgment is at hand, even if the legal authorities do not convict you of your guilt.

Since the occasion of this damnable scourge, this infernal plague, this odious calamity, my eyes have been opened to the monstrous character of the Catholic priesthood! Oh, the sacrilege, the corruption, the whoredoms of that loathsome Church! And such blind obedience on behalf of the wayward brood! The miserable rabble refuses to acknowledge American republicanism over their hierarchy.

"Is it possible that in this land of free men and enlightened minds, a population of people such as these Catholics can be so ignorant as to allow themselves to be bewitched by a lecherous and shameless clergy? These immigrants recognize their duties to their bishops and priests and regard the dictates of their Church as superior to our laws! Was this not the case with my wife before she was rescued from the quagmire of popery? Indeed it was!

"I have even learned that their bishops take an oath of fidelity to the pope binding them to further the schemes of the Church! If this priest escapes justice through the hocus-pocus it will prove that the Romish influence has taken over our shores.

After his initial anger, Roman said to Thomas, "One thing's for certain. For Protestants who can't agree on doctrine or practice, they are able to agree on one thing—my guilt. They were at each other's throats until I came to town. The Irish and German Catholics are also united. I guess I should be happy that all this has brought about the unity the bishop wanted."

"Of course, it has cost us dearly, being bought at the price of your head." Thomas said. "You're a victim of the sacramental seal, sacrificed upon the altar of freedom of the press."

The American dream. What a nightmare.

Roman despised Martin Schmoll far more than Anna Maria.

Chapter 15

Tragedy in the Woods

September of 1842 had found Roman ready to go on trial, but due to the birth of Mrs. Schmoll's baby girl, the trial was postponed until March 1843.

Therefore at the end of September he accompanied Father Deydier and Francis Xavier Linck, Sr., and his wife, to the Sisters of Providence at their community of *St. Mary-of-the-Woods* near Terre Haute. The occasion was to witness the Linck's daughter, Augusta, profess her vows as a Sister of Providence and join their religious community. When they arrived, Mother Theodore greeted the pilgrims at the gate.

She explained how she was so proud of Augusta, indicating that the novice had been well taught by both parents and priests. Roman smiled at Mother, pleased that he may have somehow contributed to the spiritual life of the nineteen year old.

"She is to become Sister Mary Magdalene. The other sisters call her the 'angel of the novitiate.'" Mother Theodore smiled.

Roman learned from Mother Theodore the trials of their fledgling community. The anti-Catholic sentiment had followed them into the woods of Vigo County. He didn't have to imagine the anguish she was experiencing. As it was, one of her sisters had left the community and was guilty of slandering Mother Theodore. Not only that, but the woman was now in the process of establishing a rival school for girls. Already, several of Mother's students had withdrawn from her school and had opted to enroll in the new school instead. And not only that, but the inimical opinion of His Lordship was now so fervent, in part because of his support for the sisters' school, but also his defense of Roman, that there were threats to somehow get rid of him too.

The investiture occurred on the thirtieth of September. Roman planned to remain at the Woods for the week-long retreat since Deydier was the retreat master.

That Sunday began with High Mass followed by the noon meal. After the dinner and rosary, Roman retired to the chaplain's quarters. No more than a quarter of an hour later while lying on his bed, he suddenly heard the chapel bell ringing and female voices crying out, "Fire! Fire! Everyone, get to the well!"

He sprang off his pallet, and emerged from the room as if experiencing a nightmare. The farmhouse was ablaze, the roof lifting up like so much parchment thrown upon an open flame, and a shower of glowing stubble ignited the dry October grass and broken stalks from the harvested corn-rows. Flaming wood and straw ash descended like a hellfire snow setting aflame the straw at the barn door, while the wind gusts fueled the blaze like kerosene, flames racing fifty feet in the air.

The sisters raced to save some of the animals and farm implements while the postulants and students frantically scrambled for anything that might serve as a pail or pan to take water from the well to the burning structures. The surrogate female fire brigade stood no chance against the consuming firestorm. Roman joined them in their fight and carried a pail to the fiery wall. He winced from the pungent heat and noxious smoke while two of the sisters escaped the blazing oven and collapsed just feet from the doors before the barn erupted into an explosion of fire.

The hired men came up from the horse stables aiding in the effort to douse the raging inferno. All together they desperately tried to smother the flames and ransom wagons, plows, and wheelbarrows, in a vain attempt to salvage Mother Theodore's dream. A cyclone of flame leapt from the house and barn, climbing into the sky, licking the adjacent woods and enkindling more fires. The hottest flames ate the freshly thrashed grain, cremating it into a crackling glittering glow, an orange blue serpent, sinuously streaming upward into the lengthening shadows.

The foreman of the workers shouted to everyone that it was useless. "Get out of there! Let it burn! Just save the fence and the stables!"

As Roman looked to the unfinished church, Mother Theodore and Father Deydier, both in tears, came running out from the chapel.

"Sweet Jesus, how did this ever start?" Mother cringed.

Roman led two horses away. They were wild, kicking and neighing to break loose. Mother Theodore took their reins as Roman returned to the blaze.

189

The workmen called on everyone to save the church and the convent and chapel. The foreman held up an axe and turned to Roman. "You, priest! Do you know how to handle an axe?"

"Yes."

"Good! Start chopping those trees to the east! We'll make a break in the fire's path."

He joined a group of six other men, hacking at the hardwood, lopping off chucks of bark and limbs.

Roman chopped, anxious to know how the fire had started. In the midst of felling a tree, he dropped his axe as a sharp pain raced across his left side. He turned to see his left cassock sleeve on fire. He fell to the ground, rolling himself out in the dirt. One of his fellow axe men was shouting blasphemies. His hair was aflame. One of his fellows covered him. The fire was by then surrounding them all. Roman could barely breathe at one point, the smoke thick and sparks intense. A dozen chickens and roosters fled the barn, while three pigs and a couple of sheep scattered, as if fleeing Armageddon. The workmen all began shouting and cursing.

Such a dear holocaust, a costly oblation to the incarnate firedrake which greedily devoured the contents of the granary—the hellacious conflagration reaping the entire harvest and consuming the buildings along with all the autumn foliage in its path, wicked as the eternal flames prepared for the devil and his angels.

By nightfall the wind ceased blowing and the fire burnt in place, a smoldering pyre of charred timbers and blackened beams. Mother Theodore had received burns to her hands as did many of those fighting the flames. Deydier wept as he prayed vespers with the sisters in the darkened, candlelit chapel.

Mother Theodore was kneeling before Christ in the Blessed Sacrament. Soot smeared her face and a bandage covered her left hand from where she had tried to extinguish the blaze. Roman stayed in the chapel until everyone had left—except for Mother. He approached her as she crossed herself and appeared ready to depart her prie-dieu.

"Mother, please."

"Yes, Father Roman?"

"I fear I am to blame for the fire. Had I not been here, your academy would have never burned."

"Nonsense, Father. The Nativists did not need you for an excuse to attack a group of immigrant Catholic sisters. We have enemies as well." She looked up at the crucifix and fingered her rosary beads that dangled from the cincture around her habit.

Roman looked at her. "The anti-Christ is here."

The woman of forty, her face aglow in the candle light with the radiance of Moses after descending Mount Horeb and with a certain aura of wisdom beyond her years, turned, saying, "Yes, but never forget *'where sin abounds, God's grace more and more abounds.* Father Roman, I have learned that the more one is stripped of in this life, the more one learns from Providence that the greatest treasure we are given is the cross. Always the Cross. Recall our Savior's first and final temptation. Avoid the cross."

She paused and took Roman's hand. "You must embrace your cross. You must take it up. Unite your suffering to those of our Lord. You are sharing in his Passion. Remember that."

"Yes, Mother."

"Never underestimate the grace of God. God will not be outdone in generosity. The Lord places certain people in our lives in order to help us learn how to love Him better, more completely, by learning to love them. Sometimes it's painful to love—and forgive—our neighbor, especially an enemy, yet Christ forgave those who scourged him and nailed him to the gibbet of the cross upon Golgotha.

"Saint Augustine prayed, 'Lord, by loving the unlovable you have made them lovable.' Perchance the Lord is asking you to pray for this Schmoll woman. If we love others we have the power to enable them to love God."

Look at what this woman has done to *me*, he wanted to say, but said instead, "Look at what this woman has done to the Church."

"Father Roman, I have a story to tell. My father was an officer in the French navy. He was away for years at a time. Once while he was away, our house at *Etables-sur-Mer* caught fire and my younger brothers perished. The tragedy was nearly unbearable for our family." She stopped and glanced up at the tabernacle as if for strength. "When I was fifteen, my father was granted a long awaited shore leave. He had written to us of his excitement at the prospect of his returning to see us. At Avignon, as he was making his way north to our village, he was attacked by brigands and was stabbed and killed. His murderer was never discovered. My mother was left all alone to care for my younger sister and me.

"I stood by my mother in the hours of her darkest despair. At first I was filled with hatred for my father's killer, but through prayer and hearing mass I discovered that I must pray for that murderer. I must pray for him—and forgive him. I must love that man, for Christ mounted the cross for him as well as for me. Jesus said, '*Forgive as I have forgiven thee.*'

"Before I left France, there was a notorious criminal executed upon the gallows of the guillotine. It had been reported in all the papers that he had claimed to have killed many men in his lifetime and was proud of his wicked deeds. While many were eager to be rid of him, I decided to pray for him. After his execution it was reported in the papers that he had become a model prisoner in his last days, even renouncing his wickedness and requesting the chaplain for the Last Rites the morning of his execution.

"Now, even if he wasn't the man who murdered my father, I believe God was calling me to give Him all of my anger and hatred, placing the matter in His hands." She took her hand away from his and folded her hands in prayer. "So, Father Roman, take heart. There are others who know a little of what you might be experiencing."

"*Merci beaucoup*, Mother." He sighed through his nose, touched by her story, and thinking how selfish he had been to only think of himself. He squeezed his rosary beads. "There must be a reason for me to be here, Mother Theodore."

"*Mais oui.* There is always a reason for being."

"Yes, but I can't quit thinking about everything. Even when I try to pray, I can't."

"Courage, my son. Recall Saint Paul's admonition in the book of Hebrews, 'my son, do not disdain the discipline of the Lord, nor lose heart when he reproves you; for whom the Lord loves, he disciplines.'"

"I could accept it more readily if I was being disciplined for doing something wrong."

"Saint Teresa of Avila said our Lord grants his cross to his friends."

"And she said that must be why he has so few friends." Roman quipped.

"Yes." Rising, she smiled and kissed him on the forehead. "Be at peace, my son. The Lord will provide a way for you—for all of us.

"The young woman who accuses you of an unspeakable crime—I do not believe she is sole to blame for your predicament. She is an example as to why I believe so firmly that we must open more schools for young women here in America, Catholic and Protestant alike. Education can free the souls of women from the tyranny of ignorance. Had this girl been given a decent opportunity to better herself through the arts and literature, I do not believe any of this would have happened."

Roman was not ready to exonerate his accuser so easily.

"We must beg God's mercy, especially for those in most need of mercy, and let us pray for our enemies. The Lord would have it no other way."

He heard her words, but all he felt like doing was cursing his enemies. It was a strange dichotomy, these two women in his life, Anna Maria Schmoll and Mother Theodore Guérin—sinner and saint.

****

Advent and Christmas came and winter thawed into the spring of Lent. The solace of Christmas had given him some measure of comfort before he was to take up the cross of Lent. A feeling gnawed away at Roman about what was happening in Evansville. Being removed from Evansville for months, the memory of early May 1842 began to fade. He even forgot about the charges at times wondering whether it was nothing but a bad dream. He busied himself with his office, prayers, mass, and rosary. His life was becoming easier, almost too easy. Would he awaken one morning to discover that all the charges were forgotten?

Yet the war between the Democratic and Whig presses had spread the story of the alleged confessional rape far and wide and despite his self-discipline and theological training, he found it difficult to pray. And even when he did pray he felt no consolation.

Waiting for the trial was like trying to hurry the sun in its course across the sky. A year of delays made the wait even more agonizing.

In another way it was as if he had experienced an interrupted night's sleep only to awaken at dawn to discover that the night had passed and the orient was on high.

John William McMullen

February came, and after spending time with his attorneys, prepared or not, the moment was now upon him. Ash Wednesday was days away and it felt as if the entire Church was shrouded in violet penitential cloth as if to veil it from the scandal of which Roman was the focal point, a festering wound upon the Body of Christ which was about to be reopened.

He would be as silent as his master was in the presence of Herod, like a sheep before the shearer, opening not his mouth.

Chapter 16

Lenten Journey

March 1843

On the eve before Roman was to leave for Evansville he learned that the trial had again been postponed until September. *Another delay in justice.*

Late in March, Bishop Hailandière summoned him to the chancery. When Sister Angelique opened the door, Roman heard His Lordship Hailandière speaking to someone. Sister Angelique seated Roman in one of the hallway chairs where he tried not to eavesdrop though the study door was slightly open.

"My Lord, I leave for France on the first of May," said a familiar female voice.

"Well then, when you return from Europe do not be surprised to learn that I have appointed your sisters to the school here in Vincennes." The bishop snorted a laugh.

"You would not."

"I would. You are under *my* rule."

"We have our own Rule. I am the Mother Superior." The voice belonged to Mother Theodore Guérin.

"Not as long as you are in my diocese."

"Bishop, you are in clear violation of Canon Law. You violate our Rule by—"

"With that kind of rebellious talk, I would have you leave the diocese," the bishop raised his voice.

"You have been threatening to send us away for over a year now."

"You know very well that I have not and never did have that thought."

There was a brief pause in the exchange.

"My Lord, if you had founded our order you would be the Superior, but we are independent—"

"How dare you talk to me as an equal, Sister. I am the bishop. You owe me respect as a successor of Christ's apostles. And there is no independence movement in the Church. Oh, there are those who think there should be."

"I beg you forgiveness, *mea culpa*, but if you will not allow us to follow our rule, then we will leave, my Lord, since that appears to be what you desire."

"Why would I want you to leave? What have I not done to try and keep you at Saint Mary's." The bishop's voice grew soft. "And as for a superior, you are the only one capable of being superior."

"Then allow us to follow our Rule or we will leave. My Lord, with us gone, you can found your own order–one that you can control. Our Rule prohibits you. I am grieved by the trouble I have caused you. We will stay long enough to instruct your new sisters."

"You will most certainly not leave!" His Lordship barked. "Nobody loves or respects you–you and your sisters–more than me! You are wicked to suggest leaving me–the diocese, I mean. Why, I would never be able to find another woman as qualified as you to be placed at the head of a community."

"My Lord, nothing is more odious in America than the office of Superior, for from it flow dependence and submission—virtues which Americans do not realize. My postulants are infected with this republican spirit at every turn. It is tremendously hard for them to submit to any authority–even the authority of God."

"Ah, how well I know. You and I have much in common, Sister Theodore. Do you remember when we were in Rennes. I was at the parish and you were in charge of the school. Those were simpler days, were they not?" There was a smile in his tone.

"Perhaps, my Lord, but what about Sister Theodore and Monseigneur Hailandière in Vincennes? How will we remember our time here together?"

"Are you implying that I am the young, inexperienced bishop of Vincennes?"

"Lordship, I said nothing of the kind."

"You insinuate!"

"Never." Her response was in a measured tone.

"*Oui*, you are too debonair for that," the bishop harrumphed.

"I ask that you stop investing sisters into the order without my approval. You cannot continue to dispense with the period of discernment. I would rather have five good sisters than twenty incompetent ones."

196

"So you are saying that the sisters I have brought to y
incompetent?"

"No."

"Then am I the incompetent one?"

"Bishop–"

"You are impossible."

"Am I? You have given the youngest priests of the diocese more
control over our sisters than I have as their Mother Superior—"

"I am the proprietor of your community–in both spiritual and
temporal matters! I can forbid you to take a step or send you away at
once!"

"My Lord," Mother Theodore's voice raised, "the weather does
not change as often as you change your mind!"

"You know I have loved your community from the beginning.
Who invited your sisters here in the first place?"

"You, my Lord."

"Do you think I enjoy the fact that some of my priests have left
me because I have favored you and your sisters so highly?"

"I am grieved, but we are not your property."

"Sister Theodore, I am suffering so much for I have loved your
community too much—and the regard I have for you is not small. I
may resign, and if I do, know that it would be due to the grief you
have caused me. The mere mention of your name can send me into a
fit of emotion."

"Are you finished?"

"For now, yes, but do remember what I said about changing your
meal times, and do not forget that I am going to change your style of
habit. Oh, and I don't think you should allow your novices and
postulants to eat with the fully professed Sisters."

"My Lord, you have an entire diocese to govern. I believe I can be
responsible for twelve sisters, making sure they are fed on time and
get enough sleep."

"I am their Bishop!"

"I am their Mother."

"With such an attitude I would have you removed as Superior.
You do realize that I could inform your community to elect your
successor while I require that you remain here in Vincennes?"

"If I may be excused, I am off to visit my missions in Jasper and
Saint Francisville."

"*My* missions. Sister."

"*Your* missions?"

"I am your *bishop*."

"And I am their *Mother*."

"Woman, you have crossed the line! If Bishop Bruté were still alive, he would have already excommunicated you."

"I would never presume to speak for the dead. I have spent time praying at his tomb in the crypt. It's something I'd recommend."

"Are you saying I do not pray? By God, woman, I do pray! And I pray for you daily."

Roman could now see the back of Mother Theodore's habit as she was standing in the open doorway. She turned around and acknowledged his presence with a slight bow of her head. "Father."

"I will show you to the door." His Lordship charged out of his study as she opened the door. Simon, the cat, ran out through the opening and skittered down the hallway towards the dining room.

"I will see myself out." Mother Theodore turned her back on the bishop.

"You did not kiss my ring."

"*Mea culpa*, my Lord." She stopped and genuflected on her right knee in front of the bishop, barely touching his ring with her lips before rising.

"Please do not leave me with bitterness in your heart. Try, my dear, to see all the esteem and affection I have for you in my soul, and put off judging or condemning me. You will then understand that the bishop of Vincennes fails in many things, some because he is unable to do them, and others because he does not know how to do them, but know that in all things he highly esteems you and your community. You must pray for him. What I am for you, frightens me; what I am with you, consoles me."

"I shall continue to do so," she said, looking up at him. "*Adieu*."

"*Adieu*." With that she turned, brushing past Roman, and glided down the steps, her black habit flowing in the spring air.

Sister Angelique had returned to the foyer. "My Lord, Father Roman Weinzoepfel is here to see you."

"*Oui*. I can see that. That will be all, Sister." She disappeared as Roman removed his biretta and knelt, reverencing the bishop's ring. He lifted Roman by his right arm. "*Entre*, my son."

Roman, took a seat in the high-backed red silk-covered chair in front of Hailandière's large desk, straightened his soutane, and balanced his biretta on his knee.

Simon, the bishop's Chartreux blue cat, sneaked around the back of Roman's chair, rubbed up against his soutane, and shed wooly fur on the black cloth. Soon the cat was jumping on Roman's lap, batting his soutane's sash and the rosary beads hanging from his hand.

"*Simon, come here,*" Hailandière called. The cat sprang across the floor and hopped up into his lap. "*Mon cher.*" He petted the cat, and smiled at Roman. "He's so sweet, isn't he?"

"*Oui*, Your Excellency." Simon purred loud. Roman thought it obnoxious.

"Did you ever visit Chartreux?"

"No."

"Simon's ancestors were companions to the Carthusian monks there."

Simon licked his front paws, the sound of his coarse tongue scraping fur audible. In a moment's rest from licking, the cat looked to be smiling as it batted its wide orange eyes across the desk at Roman.

"*Mon petit,*" the bishop looked into Simon's face before his eyes returned to Roman's. "Father Roman, I am appointing you rector of the seminary—effective the eighteenth of April, Easter Monday."

"Pardon?" Roman knew that one of his brother priests was currently the rector.

"You heard me."

"But the current rector, Father—"

"He *was* the rector. He failed me miserably. I have relieved him of his office—and of his priestly faculties. May God forgive me for ordaining him."

"But—"

"What? You heard me." Simon jumped off his lap and darted behind the lace window curtains. "It is my decision. You will assume the duties of rector of the seminary, appointing spiritual directors for the seminarians, teaching theology, and, of course, with your knowledge of language, you will continue to teach the young scholars Latin. You will also retain your responsibilities to the German speaking Catholics here in Vincennes." Simon rolled on his back and pawed at the curtains.

Hailandière stood. "You are in my prayers—go with my blessing." Coming around in front of his desk, the bishop traced a cross in the air.

Simon stretched out on the Oriental rug, clawed at the carpet, and looked up at Roman.

Roman stood—though momentarily distracted by the cat—to follow protocol, not knowing what to say. *How does one refuse Hailandière?* He wanted to protest, but his vow of obedience precluded any such protestations—and this was Bishop Hailandière, not Vicar General Monseigneur Martin.

Obediently, he submitted to His Lordship, returning to his quarters at the seminary. In the two years since his ordination, the bishop had built a new seminary north of the cathedral grounds. It was on Fifth Street on a new street appropriately named Seminary. On the corner opposite was the bishop's palacial mansion, still under construction.

Safety still a concern, he was careful not to leave the seminary grounds by himself or travel to the chancery or cathedral grounds alone, for it was a good distance, nearly a mile. Even though he acquiesced to his superiors's fears, he found it difficult to find the necessary solitude. He also missed the freedom of riding his horse.

He dutifully chanted *Matins*, *Prime*, *Lauds*, and *Vespers* in choir, said his morning mass, prayed the little hours of *Terce*, *Sext*, and *None*, practiced *lectio divina*, told the beads of his rosary, made his nightly *examen*, and ended his day with *Compline*. Yet no matter how much he prayed or fasted or offered the sufferings his penitential hairshirt inflicted upon him, he felt no consolation in his prayers. Monseigneur Martin continued to reassure him that feelings are fleeting. What was important was obedience to prayer.

Yet it was becoming more and more difficult.

****

Quasimodo Sunday

It was now the Easter Season and Roman glanced up into the sanctuary above the high altar and saw the crucifix unveiled from the Lenten Violet. He genuflected and knelt, glorying in the Cross of the Lord Jesus. After a *Pater* and an *Ave*, he rose and took his place in one of the choir seats in the apse of the cathedral. As the *Gloria* rang out on the ranks of the pipe organ an acolyte rang the steeple bell while two servers rang the sanctuary bells. It was so refreshing to hear the pipe organ for it had been silent all throughout Lent.

Roman reflected upon the scripture as he flipped the violet ribbon of his breviary. *Christ humbled himself, and became obedient unto death, even death on a cross. Christ suffered for you leaving you an example that you should follow in his footsteps. He committed no sin, no guile was found upon his lips. When he was insulted, he returned no insult. When he suffered, he did not threaten; instead, he entrusted himself to the one who judges justly. He himself bore our sins in his body upon the cross, so that, dead to sin, we might live for righteousness.*

Roman thought of his own unwillingness to forgive Anna Maria Schmoll. Or was it an inability to forgive?

He closed his eyes and renewed his priestly promises as the melismatic harmonies of the Gregorian plainchant with its single syllables stretching out over a host of multiple notes ascended to the apse's crucifix, descending upon all gathered in the nave.

After the solemn Mass the bishop, draped in his ornate golden silk cope, took the incenser and swung it in front of the monstrance containing the Blessed Sacrament. The mantled bishop received the humeral veil, covered his hands, and stepped up to the high altar. Taking the monstrance in his hands, he raised it, turned to the congregration, traced a cross in the air, and blessed the congregation while an acolyte thrice rang the sanctuary bells.

The smoldering incense smoke floated high to the cathedral ceiling while the cantors chanted the hymn, *Pange lingua.* The sweet smell of incense overwhelmed Roman as he knelt. After restoring the Eucharistic host to the ciborium within the tabernacle, His Lordship offered a benediction and joined the others in kneeling in silence until Vespers.

After Vespers, Roman continued kneeling, his eyes closed in meditation. Once the church emptied and grew silent, he descended to the crypt. There in the quiet darkness he discovered the bishop prostrate on the stone floor of the subterranean chapel before the tabernacle. He knelt, joining His Lordship in prayer at Bruté's tomb in the Divine Presence.

He gazed at the crucifix as if he was at the foot of the Cross upon Golgotha. The ninety-fourth psalm moved across his lips. *Come, let*

201

us adore and bow down before God, let us weep in the presence of the Lord who made us, for He is indeed the Lord our God.

We adore Thy holy cross, O Lord: and we praise and glorify Thy holy resurrection: for behold by the wood of the Cross joy came into the whole world.

Roman spent a portion of that evening in silent adoration before the Blessed Sacrament in the glow of ruby-red vigil candles. When he ended his prayers, the bishop was still face down, prostrate in prayer, an enigma to many, including Roman.

Though Roman had marked the joyous beginnings of Easter, there was no exultation of spirit. Even after the *Exultet* had been sung, the new fire and new water had been blessed, the bells had pealed once more, and the violet strands and shrouds had given way to white and gold vestments in the light of Resurrection joy, Roman was still in the heart of Good Friday and the somber mood of Lent—his resurrection still uncertain, inextricably linked to his future. He felt his life hanging in the balance of American justice.

Chapter 17

Limbo

September 1843

Summer quickly went and seminary classes resumed in September, after the labor of the harvest season was complete. The classes provided Roman a way to get his mind off of his approaching trial. He prepared his notes from the Church Fathers' reflections.

The priest as *alter Christus* must willingly be a victim, like his Lord, immolated for the glory of God and the salvation of souls. If a man seeks to share in Christ's priesthood, then he must be prepared to share in his victimhood, placing himself upon the altar as an oblation in union with Christ the Savior.

While on earth, Christ's Divinity was veiled within his Humanity. Though the priest is a man, subject to the vicissitudes of this mortal life, within himself he conceals the splendor of the priesthood. Therefore, he must be convinced of his dignity. Saint Thomas Aquinas said *being raised to such an exalted ministry, priests cannot be satisfied with a mediocre moral goodness: eminent virtue is required of them.*

He looked up from his notes and focused his eyes upon the crucifix above his desk in the rector's office. He knew that he was to leave for Evansville on the morrow. The eve of his trial had arrived.

****

Leaving Vincennes, Vicar General Monseigneur Martin was appointed rector *pro tem* of the seminary, while Roman was escorted by a group of well armed French Americans and German immigrants, over two dozen men in all, en route to Evansville.

Upon arriving at *The Mansion House*, he met with his attorneys. James Jones explained how they were actively seeking another attorney for the defense team, and had asked for a postponement until they could obtain another competent attorney to represent his case."

"Where is Mr. Thomas?"

"That's something I need to tell you—"

"Is he well?"

"Yes, but he is involved in a Philadelphia trial that has taken longer than he expected. He is not expected to return until the middle of October." Jones cleared his throat. "However, I cautioned him against requesting a change of venue, believing that the atmosphere in Evansville had changed. The Schmolls had been separated since March. There are rumors that Mr. Schmoll had beaten Anna Maria and their baby girl. A riverboat captain claims that the missing attorney, Jay Davis, was romantically involved with Mrs. Schmoll, and half the town is talking about how she is back to her habit of frequenting taverns. She's living with her father and sister now, but the saddest thing of all is that her child died last week. The latest story I've heard from John Chandler himself is that Anna Maria is preparing to sue Martin Schmoll for divorce."

Roman didn't need to hear any sordid details of Anna Maria's sins or her failed marriage. He was, however, grieved at the news of the child's death.

"Nevertheless," Jones continued, "Mr. Thomas petitioned the Court for a change of venue hoping that it would be sent to Mt. Vernon, Indiana. There are a number of Catholics in Posey County. But I doubt it will be moved."

The following day, Roman visited Father Antony Deydier who spoke of the death of the Schmoll baby on the fifteenth of September. "Our Lady of Sorrows," explained Deydier. "Maria Caroline. The poor little thing died two days after her first birthday. I was called to the Long farm last week when the Schmoll child was deathly ill. When I arrived, I baptized her and administered Extreme Unction. Old man Long and Mrs. Schmoll could not have been more cordial. I received word the next day that the child had passed. They asked for a *Requiem* so I obliged. The child was even interred in our church cemetery."

As Deydier related the events, Roman found himself growing more and more agitated at his former pastor.

"I cannot believe you would even visit the Long home after all the damage that Mrs. Schmoll had brought upon the brow of the Church! And after all that she did to me, and all the aspersion she has brought down upon the Church, you drop everything to ride up to old man Long's and visit her?"

"The child is innocent, Father Roman."

"I understand," his head hurt as his breathing became deeper, "but—"

"Are you sure?"

"What have they ever done for you?"

"That is immaterial. Father Roman, I know that you have suffered much at the word of the woman, but she is still a member of the fold—no matter what she may have done."

Roman had no words at the rebuke, only more resentment. And it built. His breathing became labored, his stomach tightened, and he felt his teeth grind and a sharp pain radiate through his right ear. He crossed his arms across his chest.

"Regardless," Deydier repeated. "Otherwise one wallows in hatred. And I know that hatred only destroys charity, especially in the heart of the one who has been wronged."

Roman was silent.

"You only hurt yourself by remaining angry, Father Roman."

"I'm not angry, so quit insinuating that I am." Even before the words had completely escaped his lips, he knew he wasn't being honest—either with Deydier or with himself. Roman relaxed his jaw and repositioned his arms.

"Mercy, Father. Compassion. Charity. Forgiveness. Those virtues are at the heart of the gospel. You know this just as well as I do."

"I know, I know."

"But do you believe?"

Roman stared at Deydier, balancing his biretta on his fingertips.

"In your heart, Father Roman?"

Roman lowered his eyes to his breviary that was sitting on the table.

Deydier turned, looking at the book and regaining eye contact. "All the knowledge in the world, all the wisdom—even the faith to move a mountain—is not equal to the power of charity. Saint Paul said that without charity—"

"You weren't the one nearly killed by a drunken posse." In his mind, Roman knew the passage well, though it rang hollow in his heart.

There followed an uncomfortable silence before Deydier continued. "You must forgive, Father. Saint John Chrysostom said, for those who claim they honor Christ's body while neglecting their neighbor, a hell awaits them with an inextinguishable fire and torment

205

in the company of the demons. One must not ignore his afflicted brother—or sister—for he is the most precious temple of all. *Whatsoever you do for the least of My people, that you do unto Me...*

"Saint Thomas Aquinas reminds us that a good priest is one with Christ in charity. The duty of a good priest is charity, just as the good shepherd gives his life for his sheep. Aquinas even went further when he taught that the priest must be willing to endure the loss of his bodily life for the salvation of the flock—or even one straying sheep—since the spiritual good of the flock is more important than his bodily life, especially when danger threatens the salvation of the flock. The evangelist reminds us, *the good shepherd lays down his life for his sheep.*

"Roman, it has been my experience that one does not understand joy until he faces sorrow or appreciates his faith until it has been tested."

How can I trust after being betrayed.

"Pray, pray, pray, especially for sinners, and be patient with others-and yourself," Deydier advised, bringing his hands together. "Saint Vincent de Paul was captured by Turkish pirates and taken to Tunis where he was sold as a slave, but he escaped by converting his cruel master. Of course, the rest of Vincent's life was dedicated to ministering to the poor, condemned convicts, and galley slaves. Had he held a grudge against his captors, perhaps he would have never escaped his life as a slave.

"Father Roman, the overwhelming majority of Protestants are decent citizens and are not our enemies. They're just as mortified by the actions of a few zealots as you and I."

"I understand." In his mind he did, but his heart was heavy with feelings of anger towards them just the same.

****

Later in the day, James Jones met with Roman to share new information regarding his trial. "Martin Schmoll is relishing in the knowledge that *your* bastard child is dead. The long walk north to Blue Grass to the Long farm had caused it to catch pneumonia; all summer long the baby struggled." Jones described how Mr. Schmoll was so insecure that he had calculated from the time that his wife had gone to confession at Christmas—about a week before their marriage—to the time to its birth. "He's convinced the child is yours.

I have it for fact that Mrs. Schmoll is planning to divorce her husband and has hired John Chandler to defend her.

"Speaking of the Prosecuting attorney, Chandler presented the court with reasons to postpone the trial, the death of the Schmolls' child being the principle one. However, the strife between the Schmolls over the paternity of the child, and the speculative rumors concerning Jay Davis' real reason for dropping Mrs. Schmoll's case could also be reasons. But there are other tales in town. Mrs. Schmoll's sister, Caroline Long is with child. As you know, she isn't married. This has given rise to another more insidious rumor that Martin Schmoll is the father of his sister-in-law's unborn child."

"Please, no more." Roman waved James off.

"The plot thickens," Jones said. "I just wanted you to be aware."

****

Once court was convened, the judge rendered his decision that evening. With Jones by his side, Roman listened intently as the judge gave the details. Due to the death of the Schmoll baby and the absence of Mr. Thomas, the trial was to be postponed until March, 1844, and venued to Gibson County Court, in Princeton, Indiana. "Mrs. Schmoll is ill with grief, and understandably so," the judge said. "Therefore the defendant must be placed in custody before such time. The Vanderburgh County Sheriff will escort him to the Gibson County Courthouse in Princeton and the defendant is ordered to be incarcerated there until the time of the March trial. His bail will be five thousand dollars."

Immediately, Roman's headache returned and with it severe stomach pain. He was now on his way, under arrest and in chains, to a Protestant town where he would remain in jail for at least six months.

Once in the Princeton jail, Roman sent word to Monseigneur Martin to send money for his bail. Three days later he received word from Hailandière that the diocesan treasury was bankrupt. Roman knew that the funds had all been spent on His Lordship's building projects. In the jail cell Roman felt abandoned by God, and utterly rejected. He flipped through the psalms, praying out of his distress.

Have mercy on me, O Lord, I have no strength. How long shall my enemy prevail? How can I restore what I have never taken?

By week's end, Roman's sixth day in jail, Elisha Durbin and James Jones came to his cell with the good news that they had secured his bail. The former lieutenant governor of Indiana, a resident of Gibson County, had posted bail. Though the man was a prominent Protestant Whig attorney, he held an objective view of Roman's case and said justice demanded that Roman have his freedom until the March trial." Again, Roman was surprised that another Protestant had shown mercy on his behalf.

Upon his release, he returned to Vincennes where he continued to serve as rector of the seminary, teaching, and ministering to the German-speaking congregation, but as for his effectiveness he wouldn't hazard a guess. By November, his migraines were increasing in intensity and the mental stress seemed to be making him more ill everyday. Besides his migraines, he now had a persistent cough.

****

After a few weeks of resuming his duties as rector, he evidently had caused some concern among his fellow priest-professors. Bishop Hailandière summoned Roman to the chancery.

"I don't think I can do it any more," he said to His Lordship, "teach, that is."

"You need to eat more," Hailandière huffed. "You are skin and bones. You have to keep up your strength—and quit thinking about that damned woman. And Father Roman...I know this is an odd question, but are you practicing any other means of mortification?"

"Whatever do you mean, your Excellency?"

"Are you, by chance, wearing the *cilice*?"

"*Cilicium*? Why do you ask?" He wondered if someone had told him about his hairshirt.

"Answer *my* question first. Are you wearing a *cilicium*?"

"Yes, my Lord. I am in the habit of doing penance by wearing one."

"Please tell me you do not employ the *flagellum* as well."

"That I do not, my Lord."

"Then I ask that you remove the *cilicium*."

"But it is my penance."

"Then consider its removal a penance." He leaned down and his cat jumped into his arms. "Tell me, where did you get this *cilice*?"

"I've had it since my days in Strasbourg. My pastor in Ungersheim gave it to me when I went away to study for the priesthood."

"I see. Well, from now on consider that being a missionary is penance enough. I recall one of the saints—though I can't recall his name—who claimed that his neighbor was his *cilicium*."

"I recall the saying—"

"A little Catholic humor, Father." He let Simon jump down from his arms.

"Yes, my Lord." Roman removed his handkerchief and wiped his nose.

Hailandière told Roman to join him in the kitchen. After sending Sisters Jeanne and Angelique away, Hailandière began to draw a bath, pouring from kettles of hot water that hung over the large fireplace. Roman wondered if his Lordship's mind had completely come unhinged. *Does he want me to bathe him?*

"Father Roman, do you know what you need?"

"No, my Lord."

"You need a nice warm bath. You know Thomas Aquinas was keenly aware of what pain and sorrow can wreak upon a man's body and soul. He prescribes a refreshing warm bath for men in such a state of mind as you are. Don't think I have not found myself soaking in here, basking in the warmth after a difficult day—or week in my situation."

The bishop left Roman to undress and immerse himself in the round, coopered vat. Roman felt very sleepy as he sat with his back against the side of the tub resting his head. His Lordship returned. "Sleepy, eh? That's a good sign. Saint Thomas said sleep is the other remedy for melancholia. Our angelic doctor had some very human antidotes for poisoned souls."

Roman looked over to the chair where he had placed his cassock and undergarments. Simon had pounced on the *cilicium* and was rolling around on the floor fighting with it. Roman looked again and saw the cat defecating upon it. The bishop cried out, "Simon, go outside and do that!" Simon dashed away at the angry voice of his master.

Hailandière snatched up the penitential garb. "Well, you won't be wearing this anymore. I don't think anyone will be." He threw it into the fire and turned back to Roman. "You may use the guestroom for a nap once you're finished with your bath. Join me for dinner this evening after the Vesper hour. You may also spend the night if you'd like—I don't think you ought to return to the seminary tonight."

"Why?"

"You need your rest."

"I haven't felt well for some time now."

"You wish to be removed as rector?"

"I have had the thought."

"You are an able rector."

"I miss riding the circuit—"

"I never said you could not ride."

"No, I mean on the missions. I don't know, Bishop. In the past few months I have found myself questioning everything—even my being a priest."

"Nonsense."

"I'm not so sure." Roman squeezed his eyes shut and held back the emotion. He covered his face with his right hand, pressed his fingers over his eyes, and moved his fingers and thumb together until they pinched the bridge of his nose.

"What do you need, my son?" Hailandière was never more the kindly pastor, his voice nearly breaking, "A retreat or some time away in a monastery or religious community?"

"I can't leave America."

"There are orders here in the states. The Jesuits in St. Louis, the Capuchins in Natchitoches, the Sulpicians in Baltimore, and our own Holy Cross Fathers at *Notre Dame du Lac*. Perhaps I should send you to St. Thomas Seminary in Bardstown—"

"Your Excellency—please—no more teaching posts," he interrupted the bishop, nearly forgetting to whom he was speaking.

"*I* will decide to which posts you will be assigned." Hailandière bristled and rose from his chair beside the tub. "As for the present you will remain the rector of my seminary."

Meanwhile Simon the cat sprawled across the floor with one of his hind legs stretched out and up behind his head as he busily licked his front paws and rubbed them over his face.

Roman looked into the hearth at all that was left of his hairshirt. It was nothing but ash.

****

The following week, Roman heard a knock at his door while teaching his sacraments class. It was His Lordship. He entered the room and all the students stood at attention. "Father Roman, I need to see you in the hall." Roman knelt and performed the customary ritual and departed with the bishop into the hallway. Hailandière closed the door. "Father Roman, as of this morning, I am relieving you of your duties as rector. I have appointed someone else as rector. As for you—I am sending you away. By the beginning of Advent you will be out in missionary territory. I believe you need time away."

"Where, my Lord?"

"I have assigned you to the missions of Jennings County, Indiana. You will live in the log house at the chapel in Scipio. It will do you well to get out in the open air."

"But Scipio's in the middle of the Indiana forest. It's a good two to three days ride from here and two days from Louisville—"

"I know how secluded it is—I am being mindful of your safety. There you will be safe from the idiotic Americans who want to kill you. Just be careful and watch for the bear and panthers. I will permit you to carry a rifle if you wish. Just think of the freedom you will have astride your horse."

"I will need a horse."

"I have secured one for you—actually a Catholic doctor from Evansville sent the horse to you."

"Doctor MacDonald?"

"Yes, that was his name. He says the horse was yours before you were forced to flee Evansville. Seems a horse thief was apprehended and they found your horse in his possession."

"He found Shadow?"

"Yes, a black beauty I might say. So Shadow shall be your companion." He paused, placing his right hand on Roman's left shoulder, looking into his eyes. "Father Roman, I tell you the fight for the emancipation of Roman Catholics in America might be playing out right now, here in our diocese. We do not know what will become of our people. There is legislation in Washington that would require immigrants to live here twenty-one years before they could be granted citizenship. There are others, more vocal extremists, who wish to send all Catholic immigrants back to Europe and Ireland. It appears that you were the *Roman Catholic* scapegoat that the Nativists needed in order to make their case through the American press."

211

****

Roman met with Benjamin Thomas who just recently returned from his Philadelphia trial. Thomas told him that the Schmolls had in fact separated and with the scandal of the birth of Caroline Long's illegitimate child, the people in Evansville were now rethinking whether the charges against Roman were true. But it was too late— the trial had already been venued to Gibson County. It didn't take long before people began to recall that Miss Caroline Long had stayed with Martin during February and early March and the baby had been born in September.

"Now if we can only find another able-minded attorney," Thomas mused. "Maybe we could get a prominent Whig to cross party lines and defend you."

"Could you somehow convince Former President Van Buren to get involved?" Roman suggested. "He's a New York attorney, and he was on hand when we laid the cornerstone to Assumption Church."

"That'd be a long shot," Thomas sighed, "but I do have a couple of attorneys in mind. Abraham Lincoln for one. *Honest Abe*, they call him. He was born in Kentucky but when he was a boy his folks moved to Indiana."

"Where is he now?"

"Springfield, Illinois. He gets through these parts now and then."

"Do you think he could help?"

"I'm not for sure. He's a very knowledgeable chap, but he's a bit eccentric. Some folks think he's an idiot."

"Do you have anyone else in mind?"

"An attorney from Henderson, Kentucky, by the name of Archibald Dixon. He's running for the office of lieutenant governor for Kentucky."

"Is he a Catholic?"

"No."

"Is he a Democrat?"

"No."

"What is he?"

"He's a Whig, a Protestant, a Freemason, and he owns a hundred slaves."

"What on earth would I want with a man like that?"

"He's one of the best trial lawyers this side of the Alleghenies."

"This Kentucky lawyer—what's his name again?"

"Archibald Dixon."

"Does he believe I'm innocent?"

"He is trained—as are all attorneys—to show to a jury that if there is any reasonable doubt, the defendant must be acquitted."

Thomas hadn't answered the question, but Roman understood.

****

By mid-November, a week before Roman was to leave for Scipio, Thomas had asked Van Buren but the former president declined to take the case due to his embroilment in the abolitionist movement and his subsequent ouster from the Democratic party over his recent change of position on the issue of slavery. "The Democratic leadership had shunned him and rejected his bid for the Presidency."

The thought that Van Buren might become one of his defense attorneys had cheered Roman's heart. Thomas' friend, Abraham Lincoln, was also unable to defend Roman due to his own legal commitments in Springfield during the March term. There was still hope that the Kentuckian, Dixon, might take up the offer, so Thomas arranged for him to meet with Roman.

"One can only imagine the grief I felt once I learned that former President Van Buren wouldn't be defending me," Roman said to Benjamin Thomas as he traveled by carriage to Evansville. He was to meet with Father Elisha J. Durbin and the eighty year old prelate, Bishop Benedict Joseph Flagét of Louisville at the Linck's *Mansion House* in Evansville. Roman was careful to appear incognito as they reentered the city where *all hell had broken loose in the first place*, as Thomas was wont to say.

Roman entered the Linck's hotel while Thomas led him to one of the parlors where Deydier, Durbin, and Flagét were waiting with the renowned Kentucky attorney and Whig politician, Archibald Dixon. When Roman and his companion entered the room, a tall, white-haired man stepped forward. "Benjamin Thomas, I presume?"

"I am, Sir," Thomas extended his right hand. "You must be Archibald Dixon."

"The one and only." The two lawyers shook hands.

After some pleasantries, Dixon took charge of the meeting. "Let's talk turkey, gentlemen." Dixon spoke in his Southern drawl. "I'm a busy man, no time to waste. I realize that the other attorneys for the

213

defendant are Democrats and the governor of Indiana is a Democrat. That won't get you very far with me. I'm a Whig—a Cotton Whig at that."

"I'm myself a native, man," Durbin cleared his throat, sitting tall in his chair. "My family came over well before the Revolutionary war."

"I'll bet your collar that your family wasn't always Catholic."

"Must you Americans hazard bets all the time?" Flaget pondered aloud.

"Our family has always been Catholic," Durbin replied. "That's why our family came to America—to enjoy religious liberty. Due to anti-Catholic bigotry they settled in Kentucky. I hope my ancestors weren't wrong in reading the Constitution literally."

"Very well. I'm not a very religious man. I'm a Freemason and I understand that every pope back to Saint Peter has condemned us."

"Not exactly. Only in recent years has Freemasonry come under the scrutiny of our Holy Office." Flagét sighed. "Mozart was a Catholic and he was a Mason."

"Well, whatever, I'm a busy man. It's an election year you know. I'm on the Kentucky ballot for lieutenant governor, but I know y'all didn't come here to talk politics."

"We want you to represent Father Roman Weinzoepfel at his trial." Thomas regained control of the conversation and pointed to Roman at his left.

"This is Roman? Roman Weinzoepfel? The ravisher himself?"

"The *alleged* ravisher, Sir." Durbin said.

"I expected a bigger man. I apologize. It's just, that, well, who hasn't been following his story? It's the biggest news since *Maria Monk* or when those maverick Mormons shot the Governor of Missouri."

"Yes, Mrs. Schmoll's charges have caused quite a furor. Even the presidential candidates and the pope in Rome are following the story." Thomas asserted.

"On top of being a Cotton Whig, I own me about a hundred slaves. Not exactly an ally to Catholics, or at least the Catholic abolitionists. Why do you want *my* legal representation?"

"We believe it will give Father Roman's defense much more credibility in front of a Protestant jury," Thomas explained, "and send a message through the press that Catholics and their priests are not foreign invaders, a threat to the American Republic."

"Well, I won't go it alone, that's for sure. Who else is defending him?"

"James G. and Wilbur Jones of Evansville." Thomas answered.

"Impressive. I don't see eye to eye with them on the slavery question, but I respect them nonetheless. They're both men of principle. If you have them, what do you need me for?"

"Because we're up against the likes of John Chandler and Judge Lockhart."

"John Chandler and 'Lockhorns' Lockhart are prosecuting this case?"

"Yes. Is something wrong?"

"No, it's just that, well, Chandler and his brother, Will, and I— well let's just say there's bad blood between us Dixons and Chandlers. That's all I'll say. I won't say what about."

"Does this change things?"

"No, not at all. On the contrary, I'll do it." He paused, only to stand up and exclaim, "I'll do it, gladly, and with no expense to you. I owe the bishop here a good turn, but I owe the Chandlers something else. It's been a long time since I squared off with those boys! It'll be my pleasure, Father Weinzoepfel." Dixon extended his hand and with a firm grip shook his hand.

"No personal vendettas, Sir." Roman cautioned.

"How can it not be personal? You want to clear your name, don't you? Let me do my job."

Thomas explained to Dixon the tactic that he and the Jones brothers planned to use in the defense. The men ventured off into the language that only lawyers speak. Roman was reminded of a passage from one of the psalms. *Put no trust in princes, in mortal men in whom there is no help.* He excused himself and joined Bishop Flagét and Fathers Deydier and Durbin in the opposite parlor where they were to pray Vespers before taking dinner with the Lincks.

Elisha Durbin handed Roman a breviary. It was Roman's from nearly two years before. "You thought I'd lost it, didn't you?" Durbin smiled.

****

215

The next morning, Francis Linck, Jr, drove Roman as far north as Saint Wendel where he spent the night. The next day he traveled by stage on to Vincennes.

Glad to see Shadow, he saddled up and left Vincennes, arriving at his new mission at Scipio at the end of November. Celebrating Advent and Christmas there, he also visited the neighboring missions in Jefferson, Franklin, Ripley, and Dearborn Counties. The winter was excruciatingly cold and the January and February snowfalls piled high, in some places more than six feet. Even the railway train from Madison to Scipio stopped its operation through January and into February. Nevertheless, as February thawed, he served the Catholic parishes in and around Jennings County and Madison, Indiana.

Overall, Roman was alone in the southern Indiana forest, except for a hunting pioneer he had met. This bearded, thick haired man, with unshaven neck, under a felt hat with tall crown and broad brim, grey oversized handkerchief bandana, a bear hide blanket coat, homemade trousers, and deer skin moccasins, dwelt in a log hut. Astride his unshorn horse, he carried his four foot long barreled rifle slung over his shoulder, his leather bullet pouch and a bull's horn powder flask hanging at his side. Dangling from his rope belt was a sheath with a large knife and also a tomahawk. He preferred to dwell in the thick of the woods, living off nature's produce, surviving on the fruit gleaned by his rifle and the catch of his traps. Roman came to call him *Hoosier Hunter* for he refused to till the soil, fell trees, or domesticate the beasts of the field. He told Roman on numerous occasions that the wood was his. "Ain't nobody going to chop down the Hoosier forest."

Despite Roman's solitude, it was more and more difficult to pray. There were times he would look at his unopened breviary on his night stand, the violet, red, green, white, and black ribbons untouched from the previous days. There had even been a few days where he had avoided praying the office altogether except for the psalms he had memorized. What's the use? He hadn't prayed it yesterday or the day before, so what was one more day?

Trying to pray the beads, his mind wandered to the profane and mundane—chopping wood, shoeing Shadow, and securing food. The sacred reentered from time to time as he visited the sick and said mass.

216

Pray the mass, Father. Don't simply *say* mass. Both Abbé Martin and his Jesuit professors had said it again and again. The Holy Sacrifice of the Mass is the life of the Church. With such knowledge, how could he ever simply *say* mass?

The low moan of the railway locomotive's steam whistle was like a funeral lament from a *Requiem* in the bleakness of winter. The best the sun could do was illumine the grey clouds from behind a pale horizon and the dismal season matched his feelings as he anxiously dreaded his impending court date, just wanting the whole ordeal to be over and done with. If the first hearing had been purgatorial, he knew the trial would be infernal. Having lots of time alone to think and pray, he actually did little of both so anxious was he for his March trial.

He composed a letter to his brother, Michael, wherein he revealed his heart. *I cannot begin to describe the sorrow and suffering that I have experienced since the first moment of the accusations made against me. I had hoped peace of mind, serenity of heart, and tranquility of soul would accompany me in my mission to the middle of the Indiana forest among the rivers and creeks, hills and glades. There are few Catholics in these parts of the state. The charges against me and the impending trial weighs upon my heart to the point where I can think of little else. I confess this to you to my shame, and I am so melancholy that there have been days where I have had a mind of abandoning everything if I cannot attain some sense of sanity in the midst of all this chaos. Pray God it all ends soon.*

The Christmas season came and went without so much as a smile, and I am exhausted with grief. Yet I pray everyday that none of my feelings of disgust or anger I bear toward my accuser and her husband who have ensnared me in their vicious trap is directed to the good God who has vouchsafed to protect me thus far. I believe God has chastised me harshly, yes, nevertheless, I should hope and pray that these terrible wounds, however deep and long they be, are to be for me profitable unto my salvation. Pray that I have the strength to endure this ordeal to the end. We were always taught to believe that God allows the burden of His Son's Cross to be placed upon our shoulders for some greater purpose.

The American presses are perpetrating this cruel travesty of justice that has been foisted upon me for they thrive on personal

217

tragedy. Now I understand that there are French, German, Italian, and English journalists here reporting upon my predicament.

Please know that my suffering is as nothing when compared to yours. There are days when I awaken thinking that all that I have been through was nothing more than one terrible nightmare, but of course it is reality. Were I a man of no faith, I probably would have already taken my own life, for the torment I have suffered seems too much for one man to bear. There have been several sleepless nights when I have even prayed for death.

He looked up from the page and prayed aloud. *Lord, I believe; help my unbelief.*

Finishing his letter, he asked for prayers and assured Michael that one day they would see each other again face to face. *Give my love to all.* He leaned back in his chair with a hollowed out feeling as he thought of his family.

February 1844

Winter melted into spring and by Ash Wednesday in mid February he began to pack his books and few belongings, bade his adieus to the parishioners of Scipio, and mounted Shadow returning to Vincennes so as to be ready for his trial in Princeton, Indiana. Melting snow filled streams and rivers, as muddy valleys and miry forest paths made his trip three long, cold, wet days as he journeyed to what he feared would be his most fateful trial.

While on his way, he came upon a group of ten well-armed men, shooting their rifles and pistols. He feared they had been sent by some of the Schmoll supporters to kill him. His heart raced as he reined in Shadow, who had already startled, and headed the opposite direction achieving full gallop ahead of gunfire from all directions. Turning around at the sounds of more shots, he realized the men were drunk and were shooting at a herd of deer.

Ever since his arrival in the United States he was amazed at the way the pioneers cared for and nurtured their guns. Hunting had become sport long after it had ceased to be a necessary way of life. He thought there was something in these pioneers' blood that drove them to the woods to shoot game.

From Vincennes, accompanied by armed guards, he traveled to the Princeton Courthouse. A dozen Irishmen on horseback had volunteered to ride ahead of and behind the stagecoach in which he was riding. He was humiliated that he had to ride encumbered in a cramped coach rather than atop a horse. Such were the conditions to ensure his safety.

The Reverends Deydier, Durbin, Shawe, and Monseigneur Augustin Martin were on hand for his trial, but still no sign of the bishop. Roman had overheard Shawe and the Vicar General Monseigneur Martin discussing his Lordship the night before they all left for Princeton.

"I fear this time that His Lordship's mind has truly become unhinged," Shawe had said.

"*Oui*. He's rarely in Vincennes for more than a few days at a time. He's been spending an inordinate amount of time at St. Mary-of-the-Woods, especially since Mother Theodore returned to France. He considers himself the superior of the congregation of the Sisters of Providence." Monseigneur Martin sighed, dropping his face into his hands.

****

Roman reported to the sheriff's office where he was escorted to his cell to await the trial. Sheriff Kirkman told him how surprised he was to see him return. "There were so many stories circulating about you. Some said you escaped to Europe, others said you'd gone mad and raped again. There was a stir a month ago when we heard that you had renounced the priesthood, admitted your guilt and committed suicide by throwing yourself in front of the Madison train. Then word on the street just last week was that you were stabbed and killed in Cincinnati."

After the sheriff departed his cell, Roman bent his knees and prayed.

Chapter 18

The Trial

5 March 1844

Roman tried to keep his mind from Mrs. Schmoll's accusations even though the long awaited trial was finally upon him. As time pressed on, he remembered less and less of the events that led up to the charges. Nevertheless, the cross of Christ loomed as his own as he prepared for the next morning.

The attorney, Jay Davis, was completely absent, not only from the court case at hand and the ensuing trial, but he was absent from Evansville itself. Many people thought that he must have certainly unearthed the true side to Anna Maria Schmoll, causing him to be so embarrassed he fled town to avoid public humiliation. In the spring of 1843 Mrs. Schmoll had accompanied Davis to Cincinnati to obtain affidavits to establish her good reputation. There was also a rumor that Davis had fled Evansville since he and Mrs. Schmoll had become lovers, allegedly discovered together in a compromising situation aboard the riverboat en route to Cincinnati.

One of the constables repeated a story that was circulating the town that a drunken Martin Schmoll had disturbed the peace, assaulted Anna Maria, and evicted her and the baby out of his house a year before. Some claimed it was in response to his discovery that Anna and Davis were involved. Anna Maria had not been seen for weeks, even months. The Catholics said that she was staying with her father at the Blue Grass settlement where she and the baby were said to be very ill. Mr. Schmoll for his part said nothing except now and again when he would drink to excess at *Wood's Tavern* and boast how *that priest* was going to pay for his crime.

Roman hated rumors.

The day before the trial, he hadn't slept at all. Though his brother priests had accompanied him, he thought that his Lordship should also be there. As it was, His Lordship had no intention of showing.

It was a crispy, clear, dark blue Tuesday morning in March, when Roman entered the courtroom with Benjamin Thomas and the Jones brothers, James and Wilbur, and the Kentuckian, Archibald Dixon.

Judge Embree of Vanderburgh County entered and called the room to order. He directed Sheriff Kirkman of Vanderburgh County to bring in the potential members of the jury. The officer opened the door and about twenty men accompanied him down the aisle of the courtroom. As the prospective jurors filed by one by one, answering questions put to them by both legal counsels pertaining to the case, Roman felt like a specimen under a microscope. An hour and a half passed before jury selection was complete. After the final juror was selected, the sheriff called their names and swore them in. The judge then explained to them their legal responsibilities.

All the talk of a trial for so long had made it seem unreal and so far away, yet with the first clap of the judge's gavel came a moment of spectacular clarity, and Roman realized that the moment he had so anxiously—and his enemies had so eagerly—awaited, had finally arrived. And it was exceedingly real.

After the jury was sworn in and seated, Judge Embree asked the defense and prosecution, "Before opening arguments, are there any preliminary motions?"

"The defense requests for separation of witnesses during the trial." James Jones stood.

"Does the State object?"

"No. We concur," replied James Lockhart, prosecutor for the state.

"So ordered." Judge Embree nodded. "Any further requests?"

The lawyers looked at each other but no one spoke.

"Very well, Sheriff Kirkman is charged with maintaining order. Officer John Curl will be the bailiff. The prosecution will be granted equal time with the defense." The judge looked to the jurors. "The jury will remember that the burden of proof rests upon the prosecution. And the jury must remember that the silence of the defendant cannot be interpreted or inferred as an indication of guilt. The defendant is presumed innocent until proven guilty, and any conviction must be based on your belief that the accused is guilty beyond a reasonable doubt, and your verdict must be unanimous."

The judge looked at the prosecution's counsel. "The prosecuting attorney for the state will please read the indictment."

Roman breathed deeply, folded his arms close to his chest, and put his head down as the all too familiar accusation was about to be read as a criminal charge against him. *If only I had not come to America. If only I had listened to Franz. If only I had not pushed her and Martin on the marriage agreement. If only this, if only that...* Thoughts raced through his head as his heartbeat throbbed in the blood vessels in his neck and he focused upon his every breath.

The lead Prosecutor, James Lockhart, then stepped forward to read to the jury the indictment. "The grand jurors duly sworn to make inquiry for the State of Indiana in this county of Vanderburgh, upon their oath allege that the defendant, the Reverend Mr. Roman Weinzoepfel, of Evansville, on the fourth day of May, in the year of our Lord, eighteen hundred and forty-two, with force and arms, upon Anna Maria Schmoll, the wife of Martin Schmoll, also of Vanderburgh County, did then and there violently and feloniously make an assault at and against the person of Anna Maria Schmoll, and then and there did feloniously rape and carnally know the said Anna Maria Schmoll, by force and against her will, contrary to the form of the statute in such case made and provided, and against the peace and dignity of the State of Indiana.

"And the jurors aforesaid, upon their oath aforesaid, do further present, that Roman Weinzoepfel, of the County of Vanderburgh County, in the State of Indiana, on the fourth day of May, in the year of our Lord one thousand eight hundred and forty-two, with force and arms, and in the county aforesaid, and upon the body of Anna Maria Schmoll, then and there did make an assault on her person, the said Anna Maria Schmoll, then and there did, in a rude, insolent, and angry manner, unlawfully touch, strike, beat, wound, and ill-treat, with intent, her, the said Anna Maria Schmoll, then and there feloniously to rape and carnally know, by force and against her will, contrary to the form of the statute in such case made and provided, and against the peace and dignity of the State of Indiana.

"And the jurors aforesaid, upon their oath aforesaid, do further present, that Roman Weinzoepfel, of the County of Vanderburgh County, in the State of Indiana, on the fourth day of May, in the year of our Lord one thousand eight hundred and forty-two, with force and arms, and in the county aforesaid, in and upon the body of Anna Maria Schmoll, then and there did make an assault, with intent her, the said Anna Maria Schmoll, then and there feloniously to rape and carnally know, by force and against her will, contrary to the form of the statute in such case made and provided, and against the peace and dignity of the State of Indiana."

Roman prayed that this would be the last time he would ever have to hear that indictment read aloud. He looked around at the gathered assembly. They seemed calmer than the agitated and drunken mob of two years before. He recalled his escape from Evansville, his being dressed as woman and running the route of runaway slaves. He bounced his biretta on his hands in his lap.

Lockhart began the opening arguments explaining how the prosecution would prove that Mr. Roman Weinzoepfel did commit all allegations contained in the indictment. Every time Lockhart referred to Roman as *Mr.* Weinzoepfel rather than Reverend or Father, it was as if a sword was piercing him in the heart. Lockhart swung his arms and rambled on and on about why *Mister* Weinzoepfel, *the priest,* was guilty beyond reasonable doubt. Roman looked up only when the tirade was finally at an end.

"The jury is with the defense for its opening statements," the judge explained.

James Jones stepped forward. "Gentlemen, my opening statement will be brief and to the point. To all the aforementioned charges, our client pleads not guilty. In the ensuing trial and testimony of witnesses, you likewise will reach this inescapable conclusion. The evidence will demonstrate that all the charges are false."

At that time the judge called counsel for the state and defendant to the bench. Both counsels had secured interpreters on behalf of the German speaking witnesses. Judge Embree announced the names of the two interpreters and the attorneys made their way back to their places.

"Very well. The prosecution may begin with testimony from its witnesses," the judge continued. "Mr. Chandler, you may call your first witness."

"The prosecution calls Mrs. Anna Maria Schmoll."

"If the bailiff, would please..." The bailiff stepped out into the hallway outside the courtroom calling her name and shortly returning with her. She took the stand, raised her right hand, placed her left upon the Bible, and swore before God and Man to speak the truth, the whole truth, and nothing but the truth. As she sat down, Roman silently prayed that she would abide by her oath.

"Mrs. Schmoll, do you understand the oath you just took."

"*Ja. Wirklich.*"

"State to the jury, if you please, the events and circumstances referred to in the indictment."

"On the day before Ascension, 1842, I ast mein husband, Herr Schmoll, to go to Herr Heinrich's home. He and Frau Heinrich are Katolisch and the priest sometimes ate vith them. I ast mein husband to ast them ven confessions were to be held."

Dixon interrupted the prosecutor. "May it please the Court, it seems to me that the witness can answer questions without the aid of the interpreter.

"Can you reply in English?" Judge Embree asked.

"*Ja*, a leetle."

"Then could you try in English?"

"I vill try." From then on she used the interpreter on and off.

She proceeded to repeat her version of events. She had entered the confessional and confessed her sins, claiming that Roman had asked her a barrage of risqué questions concerning her and her husband's conjugal relations. Then, after he was finished, he gave her a penance, but as she knelt in the darkened confessional reading her prayer book, she said he bounded out of the confessional and pulled Anna Maria out of the compartment. Throwing her upon the floor, he allegedly committed the rape. That's when she said she fainted. The prosecutor had her repeat her testimony that she did not faint away unconscious until after the consummation of the act had occurred. She related the details of the rape and spoke of her being penetrated before losing consciousness. Roman was mortified at the testimony and direct examination, numb from all the talk. He squeezed his beads between his thumb, index, and middle fingers as she continued by describing how he had lifted her up and placed her on a bench, sprinkling her face with water.

She then described how she finally came to reveal the entire matter to her husband. Roman remembered all too well the morning that Martin Schmoll nearly broke through the church door, announcing the charge for the first time.

The defense counsel, James Jones, began cross-examining Anna Maria. Roman watched to see if she would ever look his way. She had yet to make eye contact with him since leveling the charges against him.

He fumbled through his breviary, struggling to place his trust in God, drifting off into prayer, yet not sure it was prayer as much as it was simply reciting empty words to a seemingly aloof God. Glancing up from the page, he questioned why God had allowed him to come to this? *Why?* His emotional prayer startled him. Bowing his head, he reached for his rosary and pulled it out of his cassock. He rubbed each bead slowly, holding them briefly before thumbing on to the next one.

Martin Schmoll was called next. Roman slowly looked up. Martin Schmoll appeared. His clean shaven face, high starched collar, blue cravat and matching top coat with brass buttons made him look like a statesman.

As Schmoll swore and took the stand, Chandler began his questioning. "Mr. Schmoll, would you describe to the jury what happened between you and your wife on the Eve of Ascension Day, 1842?"

"Gladly." The trace of a German accent was still there in his voice, yet he had taken every effort to speak English. "Like you said, it was Ascension Eve and my wife asked me to inquire with the Heinrichs as to the time of public confessions at the Catholic Church on Second Street. When I returned I told her the priest would be in the church from five until six o'clock, so she left for the church sometime during that hour."

"What time exactly?" Chandler grimaced.

"I'm not sure. I gave her much freedom, so I didn't know her every move."

"Please continue."

"She returned home near nightfall."

"Was there much daylight?"

"No. It was dark."

"Continue." Chandler nodded and motioned the witness on with his right hand.

"I asked her why she had stayed so long. She told me that she could come no sooner. She seemed to be avoiding me and tried to go into the house through the front door, but it was bolted. She came back and walked past me so I asked her to go get my supper since I was hungry. As I looked at her, I suspected that something was wrong. She was not her normal self. She looked down in the mouth and she sighed all evening and through supper. After supper we went to bed. I went to bed first and as she was dressing, she kept sighing. I

225

didn't know what to make of it. I always thought that when a Catholic goes to confession, they return home more lively, refreshed, and happy. She experienced none of that."

"Did you ask her again what was wrong?" Chandler leaned towards him in the witness box.

"Yes. I asked her what was the matter and she told me that something had happened in the church with the priest. Well, I got out of bed and demanded to know what it was. She said it was something that had never happened to her before! Something she'd never heard of happening before. I was more upset than ever and I asked her several times what had happened."

"Did she answer you?" Chandler looked over at Roman.

"Yes. She told me that the priest—"

"The defendant?" Chandler turned to Mr. Schmoll.

"Yes, *him*." Martin glared at Roman. "He demanded to know information about our sexual relations! She said that was all she would say until after she had gone to Mass that next morning. The next morning her brother and sister came to call and so the three of them went off to church together. Around eleven or twelve o'clock she came back home with her sister and brother and had dinner. Finally, after her family left, I asked her to finish telling me what the priest did to her and that was when she made known to me that he had dragged her from the confessional and raped her! He had his way with her on the church floor!" Schmoll stood and pointed angrily at Roman. "That priest violated my bride! His influence upon my wife robbed me of her and a family! Rapist!"

"Mr. Schmoll, you will control yourself!" The judge pounded his hammer on his desk.

Martin continued to recount the rest of the details to the jury, how he had waited until early Friday morning to confront Roman with the charges.

Mr. Chandler disrupted Schmoll's memory. "Did her crying keep you awake that night?"

"No. The thought of what had happened to her kept me awake. The next day when she told me the rest of the story I took my pistol, and was on my way to shoot the priest. You can't blame me for being angry. But she begged me not to do it, so I didn't. The next morning I went to see him, demanding that he hand over the marriage agreement I had signed the previous Sunday."

"Why did you sign that agreement?" Chandler curled his face and lip.

"So that the expected child might be brought up as a Catholic."

"Did you agree to that?"

"Reluctantly so. Her father and that priest pressured me until I did."

"No further questions. Defense, your witness."

Jones made his way to the stand. "What did you make of your wife being late that night?"

"I don't trust a religion that allows a man's wife to go to a priest and stay as long as she pleases only to be told that she is forbidden to speak a word of what transpired between the two."

"No. Did you suspect that she and the priest may have been ... involved, should we say?"

"At the time, not exactly, but since then, yes."

"Did you believe the child your wife was carrying might be the offspring of the defendant?"

"The thought did cross my mind a time or two."

"Did you suspect your wife was guilty of adultery even before the alleged attack?"

"Objection to the question." Lockhart rose.

At that, Dixon sauntered up to Martin. "Mr. Schmoll, are you a Catholic or a Protestant."

"I am not a Catholic."

"Did you lift your wife's dress upon her return from the church and make an examination of her, uh, her, her genitalia?"

"Yes."

"What was your purpose in doing that?"

"I object to that question!" Chandler cried out from his chair.

"Sustained."

"Very well. Mr. Schmoll, did you observe anything suspicious?"

"No."

"How did Mrs. Schmoll respond?"

"She did not approve of my doing it."

"I wouldn't suppose she would," Dixon laughed. "Did you ever think that Mrs. Schmoll may have fabricated a tale of being raped?"

"Impossible."

"Then when she returned from the confessional, did you observe anything of her clothing out of order?"

"Yes. Her bonnet was scratched, maybe slightly bent on one side."

"What about her dress?"

"It was fine. There was nothing wrong with it."

"Did your wife ever tell you how the defendant was dressed once she regained consciousness?"

"She said his pantaloons were loose and when she looked again his pants were buttoned."

"But if he was standing, as both of you have testified, then would his cassock not have been covering his pants?"

"I don't know. I'm only telling you what she told me."

"Did you ever speak to a Mrs. Mary Good about any of the alleged actions of the defendant?"

"No. And neither did my wife."

"I believe your estranged wife should answer for herself," Dixon smiled. "Recently, we have learned that you and Mrs. Schmoll have separated. When did you turn her out of your house?"

"The middle of February, 1843, two weeks before the trial was scheduled to begin last March."

"How old was your baby?"

"*Her* baby was five months old." His emphasis left little for interpretation.

"You question its paternity?" Dixon reached in his pocket for his pipe.

"Objection, your Honor!" Chandler carped

"Yes," Martin Schmoll answered anyway.

"Did you threaten to starve your child?" Dixon examined the contents of the pipe's bowl.

"Objection! The question is irrelevant to the evidence." Lockhart joined his colleague in protest.

"Don't answer that question," the judge said, leaning over his bench.

"It wasn't my child!" Martin spoke out of turn again.

"That is all, Your Honor. No more questions." Dixon returned to his seat and worked to light his pipe.

Martin Schmoll left the courtroom harrumphing.

The judge and legal counsel spoke a language all their own, which, in many ways, was far more than Roman cared to understand. While the banter continued among the lawyers, judge, and witnesses, Roman focused upon his Rosary despite his ability to only pray half of it so completely divided was his mind. By all accounts, the day should have dragged on for an eternity, but instead it slipped away into a slur of arguments, objections, and exhausting testimony as the daylight waned. The judge adjourned as the sun sank into the western clouds.

Roman went back to his cell, buried his head in the pillow, and hid under the blankets. He would've cried had he not been so angry. He didn't feel like eating and his night was filled with an anxious restlessness.

6 March 1844

The next morning Roman didn't want to crawl out of bed. He wrestled with fatigue as he worked to sit upright. Soon he found himself back at the defense table in the courtroom for the second day of his trial.

The prosecution proceeded with its presentation of evidence. Some of the witnesses were from Cincinnati and had traveled to Evansville to testify on Mrs. Schmoll's behalf.

Roman's mind wandered away as he held his head in his hands. All the testimonies began to run together into one long blur of sound.

Members of the parish who were in the church near the hour when the alleged rape took place were summoned. All of them claimed that they had eaten without the aid of candlelight, establishing that it could not have been as dark inside the church as Mrs. Schmoll claimed.

Both counsels questioned the Heinrichs more thoroughly since Roman had taken his supper with them immediately following hearing confessions at Assumption Church.

The prosecutor, Lockhart, examined Mr. Heinrich. "So, the priest took his meals with you?"

"*Javoll.*"

"Did the defendant seem out of sorts that evening?"

"He was fine, except for a headache. But that was not unusual for him since he suffers from migraines. I told him to take a little peach brandy."

"I see. Do you have anything else to add, sir?"

"*Nein. Das ist alles*. That's all."

"No more questions, Your Honor. Defense, your witness." The defense merely had Heinrich repeat his account of their dinner that night.

Roman looked at the sad face of Mr. Heinrich as the man stepped out of the witness box. Roman missed their quiet evenings together, watching the steamboats and flatboats float along the lazy river, listening to the sounds of boat and horse and carriage, cicadae droning on, crickets chirping their evening hymns, and birds singing their carols. These often neglected pleasures of life and others like them were small delights of which Roman had either been deprived or prevented from enjoying since his ordeal began.

Chapter 19

Syncope

As Roman thought of Anna Maria and her estranged husband he tried to pray for them, but all that kept coming out of his heart was the cursing psalms. Outwardly, he was holding up rather well, but inwardly he knew he lacked any consolation of spirit. He just wanted it to all be over, either to be set at liberty or found guilty as charged and consigned to the dungeon. But whichever it would be, the judgment couldn't come soon enough.

The next witness the prosecution called was a doctor. He elaborated on the medical condition of syncope. "Some people call it fainting, but syncope may be caused by anything which excites the nerves or blood flow. A sudden rising up from a seated or kneeling position may cause it. An emotional response can cause it as can grief or fear. Pregnancy could have been another contributing factor. Even the milk sickness has been known to bring it on. Syncope begins with the loss of muscle control, and can end with eventual loss of consciousness, but it does not always end in unconsciousness. Syncope is a condition that some persons are more prone to experience than others, and women more likely than men."

Roman's attorneys yielded nothing in their cross examination.

The prosecution called forth another doctor. He was more distinguished than the first and contradicted him by claiming that there are three levels to syncope, not two. He was a graduate of Yale Medical School. "The first stage is vertigo, mere dizziness. The second is fainting due to an interruption in the heart and arteries. The senses also vitiate at these first two levels. The third stage is swooning, whereby all sensation is completely extinguished and the patient is oblivious to all in this state. The patient might be out for some time, maybe an hour or two. It used to be that swooning and fainting were interchangeable terms. Not so, today."

Roman remembered her saying that she felt lightheaded as she left the confessional, but as for a two-hour debate over an alleged fainting spell he could not care less.

Jones began the cross-examination for the defense. "Might a violent shock cause syncope?"

"Yes."

"Say, for instance, a man attacking a woman with the intent to ravish her?"

"Definitely, yes," the doctor replied.

"Yet you have testified that a person who syncopates, for the lack of a better word, might not fully recover his or her strength for some time. In your humble opinion, is it possible that Mrs. Schmoll was able to recover as quickly as she states that she did?"

"I'm not an expert, but in many cases the patient may take upwards of an hour or two, perhaps three, to fully recover his strength."

"So, do you think that it possible that Mrs. Schmoll might have been unconscious longer than she realizes it?" Jones squinted at the Doctor.

"It is quite possible."

"So, instead of being unconscious only for a few minutes, two hours or so might have elapsed?"

"It is conceivable. Yes."

"But the witness testifies that when she went to the church it was near sunset and when she returned home it was just the beginning of nightfall. This would seem to be no more than half an hour at the most." Jones asked.

"I don't know."

"For the sake of argument, is it not possible?"

"Yes, but there are always exceptions to the rule," the doctor argued loudly.

"Thank you, Doctor. Now allow me to return to the actual statement of Mrs. Schmoll. She has told us that she went unconscious immediately after being debauched. Now, could she be completely powerless, and yet retain the cognitive powers?"

"Yes, there may be such a thing as a complete loss of the strength for motion, but the power of thinking may be intact."

"In other words the person may know what is going on but not have the power to defend himself, let us say, from an attacker?" Jones mused.

"Yes. One may be conscious yet have no muscular power."

"Very well, then. If this is, in fact, what happened to the state's witness, Mrs. Schmoll, do you think it would be possible for a woman, who has lost her ability to move or reason, to sit on a bench with no support?"

"Yes."

"Really?" Dixon laughed and came to his feet to enter the examination while Jones backed away and moved toward the defense table.

"Rigor mortis has caused corpses to sit up for an undertaker," the doctor continued. "Who among us hasn't heard tales of people being buried alive? They were thought to be dead, but they were only experiencing syncope."

"But are you for certain?" Dixon chewed the end of his pipe.

"The condition is referred to as catalepsy."

"Mr. Jones asked if it were possible, but do you think it probable that Mrs. Schmoll could have sat up on her own—under the given circumstances?"

"No, it would be very improbable."

"Thank you." Dixon sat down and worked to empty the bowl of his pipe.

Mr. Jones resumed his position and questioned the witness. "Let me pose another scenario. Let us say that someone told you that they 'fell down dead,' would he—could he—claim to have consciousness?"

"Not according to the definition of 'dead.'"

"Explain what you mean?"

"Well, if someone is dead, that means they's 'dead.'"

"So being 'dead' means that one has lost all consciousness?"

"Yes. That seems rather elementary."

"You would think, wouldn't you? But what if someone told you that he was dead but really alive?" Jones walked away and turned towards the jury.

"Is there some humor in this?" the witness asked.

"None at all," Jones spun around and faced the doctor. "Please answer the question."

"Well I would think that he was unhinged in the mind."

"That's interesting. But there is a witness who claims that Mrs. Schmoll told her that as soon as the defendant took hold of her arm she fell down dead. Are you prepared to diagnose the State's lead witness to be of unhinged mind?"

"No."

"Then do you think her statement to be irrational."

"Conceivably so."

"Then are you insinuating or implying that Mrs. Schmoll is irrational?"

"Not in the least, perchance unhinged, but not irrational."

"Thank you for your perfectly ambiguous clarification," Jones smiled. "Moving on to another point, would a woman in the state of syncope be easily violated?"

"It depends upon the patient. A natural instinct would be to avoid such a thing."

"In the case of Mrs. Schmoll, she was pregnant at the time of the alleged attack. What do you know of pregnancy?"

"Pregnant women are predisposed to fainting."

"Is it true that you witnessed Mrs. Schmoll faint in the courthouse in early May of 1842?"

"Yes."

"In your opinion what might have caused that display?"

"She was between the fourth and fifth month of her pregnancy. That's about the time of the quickening process. A woman's liable to experience syncope then."

"Please describe her physical condition at the time."

"She was short of breath, nervous, and apparently hysterical. She kept sighing. Loud sighs. That's what I remember right before she plunged to the floor."

"Thank you." Jones removed his pocket watch, acknowledging the passage of time. "With all possible haste, Sir, would you please describe some of the physical conditions that a person who's hallucinating will experience?"

"Shortness of breath, agitation, nervousness. Hysteria. Given to great excitement. Sometimes the shortness of breath will give way to hyperventilation."

"Doctor, your description of Mrs. Schmoll's physical condition at the time of her fainting spell and your description of the physical conditions associated with hallucinations are practically the same. May I ask if you think she may have hallucinated the whole affair?"

"No, I don't think that."

"But is it not possible that she hallucinated it?"

"There is some possibility."

"Explain."

"Well, there are those who have nightmares that seem so vivid that the person experiencing them would swear under oath that it actually happened."

"Is it not also true that if someone wants something so badly that he might imagine that it happened?"

"Yes, but you don't need a physician to tell you that."

"Correct, nevertheless, let us suppose that the patient is a woman in an unhappy marriage and her priest is a young man, just a few years older than she and he lends her a sympathetic ear. Is it not possible that she might develop a fancy for the man, even though he is vowed to abstain from romance and the marital act?"

"I suppose, but why are you asking me these questions?"

"Because you seem to be an objective man of science. Do you think it possible that if Mrs. Schmoll had a romantic attachment to the priest, and he, giving her the mitten as it were, rejecting her, that she then could have hallucinated this alleged attack?"

"Objection!" Lockhart and Chandler called out simultaneously.

"Sustained," the judge replied. "Mr. Jones, you are fishing in dreadfully shallow waters. Do you remember what the doctor was called to speak on?"

"Yes, your Honor." He turned to the doctor. "Is there anything else you would like to say concerning syncope?"

"Not exactly, but it might be slightly related to the subject."

"Go on." Jones nodded.

"I've been studying the new scientific field of Phrenology and—"

"For the benefit of the jury, please define *Phrenology*?"

"We in the medical profession are finding that by carefully examining a man's skull, studying the sizes and shapes of the skull's protuberances, a person's character and mental capacities can be determined."

"Fascinating, doctor." Jones's eyes widened as he pursed his lips.

"Yes 'tis. There are also criminologists using it in their analysis of criminals, murderers, thieves, and rapists. I shall have liked to examine the head of the defendant to determine if he was predisposed to such deviant behavior. From here, you will notice his high forehead and prominent cheekbones, almost angular, a volatile type. I know the look."

"And so do I," Dixon bounded out of his seat. "Listen Doctor, with that kind of quackery, you'd have to examine Judge Embree's head, and Mr. Chandler's as well."

"You should have your head examined, Mister!" Chandler turned angrily, facing Dixon. "But perhaps the doctor would have too much trouble distinguishing your head from your backside, Mr. Arch-i-bald Dixon."

"John Chandler—" Dixon left his thought unfinished.

Judge Embree said nothing but twice pounded the gavel. The lawyers went mute.

Roman once again was humiliated. Using those criteria, nearly every man in the courtroom was criminal. He was more confused than ever.

"The prosecution would like to call Doctor William Trafton to the witness stand."

The bailiff said something to the sheriff and they both went to the judge.

Chandler stood and addressed the judge's bench. "If it please the Court, may I ask the whereabouts of the witness, Doctor William Trafton?"

"He could not be located," the judge explained. "The sheriff attempted to serve him a subpoena, but he was nowhere to be found. No one seems to know where he has been for a while."

"Well, well, well, Mr. Chandler. Isn't that timely?" Dixon's rhetorical question brought the blood to Chandler's face. "I'm sure the good doctor is out making his rounds, curing people of the milk-sickness."

Roman wondered if Anna Maria's tongue was black with perjury.

The counsel next called the third and final doctor to the stand. Roman listened as he detailed his theory on syncope. "That scent of incense that Catholics use in their rituals can bring on the syncope. I've seen it happen with foul smells like horse-apples, or even disgusting cooking odors. Even a dusty room can spark off an episode."

Jones cross-examined the physician. "What are your credentials?"

"I started out as a barber. I still cut hair and all, but I've pert near perfected bloodletting. Some folks are scared of leeches and the like, but I been using ticks, now and again. My friends say I got the eye of a hoot owl when it comes to spotting what's ailing somebody."

"Where did you go to medical school?"

"Back in the good old days you didn't have to have nobody tell you you could go doctoring on nobody."

"So you have no diploma?"

"No, sir. I don't need no piece a paper to tell me I'm no doctor."

"I see. Then how did you become a doctor?"

"I'm a doctor, damnit. I don't need no fancy school out east telling me what I done ready know I know how to do. Enough of that, I say. Danged intellectuals done hoodwinked Washington. Now Congress is a telling us that we gots to send our children to the schoolhouse to learn them. As if some stranger's gonna know more about teaching my youngins than I do."

"And how long have you been doctoring, as you say?"

"Be twenty years come this October. You ain't doubting me, are you? Plenty of folks round these here parts can tell you how I been their doctor. Syncope has been associated with the milk sickness..."

Roman looked at the self-proclaimed physician. For a moment he thought that he might be the same man who had tried to sell him a headache cure four years before.

"Bloodletting is one of the four humors of medicine—"

"They're humorous, all right." Roman heard Dixon utter under his breath. "But won't patients die if they have no blood?"

"Yeah, but we don't drain them dry, just enough to get them healthy. Bleeding, purging, blistering, and vomiting. You got to purge their system. You can axe ol' Doc Trafton in Evansville. He blood lets all his patients."

"Does he now? Isn't he a friend of Mr. Chandler?"

"Believe he is."

"Is it necessary to let blood?"

"Necessary for diagnosis of the ailment."

"This Doc Trafton you speak of, wasn't he recognized for developing a cure for the milk sickness or black tongue?"

"Yeah, that him."

"A large quantity of whiskey is considered medically beneficial?"

"Brandy with honey would work, for womenfolk."

"Mr. Dixon!" The judge hammered again. "Would you please! You are cross-examining the witness concerning syncope, not the milk sickness!"

"Mr. Dixon doesn't know any better, your Honor." Chandler laughed.

"Yes, the reputable doctor doesn't have his office in *Ansel Wood's Tavern* like Trafton does," Dixon volleyed.

"Gentlemen!" Embree was on his feet.

"Doctor, is there anything else you would like to tell us about syncope?" Dixon hurriedly returned to the subject.

"Oh, I seen this one woman laying like she was dead for days, nine, ten days. Her kin wanted to call the parson out because they said she's dead, but I told them she was alive. It was the dangdest thing. She finally got up about two weeks later and cooked them a Sunday dinner! It's hard to believe, but you'd all be surprised how many people is buried alive. Old Asa Adams, east of Boonville, was buried alive and he clawed at his coffin lid all night and pried the lid halfway off—"

"Thank you, doctor. That's quite sufficient for dinner conversation. Does the prosecution have anything else for the good doctor?"

"No, that will be enough." Lockhart rubbed his eyes.

"The witness may step down." As the doctor walked out of the courtroom, Dixon could hardly contain himself. "Great witness, Mr. Chandler," Dixon whispered with a contagious smile. "Where do you come up with these characters? He should have been one of our witnesses."

"Just you wait," Chandler whispered back loudly. "We haven't examined your witnesses yet."

A motion for a midday recess was called and court adjourned for lunch.

****

When the court reconvened, Officers John Curl and Zachariah Aydelott were placed on the stand. With the arrest warrant, both men claimed that when they arrived at the Fitzwilliams' farmhouse Roman was walking up the lane, reading from a book. At the time of the arrest, he had uttered under his breath, "Schmoll! Traitor!"

Caroline Long was next called to the witness stand. Caroline had stayed with Martin Schmoll to care for Anna Maria's child during February of 1843 while Anna Maria and the attorney, Jay Davis, had gone to Cincinnati on legal business. When Anna Maria returned by herself, she and the baby were turned out of his house; Jay Davis was nowhere to be found; and in November of that same year, Caroline gave birth to her bastard child. The seventeen or eighteen-year-old Caroline shivered like a frightened lamb, the attorneys pacing in front of her, ruminating upon the case, towering over her, asking their questions.

The prosecution then called forth another witness. The man smiled at John Chandler as he gave his testimony. "Me and my buddy went over to the Catholic Church to see how easy it'd be to yank a fellow out of the box like that there priest did to that Schmoll woman. Anyway, I had him kneel down in the box and I threw back the drape and took him by the shoulders. I throwed him about ten feet, maybe twelve, no problem."

James Jones began the cross-examination. "Did you throw your friend to the floor?"

"Not exactly."

"Why not?"

"I didn't want to get his clothes dirty."

"But when Mrs. Schmoll was thrown to the floor, she said her dress was not soiled. Her husband says the same. Yet you seem to be saying that the floor was dirty. Is that true?"

"Yeah, there was lots of dirt and dust."

"Do you think that an unsuspecting woman could manage to catch herself like your friend did?"

"No."

"Do you think a woman on the verge of syncope could have avoided falling to the floor?"

"No."

"Do you think the woman's dress would have been soiled had she been tossed about on the church floor like Mrs. Schmoll claims that she was?"

"Probably so."

The State not having any other witnesses to call, the judge adjourned for the day. "We shall continue tomorrow with testimony when the defense will begin calling its witnesses. Court is adjourned until tomorrow at nine." Judge Embree smacked the hammer then stood and stretched.

Roman was escorted back to the jail where he remained under close watch, protected by several constables keeping vigil.

Chapter 20

Virtue and Vice

7 March 1844

On Thursday, the third day of the trial, the judge called the court to order. As soon as he took his seat, Roman's counsel, Benjamin Thomas, was on his feet calling witnesses to discredit Anna Maria Schmoll's character.

Some of the witnesses from Cincinnati told stories of a young, lustful, criminal Anna Maria. One witness told of how Anna Maria's brothers, Jacob and Louis, confirmed her bad character by saying that she had desperately wanted to get married, and "longed for a husband," but her father was strict and very much opposed the idea. She said that Anna Maria resented her father and mother. She had taken a housekeeper job and while there she stole from the family and violated her curfew.

According to one man's testimony, "Anna Maria was always out with strange men, drinking and showing off her legs, at all hours of the night. I heard a story of how Anna's own brother, Jacob, called her a whore, and slapped her up a'side the head a time or two. She got all mad and left Cincinnati."

Roman paged through his breviary, meditating upon the psalms while Chandler went to work in an attempt to dismantle every witness's story.

For a few moments, Roman found himself pitying the poor girl, seemingly driven to the dregs of society as a result of her unhappy childhood. More witnesses testified that she did not want to work for a living and said she was a thief and a drinker who slept during the day and caroused at all hours of the night. Another witness testified that Anna Maria was in the custom of giving herself over to young roughs at a certain Cincinnati tavern.

Roman remembered the first night he met her and he felt a wave of anger go through him. His stomach ached. He despised the Schmolls. He knew he shouldn't. He couldn't. It was a sin. But he couldn't help it. Clenching his fists, he unintentionally broke his rosary, having forgotten that he was clutching it in his right hand. As it came apart *Ave* beads bounced across the floor, momentarily distracting everyone's attention. He knelt down and collected the loose orbs which were shooting over the floor like errant bullets. As he diligently worked to restore the relic, heads turned and whispers rustled like a northern wind through autumn leaves. The judge hammered his gavel to call the courtroom back to order. Roman was angry at himself for being angry. Now he was embarrassed that he had made a scene. Getting up from the floor, he labored to mend the chain. He mouthed the *Ave* beads and ignored the proceedings for a while.

Thomas roused Roman from his prayer telling him that the next witness had an interesting tale. A woman was called to the stand and Thomas took to the floor, asking her to tell her story.

"One autumn evening of 1841, I was out with a fine young man, Ignatz Yeager, when Anna Long stopped us on the street. In the midst of our conversation, she had the audacity to invite Mr. Yeager to come see her when he tired of me. She said, 'everything is convenient. My bedroom is over the kitchen, so it's always warm up there.' I was outraged, so I thought of a way to distract her. I knew that she had fallen and hurt her leg recently, so I asked her if she did not need to go home and rest her leg. She replied, 'Oh, no. It is healing nicely.' I thoughtlessly said, 'I'm sure.' Well, when I said that, at once she lifted her dress up over her knee to show off the wound. Then she asked my male friend if he had ever seen a healthier leg than hers. Several men on the street turned to gawk."

On cross-examination, Chandler tried to paint the woman as a bitter spinster.

The defense surprised the prosecution by calling Ignatz Yeager to the stand. He had been located after several weeks of searching. Wilbur Jones had been missing from the trial since the morning and Yeager entered the courtroom with him.

The prosecution strenuously objected to Yeager as a surprise witness. Wilbur Jones responded, "If the prosecution will recall, we identified Mr. Yeager as a possible witness early on. The only surprise is that we were actually able to locate him."

The judge then reviewed the pre-trial submissions and found that Yeager had indeed been listed as a potential defense witness. "Your objection is overruled. The witness was properly identified by the defense. It is irrelevant that the prosecution assumed he would not be produced."

There were hisses and boos from the prosecution side aimed at the defense. After the judge tapped his gavel, Yeager took the stand. "I first met Anna Maria, or Maria as she was calling herself then, Miss Maria Long, or now I suppose I should say, Mrs. Schmoll, but whatever she calls herself, I think she's a whore."

"Objection, your honor! The witness is vulgar and sarcastic."

"The witness must adhere to proper decorum."

Yeager continued, describing the first time he met Mrs. Schmoll. "I was courting another woman. I had come calling on her a time or two, but then one day the creature, Maria Long, raised her dress and showed me her hairy legs. I'm not a blind man. The girl was trying to seduce me, if the truth be known. It repulsed me, to be honest. She might as well have pulled off her dress. There were other witnesses, ask them. That is all I care to say."

Chandler rose for the cross exam, "You drink, don't you Mr. Yeager?"

"That's none of your business."

"The witness is reminded that he is under oath," the judge spoke. "Answer the question."

"Yes, I'm a drinking man."

"And the reason it took so long for the defense counsel to get you on the stand here," Chandler smirked, "was due to the fact that you've been laying drunk in a gunboat bobbing up and down on the Ohio, isn't that the truth?"

"I don't have to answer that." He strained to look at Thomas as if pleading for help.

"That's right," Chandler laughed. "You didn't have to answer any of the defense's questions either...but let's get this straight. You came here today to maliciously smear the reputation of a beautiful— creature—to use your words, and yet you yourself still smell of the perfume of a boatload of harlots! How much did the defense counselors pay you to wash up and put on decent clothes?"

"Objection!" Thomas and both Jones brothers cried out in unison. The witness reared up out of the seat and doubled up his fist as if to hit the prosecutor.

The bailiff and sheriff both lurched in that direction, but Chandler slid across the floor in front of the jury box. "Messrs Jones and

Thomas. Shame on you! Does the sanctity of the courtroom mean this little to you?" Chandler shot them a staged glare. "Calm your witnesses down prior to bringing them before the court—and sober them up too! No sense in anyone getting hurt. If it please the Court, perhaps a doctor should be called, for I do believe Mr. Yeager is about to have an epizootic!"

Roman sank into his chair and covered his eyes as the bailiff escorted Yeager out. The prosecution team challenged the defense that Roman was on trial, not Anna Maria. Roman feared that by attempting to discredit Anna his attorneys had tainted his chance for exoneration.

Once order was restored, Thomas recalled Anna Maria Schmoll to the stand. "Mrs. Schmoll, we have heard from some residents of Cincinnati, and we have all heard many of them state that you are a girl of loose morals, a thief, a liar, and known to drink to excess. Even some of the witnesses for the prosecution affirmed this."

"Objection, your Honor. The defense, as always, is conducting an inquisition against our helpless victim! I have always believed this poor woman. But when I see the magnitude of the forces which are arrayed against her, ready to discredit her as a whore, when in reality she is a witness to chastity and morality, I am cut to the core."

"Overruled!"

Wilbur Jones arose. "Two of the witnesses swore that they would not believe her, even if she were to swear to tell the truth."

"Objection, your Honor!"

"Yes, Mr. Chandler, what is your objection?" the judge asked. "Or are you simply objecting to be objecting?"

"Gentlemen of the jury, see, once again, that these witnesses clearly are not consistent!"

"Mr. Chandler!" the judge spoke again.

"The only witnesses who have said anything against Mrs. Schmoll's impeccable character have been witnesses sympathetic to the Catholic priesthood."

"Mr. Chandler—"

"That should show you who's trying to subvert justice in this case." Chandler threw up his arms.

"Mr. Chandler, you're out of order!" the judge shouted.

"That's not in evidence!" Thomas shouted. "See how Mr. Chandler reeks of prejudice against the Catholic religion! What about the previous prosecuting attorney, Jay Davis? Where is he? Why has he abandoned this case? Why does he now refuse to stand by the victim?" Thomas was getting red in the face.

"Your Honor, this is not irrelevant to the case!" Chandler shouted back. "If the truth be known, Mr. Davis had debts. His flight from Evansville has nothing to do with the character of Mrs. Schmoll, but everything to do with angry creditors."

"Order, gentlemen! This exchange is inappropriate and distracting to the jury!" The judge grabbed his gavel and hammered it hard upon the desk. "Counsel will meet in my chambers! *Now!*"

Roman watched as the lawyers angrily stamped out of the courtroom allowing the assembly to erupt into noise. He looked up to see Mrs. Schmoll still seated in the witness box, her head down, eyes closed. The sheriff was standing halfway between the two, eyeing Roman as if he was to spring out of his chair any moment to do her bodily harm. Roman's attention turned to loud voices coming from the judges' chamber as the door opened. The men spilled out into the courtroom and returned to their positions.

"Order, order." Embree pounded his gavel. "Court is back in session!" He took his seat and looked at James Jones. "I believe the defense was cross examining the witness. Mr. Jones, please continue."

"Mrs. Schmoll, could you kindly inform the court where you and your infant now reside?"

"With my father at Blue Grass."

"Is it true that your husband did violence to your person and that of your child on the night of March third?"

"*Ja,* jest a leetle."

"Why did he treat you thus?"

"He was trinking."

"Are you being forced to repeat the calumny against the priest?"

"*Nein.*"

"Do you fear your husband?"

"Only when he has been trinking."

"Why did he threaten your life and force you and your child to walk six miles in the snow, sleet, and rain?"

"Objection!" Chandler was on his feet. "The defense is badgering the witness!"

"Sustained," said the judge. "Defense will ask questions pertaining to the charge of rape against the defendant."

Where all of this was going, Roman had no idea. His strict, structured world had given way to a hurricane of chaos. Roman's life was no longer the ordered universe of a Mozart concerto, but rather that of an eruptive, fiery Beethoven crescendo. He recalled hearing Beethoven's Ninth Symphony in Strasbourg the first year he had entered the seminary. The cacophony of the first two movements that had made no sense to him then now took on meaning. He could only hope that as that symphony's tumultuous beginning had culminated in a triumphal resolution, so would his own trial and tribulations give way to new life. His reverie of the pounding timpani gave way to the banging gavel.

Archibald Dixon, the Kentucky attorney, then rose to cross-examine Anna Maria.

"Did you not on the Friday evening after Ascension day speak to a Mrs. Mary Good concerning the alleged incident?"

"I never spoke to that woman!"

"That's not what she says," Dixon said as he lit his pipe.

"The witness says she never spoke with her!" Chandler shouted from his chair.

"She remembered before." Dixon puffed out smoke. "Why can't she recall it now?"

"She can't remember saying something that she never said."

"Is that it?" Dixon held his pipe, inhaling. "Well, that's what she says now."

"No, that's what she's always said," Chandler replied calmly.

"I thought you said she never said anything." Dixon removed the pipe slowly and turned toward the jury box.

"I know what the woman said!"

"Good. We may want to call you as a witness later, Mr. Chandler."

"Gentlemen, another outburst like that, and—" Judge Embree hammered the gavel.

"The gentleman from Kentucky didn't mean anything by it." Chandler said.

"If you don't mind, I can speak for myself, Mr. Chandler." Dixon took the pipe from his mouth and puffed out smoke. "I mean everything *I* say. If you don't know that, then you don't know me. We're liable to lock horns again, your Honor."

"Mr. Dixon, I am aware of your reputation through Kentucky and Southern Indiana and I believe you would like to leave it intact—"

"Understood. I beg your pardon. Could we resume?"

"Certainly." Judge Embree sighed.

"Mrs. Schmoll," Dixon moved toward Anna Maria. "Did you faint immediately whereupon you charge that the defendant took you by force?"

"No..." She paused and spoke in German to the interpreter.

"She says," spoke the interpreter, "that she fainted immediately after the defendant penetrated her."

Roman covered his eyes with his hands.

Dixon went on with his questions. "Was this against your will?"

"Javoll!"

"Then the defendant threw you on the floor, yet your clothes were not soiled?"

"I suppose the sexton, Herr Stahlhofer, had just cleaned."

Dixon further questioned her at length concerning her reason for returning to the church the following morning for Ascension Mass. "If the defendant had ravished you the evening before, do you expect me to believe that you returned to his church the next day?"

The interpreter indicated that she did not understand the question.

"Why did you return to the church the next day?" Dixon repeated the question.

"To take communion. It was a holy day. I feared that if I were to abstain from the sacrament, then I would be lost forever." Anna sighed.

"But the night before the same priest had violated you in the most vicious manner, yet you returned and placed your sister in peril of the same outrage?" Dixon's voice increased in intensity as he smoked his pipe.

"The graces of the Sacraments do not depend upon the holiness of the priest," Chandler called out from his chair.

"Very good, Mr. Chandler!" Dixon bowed his head. "She makes a fine marionette. Why, I can't even detect any of the strings!"

"Mr. Dixon..." the judge growled.

Dixon sat back down and placed his pipe firmly in his mouth, chomping the end.

James Jones had more questions for the witness. "Mrs. Schmoll, did you ever tell a Mrs. Mary Good anything about the alleged ravishing?"

"No. Never."

"You never spoke to anyone, not even a Mrs. Bruner in Cincinnati?" Jones asked.

"That is true. I would never talk about such a thing to a stranger."

"You've tutored the witness quite well, John," Dixon said, as he puffed smoke from his pipe.

Chandler and Jones both ignored Dixon.

Jones quickly asked his next question. "Were you kneeling when the defendant allegedly took hold of you?"

"Yes, I was praying."

"You state that after you received your penance, you said a prayer..."

"Yes, when I get my penance, I kneel down to say a leetle prayer I learnt in Germany. I was kneeling when he came into the box and took holt of me."

"Did you try to resist him?" James Jones paced in front of her.

"No. I could not. I was too scared."

"I thought you said you fainted as soon as he took you out?" Jones stopped, looking at her.

"I don't know." She looked over to Chandler.

"Well," Dixon smiled, puffing away on his pipe, staring at Chandler.

Again, Jones seemed to be ignoring Dixon and fired off another question. "What were you wearing at the time you claim the defendant ravished you?"

"My blue dress and a straw bonnet."

"What color was the bonnet?"

"White."

"After being thrown to the floor, was the bonnet damaged in any way?"

"Yes, it was broken in front and back."

"Did you tell your husband that you pulled the defendant's hair?"

"Did he say that?" she cringed.

"The witness should answer the question," came the voice of the judge.

"No."

"On that evening was there anyone else in the church besides you and the defendant?"

"There was when I first arrived. When he threw me out of the box, I was so confused. I could not tell if there was anyone else there or not. I only saw him."

"You saw *him*?"

"Yes."

"Identify *him*."

"*Roman* Weinzoepfel." She pointed at Roman, saying his name as she had that cold December night of 1841.

"What were you doing in the confessional when the defendant took hold of you?"

"I was praying."

"From a book or from memory?"

"I had my book with me."

"Were you able to read the prayer-book?"

"A leetle, but it was so dark."

"How dark?"

"Twilight."

"How long were you unconscious?"

"I do not know."

"When you regained your consciousness, did you find your prayer-book?"

"Yes. When I came to my senses after he had violated me I saw my book on the bench."

"When did you first make the acquaintance of the defendant, Father Weinzoepfel?"

"Father Roman was the priest at the Evansville church. I met him at my father's house. Shortly before my mother died he came there to give her the Last Rites."

"Did you ever go to confession with the defendant prior to the incident on Ascension eve 1842?"

"Yes. I believe it was Christmas Eve of 1841."

"When were you and Martin Schmoll married?"

"New Year's eve 1841."

"How long had you known your husband prior to the marriage?"

"Not more than a week. We met at the Mill a mile or so from my father's house."

"When was your child born?"

She sniffled and wiped away a tear from her eye before speaking. "The sixteenth of September, 1842." Her voice dissolved into sobs.

"Did your husband question the paternity of your daughter?"

The judge hammered the gavel. "Mr. Jones! Can't you see you're driving the witness over the edge? The witness will not answer that question."

Jones moved near Roman and pointed to him. "Are you absolutely sure the defendant was the man in the confessional that evening?"

"Yes." Anna Maria's eyes met Roman's for the briefest moment before she glanced away. "I saw him through the lattice window."

"How old are you, Ma'am?"

"Twenty-two. I will turn twenty-three on the sixteenth of June."

"You were twenty-one at the time of the alleged assault?"

"Yes."

"Mrs. Schmoll, did you have a conversation with Mrs. Good on the Friday following Ascension day, 1842?"

Even before Jones had finished the question, Roman saw Anna Maria turn away in tears.

"I have suffered so much from an illness, and the death of my child September last, and the matter of my separation from my husband, that I am afraid my memory has been weakened."

"But can you remember having a conversation with the woman following the alleged crime perpetrated by the defendant?"

"I cannot be for sure."

"Did you not converse with Mrs. Good at your house that Friday afternoon after returning from the courthouse where you had filed charges against the defendant?"

"I do not remember, Sir."

"Did you not tell her that when the priest took hold of your arm you fell down dead?"

"I cannot remember."

"Do you deny it? You admit that you cannot recall saying—"

"Objection, counsel is interrogating the witness!"

"Overruled!" the judge answered. "Let us give reasonable scope to their questioning. Defense counsel may proceed with the witness."

"On the night after you returned from confession, did not your husband, Martin Schmoll, demand that you tell him what happened to you in the church?"

"Objection, your Honor!" Chandler smacked his hand down on his table in front of him and stood. "I have about had all that I care to endure. Counsel is cross-examining his own witness before examining her directly! These questions have already been asked and answered. It has been nearly two years since her assault and she doesn't need to be put through any more misery! Her heartless husband has already put her through enough as it is!"

"Mr. Chandler, *I* am the judge, not you. We are disposed to give all legitimate breadth to this examination. You're overruled. Mr. Jones, please proceed. The witness will answer the question."

Anna Maria recounted the same details that she had told the prosecution two days earlier. Roman did become interested again as his counselors asked about Anna Maria and Martin's marriage.

"Mrs. Schmoll, we want to know exactly when Mr. Schmoll forced you out of his house?"

She said it was the middle of February 1843 and she had just returned from Cincinnati after assisting the attorney, Jay Davis, in obtaining depositions for the trial scheduled for March of 1843.

"How old was your baby?"

"Five months old."

"Was it a boy or a girl?"

"A baby girl."

"My sympathy to you in your loss... What did you name her?"

"Maria Caroline. After my middle name and my sister."

"Uh, huh. How did your husband tell you to leave his house?"

Through the interpreter, she answered. "Mr. Schmoll was in a drunken, jealous rage and accused me of infidelity. Then he told me to leave or else he would kill us both."

"How?"

"He threatened to starve me and the baby to death. He treated me badly...he turned me out with our child leaving us to walk in the sleet and snow for the ten miles north to my father's house. We both took ill, but in the next week as I recovered, the baby grew sicker and sicker. That was early March 1843, but by September my...my baby, my baby was dead... after she died, I thought it was the curse of God. The curse of God for taking one of his priests to court."

Roman heard the same trepidation in her voice that he had heard that evening more than a year and a half before. Her voice went silent

251

as she wept bitterly. This was not the same Anna Maria that had taken the stand at Evansville in May of 1842.

Were these tears of contrition? Roman wondered. The priest in him had pity for her. She was a soul in peril; a soul for whom he had vowed to lay down his life. *How great Thy cross, O Lord. Father, forgive them for they know not what they do.* The words of Christ had never meant so much as they did now.

"What is the relationship between you and your husband today?"

"He is my greatest enemy!" she answered for herself.

"Even greater than the defendant?"

"Objection—"

"Allow the Court to intervene for once, Mr. Chandler!" The judge called out. "I was about to beg the gentleman off. Mr. Jones, I believe you have pressed this matter far enough!"

"Hell hath no fury like a woman scorned," Thomas leaned over and whispered loud enough for Roman to hear. Dixon chuckled.

The judge turned to Mrs. Schmoll. "The witness may be excused—subject to recall." She put her handkerchief to her eyes as the bailiff conducted her out of the courtroom.

Chapter 21

Of Bonnets and Prie-Dieus

The judge called for a midafternoon recess so the jurors could make toilet and stretch their legs. Once the judge reconvened the trial, the proceedings resumed.

"The Court now recognizes Mr. James G. Jones on behalf of the defendant. You may proceed with your witnesses."

Roman watched as the Heinrichs were called to the stand and questioned. Mr. Heinrich explained, "I told my wife that we should let Mrs. Schmoll go to confession ahead of us since her husband wanted her home. But when we told her to go first, she stayed in her pew, ignoring our offer. For some time the priest was alone in the confessional waiting because we kept waiting for Mrs. Schmoll to go. Finally we went to confession. Afterwards, my wife and I prayed our penance in the church. Mrs. Schmoll finally went to confession, but my wife and I left the church before she was finished confessing. She was still in the confessional with Father Roman when we left."

Mrs. Heinrich was called next. Due to her inability to speak English well, the interpreter was utilized. "When my husband and I entered the church Mr. Karges was already in the church. The priest was not yet in the confessional. Once he entered the confessional, we asked Frau Schmoll to go first, but she wouldn't. My husband and I went ahead to confession because Frau Schmoll insisted that she be the last to go to confession. The next time I saw the defendant was at our house for supper no more than an hour later. It was yet daylight because we did not need to light the candles. He often took his meals with us."

Meanwhile Roman reminisced the many evenings he had shared with the Heinrichs.

Josiah Stahlhofer was summoned next. Jones asked him, "What is your relationship to the defendant?"

"I am the sacristan and sexton of the Kirche, the church."

"What does a sacristan do?"

"I schveep and clean the Kirche. I take care of the chalices and patens, and I set up for the priest ven he says Mass."

"You were in the churchyard when Mrs. Schmoll came to confession that Ascension eve. Tell the jury about a conversation you had with her moments before she entered the church."

"I vas sveeping the sidevalk und schteps of the Kirche, ven Frau Schmoll came upon me. She ast if the priest vas hearing confessions. 'Javoll,' I say to her."

"Then what?"

"She say something like, 'I schvear that priest best absolve me or I don't know vhat I do.'"

"Were those the words she used?"

"I schvear the priest best grant me absolution or I don't know vhat I do.'"

"Are you sure those were her exact words?"

"I denk so."

"So, it was a threat?"

"It sounded like vone to me."

"Did Mrs. Schmoll threaten to do some type of harm to the defendant?"

"She swore. Das ist alles. To schvear revenge on a *Pater* is no good. It's a mortal sin."

"Why would Father Weinzoepfel withhold absolution in the confessional?"

"I do not know."

"What did you think when she said this to you?"

"It is not everyday that a young Katolisch voman tells a sacristan that her priest vithheld absolution from her. What is a man to think of such a voman? Only mortal sins came to my mind."

"Did you tell the defendant what the woman said to you?"

"Not right away. I forgot."

"How could you forget something like a threat to your priest?"

"I forget tings."

"When did you tell the defendant what Mrs. Schmoll said to you?"

"De nochxt morgen after Mass."

"Which day?"

"Friday morning."

"What did he say?"

"He vas full of angst, but he vould not let me tell anyone. He say 'vait.'"

254

"Did you perchance see the woman go to confession?"

"Nein."

"Did you see the defendant go in to church that evening to hear confessions?"

"Javoll."

"At what time?"

"Five o'clock."

"How was he dressed?"

"He was wearing a cassock and surplice with the purple stole around his neck."

"For the sake of the jury, what is a cassock and surplice?"

Stahlhofer described the cassock as a long, ankle-length black robe buttoned from top to bottom and the surplice as a white garment worn over the shoulders, covering the upper torso. "The stole goes around the neck and crosses in front of him. It is a sign of his priestly authority."

"How easy is it for a priest to get out of his clerical garb?"

"Not very." He explained there was a prayer that accompanies the putting on of every piece of clothing.

"I suppose if one of the Reverend gentlemen would stand, they could show all of us," laughed Chandler.

"Prosecution, you may cross-examine the witness," the judge tapped his gavel.

Chandler stepped up in front of the witness stand. "Thank you, Mr. Jones." He turned to Stahlhofer. "So, you are a German immigrant?"

"Javoll."

"And you are both the church's sacristan and sexton?"

"Ja."

"Would you say that Mrs. Schmoll was troubled in spirit that evening?"

"I do not know."

"She was perturbed in spirit, otherwise she wouldn't have come to the church for confession. Now tell the jury what she said to you again."

"I schvear that priest best grant me absolution or I don't know vhat I do.'"

"Are you sure? You've changed the wording several times."

"I denk."

"It means nothing. There was no veiled threat. How did you know she was threatening revenge? Revenge for what?

"It was the way she said it…I schvear, that young priest best grant me absolution."

"So, there was no threat."

"Nein, there vas not."

"Your testimony seems to indicate that the priest may have harassed her in the confessional on an earlier date."

Jones stood, interrupting Chandler's cross-examination. "The state's witness has testified under oath that the only other time she went to confession with the priest was on the second day of Christmas, 1841. Five days before she and Martin Schmoll were married."

"Precisely, Mr. Jones," Chandler snapped. "It only took once for the woman to become wise. He must have denied her absolution that December."

"Not *must* have. *May* have." Jones nodded.

"May have. Thank you, Mr. Jones."

"Herr Stahlhofer, you said the priest wore a stole which symbolized his priestly authority. What authority does a priest have in the confessional?"

"The authority to forgive sins."

"Herr Stahlhofer, I have no further questions." Chandler bowed to the judge.

For the defense, Jones asked the witness to repeat the alleged threat that Mrs. Schmoll made against Roman and then excused the witness.

Jones then called John Karges forth. "What do you do?"

"I work at Linck's sawmill and in my free time I make tables and chairs. I made all the prie-dieus at Assumption Church."

"What are pray-doos?"

"Kneeler benches."

"Let us proceed with your account of Ascension eve. What was the priest wearing when you first saw him that evening?"

"He was wearing his cassock and white surplice."

"Do you go to church often?"

"I'm not a holy man, but I do practice my religion."

"How easy is it for a priest to get out of his clerical garb?"

"I'm not for certain. It would seem to be rather complicated."

"Thank you, Mr. Karges." Jones backed off. "Your witness, counsel."

Lockhart for the prosecution cross-examined. "Mr. Karges, were you in the church when Mrs. Schmoll went to confession?"

"No. I was the first to confess that evening and I left the church shortly after praying my penance."

"So you left the church before the priest?"

"Yes. I left before the other three penitents were finished."

"So you did not actually see the priest leave the church fully dressed?"

"No."

Roman was disgusted at the innuendo.

"Thank you." Chandler smiled across the bench.

Jones then had Patrick Fitzwilliams recount to the court how his wife had given birth that Friday morning after Ascension and he had ridden to Evansville to invite the priest to dinner in hopes he would baptize the child that day. From there he told how once arrived at his farm, Roman used the time to pray before dinner was served. Just as they were about to sit down and eat, officer Curl arrested the defendant.

Chandler cross-examined. "Where was the defendant going on this particular morning?"

"He said he was to leave for Vincennes after he baptized our baby."

"Where was the defendant going before you invited him to your house for dinner?"

"I don't know." Mr. Fitzwilliams shrugged his shoulders.

"Isn't it true that he was thinking of fleeing from justice?" Chandler spoke loudly. "He realized that his deed was known so he saddled up his horse to claim sanctuary at the Cathedral in Vincennes or perhaps he was going to board a steamboat to New Orleans and sail back to Europe?"

"Sir, I don't know." Fitzwilliams shook his head.

"Well I wish you would know! Think for a minute and perhaps your memory will return."

"I've told ye over and over, can't ye hear me? I tell ye I don't know!"

"Mr. Chandler," the judge cleared his throat. "The man is under oath. If he says he doesn't know, then he doesn't know."

Mrs. Mary Good was then called and sworn. Mr. Jones began, "Mrs. Good, please tell the jury when you saw the defendant on the eve of Ascension?"

"She was just returning from the church"

"What was she wearing?"

"A blue dress and a white bonnet."

"Did she seem distraught?" Jones cocked his head and scratched his beard.

"No." Mrs. Good looked at Anna Maria.

"Were her clothes disheveled?"

"No."

"Was her dress dirty at all, like it might have been if she had rolled upon a dirty floor?"

"No. It was clean."

"Did her bonnet appear to be broken or damaged?" Jones pinched at the end of his beard.

"No."

"What transpired after you saw her return from the church?"

"Her husband yelled at her and made her prepare his supper."

"Had the two been fighting?"

"I only heard them arguing."

"How long did that go on?"

"Into the evening."

"When was the next time you saw Mrs. Schmoll?"

"The following morning. She and her brother and sister went off to the church together."

"How did you know they went to church?"

"I watched them walk in. They were having an obligatory Thursday morning services."

"How was Mrs. Schmoll dressed?"

"She was wearing the same blue dress that she had worn to the church the night before."

"And what about her bonnet?"

"She was wearing either a red or maroon scarf, but her sister was wearing the bonnet."

"The same bonnet belonging to Mrs. Schmoll?"

"Yes."

"The white bonnet?" Jones turned, saying his words to the jury.

"Yes, it was a white bonnet."

"Did the bonnet appear to be in order?"

"Yes."

"In the light of day, did her dress and the bonnet appear to be soiled at all?" Jones continued speaking to the jury.

"No, not in the least."

"Of the people going into the Catholic Church that morning, how were they dressed?"

"Everyone of them dressed in their 'Sunday go-to-meeting clothes.'"

"Did Mrs. Schmoll usually dress well?"

"If there was anything that girl would never do, it was to be seen in public wearing soiled clothes. She was always keeping up with the latest fashions."

"A charming footnote." Jones smiled at the jury and then at Roman. "Mrs. Good, tell us about the next day."

"That would be Friday?"

"Yes, tell us what Mrs. Schmoll told you?"

Roman listened to every word as he sat on the edge of his chair balancing his biretta on the tips of his fingers.

"Well, she and her husband just come back to the house from the courthouse. So I asked her what they was doing there. She said that her priest had ravished her in the church. So, naturally, I asked her if she tried to fend him off, but she said, 'I could not. As soon as he took hold of me, I fell down as one dead.'"

"What did she say?"

"She was dead."

"My, my, then what did you say to that?"

"If you was dead, how do you know that he did anything to you?" She paused in Chandler's stare.

"Yes? Go on." Jones turned back to Chandler.

"She said that when she came to her senses, he—" Mrs. Good's eyes were bouncing back and forth between Jones and Chandler.

"The defendant?" Jones moved close to her.

"Yes," Mrs. Good nervously answered. "When she came to her senses, he had hold of her arm."

"That was her proof positive that she had been ravished in the vilest manner?"

"She said she knew it happened because he kept her in church for so long a time."

"How did you respond to that?"

"I told her 'that was no evidence.'" She looked at Anna Maria seated with her attorneys.

"Did either of you say anything else about the matter?"

"No, we couldn't. About that time her husband came out on the porch and told her to get inside the house."

"Was he friendly?"

"Not at all. He seemed very angry, but then that was his normal mood."

"Returning to her account of the ravishing, are you absolutely sure that she said she became unconscious immediately *after* the defendant took hold of her arm?" Jones glanced to Anna Maria.

"Why, yes," Mrs. Good acknowledged ardently.

"Are you sure that she did not say that she became unconscious immediately *after* the defendant had ravished her?"

"Yes, I'm sure. Otherwise I wouldn't have asked her all those questions."

"Was Mrs. Schmoll friendly towards you?"

"Oh, yes. Sometimes, when she had been scolded by her husband she would come to me for, well you know, womanly advice on marriage and the like."

"Yes, yes, I'm sure that was often." Jones' remark elicited a few laughs from the gallery. "But can you think of a reason why Mrs. Schmoll would testify that she did not speak to you about the matter?"

"My husband says her version of the story is different."

"Once again, for the benefit of the jury, she told you that she was unconscious from the very moment that the priest took hold of her?"

"Yes."

"And the deed was consummated while she was unconscious?"

"Yes."

"And that her proof of being ravished was the fact that when she revived it was dark outside and the defendant was holding her arm?"

"Yes."

Roman had heard enough, yet he knew there would be more.

Chandler rose for the cross-examination. "Mrs. Good, we are not here to discredit your reputation, but, my goodness, if you knew all of this, why didn't you make yourself known two years ago?"

"Well, a woman's place is in the home."

"That is a matter of disputed opinion these days, but why did you only come forward now?"

"My husband didn't want me to get him involved."

"Madam, you're the one to whom Mrs. Schmoll told the story. Your husband hasn't been called as a witness nor is he on the stand, you are. Now tell us why you failed to disclose this information before today? A man's life is at stake."

"My husband feared for our safety. Mr. Schmoll can be a beast, you know."

"No, I don't know from first hand experience, but I am hearing a whole heap and plenty about him." Chandler chuckled. "So much so that I am considering representing Mrs. Schmoll in divorce court."

"Objection! Counsel is trying to gain sympathy from the jury." Jones cried out.

"Sustained."

"Now, Mrs. Good," Chandler continued, walking slowly in front of her, "call to mind that you are under oath. Tell the Court the truth. Mrs. Schmoll never told you any of the things you have sworn that she did, did she?"

"That's not so! I was there, not you. The woman was preparing her husband's dinner when she told me." Mrs. Good seemed at the point of crying.

"That's another lie! Both Mr. and Mrs. Schmoll have testified that they did not eat their noon meal that Friday owing to their distress at lodging charges against the defendant."

The harangue went on and on, the prosecution accusing Mrs. Good of being a liar. The defense tried to reassert her story, but she had been strong-armed by Chandler so much that she began to babble.

Once she took leave, the defense recalled Martin Schmoll, but he said the same thing over again.

Roman's stomach hurt as a migraine assailed him. The only relief was in knowing that by evening the testimonies would cease.

James Jones was convinced that the attitude in Evansville had turned against the Schmolls. Maybe there was hope after all.

Having no more witnesses to call or cross-examine, the judge cleared his throat and spoke. "If there is no further evidence to be presented on either side, then I will close the trial to evidence and adjourn this court until tomorrow at which time closing arguments will begin. Following which time the jury will then deliberate until a verdict is reached." He banged his gavel. "Court adjourned."

Roman was exhausted and yet that night he kicked at his blankets, his restless legs moving under the blankets as if he were running for his life. What little sleep he experienced was filled with nightmares of the gallows, the guillotine, and the fiery pyre.

Chapter 22

Closing Arguments Begin

8 March 1844

With Friday morning came great drowsiness. Roman surveyed the sunrise through the window. The sheriff arrived within the hour giving him two cornbread biscuits and real coffee before escorting him to the courthouse

Judge Embree called the court to order. "By agreement of both counsels, it is the decision of the court to allow the three lawyers for the prosecution to each give closing arguments and likewise for the defense. The prosecution will begin and the prosecutor, Lockhart, will go last. At this time the argument may proceed. The court recognizes Mr. Blythe for the prosecution." Of all the prosecution team, Blythe was the least involved in the proceedings prior to this point.

Blythe walked out in front of the jury and began. "Gentlemen of the jury: I do not doubt that you have listened with due respect and patience to the evidence of this case detailed to you by the state's witnesses and those of the defendant. The issue before you is whether the defendant will be set at liberty or be consigned to the doom of the penitentiary. Oh, the gloom one must feel within its walls, the consuming loneliness, the chains and shackles, and overall moribund existence." Roman's imagination immersed him into the darkness of suffering.

"This unfortunate woman appeals to you not for protection, oh no, it is too late for that, what's done is done. No, gentlemen, she seeks retribution." He looked over to Roman and his counsel. "I realize there are those among us who seek for you to fully exonerate her violator, and drive her to the very brink of despair. Therefore I will call your attention to the evidence of this case as it has been explained to you. Allow me to lift the curtain of this tragic drama and introduce you to the principal players upon its stage. Our scene opens with the Schmolls clandestine marriage. Anna Maria was a Catholic, her husband Martin Schmoll, a Protestant, yet family, friends, and her Church opposed this marital union. Her vows were not exchanged in a

Catholic sanctuary, they were not consecrated before the altar and crucifix, and they were not celebrated with the solemnities of a sacrament, but rather were performed and witnessed by a magistrate of the State of Indiana, the Squire Joseph Wheeler.

"Would to God that this marriage had never taken place. It was the beginning of all her heartaches and sorrows, stripping her of friends and family, a husband's love and affection, and, ultimately, the curse of which took the life of her only child of this most unhappy union. Further tragedies includes her being severed from the faith of her ancestors, deprived of communion with the Catholic Church, until the time her husband would most reluctantly sign an agreement that his and his wife's children would be reared and educated in the Catholic faith. Whether this demand is just or unjust is not our question presently, but it would make for an interesting exhibition I am sure." Roman turned to Reverend Shawe who slowly shook his head conveying to Roman that there would probably be plenty more stabs to the Church.

"Of course, Mr. Schmoll yielded to the requirement and Anna Maria thought herself about to be restored to the bosom of the Church. With the firm hope of being reconciled to her faith, she was eager to participate in the Holy Day of Ascension Thursday. As she longed for that sacred day, she would have never dreamed of the dark storm swirling overhead which was about to envelop her, deadening her to her husband and the world, the cloak of agony swaddling her like a shroud."

"At about the same time that she entered the box, the other parties had already departed the church. Alone with her priest, she knelt down, revealing to him her heart, concealing nothing from the young father confessor. But gentlemen, he wanted more. Her confession was not enough to satisfy his hungry heart. Oh, I shall not repeat the lewd questions to you for the sake of decorum; besides you have already heard them from the lips of the pitiable creature herself and are undoubtedly still fresh in your mind. But my good men, the defendant had a point in all this. There can be no question that his aim, his target was Mrs. Schmoll herself. He had known her before as a member of his congregation and he wished to know her even better." There were a few muted laughs.

"Mr. Blythe," the judge cleared his throat. "We get the point. Continue, mindful of the need for decorum."

Roman clutched his rosary beads as Blythe blathered on and on.

"The next thing we know, the defendant is north of town in the German settlement, supposedly on his way to baptize the child of the Irishman Patrick Fitzwilliams. The officers of the Law both informed us that the defendant, upon being placed under arrest, uttered under his breath, 'Mrs. Schmoll, traitor!' Betrayed him? How so? I think we all know.

"Gentlemen, I step aside now, merely a player upon the stage of this unfolding drama. In the words of Shakespeare, 'All the world's a stage and all the men and women merely players; they have their exits and their entrances, and one man in his time plays many parts...' Well, this was the part I played today. I have discharged my mind and fulfilled my obligation for the sake of justice. It will soon be time for you to discharge your duty and fulfill your obligations as jurors to acquit or condemn the prisoner at the bar. If you are satisfied beyond a reasonable doubt that he is guilty as charged, then you must condemn him. Should he not be required to drink from the dregs of his own lusts in order to redress his victim for the horrendous outrage he committed against her? Yet even if it were the very punishment of hell, it would not compensate her for what he has taken from her! No penance, no prison term, no compunction regardless of sincerity can ever regenerate her life as it was before she knelt before him in that confessional!

"Therefore, gentlemen, I close my arguments. Execute your duties faithfully for you are the minister of the law. Keep in mind the prisoner, the prosecuting witness, and the rule of law, so that in the sunset of your life you may look back upon the road you trod and can say, with all your heart, in the name of Almighty God, I did what I had to do.'"

Mr. Blythe closed his eyes and slowly walked over to his table.

"Thank you, counsel." The judge cleared his throat and looked to the defendant's counsel. "If the lawyer for the defense would please step forward to argue the case."

Mr. Thomas swayed out in front of the jury box. "Gentlemen of the jury: It is not by my choice that I appear before you today. Our first proposal, of which I favored, both professionally and personally, was that Mr. Jones would close with his arguments for the defense and Mr. Lockhart for the prosecution. But as you can see the young ambitious attorney, Mr. Chandler, is all too eager to get in the fray of things, so now all three attorneys for both sides will argue before you. There's no telling when we'll leave these chambers...."

"Gentlemen, I have with patience endured the prosecuting attorney and his assassination of the good character of the defendant! I do not think I can go on much longer, standing here before you, listening to the ignominious insults upon the Catholic Church, atrociously abominable accusations against the defendant, complete with detestable and odious lies about other liaisons with female penitents in Vincennes and elsewhere! Oh, I am sick with a grief of which there is no cure when I think upon the dignity of the priest seated here before you and the honor of his Church which has been so violently attacked during this trial which has become a national spectacle, turning this courtroom into a circus of sorts and the priest and his Church into a side-show! I am surprised the prosecution did not sell tickets!

"Even the mere proposition that the priest and Mrs. Schmoll might have entertained a consensual voluntary relationship, is so repugnant to my mind and revolting to the mind of the defendant, as to dishonor his Church and breach his duty to God! Not only is the defendant innocent of the charge of rape, but also he is entirely free of any impropriety towards Mrs. Schmoll, or any female penitents for that matter! Would that this poor man had never willingly left the shores of Europe to dare the Atlantic! Did he come to America only to experience torment at American hands? From our presence here it appears to be so.

"The supposition proffered by the prosecution is even more monstrous than the thought that Fr Weinzoepfel was untrue to his sacred vows! The whole Catholic world is waiting to see how one of its own ministers of the gospel is treated in this, the land epitomized as the land of religious liberty. If the accusations against the defendant had been true, then he would have been disowned by the Church and exposed to desolation, rejected and spurned, left miserably alone, being cast away into the outer darkness, left to wail and gnash his teeth, cut off from the land of the living, an excommunicate, defrocked, and reprobate priest! But no, this is not the case, not at all, not at all!

"If it please the Court, let me paint the picture for you, explaining how Mrs. Schmoll came to the decision to accuse the defendant of forced intercourse. I propose that the charges were instigated by her desire for revenge upon her priest. Again, here I am merely speculating. This is my opinion, my theory, although a plausible one. The priest is under the seal of the sacrament of confession and cannot even affirm that Mrs. Schmoll actually entered his confessional on that fateful evening of May the fourth, 1842. And let it be known that the priest has not told me anything concerning the subject of their confession, nor has he even intimated that Mrs. Schmoll was a penitent in his confessional, but I believe what happened in the confessional on that dreadful day was that the Reverend Roman Weinzoepfel, plain and simple, refused to grant Mrs. Schmoll absolution from her sins."

Roman squeezed his rosary beads tightly and held his breath at the theory proffered on his behalf in order to divine a motive for Mrs. Schmoll's charges against him. He could have stood and stopped the proceedings, explaining what truly happened, but he would not.

"No, what this entire scandal is centered upon is the personal vendetta of the Schmolls and the anti-Catholic, anti-immigrant agenda of the Nativists of this fine country," Thomas thundered "From start to finish this trial has been to discredit the Catholic Church in the eyes of the citizens of America and to denigrate the nature of the Catholic priesthood. The enemies of the religion of Reverend Weinzoepfel have prostituted the freedom of the press, especially the Whig party and their politically motivated editors. To the point, it is clear that the machinations of such presses originated here in Evansville at the desk of none other than William Chandler, the editor of the Whig publication, *The Evansville Journal*! And I might add that the same William Chandler is the very brother of one of the prosecuting attorney in this case, John Chandler!" There were groans from the prosecution side of the courtroom. The judge hammered his gavel to stop the murmuring. Roman looked up to see a red-faced John Chandler making eye contact with someone in the rear of the courtroom gallery. Turning around, Roman saw William Chandler holding his signature speckled hat standing in the rear of the room, leaning against the wall near the doorway.

"Hence, these Nativist Americans have destroyed the foundation upon which American justice is founded, namely, that the accused is innocent until proven guilty. From the way some of my fellow countrymen have behaved, I am amazed that the trial by jury is still intact in our nation!

"*The Evansville Journal* has been, from the first word of these accusations, the manufacturer of popular opinion. Note that just six days after the priest was charged, in its issue of the twelfth of May, 1842, a most biased account of the charges and attempt at a first trial appeared." Thomas held up a copy of the newspaper to the eyes of the jury. "This article, rather than reporting the story in an objective manner as journalists ought to do, is anything but an unprejudiced, objective account that it purports to be, but it was passed off to be an honest and fair account. In it the prosecution and its chief witness, Mrs. Schmoll, are lauded as bastions of truth, whereas it condemned the defendant as guilty of the charges, and not only the charges placed by Mrs. Schmoll, but *other, more serious charges*, of which, by the way, have never surfaced.

"Now allow me to defend Mr. Chandler in his initial newspaper account. Let us grant him the benefit of the doubt for his May Twelfth editorial. One could rightly exonerate him for his primal response of outrage and indignation, but it is in his subsequent newspaper accounts that he reveals the true nature of his purpose in repeating the calumny. But that is not the end of it, my dear jurors. Oh, no, the *Journal's* articles have now been supplemented by a pamphlet, purportedly written by Mr. Martin Schmoll, yet published by Mr. Chandler's press, reportedly to be, and I quote, '*a full and circumstantial account of the outrage.*' I happen to have a copy with me now." He held it up for the judge and jury to behold. "It is indisputably obvious that it was intended to taint public opinion, rendering it nearly, if not completely, impossible for the defendant to receive a fair and impartial trial!

"Permit me to read from it, if only for the length of a paragraph or two." Opening to the first few pages, he began to read aloud. "'Oh thou hoary lecher...thy polluted priesthood...who hast through all time filled thy land with whoredoms and iniquities...you cannot escape forever! Even now the laws of man are about to expose your fiendish and hellish wickedness...Dost thou not tremble at the fate that awaits you and your miserable fraternity?'" Thomas closed the pamphlet, returning it to the defense table.

"Now, honestly, gentlemen, can that be considered the work of an objective journalist? Is it not rather the work of a prejudiced mind? I am convinced, that the prosecution and the press, together, of which one member is John Chandler, and the brother to the very editor of

The Evansville Journal, have conspired to convict the defendant. However, for the sake of decorum, I will not knit together a theory from that connection, but I believe that it should be most obvious for any passerby to see the design of their motive.

"The combination of the prosecution and the press shows a conspiracy was afoot from subsequent articles." The lawyer opened a newspaper, preparing to read from it. "In one story, the editor wrote as if he knew what Mr. Schmoll was going to say on the stand, when in actuality, Mr. Schmoll never took the stand. Listen to this sentence: *it was to detail this conversation that Mr. Schmoll was sworn as a witness.* Excuse me, gentlemen, but I was not born yesterday and dare I hope you weren't either? How could the editor of the newspaper, a mere reporter, know of such an intimate detail? Mr. Schmoll was prevented from being examined by the prosecution or defense because the mob intervened in the administration of justice. There is no way the editor could claim such privileged knowledge unless he was privy to a prearranged plot or at least conversation with the lawyers or Martin Schmoll or both.

"Here is Mrs. Schmoll, a woman of loose morals, one who holds her own religion in disdain, yet mockingly seeks its sacramental treasures in hopes of cloaking her malicious heart. This is revenge, pure and simple. While endeavoring to obtain the grace of the sacraments, she was, at the very same time, treading upon and violating all of its sacred precepts. Almost immediately after receiving Holy Communion at Christmas Mass, she eloped with Martin Schmoll, a man she barely knew for a week, hence disregarding her father's best wishes, entering a covert marriage, yet desecrating another solemn sacrament of her Church.

"So what has Mrs. Schmoll gained? It causes her to be cut off from her father's affections, she is excommunicated from her Church, and she has since been degraded into an object of scorn among her family and former friends. Now, she has entered upon a marriage that she takes steps to rectify in the eyes of the Church. In that process her husband reluctantly enters into agreement that the children should be educated in the Catholic Church, and she then exhibits an obtuseness of spirit that takes her to the confessional where, in the words of one witness, Mr. Josiah Stahlhofer, she threatens to have revenge upon the priest if absolution is not granted her. Is that the attitude or disposition of a repentant sinner?

"And for those who say that she must have received absolution simply because she received communion on that morning of Ascension Thursday, must remember that it does not necessarily follow that she had received absolution, since a priest is strictly forbidden to deny holy communion to any of the faithful, except public, notorious, or scandalous sinners who have not done public penance. So with these exceptions, the Church forbids her priests from withholding communion from the communicant, whether he or she has received absolution or not, because by refusing the person the sacrament, it would cause suspicions among others and bring infamy upon the penitent. So to consider her reception of communion on the morning of the fifth of May 1842 to be proof positive that she received absolution is in error. Revenge is still a valid motive for her accusations against Reverend Weinzoepfel.

"So, you see, the priest could not have refused communion to her, although absolution may have been withheld, and this is more particularly the case since she went to confession while others were present. She, like Judas Iscariot, was free to eat of the Lord's body, hence eating her own condemnation, if she chose to do so. Her motive for receiving communion that morning is clearly evident. She defies the priest, and like Judas, dips her hand in the same dish, and goes out to betray him.

"Mrs. Schmoll claims that she was unconscious at the time of the pretended rape, yet she contradicted herself in front of witnesses. If she was unconscious, then how did she know she was ravished? I will not attempt to repeat everything that the witnesses said to indicate the alleged victim's contradictions in testimony, but I will reiterate some of the glaring inconsistencies.

"The jury will take note that Mrs. Schmoll claimed that she knew what was done to her until she was thrown on the floor, and then she lost her mind. Of course, I will not offer any commentary upon that remark. I believe the witness was referring to her losing consciousness.

"Allow me to draw upon another witness for the prosecution, Mrs. Webb. She is a resident of Cincinnati. While Mrs. Schmoll was in that fair city assisting the former prosecuting attorney, Jay Davis, in obtaining depositions for this trial, Mrs. Schmoll told Mrs. Webb that after the priest had grabbed her by the arm the two of them struggled on the floor for nearly ten minutes. It was when she tried to cry out that she passed out.

"Now, may I ask why did she not cry out at once instead of waiting until ten minutes into the struggle? And why has she swore that she fell down as one dead at the first touch of the priest, yet she told Mrs. Webb that they hauled about on the floor for ten minutes? And if she had been dragged across the floor, why then did her husband not notice his wife's soiled dress?

"Had she cried out, she surely would have been heard for the Catholic Church here is near the courthouse and in the midst of residences, not to mention the alleged victim's own home. No, she has reasoned carefully that since she has no alibi in failing to cry out, she has instead fabricated this ludicrous tale that she fainted immediately upon being touched. So, then, are we not allowed to ask, how she could know that the crime had actually been committed? Are we expected to actually believe this rubbish, no, pernicious, insidious prattle, that a person can be at the same time both alive and dead, or am I the only man in America who has laughed himself to sleep thinking upon such a ridiculous thought? No, gentlemen, what we have here is a calculated plot supplied by her prompters, those who think that the American mind is too sluggish to question someone claiming to be both dead and alive at the same time. I hold the American public to be a bit more reasonable than the Prosecutrix and her lawyers!"

Mr. Thomas then walked back to his seat and picked up the pamphlet. Holding it up high, he began again. "Mr. Schmoll, in his eloquent diatribe, claims that his wife did not communicate the particulars to him until the following Thursday afternoon after their noon meal. You will recall that the alleged crime took place the evening before, where, as several of the witness have testified, Mrs. Schmoll said she told her husband the details immediately after returning home from the church.

"I would also like to point out that on the evening of the alleged assault Mrs. Schmoll is said to have passed out immediately upon being touched by the priest, yet in an earlier sworn statement, she said she went into a frenzy and in her first words, she said she fell into a fit. Yet now she has her story all together and has chosen to ignore her earlier version. She has not said anything about a fit, has she? I would like to know which it is, did she have an epizootic, or did she up and die as she now wants us to believe? Or should I put the question again to her handlers, have the good gentlemen decided which it is going to be?

"While they attempt to understand that question—and you seek to answer it—I will return to the night when she returned home from the alleged crime scene. She claims that she was afraid to tell her husband of the outrage out of a fear that he would do injury to himself. But I ask, could it be that she feared being prohibited from attending the holy day Mass the following morning? Did she fear her husband's wrath due to the fact she had spent more time than he had anticipated in the church? Or did she not tell her husband of the abomination because she wanted to take communion the next day?

"No, what was going on, gentlemen of the jury, was that Mr. Martin Schmoll, knew that Catholic priests cannot reveal anything said in the confessional. So, in his unabashed hatred for the Catholic Church, he clearly orchestrated that his wife's tale of debauchery should occur during the act of confessing her sins in the confessional. Therefore, my dear jurors, the Schmolls were well aware that the priest could never take the stand to defend himself against the nefarious, calumnious charges.

"What will it take for you to see that the seal of confession is so sacred to a Catholic that the defendant would rather suffer an earthly injustice than breach the inviolability of the sacrament and sin against God and his Church, thereby suffering eternal damnation. Oh, yes, he would save his life, and he would walk away a free man, but he would lose his soul, and be defrocked and excommunicated.

"The seal of the sacrament is actually established for the benefit of the penitent, just as the law of jurisprudence places the legal counselor under obligation of secrecy to ensure the rights of the client. Only the client can reveal secrets, and so it is with the penitent. Only he or she can reveal the details of the confessional. The confessor is bound by his priestly vows and Canon Law to remain silent, even if under the threat of being sent to prison, unjustly accused of a crime he did not commit! I think we can look upon the Reverend Roman Weinzoepfel and see one who has truly fulfilled his moral obligations and is no purveyor of injustice!

"Mrs. Schmoll says it was so dark in the church, that she could scarcely see to read her prayer book, yet Mrs. Heinrich has sworn that when the priest joined them for dinner following hearing confessions that Wednesday evening, it was still daylight, there was enough light that they did not require candlelight at table.

"And upon this subject of daylight, let us turn to the prayer-book. Mrs. Schmoll claims that she carried her prayer-book with her to church and then also carried it home with her. Now, honestly, how did she manage that? If she was violently assaulted and ravished as she would have us believe, then when did she retrieve it? Now if she passed out and was dragged out of the confessional, sprawled upon the floor, and flung over a bench, where did she find it and when did she find time to find it if she was in the act of fleeing from the assailant? Did she drop it in the confessional? She says she had no muscular control, and yet we are to believe she could locate the missing book, pick it up, and all without the hindrance of the priest who just moments before had assaulted her in a way most odious!

"Did she retrieve the book after being assaulted in the most vile nature? Would not the prayer book be the least thing on her mind after receiving such treatment, particularly at the hands of her priest? Or was the priest so polite that after forcing himself upon his helpless victim he recovered the prayer book out from under one of the pews and kindly gave it to Mrs. Schmoll as she made her way out of the church? 'And, oh, Anna, dear, here is your prayer-book. You must have dropped it. I am glad I found it otherwise you would not be able and pray your penance.' Preposterous! The probabilities of her taking the time to find her book are zero to none! How absurd!

"Nay, this is further proof that nothing happened-absolutely nothing happened between Mrs. Schmoll and the defendant save that of the act of confession! There was no fainting, there was no seizure, there was no fit, there was no syncope, there was no loss of consciousness, nor was there a loss of the power of her limbs, and the utter falsity of these claims can be garnered and deduced from the mere fact that she carried her prayer-book home with her. Nothing happened! Otherwise someone else would have found her prayer book scattered to the floor the next morning.

"And pertaining to this business about her trying to read her prayer-book in the darkened confessional—let it be known that Catholics do not pray their penance in the confessional! Penitents only remain in the confessional for the duration of the confession and absolution, and then they depart to make way for the next penitent. A faithful Catholic says his prayers of penance in the church. To the devout Catholic the statements by Mrs. Schmoll concerning the sacrament of confession indicate that she is either not used to going to confession or else she is so unfamiliar with her Catholic faith, and its customs and traditions, so as to be ignorant and negligent of these important details. This definitely should leave one questioning whether she is Catholic at all. And if the ravishing did occur during the public hours while the priest was hearing confessions, would not any simpleton have invited his intended victim to an anteroom that would have been less visible to the public eye? As it was, they accuse Reverend Weinzoepfel of committing the outrage in the very sanctuary where he communes with God everyday. And as it is, Weinzoepfel is no simpleton! Far from it! He speaks four languages French, German, English, and Latin and is currently a professor at the Catholic Seminary in Vincennes!"

"Gentlemen of the jury, there is one last set of questions that you must help me grasp with understanding. These deal with Mrs. Schmoll returning to church the following day after the alleged crime. Who among us, would allow our own sister, to not only place herself in the very same confessional booth with a lecherous priest where just hours earlier the same priest had ravished a woman, but would also allow her to receive the communion from the hand of the same priest, a hand, mind you, which will place the wafer upon her very tongue? Who would even think of placing his sister in such danger of lechery? Yet Mrs. Schmoll did all of the aforementioned. If what she says about the priest is true, then why did she allow her sister to confess her sins to him and receive the Sacrament of the Altar from him? How can you seriously consider her testimony? You cannot. Therefore, you must acquit the defendant of all charges.

"Gentlemen, the more I examine this case, the more I realize that what is at stake here is the character of our nation. Little else besides this case has been spoken of in our communities for nearly two years. The volatile charges against the defendant have caused great excitement in Evansville and elsewhere in this country. According to the Bishop of Vincennes, even the pope in Rome is concerned for the fate of the defendant and indeed of the entire Church in the United States. If what I say were not so, then the stenographers from Europe would not be here in Princeton, Indiana, reporting upon and printing the proceedings of this trial in the capitals of European newspapers, now would they? No, my good men, what is at stake here is the American creed of religious freedom.

"Yet I ask, no, I beg you, to answer this question in the depths of your conscience: Shall we inflict our good Catholic citizens with the punishment due past sins of their Church during its most corrupt periods of existence? Were it not extraneous to the case at hand, I could raise the curtain upon another tragedy and the mantle I could lift would unveil a dark page from the history of Protestantism and show everyone that the weapons of fire and faggot have also been utilized by Protestants in acts of execution that would chill your blood with fear and trepidation, sending the prosecuting attorneys into sheer horror!

"So, shall we denounce and condemn Catholics for their past misdeeds while we revere Protestants who have cut the throats of Protestants and Catholics alike? Shall we crush the defendant in infamy for the sins of his Church in days gone by, while our own robes are soaked in the blood of martyrs? God forbid! To do so would do little more than resurrect the atrocities of the past and visit them upon the present.

"I can conceive of no situation more sinister than putting a Catholic priest on trial upon a charge involving the nature and character of his Church. I am not so naïve to think to be unaware of some Protestants, mostly Nativists Whigs, who have raised a hue and a cry for the condemnation of my client. Please know that there are many Protestants in Evansville who believe in the defendant's innocence, but one has not found any reports of this fact in the Whig press, such as *The Evansville Journal*. Perhaps Mr. Chandler could talk to his brother about that." There were groans from the gallery as John Chandler just stared at Thomas.

Thomas turned to the jury, pulled his golden chain from his pocket, and looked at his watch. He went back to his table and took a sip of water. He walked back near the foreman of the jury. "For the sake of your supper, I will not detain the jury much longer owing to the late hour. So, allow me to be brief as I close my arguments. Let me reiterate that the whole Church, pope, bishops, clergy, and laity alike are confident that the defendant, Reverend Roman Weinzoepfel, is innocent of all the charges placed against him. He is the innocent lamb led to the slaughter, the scapegoat weighed down with the sins of the Schmolls and driven to the city gate left to die, a symbolic sacrifice upon the altar of jealousy and prejudice!

"Oh, my good citizens and distinguished guests, this good priest has obeyed the laws of this great nation and did not flee from the arm of justice as some implied that he would! Mark my words; this man is guilty of the crime of rape no more than the rest of us! Take note, this priest has remained true to his word and true to the very country he came to serve despite some of its citizenry rising up against him to plunge him back into the violent sea.

"Would to God that men might be just! And if you find Reverend Weinzoepfel guilty and convict him—God knoweth how—he will continue to serve the Church from within his prison cell and even minister to his enemies by praying for their conversion!

"May God grant you the wisdom to discern the truth in this case." He closed his eyes briefly and sighed. "I dread that some of you may have a fear that there are too many Catholics coming to America. It is no secret that there has been arm-twisting in the taverns at night where some of you have taken your meals. Some of our friends have informed us that a couple of you jurors have received friendly *home visits* from some of the prosecution's supporters. I simply ask, that in the name of freedom and justice, and in light of the evidence we have given you, vote your conscience."

"Therefore, gentlemen, if you are able to rise above the din and influence of that biased pack of wolves called the Nativists, then you must be more than mortals. Regardless of what you do in the jury room, I beg you, for the love of justice, as well as that of religious liberty, forget that the defendant is a Catholic priest and regard him as nothing more than Mr. Roman Weinzoepfel, and I shall, with confidence, refer his case for judgment upon its own merits and utter nary a word in his defense."

He bowed his head slightly to the twelve men and then turned to Judge Embree. Over two hours had passed since Thomas had begun. The judge called for a lunch recess and the courtroom quickly emptied.

****

Following the recess, Roman reentered the courthouse with his defense team while the prosecution and Anna Maria entered from the opposite side of the chamber. The members of the jury took to the box followed by the judge. The noise of hundreds of feet on the wooden floor filled the room as everyone rose.

"Court is now in session," the judge banged his gavel. "The State of Indiana versus the Reverend Roman Weinzoepfel will now continue. If the lawyers for the parties would please approach the bench." After an initial meeting, the judge signaled for Chandler to come forward.

John Chandler strode around to the front of the courtroom as if it was his finest hour. Roman recited his beads but no longer so sure of their efficacy.

Roman sunk in his chair feeling like a caged animal. How he longed to be back home in Alsace riding *Bijou* through the valleys and forests where he grew up, taking his meals with his brothers and sisters, reliving the old days with his parents.

Mr. Chandler stood near the jury box, leaning in towards the jurors.

"Gentlemen of the jury, it is with great apprehension that I arise to execute the task before me. To engage in the prosecution of a fellow human being for such a heinous crime to which the prisoner at the bar stands charged, can never be anything but the most unpleasant and unsavory thing for a lawyer. I say all this despite the fact that I have made it my business to uphold the law of this great nation and consider it my sacred duty!

"May I also remind you that I am not entrusted with a public charge, for I am not the prosecuting attorney of this county. Nay, I have painfully remained on this case, in the position that I find myself after her original lawyer fled the scene for parts unknown. Exactly why he vanished is not yet clear. Perhaps he had been threatened with violence if he pursued this case against the priest, but I must admit that is pure conjecture on my part.

"Please do not misunderstand me, gentlemen, and think that I appear here because I desire to see this immigrant priest crushed under the hand of law. Not in the least. I appear here today out of a duty to my calling as a lawyer and the fact that Judge Embree asked that I serve as a prosecuting attorney with Judge James Lockhart. Were things otherwise, I would not be standing before you this morning asking that you remove this discontented prisoner from the public square and convict him of the unspeakable crimes of which he has been accused.

"So, then, where does one begin to bring a man down? To even ponder the punishments of the penitentiary causes me to shudder. No matter how loathsome I may find this position in which I find myself, I must adhere to the dictates of law. Therefore allow me to begin by giving you some understanding as to how I ended up standing before you this morning.

"My connection to this case, was, and has been, the topic of much conversation, both in the taverns, on the streets, and on the pages of the free press. Even within the walls of this courtroom, the defense counsel, Mr. Thomas, pettifogged me like no one's business. Imagine it, a Philadelphia lawyer himself, yet he dared lambaste me as a political opportunist, a Cotton Whig, state's rights advocate, anti-immigrant, anti-Catholic, anti-Roman, anti-papal, anti-anti-anti-anti, I can't remember what all I'm against!" He laughed, as did many in the gallery. The judge tapped his gavel and restored peace.

"For the sake of the argument, please put all the vituperative criticism from the defense out of your mind and focus upon what is really at stake here this morning in Princeton, Indiana. As a jury, the decision that you make will have repercussions well into the future concerning this country. Your names may be spoken in hushed tones years from now as being twelve of the most important Americans who ever lived in Indiana, or America, for that matter! But please do not let me influence your objective view into this matter at hand, namely the ravishing of one of Evansville's finest flowers, the deflowering of which has now affected her so badly that her own sacred vows to her husband have been unhinged! But did not the almighty say in holy writ, 'What God hath joined together, let no man put asunder!' and 'Woe to that man by which scandal enters the world?'

"Now, I must not get too carried away, but can one hardly blame me? Let us consider the defense counsel. Let us count the lawyers who are arrayed against the poor victim, a woman of virtue and honesty beyond doubt. I ask, is there anyone here, or anyone anywhere, who would not have pity upon this helpless woman, abandoned like an infant amongst ravenous wolves, and defend her to the very gates of hell! Certainly! Well, gentlemen, I stumbled across this orphaned waif when I saw the strength of career lawyers allied against her, ready to devour her and deliver her up to the Inquisitorial Roman tribunal of the Catholic Church!

"The notorious crusade the lawyers for the defense orchestrated against this poverty-stricken, friendless female is disgraceful! Every arrow in the quiver of slanderers was stretched across their legal bows and aimed for the purity of her heart. Oh, the sadness she has experienced. The terror she has braved would have rendered the strongest of men weak and puny! Yet I ask, have they impeached the witness' character? No, of course not! The citizens of this fair county, indeed the entire country, have had to endure the gossiping whispers and public calumny found in the press and heard from the Catholic pulpits! Every wicked tale of crime that hatred could devise was unleashed upon this defenseless woman, Mrs. Schmoll, and she received a second ravishing, far worse than the first!

"At this juncture of these proceedings I will not attempt to recount the stack of depositions which were taken and then testimony given at the beginning of this trial. May it please the judge and jury to see that the Holy Roman Catholic Church has attempted to completely sweep away one of her own members from its communal life, working to ensure the utter desolation of its innocent daughter for having dared expose one of its father confessors as a foul, lecherous ravisher! There is actually little left for me to show you except what the papists have tried to shroud in darkness, namely the sins of one of their priests.

"It was at the time of the former trial when I was approached by some dear friends of the victim who asked if I would lend my feeble knowledge and practice of law to argue her case against an already growing legal team made up of self-aggrandized legal hounds sniffing at notoriety, fawning all over themselves in the madness to defend the immigrant priest from what they called a slanderous campaign. The tempest-tossed victim, Mrs. Schmoll, was opposed by a most invincible array of legal talent. Of course, my good men, I informed them that they should employ someone of much more expertise than I, but they insisted that they could not obtain the services of anyone except me. What was I to do?" Chandler motioned to the jurors, his hands extended.

"I believed Mrs. Schmoll had been deeply wronged and I desired to defend her honor, yet when I looked over the horizon and beheld the wealth and sway that the Catholic Church was about to exercise against her I was greatly intimidated to say the very least. But I, concerned for the cause of justice, knew that if someone did not step forward to prevent her from being carried away to prison and the guilty being set free, I determined that no matter how incapable or ineffectual I might be, I would strive to prevent a greater injustice from occurring. Needless to say, I volunteered my services, accepting the case, and I refused to accept any payment of a fee. From that day unto this very hour in and out of court, I have applied myself to the charge, doing all within my power to prove this woman true to her word, though I am hardly up to the formidable task of out-maneuvering the likes of the defense lawyers that are present in this courtroom today.

"As the slanderous rumors concerning Mrs. Schmoll's character poisoned the atmosphere, I sought to investigate everything anew. I have operated with every intention that the moment I were to learn of a flaw in the character of the State's witness I would seek to confirm it, and if true, I would have immediately abandoned her to the winds of perjury. But, with each new attempt at smearing her good name, our cause served only to be strengthened!

"God knows—and anyone who knows me knows—that I bear no ill will towards the church affiliation of the defendant. I appear before you not so much to prosecute the prisoner at the bar as much to defend the prosecuting witness, and who knows, I may never engage in another criminal prosecution, but as for the case of the misfortunes heaped upon this virtuous woman, I will remain by her side to the end, so sure I am of her innocence!

"With that out of the way, I now move forward to consider the facts of the case before you. Yet I must admit that the evidence, being so fresh in your memories, need not be repeated, but only summarized. Given the nature of the testimony of the State's witness herself, it is especially not necessary to repeat for she was *and is* her own best advocate. Her very presence and narration of the events of that terrible evening, May the fourth, eighteen hundred and forty-two, a date which will be etched in her memory forever as well as all of our hearts in America, manifested to all who beheld her testimony under oath such eloquence of spirit that there can be no doubt that what she has said is true. In fact, I might as well sit down and rest my case with confidence that the conviction of the defendant must follow. I am sure that all involved would welcome the opportunity to go home and resume their regular routine.

"Nevertheless, and however desirable that might be for me, or for all of you, I am compelled to persist and must remain on my feet for the duration of my closing arguments. As we saw, the defense tried to discredit the chief witness' reputation, but they have failed, and miserably so. No motive has been found, nor could one ever be found for this absurd idea that she has fabricated the charges. Her testimony alone must stand if conviction is to be the result of this tribunal's deliberation. Whether it stands or falls we shall, I believe, discover forthwith. But allow me to state that of all the cases of rape reported, I challenge the defense to show me where the testimony of the victim was not sufficient enough to secure conviction of the offender. The nature of rape is such that normally it excludes the possibility for witnesses other than the perpetrator and the victim. Therefore, if we are to follow the logic of the defense and apply it unilaterally to all of jurisprudence, one must forever shut the door of justice to the victims of rape unless there are other witnesses besides the victim herself! Preposterous, I say, and I dare say, you say as well!"

"As for the supposed contradictions in Mrs. Schmoll's testimony which the defense counsel seems intent in placing all the hopes for acquittal are actually of the most inconsequential and immaterial nature. Is it right, is it fair to allow our trust in Mrs. Schmoll to be shaken because over the past nine months she, in deep sorrow and agony of spirit, has given slight variations upon exactly what happened in the hours following her gruesome violation? Who among us could say we could hold our memory intact or responsible for all that may have been said since the occurrence of this perpetually talked of sordid affair?

"Is our witness not of good fame? There is no blemish upon her soul. Yet Messrs Jones and Jones and Dixon and Thomas have all claimed that she has no general character! What, you say? She has endured the past months and has been the constant subject of the talk of this whole country! And during all this time she has been under close surveillance of her legion of enemies!

"No character! Oh, yes, we are all aware that the holy doctor of theology, the Right Reverend De La Hailandière, the Catholic bishop of Vincennes, has pronounced her as a 'notorious, lying, shameless girl.' And in strict compliance with the mandate of their bishop, his obedient sheep have charged her with every sin known to man! Why, I must say, that in the space of an hour or an afternoon, or a day, I have been taunted by the devotees of the defendant and heard outrageous tales that the defenseless Mrs. Schmoll is guilty of lying, perjury, theft, and prostitution in all its forms, from simple adultery up to incest with her bald-headed father, who I hear is now quite ill, very possibly on his deathbed even as I speak, so sickened by the abuse that he and his beautiful daughter have had to endure.

"She has been painted as black as Satan himself, yet she is as white as snow. There is nothing her lynx-eyed enemies won't do to try and destroy her reputation. But I ask, why is it that they have so vilified our client? I believe it is simply because she dared reveal the sins of this criminal priest!

"Gentlemen, the prosecuting witness is of good reputation, no, I say of the very best name, which has enabled her to walk through the furnace of hatred and has come forth not only intact, but like Meshach, Shadrach, and Abednigo of old, she has emerged from the fiery heat of calumny without even a scent of smoke! Oh, I tell you I am so proud of her demeanor throughout this whole ordeal.

"Now the defense has made a point to show that the victim did not report the incident immediately and wondered why the delay. The answer is plain and simple. She was influenced by undo fear of her ravisher. As you will see, there was a good reason to not reveal the entire matter to her husband immediately.

"The truth is that from the time of the crime until after she had returned from receiving the sacrament of the altar there was a space of eighteen hours. It is true that she told some of the tale to her husband, yet she did not complete the account until after she had returned from the Holy Day Mass. The defense then raised the question in everyone's mind exactly why the victim of a horrendous outrage, as was committed against Mrs. Schmoll, would return less than eighteen hours to the presence of the ravisher and receive from the same hands which had polluted her the most holy sacrament of the Eucharist! What an infernal and freakish inconsistency! Who could believe the woman who would return to the same man she claims violently ravished her the previous evening? I know that I certainly would not. But the circumstances of this case are unique and quite different, my good men, and as I have said, there are exceptions to every rule. This is one such case.

"For those who are not acquainted with the Catholic faith or enlightened concerning the necessity of taking the sacrament during the Easter Season, allow me to explain. The dogmas, doctrines, and customs of that church are quite foreign to our way of thinking. Those of us who have taken the time to decipher the motives that commanded her to go to church understand why she did what she did. I dare say that the defense knows exactly why as well, but were they to admit it; they would reveal that Mrs. Schmoll's testimony is anything but pretended.

"For a 'good Catholic' is known to regard the minister of his faith as another Christ and therefore that of itself would be sufficient reason for anyone to pause in their thoughts whether to expose the priest or not. In their doctrine, the priest sits in the tribunal of penance as the penitent's legitimate judge. The Catholic honors the priest as he would Christ, and it is out of this belief that Mrs. Schmoll would have feared the ravisher. Given the devotion of a Catholic to his church, it is not hard to see why she was reluctant to expose the pastor to the law knowing what disgrace and dishonor would befall her church, in fact, the entire Roman Church.

"One might say, 'all right, that accounts for her delay in telling her husband, but why would she dare return to the reprobate within the same twenty-four hour period? Why would she risk herself to receive from the foul priest the consecrated wafer in which she believed her Savior to be truly present?' The witness herself gave the reason on the first day of examination when she stated that she took the sacrament on Ascension in order to fulfill her duty, it being a holy day, upon which the Church obligates her to attend Mass. Had this not been the case, she probably would have not received the Eucharist, let alone attend Mass. The next day, you will recall, the witness was recalled and stated that according to the customs of her church, she could not eat until she had partaken of the sacrament, which, to me, seems a tolerably strong motive and she was of the impression that if she did not do so, she would be forever lost!

"She had been taught from the time she was a little girl that she must observe the 'Easter duty,' that is confess ones sins and take the sacrament of the altar within the Easter Season, otherwise suffer eternal perdition! So, you see, if she had told her husband of the outrage, he would have naturally prevented her from doing so. No, her behavior was exemplary! It was done out of a fear of hell and the loss of heaven! The counsel for the defense is missing the opportunity to honor one of their own as a champion of Church Doctrine and Canon Law! She, being a good Catholic, has obeyed every precept of Holy Mother Church!

"If it pleases the court I shall read from the Council of Trent on the matter." He fidgeted with his spectacles, which he had been holding in his hand, raising them up to his face. Slowly pushing them over his ears and down upon the end of his nose, he continued. "It reads, 'the Church has decreed that whoever neglects to approach the Holy Communion once a year at Easter, subjects himself to excommunication.' And gentlemen, lest there be any confusion as to the length of the Easter Season, and whether Ascension Day can still be considered Easter, allow me to further impugn your ears by quoting from a Papal Bull of Pope Pius VIII." He held up a paper and read the Council of Baltimore's decision to extend Easter time in the United States to Trinity Sunday on account of the shortage of priests and the great distance between mission churches.

"So, we can clearly see that Mrs. Schmoll had a very real fear that if she were to miss Mass on account of Mr. Weinzoepfel, she may never get to Mass during Easter time. It was well known that the dear Curé of Evansville, Reverend Antony Deydier, had left town Easter night of March, 1842 and was on business in the east, so the defendant was the only sacramental minister in Evansville at the time. It was also common knowledge that the defendant was not administering the sacraments at Assumption Church every Sunday in Evansville due to his missionary assignments. Mrs. Schmoll, therefore, had no foreknowledge that she would be able to receive the Eucharist anywhere else but there on Ascension Day, the fifth of May, 1842.

"Catholics—unlike Protestants—are totally dependent upon their sacred ministers to provide for their spiritual care. This posed another dilemma for the victim. She knew that, according to the Council of Trent, only a validly ordained priest could administer to her the sacrament of the Eucharist, as it is with the sacrament of penance, or confession.

"Therefore, the priest, any priest, represents the person of Christ, and the minister of the sacrament, be he good or bad, validly consecrates and confers the sacraments. This was at all times a fixed and well defined doctrine of the church, is established beyond all doubt by the great theologian, Saint Augustine, who made it clear that the efficacy of the sacraments do not depend upon the holiness of the minister. If we can infer from the Gospel of Saint John, Judas Iscariot himself conferred baptism upon many believers, yet after he had fallen, those believers did not require to be baptized again. So it is with the Eucharist, whether it is ministered by holy or unholy hands, it is still validly consecrated. The faith of the Catholic Church teaches that the grace of the sacraments do not rely on the merit of the minister, but on the merits of our Lord and Savior, Jesus Christ! Mark my word, gentlemen, how well this teaching is in conformity with the testimony of the witness. Her treatment by the priest was irrelevant when it came to her obligation to fulfill her Easter duty. It would be presumptuous in the least to dare speak on behalf of her church, but in the State's opinion she is a faithful daughter, true to church teachings—unlike the defendant."

"Well done, Mr. Chandler, if I didn't know better, I'd think you were ready to ask for the sacraments yourself!" Mr. Thomas stood, interrupting the prosecutor. "A little more, and I shall be convinced of the defendant's guilt!"

"Thank you, Sir." He smiled at Thomas. "The defendant and his good bishop continue to denounce and slander the good name of this fine woman, Anna Maria Schmoll." Chandler began quoting from the Council of Trent and other Catholic religious authorities upon the sacred nature of the Eucharist and the confessional. It reopened Roman's wounds, pouring on the salt. He envisioned the mysteries of the rosary in his mind, mouthing the words on each bead so that he did not have to listen to that man berate his faith and his congregation to the court and the world. The louder Chandler grew, the more fervently Roman prayed. After the fifteenth mystery, and several difficult prayers for his persecutors, the prosecutors, Roman thought the voice of Chandler had shifted in its sarcasm. He tucked his rosary away and listened.

"I should like to know how a wife would be disgraced simply by marrying the man who loved her? The only disgrace I know of is a church that would dare punish a woman for disobeying its rules in order to marry the man she loves. I should also like to know where the Church gets its foundation for the idea that Anna Maria either was or could be refused forgiveness, even if she had been living in adultery. This is news to me. I had supposed that so-called mortal sin forever shut the gates of paradise to the sinner unless a humble, repentant heart wiped out the sin with the proper penance. Perhaps I am mistaken?"

285

"I have already demonstrated that Mrs. Schmoll was abiding by the explicit rules of her church to partake of the sacrament of Holy Communion under pain of excommunication, or in her words being 'forever lost.' She could only receive it from the hands of the 'officiating priest,' namely Weinzoepfel, and that it mattered not whether he was holy or unholy, since the sacrament was valid. As anyone here can see, it is obvious that she has a deep and abiding faith, albeit Catholic. Now, the question as to why the victim waited more or less eighteen hours to tell her husband of the outrage committed has, I believe, been adequately answered with the truth. This difficulty was the only circumstance that seemed to fly in the face of her story, but I trust that all acknowledge that she was bound to her God and his Church.

"Why did she not report the matter to the sheriff, you ask? Simple. She did not desire to ruin her congregation by exposing the lechery of the Evansville priest before the wide world, while at the same time she was under the feeling of responsibility to reveal the deed to her husband. It was with the hope of keeping the matter private that she was able to get Mr. Schmoll to wait until he was calm before he went to talk with the defendant.

"What woman, fresh from such a bench of perversion, would not have sought a moment of solitude before falling into her husband's arms? Yet because of her religious duties, she did not desire to tell him. Can you imagine the agony? I cannot!

"Let us recall that the place where the alleged crime occurred is twenty-five feet from the street, surrounded by a high board fence. The priest must have felt secure that he would not be discovered due to the late hour. I will give him the benefit of the doubt, nevertheless, and say that I don't believe there was much deliberation about what he did to his penitent. Quite simply, I believe he was a young priest sincerely trying to be true to his vows of chastity, a difficult experiment for an unmarried man, I might add, and quite honestly, I postulate that he was overcome by the frenzy of the moment and could restrain himself no longer. It is a wonder we do not hear more tales of situations where the frail mortals who are forced to give up natural relations in exchange for the frock. I can think of no other setting where a man would be so likely to be overcome with passion or more strongly tempted to yield to his lust and commit the most vile act of rape, than that of a lonely, young, red-blooded male, who as a

Catholic priest, has made a vow that he will not even look upon a woman, and yet in his priestly duties he places himself in the closest proximity to young and lovely penitents, whereby the lusts of the flesh and sins of desire are enkindled into red-hot flame of such an intensity that—"

"If the prosecution would refrain from titillating the jury, in fact, all in the courtroom," the judge cleared his throat, with an embarrassed look. "Please remember the need for decorum."

"My apologies to the court, your Honor." He nodded reverentially. "You will also recall that the priest never once denied the charges, either alone with Mr. Schmoll or once at the Schmoll home face to face with the victim herself. But gentlemen, can you imagine the mind of a man, who upon hearing from his victim herself, 'you are the man,' that he merely stated, 'if I did it, then I am the worst man in the world.' Recall as well the third time he is faced with the facts, learning of the charges from officer Curl, far from denying it, he angrily responded by calling Mrs. Schmoll a traitor for exposing his hellacious deed to the law!

"His excuse for seeking to leave Evansville was to go to the Fitzwilliams' farm to perform a baptism, but we know the truth, he was fleeing from the scene of his crime supposedly to inform his bishop of the matter. And if he was off for Vincennes, and not Canada, what was his motive for going to Vincennes? I dare say that he was endeavoring to procure, through the intercession of Bishop Hailandière, the benefit of clergy. It's a historical fact that the Catholic Church has declared for its clergy immunity from civil prosecution—"

"Mr. Chandler," Judge Embree interrupted, "you had best confine yourself to the evidence at hand and not conjecture upon the tenets of the Catholic Church."

"Your Honor," Mr. Jones stood up, "We have no objection to the gentlemen's course, but his comments will require us to set forth Church teachings."

"The counsel will confine himself to the evidence." The judge put his head down, possibly growing tired of the long-winded Chandler.

"I have a right to show that his motive in going to Vincennes was to secure the bishop's assistance in shielding him from the law."

"The gentlemen will refrain from insinuating that it is an historical fact that the Church asserts or asserted supremacy over civil tribunals." Embree was visibly perturbed. "Besides, this has nothing whatsoever to do with the evidence at hand!"

"Very well, Your Honor. I will therefore restate my ground and refer to the *legal* fact, and with your permission, and my good friends on the other side of the aisle not objecting, I will read from Professor Blackstone."

"You may—but only if it is pertinent to the evidence."

"Oh, it is *most pertinent*." Chandler opened a book, thumbing through the pages. He found his place and began anew. "*The benefit of clergy was the claim of the Catholic clergy to immunity and exemption from municipal jurisdiction for offenses subjecting the offender to capital and corporeal punishment.*" He slowly closed the book and looked at the jury. "Now, by no means, am I implying that this is the doctrine of the church today, but the defendant is a handsome young lad, a recent émigré to this country, with no knowledge but from what he may have read in some old books while he was shut up behind the walls of some European monastery. Therefore, his conduct confirms that he was fleeing the civil judiciary to the ecclesiastical tribunal at Vincennes, of which the distinguished Canon Lawyers, the Reverends Shawe and Monseigneur Martin were members." He looked at the priests, nodding to them.

"At this time I would like to quote an interesting poem by Jean Jacques Rousseau, a Catholic, I believe,

> A youth to his confessor went,
> his absolution to obtain,
> and undergo the punishment
> the holy father should ordain.
> 'Father,' says he, 'six times I've been,
> by carnal passions led astray.'-
> 'Six times! Oh fie! So oft to sin,
> a rosary for your penance say.'
>
> But puzzling more than all the rest,
> Was the last penitent that came,
> For me, eleven times, confessed,
> He'd played at that same carnal game.
> 'Eleven times! Vile wretch! By heaven,
> I've no such number on my roll.

Do it once more, to make it even,
then say two rosaries for the whole."

Simultaneously, James Jones, Benjamin Thomas, and Archibald Dixon were on the feet, crying out in objection.

"Counsel must limit his comments to the facts and stop putting the Catholic Church on trial!" James Jones was livid, his face red behind his beard.

"Sustained!" The judge whacked the gavel. "Mr. Chandler will confine himself to the evidence!"

Chandler only smiled and looked to the jurors. "As I can see in your eyes, my dear men, I have already transgressed upon your good natures longer than kindness can endure, so I close by recommending that you find the defendant guilty as charged. And even though I bear him no ill will personally, nor harbor any latent prejudice towards his religious affiliation or foreign status, I am convinced of his guilt. Therefore, it is with the most fervent confidence that the gentlemen of the jury will calmly yet with strong resolve and without bigotry on either side, ponder the evidence before them and convict the defendant of rape."

He turned to the judge, then the defense. Then, stepping closer towards the jury, he inhaled a deep breath and put his left hand to his mouth while his right pulled out a handkerchief. He wiped his neck and chin with it before exhaling his final words. "Gentlemen of the jury, the fate of America rests in your hands. Whether we will allow lecherous—" Chandler coughed, choking on the word, but not rendering it unintelligible. It was obvious to Roman that he had coughed out the word *priests*. Roman was seated at an angle and saw the faces of all of the Catholic clergy seated behind him. They shifted in their seats, clearly agitated. He thought Elisha Durbin was about to stand and speak when Chandler regained his composure. Roman had learned over the course of the trial what a fantastic actor John Chandler could be. "As I was saying, whether we allow lecherous *men*...to prowl our towns and cities lurking for women and girls unawares is up to you to decide." Chandler paused, stiffening his upper lip. "Whatever you decide...may God have mercy on us all." He stepped back away from the jury bench, took the handkerchief and wiped away tears and sweat from his face.

Chandler had spoken for two and a half hours. The judge adjourned about five that evening for a supper hour recess.

An hour later court was reconvened and Mr. Dixon prepared to launch his defensive on behalf of Roman. Although a Whig, Dixon held no outward prejudice towards Catholics. Actually he held no prejudices towards any organized religion since he believed that a man's conscience should be his guide as long as he lived a good life and helped his fellow man. Roman had a difficult time reconciling the man's religious indifferentism to his own deeply held convictions about the Catholic faith, as well as Dixon's view of the Negro as an inferior creature born only to serve the superior white race.

Nevertheless, Dixon had gone to the trouble of defending him and seemed to believe in his innocence. Never in his life had he ever spent so much time with so many Protestants. There was a time in his life when he would have nothing at all to do with Protestants. Now they surrounded him. And some were risking their lives and fortunes by defending him. It caused him to question his own prejudice.

Dixon pulled his matchbox from his topcoat and lit his pipe. He stepped out in front of the jury and took a few puffs before he began. "Gentlemen of the jury: some of my fellow Whigs have called me a traitor to the cause of Whiggery and charged me with treason that I would even dare approach this very courthouse to defend an alleged lecherous monk. Yet it is not by some political conspiracy that I appear before you today. There is a rumor that I am a *Big-Whig*, or one of the biggest toads in the puddle, so the learned counsel, Mr. James G. Jones of Evansville petitioned me to lend my legal services to the cause of the defendant. Indeed I had heard the cry for justice across the waters of the Ohio River in the foothills of Kentucky, so I appear before you here. I sincerely believe that an injustice committed in Indiana today may very well become a threat to justice in Kentucky tomorrow." He took another puff off the pipe and looked at John Chandler.

"Oh, the malicious rumors never cease to abound. Our client has a character at stake in this case as well, gentlemen. He is a foreigner, and when he came to the United States, he came as a volunteer missionary. His faith evidently means everything to him for he was willing to sacrifice all to come to America. His devotion to God and his love for his fellow man is second to none! Why, he has been known for his self-imposed poverty, living the most austere lifestyle, even more strict with himself than a Carthusian, wearing a hair-shirt and depriving himself of sleep so that he might pray more, fasting time and time again, living only on bread and water for days, his only nourishment being the work of God. Oh, no, one does not find the libidinous and disgraceful portrait of a wretch that the prosecution has painted for you."

Roman was embarrassed at the saintly exaggerations. He was no saint. He knew himself all too well.

Meanwhile, Dixon continued now reviewing the evidence gleaned from the testimony and he carefully and meticulously pointed out every inconsistency in the testimony of the Schmolls as compared to the defense witnesses. He talked on and on trying to emphasize to the jury the veracity of Mrs. Good's testimony. His pipe had gone out, but he still had it in his hand as he motioned with his hands.

"I must observe that one of the most inconsistent circumstances of this case concerns the alleged fainting spell. Anna Maria has testified that she fainted immediately following the act of consummation and states that she recollects being penetrated just before fading away into unconsciousness. Yet Mrs. Mary Good has testified that Anna Maria told her that as soon as the priest took hold of her while still in the confessional, she fell down as one dead and knew no more. Of course you will recall the obvious questions, 'if you fell down as one dead, then how did you know you were ravished?' You will recall that she had no answer but to say that the priest had her by the arm when she regained her consciousness and, besides, he had kept her in the church too long. She then questioned her why she did not try to resist him or cry for help, but she merely answered that she could not for she was dead. Mrs. Good then pointed out to Anna Maria that if she were dead then there would be no way for her to know anything, for the dead are dead. It should come as no surprise that the state's witness became mute at this time and would speak no further with Mrs. Good. Gentlemen, if Mrs. Good is telling the truth, and there is no compelling reason to believe she is not, then her testimony proves that the Schmolls have perjured themselves."

Dixon walked up to the jury box and looked intently at each juror, sure to make eye contact. "Gentlemen, the priest cannot be found guilty of the charges found in the indictment. And if there remains even a wee bit of a rational doubt concerning the guilt of the accused then the law requires an acquittal of the accused. Remember always

291

that the accused is cloaked with the presumption of innocence. Therefore, with that being said, I believe I can retire peacefully tonight with the full knowledge that my client is in no danger of a guilty verdict. No honest person could regard this priest as guilty for it is inconceivable that this frail priest ravished Mrs. Anna Maria Schmoll. Please know that it was not my intention to visit any more evil upon the brow of this poor woman, but for the sake of justice I did what I had to do, namely, reveal the truth."

Dixon put his pipe in his pocket and leaned on the rail of the jury box. "Gentlemen of the jury, when you begin the deliberation process, know that the eyes of the nation and even those abroad look to you to faithfully execute justice."

It was well past the Vesper hour and the lamplighters were hastening to their task when the judge adjourned court until nine o'clock the next morning.

Chapter 23

Summation

9 March 1844

The judge called for order and summoned the attorneys to approach the bench. After preliminary remarks by the judge, James G. Jones was called to address the jury.

"Gentlemen of the jury," Jones began, slowly stroking his beard with his right hand and pacing across the floor in front of the men. "I will not endeavor to close the defendant's case with a flourish. If at any time while I am speaking of testimony should I misstate it or misrepresent one of the parties involved I should like to be corrected by you or one of the counselors. I tell you this due to the sheer fact that I have been hearing testimony upon this case for upwards of twenty one months and during those nearly two years time I have thought so much of this case, actually little else, that I am having difficulty remembering what was sworn here and what I heard elsewhere. I apologize for my lack of ability, but I believe you will be gracious enough to give me the benefit of doubt.

"Here I shall freshen your memory of Mrs. Schmoll's testimony. She says that while in the confessional the defendant latched onto her arms, and throwing her backwards upon the floor, he carried out his malevolent designs. Why then did she not cry out or offer resistance? She says his grasp rendered her dumb and paralyzed every muscle and bone in her body. Although she had lost all ability to protest or resist his advances, she maintained consciousness until the deed was consummated. At that point she swooned and knew nothing more until she awoke upon a bench with the defendant splashing her face with holy water." James kept pacing back and forth in front of them.

"Why did she not then sound the alarm? Or was she still mute? Not at all, for she tells us that immediately she exclaimed in a hushed voice, Oh, God! What have you done to me?' Would not the first response be to scream and alert the neighborhood? Why, the church building is hemmed in on all sides by homes, and besides, Mr. Schmoll's home is just beyond the church some distance from the spot where the abomination is said to have been committed. He may very well have heard his wife's pleas for help. She would have had but only raise her voice and he would have been at her side to apprehend the offender at once!

"Why did she then fail to rush away and go to her husband? Was she still powerless? Not in the least for she told you that she picked up her prayer book from the bench and calmly walked home. She must have been very calm because her husband did not, as he said, see anything in her visual appearance that would have warranted a suspicion that violence had been done to her person. So rather than going straightaway to her husband, collapsing in his arms, and divulging all the horrid details of the alleged ravishment, what does she do? She avoids her husband who is waiting at the gate for her return and attempts to go in the front door of the house. Why? Why does she do this? Is this not the most unnatural behavior of such a virtuous woman as Mrs. Schmoll to act immediately after being viciously molested? Indeed it is strange. Strange indeed." Jones stopped walking, stroked his chin again, and pressed his beard upward.

"Is there any one of you in the jury box who believes that if his wife had been violated she would conceal the attack from you?" Jones leaned over the rail, eyeing each juror, pausing to a point of uncomfortable silence before continuing. "No reason whatsoever, no matter how compelling, could keep her from declaring the outrage to you. Are we not in agreement? Every sinew in your body and every feeling in your soul tells you that it is next to impossible to believe that a woman would hide such a monstrous deed from her beloved spouse. Unless the husband was not so beloved..." Looking down, he paused, and gently tugged at his beard.

"Gentlemen, the truth of this entire affair has been hidden for nearly two years from the public eye. Today, I believe the veil, which has draped the truth for so long, is about to be pulled back." His voice grew in intensity. "With your patience already strained, if I could beg your indulgence for a little longer I believe that I am about to uncover the real events of that Ascension eve some twenty-one months ago in the Church of the Assumption at Evansville, Indiana.

"Return with me, in your minds, to the moment when Mrs. Schmoll returned to her home that Wednesday evening after confessing to the defendant. She sees her husband impatiently awaiting her return to perform the rest of her household chores, not the least being her duties of getting his supper prepared! Is it any wonder why she stayed late in the church? The poor woman needed a respite from the tyranny of her husband's rage and drunkenness. He was, and is, a jealous man, and he never did like the fact that his wife had spent time with the defendant in a purely spiritual relationship, namely that of priest confessor to penitent parishioner. A relationship, I might add, is similar to the relationship between an attorney and his client.

"Yet Mr. Martin Schmoll could not see clear enough to understand this, so volatile was his jealous rage, and his suspicion wild with imaginings that the priest had plotted to have a relationship with his wife. He didn't even trust his wife with the defendant. He believed their relationship to be mutually satisfying. So when Mrs. Schmoll encountered her husband at the gate of their home that evening, she saw the look of terror in his eyes and was anxious and afraid to even walk past him for fear of what he might do to her for being away at the church for so long a time. She had seen the look on his face before. It was the look of a husband with a suspicious glare that his wife has been unfaithful. When Anna Maria Schmoll entered into the presence of her husband she saw in his eyes a jealously blazing fire of envy, that 'green-eyed monster,' which has plunged many a men into homicidal rages. Crazed with spite, he accused her of committing adultery with '*that priest*'.

"Mr. Schmoll believes that his wife copulated with her priest, insinuating that their forbidden love had been consummated inside the defendant's church! Can you imagine his thought! Oh, such forbidden fruit is so delectable! One can imagine the fiery passion Martin Schmoll's imagination conjured up between his wife and the defendant! Can you imagine what his fury must have roused in his tender, beloved wife? Horror inconceivable! I'm sure he told her to go get him his supper after berating her, accusing her of the foulest of deeds. She knew he was a jealous man, but this was the height of his explosions of temper and his surliness and overly suspicious, paranoid heart drove her over the brink of despair!

"So, why does she not at once deny the charges of unfaithfulness like any woman would have done regardless of the truth of them or not? Because denial would not satisfy her husband's ravenous and unshakable conviction that she had betrayed him.

"He had watched her go to the church and impatiently waited for her return. When her husband asked her why she stayed so late at the church, she said, 'I am not done yet.' This did not appease his anger, so she walked away. It was in her silence that she took time to ponder her alternative responses to his questions.

"That night, Schmoll and his wife retired to the bedroom, but both remained awake. He because he believed his wife to be an adulteress and she because she had been accused of adultery and assaulted in a most degrading fashion by the man who was to be her helpmate, her intimate husband, her God-ordained marital partner. She sighed long and loud, and continued doing so throughout the night until finally she thought of some means to stay her husband's hand and take away the charge of infidelity. At that, she began crying. This caused Martin to suspend his wrath for a moment and ask her if she was sick. She said, 'Oh, no; but I have something to tell you.' What was it she told him at that late hour, the details of her ravishing? No, not yet. In order to gain sympathy from the man she loved, she told him the tale about the priest's alleged inappropriate questions concerning her and her husband's connubial relations, which the defendant allegedly claimed did not belong to the confessional and told her not to tell her husband.

"Yet this did not appease the husband. Would it for any of you? Certainly not! You would forthwith demand the balance of the story! Her husband wanted to know what else the priest did. You can see the vexed man sitting up in the bed, demanding her to come out with the rest. His passion was now rekindled. Recall Mr. Schmoll's words, if he, the defendant, did that, then he did more. That's real whoremonger talk and proves to me that he is a lewd man and would not stop at that. There's something more and I must know it!'

"Well, gentlemen, she realized she had made a serious mistake, an error in judgment. What was intended to extricate herself from the target of his rage, had implicated the defendant in a deed most foul! She then tried to hide behind the benefit of Catholic doctrine by pointing out that she could not reveal anything that had taken place in the confessional.

"Oh, there would be no question if the state's witness would simply approach the bench and reveal the entire bogus tale in front of us all and put an end to our speculations and ruminations upon the truth when she has possessed it all along." Jones paused, and looked at Mrs. Schmoll. She kept her head turned away. "My question is, why did she not go on and give the remainder of the story? Is there any woman alive who would give the details of her ravishing in such a piece-meal account? No! Think about it, gentlemen. Here were the husband and wife upon their marriage bed, in the dead of night, together, talking, her husband civil and concerned for her after erupting in a flash of harsh words that evening, and yet she stops there with her narrative. Would she not have finished telling her husband the grievous details of being ravished had it truly happened?

"I am convinced that Mrs. Schmoll realized she had made matters worse. She now had to either refuse to speak any more or take more time to manufacture another tale. She compromised and said to her husband that if he would wait until morning she would reveal more details, never mind the fact that she had just told him she could say no more owing to the sacred nature of the confessional!

"Now, this was to her advantage. She reflected upon her husband's jealousy and saw that the late hour with which she departed the church, the fact that she tried to avoid him upon returning, and her cryptic reply that she was 'not done yet,' gave him reason to think she had a guilty conscience. Therefore she must have concluded that the only way for her to escape her husband's gathering storm was to admit that the priest did more than ask ribald questions. It was then that she constructed the story of how the priest had forced himself upon her. If she were pressed as to why she failed to cry out, she prepared the excuse that as soon as the priest took her by the arm she had instantaneously fallen helpless and speechless, and fainting, remaining unconscious until the defendant splashed holy water in her face!

"But, my dear men, before she was able to give her account to her husband an unexpected event took place. The morning following the alleged rape was perpetrated, Mrs. Schmoll's younger sister, Miss Caroline Long, came to her house. Miss Long has testified that she had come to see if her sister would accompany her to church to go to confession and attend the Holy Day Mass. In the process, Mrs. Schmoll explained she had confessed the evening before. She then lent her sister the white bonnet, the broken bonnet, mind you, that she had worn to the church the evening before, and sent her sister to the church alone for the purpose of confessing to the same priest whom Mrs. Schmoll alleges raped her twelve hours earlier!

"What are we to make of this? Mrs. Schmoll did not expect her sister that morning, so these facts disturb her carefully concocted story. If Mrs. Schmoll had actually suffered at the hands of the defendant the evening before, would she have ever sent a young, inexperienced girl, indeed her very sister, at such an early hour, to the same confessional, to the same priest, wearing the very same white bonnet? When she and her sister, Caroline Long, in the company of their brother, went to church for mass, Mrs. Schmoll wore the same dress she had on the evening before according to Mrs. Heinrich, sexton Josiah Stahlhofer, and Miss Caroline Long and both Mr. and Mrs. Schmoll. Only a fool or a wretch would allow her debaucher to place the Holy Communion upon her and her sister's tongues!

"Weighing all of these elements, it is a preposterous tale that the state's witness has woven, woven, mind you, in order that she might be restored to her husband's confidence. Yet, as you can see, the resulting evil has been far greater than the original evil it was intended to remove!"

John Chandler was sitting at his table, scribbling notes, passing them to Lockhart.

"Therefore, after dinner that Thursday noon, Mrs. Schmoll told the rest of the story to her husband, but only after he had asked her to tell what had happened in the church confessional. Indeed, she did not want to accuse her priest of wrongdoing, and would never have done so had she not been compelled, measure-by-measure, by the hope of retaining her husband's affections. It is unlikely that Mrs. Schmoll set out to destroy the defendant's life. I attribute no malice to her, for what she did any woman might have done in an act of desperation, even at the risk of eternal perdition. What she did was to secure the love of her husband, for I am sure that she truly desired to be loved by him. The defense counsel has no theory of a great conspiracy like the opposing counsel has of the defendant and his Church."

"How much more evidence do you need? You must imagine the defendant as a man of little sense to approach a woman the size of Anna Maria Schmoll to carnally know her in the open body of an unlocked church, within thirty feet of one residence, and three hundred some odd feet from her husband's door! Why, he was so brilliant as to know that the moment he grasped her arm, she would faint away and would not reveal his treachery to the authorities of law or her husband! And to know that his intended victim would be

298

rendered mute and immobile! Amazing, gentlemen! This defendant must be some kind of a demon, indeed the very fiend of hell, if all these alleged things are true.

"Seriously, gentlemen! Can you or any man believe any of these things? I cannot. As for the defendant being guilty of rape or even a voluntary, mutual relationship with Mrs. Schmoll, that is impossible. He is innocent of carnal knowledge of the woman either with or without consent!

"For a moment, let us think upon the estranged husband in this saga, the illustrious Mr. Martin Schmoll. The man's behavior indicates that he has never quite believed her story of ravishing. On the contrary, it appears that Mr. Schmoll has always maintained the belief that his wife and the priest were intimate as lovers, both guilty of violating their vows before God and man. It is an established fact that Mrs. Schmoll, then Miss Anna Maria Long, went to confession to the defendant within the week before she was married. The defendant again will not indicate whether this is true or false, but all the principal parties involved coincide in establishing this fact. Mr. Schmoll, as it has already been said, is a jealous man. When his daughter, Maria Caroline, God rest her soul, was born in September, 1842, all doubts in Martin Schmoll's mind concerning Anna Maria's infidelity were removed. For, you see, nine months had passed from the time of her meeting with the priest, and since both the priest and Mr. Schmoll are Dutch and black-headed, it was impossible to tell whether the baby girl was begotten by it's own daddy or not!" The courtroom erupted with shouts and catcalls. Martin Schmoll looked like an angry volcano.

"Martin Schmoll was so jealous with rage that he accused his wife of committing adultery with the priest. Schmoll then took up his pistol and prepared to execute vengeance upon the supposed violator! Anna Maria stopped her husband, begging him to spare the Reverend Father's life, but Mr. Schmoll interpreted this as an indication that she loved the priest. Perhaps Martin was merely acting like he was off to kill the priest, simply to see how his wife would respond to such a plan. He wanted to see if she would beg him not to shoot the priest. When she did, he became convinced of her infidelity. Oh, such tragic consequences of an unhappy marriage, the lies and wicked schemes that mar human relationships! Consider this, gentlemen, we find

America on the verge of national civil unrest as a result of a miserable marriage!

"Gentlemen, if you entertain a solitary rational doubt that the defendant is guilty, then I have performed my duty. If you doubt, you must acquit! And even if you believe that the defendant had carnal knowledge of Mrs. Schmoll, not only at the time specified in the indictment, but at a hundred other times, even so, if it was not obtained forcibly and against her will, then you must find the defendant not guilty. Should you find him guilty, his enemies will rejoice in triumph, but his friends will not abandon him nor will his character suffer. Those who know the man will continue to love, cherish, and honor him, even if he is a convict in the state penitentiary. Again, if any of you have a splinter of a doubt, then you must acquit!

"Furthermore, the Court will instruct you that, if the evidence is susceptible to two reasonable, yet different interpretations, one consistent with the defendant's innocence, one consistent with his guilt, you are duty bound to adopt that interpretation consistent with his innocence. In that regard, be mindful of the fatal inconsistencies in Mrs. Schmoll's testimony."

James Jones placed his right hand to his face, slowly walked back to the defense table, and sat next to Roman.

At that, the judge hammered his gavel and adjourned the court until the one o'clock hour. The Vanderburgh County Prosecutor, James Lockhart, would present the final arguments once court resumed.

****

Following the recess and the reconvening of court, James Lockhart slowly rose from his chair and sighed. "Gentlemen of the jury, this prosecution is drawing to its final hour. I hope I speak for no more than an hour, but gauging from my colleagues I may stray beyond that mark. Nevertheless, if the truth is worth having, then I suppose even six hours would not be too long. Let me say that during this extended trial I have had but one object in my view, that of fulfilling my duties of office as a prosecutor.

"Each of you has been called, in the name of your country, to sit in judgment of a man who has been charged with a crime most odious of all crimes, the crime of rape. The character and the religious office of the accused, the virtue of the state's witness, the place and context under which this crime is said to have taken place, have all commingled giving particular titillation to our nation's conscience. Therefore, I need not impress upon you the importance of a prudent, honest, and just investigation of the evidence when you go into deliberation.

"Bear in mind, gentlemen, that the same law which penalizes the guilty, also protects the innocent. I direct you to the indictment in this cause. The prisoner was arraigned on an indictment to which he pleads not guilty. The indictment contains three counts. The first count is for rape, the second and third are for an assault, and an assault and battery, with intent to commit rape. Should you find the prisoner guilty of the charge in the first count, it will be your responsibility to decide the length of his imprisonment at hard labor in the state penitentiary, no less than five and no more than twenty-one years. Should you find him guilty of either of the other two counts, his time cannot be less than two but no more than fourteen years."

Roman's eyes filled with tears as a knot developed in his throat. Twenty-one and fourteen was thirty-five. The prospect of thirty-five years meant that he would be sixty-five years old upon his release. He feared he was about to waste his life behind the walls of a prison! *O Lord,* he silently prayed, *I had so many hopes for your Church!*

The prosecutor went on and on reviewing the evidence and testimonials. Roman was sick of hearing it. *Why must he repeat it? The jury will find me guilty, of that I am sure. In a way I am grieved that I will not be hung for my alleged crime. To spend thirty-five years in prison for a crime I did not commit will be hell. At least my time in purgatory might be minimal,* he thought.

Roman looked at Anna Maria Schmoll. Their eyes met for a second, no more than the tick of a clock, a swing of the pendulum, but it seemed like an eternity. He glanced to her left and saw Martin Schmoll. Roman turned his attention to Lockhart who was dramatically illustrating why the jury must find him guilty. "Put out of your minds all the baseless speculations offered by my friend, Mr. Jones, concerning his theory of events, not to mention Messrs Dixon and Thomas's ravings. They shamelessly pushed their ideas onto you. But do you wonder at all why the poor Schmoll woman passed the night with heavy sighs and tears? Was it because she was plotting how she might destroy an innocent parish priest? Not in the least! If she was plotting anything it was how to save the defendant from being discovered as a lecherous man, possibly saving him from being lynched by a posse of citizens in a rash execution of justice. I am sure that she asked herself over and over again the same question, debating whether she ought to disclose his villainy, making known his crime. I am sure she spent most of the night in anguished prayer, pleading with God to give her the courage to do what had to be done!

"Many people have said that this priest is a holy man, not the kind to be expected to do any thing the likes of which he is accused. Yet is it not the clever criminal who pawns himself off to the world as an innocent dove? The defendant, appears to be one such man, accustomed to deceiving the unsuspecting. This man's lust lurked beneath his cassock and led him to execute the deed of darkness upon Mrs. Schmoll.

"Here is a priest, who stood before God and man in his bishop's cathedral of Vincennes and swore upon the altar of sacrifice that he would renounce marriage, and abstain from all carnal desires of the flesh, yet he allowed the devil to induce him to violate one of the most sacred commandments of the Almighty, thou shalt not covet thy neighbor's wife!

"Shall the puny arguments put forth by the defense counsel to destroy the witness so that the prisoner might go free prevail? Shall they rather not be impugned so that justice may prevail? The defense counsel accuses Mrs. Schmoll of being a tutored witness. Yet I tell you that I never spoke a word to this woman until she was placed upon the stand before this very court. And if Roman Weinzoepfel had unlawful carnal knowledge with Mrs. Schmoll or with any other woman, even with consent, he should be sent to the penitentiary for life! Any man under the sacred vows that the defendant had taken, promising eternal celibacy upon the holy altar, who then commits the egregious outrage that the defendant did in his consecrated temple, no punishment, either human or divine, could be too severe for him. The tortures of the Inquisition, with all its severity, would be mild for him.

"You have the case. The evidence before you is clear. There is no room for doubting that the defendant is guilty beyond a reasonable doubt. His guilt, associated with his office as a priest, the circumstances dealing with when and where the crime took place, exacerbates the crime. He deserves the strictest censure that the law will countenance. If he were being tried in his native land, he would have been swinging from the gallows the night the charges were revealed to the public, but as it is, we are a civilized country where we pamper our criminals in prisons, so he will be happily contented to spend his remaining years confined to the state penitentiary performing manual labor.

"Gentlemen of the jury, It is finished. I have accomplished my task. I have uttered my last. I now exit the stage. The more solemn duty of determining the guilt or innocence of the defendant is about to be assigned to you. When you retire from this jury box for deliberation, if the evidence indicates that the defendant is guilty beyond every reasonable doubt, then your verdict must render the defendant guilty. At the same time, if you do have a reasonable doubt, then you must acquit the defendant. All the same, when all is said and done, I have the utmost confidence that the twelve of you will convict the defendant, condemning him to a long life of imprisonment in the Indiana State Penitentiary at Jeffersonville."

It was over. Lockhart had spoken for over two hours. As law permits, he had summated the state's case and rebutted every point that the defense had made. Altogether, the defense had consumed eight hours in giving their closing arguments and the prosecution had matched it with nearly an equal amount of time. The judge said a few closing remarks, but they made no sense to Roman. His emotion was controlled yet within he was filled with dread.

It was now the ninth hour. *None.* The three o'clock hour when Christ had cried out from the cross abandoning himself to the Father, the hour when daylight begins to fade. Roman felt as if the light in his own life was beginning to fade.

All through the week he had sat expressionless, like a statue. He wished he were a statue, but then that would make him a saint and he knew he was no saint. No, he felt like a revolting gargoyle, set high atop a church, but not as a sentry to ward off demons, but put there to ward off Christian souls from entering. *Abandon hope all ye who enter here.* None of Christ's worst enemies had ever brought such ruin upon the Church as he had. He felt as if he had plunged into a sea of melancholia, the Stygian waters drowning his mind and heart, casting him down into a Neptunian abyss of utter darkness.

All he wanted to do was sleep

******

The judge sent the jury out of the courtroom and Benjamin Thomas, James Jones, and Archibald Dixon stepped over to Roman. He tried to stand, but his right leg was asleep. The brief but stinging pain subsided momentarily as he awaited the sheriff to lead him to the temporary cell. His brother priests tried to encourage him, but it was as if didn't hear them.

"Come along, Mr. Weinzoepfel!" said the sheriff, escorting him away. Once in the cell, Roman thumbed through his psalter, praying against his accusers. *False witnesses have risen against me. O search me, Lord, and know my heart. O test me and know my thoughts.*

Keep me safe from the snares of those who do evil. Bring my soul out of this prison and then I shall praise Thee. Reach down from your lofty height in heaven and save me, draw me out from the mighty waters and miry clay. Save me from the hands of alien foes whose mouths are filled with lies, whose hands are raised in perjury. Render them as winnowed chaff driven away by the winds. Judge them guilty, O Lord.

****

At half past the hour, he heard a commotion in the hallway outside his cell. They were coming for him. Already? Lying on the small bed frame staring up at the ceiling, resting in the quiet, he heard someone unlocking the door. There were other men, their keys rattling and boots scuffing the wooden stairs that led down to the dungeon. He managed to button his cassock and place his biretta atop his head before the constables jerked him out of the cell and hurried him along despite his shackled feet. One man on each of Roman's arms, they lifted him up the stairs, through the jailhouse, and out into the blinding sunlight, their strong hands squeezing his upper arms. Clutching his breviary close and feeling his rosary beads dangling at his side, he beheld his enemies, a pack of ravenous wolves ready to devour him, pushing and encircling him as if he was their morning carrion.

Stumbling in the dirt and dung, he struggled to keep up with the swiftness of the vulgar constables who laughed in his face. More abuse sounded forth from the lips of those gathered in the street, on the square, and in the jailhouse lawn. With the crowd following like a herd of bulls, he was taken into the Gibson County Courthouse where he met his attorneys.

"Roman! The jury's back!" Mr. Thomas was the first face to appear at the opening door. "They have a verdict!"

He said nothing as he wiped sleep from his eyes. The jury had deliberated for less than half an hour.

"They're going to row him up Salt River," Jones whispered to Thomas loud enough for Roman to hear.

"He's been through the mill," Thomas whispered back.

Dixon puffed on the end of his stogy, speaking to Messrs Thomas and Jones. "He's down lower than a steamboat snagged in the Ohio."

"Or a slave in chains?" Jones looked his southern colleague in the eye.

Dixon huffed, put off by the comment.

Meanwhile, Roman nervously walked with the sheriff. He was as ready as he ever would be.

"Now, don't worry, Roman." That was easy for Thomas to say. He wouldn't be the one going to prison for thirty-five years. He wouldn't be the one to die while digging a canal or laying ties for the railway.

Dixon had traded his pipe for a cigar as he came up behind the others. Roman, flanked by his entourage of lawyers and fellow clerics, looked at the twelve jurors, then to his accuser and her attorneys. No sooner had Roman taken his seat did the judge enter from his chambers. "All rise. Court is now in session." There was not an open seat; in fact, more people were in the chamber than had attended any session, the room warm with the crowd desiring to hear the verdict.

The judge sat and everyone followed. "Has the jury arrived at a verdict?"

"Yes, your Honor," answered the foreman.

"If the bailiff would please take the verdict from the foreman and please hand it to the clerk who will read it." The bailiff fulfilled his purpose.

Roman had the feeling that he was watching all of this transpire upon some elaborate stage, feeling himself removed, as if watching from a distance. Yet well he knew that he was more than a witness. He was the defendant.

The clerk rose from his seat and read aloud. "We, the jury," the clerk paused, (and in the brevity of that moment, though instant, for Roman the pause was eternal), "find the defendant guilty as he stands charged in the first count of the indictment, and we sentence him to five years hard labor in the state penitentiary, signed, John Hyndman, foreman of the jury.'"

Roman sighed. It was over. He was glad. Not glad that he was to be imprisoned, but that the entire lurid ordeal was at an end. What he had expected for nearly twenty-one months of preparation had now come to pass with the utterance of one word: Guilty. However, no amount of preparation for prison truly prepares a man to go to prison. Roman wanted to cry, but he was too angry. He wanted to see Anna Maria Schmoll's reaction or her husband's but he could see neither of them. A roar of noise engulfed him, nearly knocking him to the floor, both excited cheers and angry shouts.

At least his fate was decided. At last he knew where he would be for the next five years. *Deo gratias, at least it isn't a thirty year sentence. I'm glad it's over. Why did we even have this trial? The jurors had already found me guilty before they took to the box.* He studied their faces. He hated every one of them. In another way, he pitied them, victims of demagoguery, blind prejudice, and intimidation. He had long since abandoned himself to Divine Providence, even though God had seemed so remote for nearly two years now. Oh, there were moments of grace but all he could see now was the blackness of a starless night sky. He thought of the lonely prison cell that awaited him. What kind of fiends would he be placed with in the prison? It hurt even to think.

He watched the mouths of the judge and his attorneys open but he had heard enough. The faces of Dixon and Thomas became angry and the judge's gavel pounded furiously.

"Balderdash!" Dixon took the cigar from his mouth and stomped. "If that don't beat all."

"Horsefeathers!" Thomas said, dropping his head. "How in the Sam Hill could they have come to a decision so quick?"

Roman sat in his chair, slumping down. He felt as if his chair was tipping back. Tipping, tipping, falling, spiraling down, down, down. He closed his eyes into a black abyss of nothingness. How long he sat there, motionless, he wasn't for certain.

The judge pounded his gavel. "Order, order."

"Your Honor," Dixon called out, still on his feet, "I ask that the jury be polled individually to ask if they agree with the verdict."

"Very well. If the clerk would please poll the jurors."

In silence, one by one each juror affirmed the verdict.

"The verdict stands." The judge declared.

Dixon threw his cigar to the floor and crushed it out.

"Mr. Dixon, if you would be so kind as to make sure your cigar butt is removed from the floor before you leave."

"Yes, I was supposed to be sworn in as the Lieutenant Governor of Kentucky at Frankfort two days ago."

"We're all aware of your political ambition. Now if we could continue with the sentencing of the prisoner."

"Excuse me, Your Honor," the rational voice of James Jones regained his attention. Jones approached the judge's bench. "On behalf of the defendant, I seek to file a motion for a new trial."

"The court overrules Mr. Jones' motion for a new trial." Judge Embree quickly replied, reaching for his gavel.

"Objection!" Dixon leaned over the defense table, removing his cigar.

"Overruled, gentlemen." The judge shook his head, smacking the gavel down.

"Your Honor!" Thomas' shoulders fell.

James Jones stepped forth. "Your Honor, we will appeal this case to the Indiana Supreme Court in Indianapolis for its May term of this year."

"That was to be expected, Mr. Jones." The judge answered.

"I'm sure the higher court will uphold the decision of this court," Chandler smirked.

"Are there any other motions?" asked the judge as some of the assembled people began moving for the doors. "Order, Court is still in session. Those in the gallery will please be seated and observe silence." The judge popped his gavel loudly.

"No further motions from the defense," Jones answered, raising his voice, standing directly in front of the judge, "but have you forgotten something?"

Those in the chamber had seated and quieted themselves.

"No, I was about to address the defendant before sentencing him."

"Thank you." Jones sat down.

The judge looked at Roman seated in front of his bench. "Before I sentence you, I am to ask if you have anything to say."

A flutter of nausea rose from Roman's stomach and he felt as if he would suddenly vomit.

"If he doesn't, I surely have." Dixon rolled his eyes, took a seat, and glared at Chandler and the judge.

"Do you have anything to say?" The judge looked at Roman again.

Roman swallowed hard, cleared his throat, gripped his biretta in his left hand, and held his rosary's crucifix tightly within his right. He slowly rose from his seat before the silent crowd, and focused his thoughts on what he would say. "My fate has been decided, has it not? Indeed then to what purpose shall I speak? From the first moment I heard the accusation made against me, I expected justice, not mercy. I received neither.

"Christ did not defend himself before Herod so I have already spoken too much, yet with God as my witness, I am innocent of the charges for which I have been found guilty." Roman paused and turned to the prosecutors. "But it was not for the charge of rape that I was so vigilantly prosecuted, but rather that of my being an immigrant Catholic priest—"

"Stop his mouth!" John Chandler shouted to Embree. "He's an imposter, a false prophet masquerading as a champion of Christ!"

"Mr. Chandler, sit down before I hold you in contempt!" Judge Embree called out.

The room was filled with angry murmuring as Roman snatched his breviary off the table, stared straight ahead, and said nothing more.

Judge Embree paused as if to make sure Roman was finished before he stood to pronounce judgment. "Prisoner at the bar, you have been found guilty of committing rape upon the person of Anna Maria Schmoll and are thus sentenced to five years of hard labor in the State Penitentiary at Jeffersonville. You will be transported to the facility sometime tomorrow." The judge closed his eyes, concluding. "And may God have mercy on your soul." The gavel came down in a thundering boom, exploding all around Roman.

He had known all along that he would be found guilty as charged. He lamented that he had allowed his lawyers to fool him into thinking that he would somehow be exonerated. His fellow priests embraced him, offered encouraging words, and promised their prayers, but the words they spoke seemed like babble and even in their embrace he felt all alone and forgotten.

The judge spoke to some of the jurors and Mrs. Schmoll's attorneys as all in the chamber rose to leave. The two constables returned for him and removed him much in the same manner as they had transported him earlier. The sheriff led him out of the courtroom to his Gibson County jail cell. Roman replaced the biretta on his head. *At least I didn't drop it*, he laughed to himself as he was led through the crowd. He considered the murmuring crowd a hissing crowd of vipers. His legs tangled at least a dozen times before they found the wooden steps of the dungeon. Reeling as if drunk, he fell backwards upon his cot and stared at the mud-daubed timber ceiling.

Staring into the ceiling, hearing the passersby and horses, carriages and wagons, church bells, tavern dinner bells and the echo of cowbells, he ground his teeth in his hellhole, descending further and further into an inferno of prejudice himself.

He ate nothing that evening, as he hadn't eaten much of anything during the week. He had been fasting for many months now and his stomach pains were intense. Leaving his breviary unopened, he fell onto the cot, his mind vacant and heart numb.

****

Was it already morning? It felt like morning. It smelled like morning. Had he been dreaming? Was he truly in America? It was a question he had awakened to nearly every morning since the accusation was first made.

It was the smell that had first roused him, the odor of burning wood. The scent of smoke was as intense as the fire at St. Mary-of-the-Woods a year and a half before. The sunlight was hardly piercing the darkness when he heard the angry voices of men approaching the Princeton jail. Suddenly the whole room shook. A maddening chorus of angry voices chanted feverishly the *Dies Irae* as the sound of pounding sledgehammers ringing upon anvils echoed through the air while a church bell slowly tolled the funeral dirge.

Suddenly someone smashed something against his cell door, again and again until all at once the door was kicked down, ripping its hinges, and pulling the door out of its frame. Men wild with rage yanked at his arms and pulled his hair, snatching him from his underground cell. He didn't even have time to fasten his soutane, feeling like a tomato plucked prematurely from its vine. The townsfolk had arisen early to satisfy their unjustified hatred.

Everything was happening so fast. He was lifted up by hundreds of hands and thrown upon a horse drawn cart, excoriated with vicious tongues and vile epithets. Still half asleep, he called out for the sheriff and prayed that this heinous mob would not kill him. *Who are these men? Where are they taking me?*

The carriage turned a corner and he saw a tall pyre looming in the center of the town square opposite the courthouse while a plume of smoke ascended from somewhere nearby. The chant grew cacophonous, almost diabolical as it increased in strength. Roman couldn't move his arms or legs and even his eyes were fixed in his head. He tried to speak, but his tongue and jaw were locked as if his mouth was in the grip of rigor mortis.

The cart bore down upon the pyre. *Die, priest, die!* The chant became deafening. Again he tried to open his mouth and cry for help but he couldn't. To one side of the square there was a group of Catholics bewailing him, chanting the litany of the saints. As he drew closer and closer to the pyre he could acutely smell the rancid smoke while loud, obscene laughter was coming from those gathered about the pyre and the nearby crackling fire.

Roman asked to be brought a cross, but instead someone raised a serpent on a stick to his lips. He was removed from the cart, taken to the top of the woodpile, and stripped naked. Ropes were fastened around him as he was tied to the large piece of timber that rose from the pile.

"Do you renounce your Catholic faith?" A voice asked.

"Never!" Roman's mouth was unloosed.

"Then you will die!"

"I shall die for Christ!"

A military drumbeat began while someone lifted a large tree limb, dipping it into the burning flames of the fire, and setting the pyre aglow.

The smoke and heat quickly seared his nostrils, burning his lungs. The church bell tolled louder. Roman cried out as the thick smoke darkened his world. He coughed and prayed, "Jesus! O my Jesus!" He writhed in torment and agony as the flames enveloped his legs, the heat unbearable, as he felt his flesh burning and his eyes melting like wax.

"Father Weinzoepfel? Your breakfast, Sir."

Roman startled and kicked the woolen blanket off his rack aware that he was burning with sweat. He opened his eyes, squinting in the morning sun, and saw one of the constables standing over his bed with a plate of food.

The steeple bell of the Protestant church on the town square was steadily calling Sunday worshipers to prayer while the sound of the choir practicing the day's hymns wafted through the air into his cell, as did the smoke of neighboring chimney flues and kitchen fires.

Roman wiped the sweat from his forehead and face.

"You were dreaming, Sir," the constable said. "It must've been a nightmare." The constable handed Roman a steaming cup of black coffee and a plate of sausage and eggs.

Shortly thereafter Sheriff Kirkman entered Roman's cell and made him strip out of his soutane and biretta.

Roman had now, in effect, been successfully defrocked by the State of Indiana, the long sought after objective finally achieved.

Chapter 24

De Profundis

The memory of his nightmare haunted his waking as he sat on the end of his bunk. He dressed himself in the pair of denim trousers and the blue cotton shirt the sheriff had brought him. It was a small satisfaction that he was allowed to wear his own stockings and boots. He reached for the top button of his shirt working to straighten his white collar, momentarily forgetting that he had been defrocked. He recalled the passage of scripture from the Passion of Christ: *He was stripped of his garments and for his vesture they cast lots.*

******

An armed escort of at least twenty four men in twilled cotton jeans, buttoned work shirts, wide brimmed floppy felt hats and coon skin caps, bearing rifles and pistols in holsters at their sides, led Roman to the blacksmith's shop just off Main Street to be forged into the iron handcuffs, fetters, and shackles. People clamored about him, as if trying to catch a glimpse of a collared beast. As the blacksmith worked to forge the handcuffs to bind Roman's hands from celebrating the sacraments, he said to him, "You're not as terrible as they say. I was expecting a much bigger man."

The blacksmith then handed the heavy chain with forged cuffs at both ends to the sheriff. Sheriff Kirkman smiled at Roman as he fit the metal about his wrists. Another prisoner, a frail man, unshaved and in patched clothing was chained to Roman. This man explained that he had been sentenced to five years imprisonment, condemned for stealing five dollars and two loaves of bread. The man continued, sobbing in tears, "I was poor. What was I to do? My children were hungry." The blacksmith then fastened the shackles about both of Roman's ankles and those of the other prisoner.

The sheriff and his deputy, John Curl, were behind Roman and the thief as they made their way toward the stagecoach. The humiliation and ridicule was almost too much for him to bear, escorted through the streets of Princeton like a gorilla in a traveling circus, being treated like one of the freaks in the sideshow.

312

It's Sunday. Why aren't these Protestants in church? Roman angrily asked himself.

Forced into the coach, he and his companion stared blankly out the windows while Sheriff Kirkman and Officer Curl made jokes at their expense, awaiting the whip to snap the reins sending them on their way. Once on their way, Roman slumped in his seat and thought of the time five years before when he had ridden from Strasbourg to Paris before boarding a boat and traveling the *Seine* to *Le Havre*. Jarred back and forth, he listened to the weighty thump of horse hooves upon the ground, the swish of rolling wagon wheels in the slimy mud path, and the creaking of leather harnesses and splintered wood yokes. Storm clouds moved swiftly overhead as lightning flickered and thunder grumbled.

He thumbed his rosary beads, but half-heartedly mumbled the words. In his hands he held his breviary and turned the pages with restricted wrists and hands. He glanced up at his pathetic partner in chains who was silently wiping his tear-stained eyes.

Kirkman and Curl ordered the carriage stopped on several occasions wherever there was a gathering of folks. "Would you care to see the vile priest now that he's caged?" Kirkman laughed, calling out to the passersby at the mill on Pigeon Creek.

"I don't think he'll be ravishing anyone now that he's secured with a chain," Curl stood in the open door of the carriage.

It seemed that the chained torture of being paraded down the streets was worse than death by fiery pyre, hangman's rope, or guillotine blade. Here the anguish only lingered.

By Sunday evening, the carriage rolled into Evansville. When they arrived at the jail, hardly anyone was moving about. Roman and his fellow prisoner were housed in the jail's basement dungeon. Roman prayed that no one would storm the jailhouse in an attempt to exact justice from his lifeblood. He fell asleep praying his rosary, the reality of his ordeal still like an ominously long nightmare.

The next morning, the streets were surprisingly quiet. He had expected to be met by a surging crowd of Protestants and roughs come out to gloat over his imprisonment. Even the sheriff had expected a gathering. However, the only man on the street was Will Chandler standing in front of his newspaper's print shop wearing his speckled hat. He had a look of triumph across his face as Sheriff Kirkman stopped the carriage allowing John Curl to open the door.

"Mr. Chandler, Sir," Curl laughed. "The priest's on his way up the river."

"Without so much as a canoe or a paddle." Chandler tipped his hat to the officers and pouted his lips to Roman, feigning sympathy. The Sheriff snapped the reins and the horses jerked the carriage forward.

Meanwhile, Reverend Antony Deydier, Andrew Martin, Josiah Stahlhofer, Doc MacDonald, John O'Connell, and the Lincks and Heinrichs, were all standing at the corner of Second and Main with many other parishioners, men, women, and children, just down from the front of Assumption Church. Some looked on in disbelief, while others were bathed in tears. He could only imagine the explanation the parents would give their bewildered children as to why their parochial vicar—minus his collar and frock—was bound in manacles, being led away in shackles and chains about his ankles. The only chain Roman had ever desired was that of a rosary dangling from his side.

His pastor, Deydier, and his faithful followed him to the wharf where he prepared to board the boat. Deydier openly wept, as did the others who hugged Roman in prolonged embraces. With the Sheriff ostensibly chomping the bit towering over Roman and the poor man, Deydier conversed with Roman in their common French tongue.

"There will come a time when you shall be set free and these dark days of anguish and suffering will be but a fading memory." Deydier assured. "Trust in God, my son. Thank God you were spared of martyrdom"

"I'm not so sure they're finished with me yet."

"Courage, my son. In the meantime, pray as St. Paul. His greatest efforts at evangelization and witnessing to the truth of the gospel were done from his prison cell while shackled in chains."

"My mission is at an end," he answered, dispirited.

"Do not think your missionary task has ended. You must unite your suffering to the sufferings of Christ, offering up your cross for the salvation of souls. Think of all the poor tortured souls in purgatory whose release you will secure by your prayers and offerings, bearing your injustice patiently just as our Blessed Lord redeemed the world by his own suffering and death."

"Would they had done me a favor by killing me two years ago, sparing me of the torment of the abysmal penitentiary." He turned his wit against himself.

"Father Roman, never despair. Your imprisonment, which you will endure, will be no less efficacious than being fed to lions, beheaded, or placed upon the rack. Your very willingness to volunteer for the missions shows that you were prepared to shed your blood for Christ from the very beginning."

"Then pray that I can minister to some of the souls languishing in the prison."

"Saint Vincent de Paul said, 'If God is the center of your life, no words will be needed. Your mere presence will touch their hearts.'"

Roman embraced Deydier, clinging to him, lingering for the length of an *Ave*.

"If we never see each other again in this life, my son," Deydier spoke, his voice tremulous, "may we merrily meet in heaven."

Roman could say nothing, his throat swollen with emotion as he stood opposite his pastor.

"Hurry up, they're ready to leave!" Officer Curl called out, stepping onto the wharf from the boat.

At that, the sheriff took advantage of the lull in the conversation and pushed Roman along, boarding the packet boat for Jeffersonville.

"We were saying our goodbyes." Roman asserted.

"Goodbye," the sheriff turned and waved irreverently to Deydier.

Officer Curl returned and assisted the sheriff in securing Roman and his fellow prisoner onto the boat.

Once aboard the vessel, Roman was encouraged to find so many people, mostly Protestants who willingly spoke with him, convinced of his innocence. The sheriff and his deputy were visibly taken aback by the support that the Americans gave Roman.

Roman for his part fought back tears as he tried to breathe in the hills springing with green and the creeks and rivers feeding into the Ohio, ever reminded of his Alsatian homeland in the foothills of the Vosges Mountains of the Alsatian valleys.

Midway to Louisville, some of the passengers gathered about Roman as he sat on the deck of the boat. A Catholic lawyer from Terre Haute, no less a friend of Mother Theodore Guérin, said he would act as judge and soon a Protestant lawyer from Cincinnati acted as Roman's defense attorney. Twelve occupants of the boat volunteered to serve as jurors while the rest watched on as observers in an imaginary gallery.

The sentiment of the people was against Sheriff Kirkman. Soon many respectable men and women gave Kirkman a severe reprimand. Roman nervously listened and could see that the sheriff was not amused by the mockery he received. Curl was furious and threatened to arrest some of the passengers on the charge of provocation.

Roman soon became aware of a plot afoot among some of the passengers to overtake the sheriff and his deputy. Even the captain of the boat was ready to put to shore, either setting Roman at liberty or allowing the burly passengers to tie up the sheriff and his deputy only to leave them on the river bank in the middle of the wilderness somewhere between Evansville and Louisville.

Roman managed to gain the people's attention, "Please...I now suffer unjustly under the law, but I trust the higher courts will rectify the wrong that has been done to me. Therefore, I prefer to be imprisoned of my own free will and patiently await vindication. Otherwise, if I flee from justice, then I *will* become guilty of transgressing the law and render myself a fugitive. To my enemies it would appear I was guilty all along." He saw the sheriff look at him with amazement. For the remainder of the trip upriver, the sheriff treated him with kindness and even removed his manacles and shackles.

The next day they arrived at Jeffersonville. Sheriff Kirkman took Roman aside and whispered to him as they exited the boat. "Reverend. You really are innocent, aren't you?"

"Excuse me?" he asked, despite the fact that he had heard him the first time.

"I regret that it is only now that I see you are innocent. Forgive me for the way I have treated you these past two years. I didn't mean to hurt you. I never knew."

Roman didn't exactly know what to say as he nodded to Kirkman. Taken down from his hill of Calvary, he prepared to be placed in the tomb of the penitentiary. They journeyed from the docks through the muddy streets towards the ominous building which was the prison, its lookout posts watchful eyes and barbed wire fence sharpened teeth to snag those attempting to flee. The structure itself was two stories and another building was under construction next door.

Deputy John Curl clanked the knocker on the large wooden door that was the gate of the prison. A guard opened the double door and the sheriff exchanged some information before handing Roman over to him. The guard's name was Calvin Pike and he was one of the chief guards at the prison. He took the knapsack from the sheriff that contained Roman's soutane, biretta, and portable mass kit including a chalice, paten, and prayer cards.

"I won't even be allowed to celebrate Mass?"

"No, and you won't be needing these either." Pike then pried the rosary from Roman's right hand and tore his breviary from his left, ultimately consummating the act of violation that began with his being divested of the honor of soutane and biretta. "We don't need no martyrs behind these walls."

Now no vestiges of Roman's priestly nature remained save that of the unseen indelible mark of the sacrament of Holy Orders visible only to God.

The Warden of the prison, Mr. Pratt, approached. "So, you're The Reverend Roman Weinzoepfel," he said, looking at Roman. "Sheriff," he turned to Kirkman, "from the stories I've heard about this man's trial, you should've brought the judge and jury."

The Schmolls and the Chandler brothers would suit me just fine, thought Roman.

"I'm not sure about anything anymore," Kirkman shook his head. "The prisoner had a chance to escape on our way here, yet he remained with me and my deputy, insisting that if he was to escape then he *would* be guilty of a crime. Perhaps I should have let him go free."

John Curl spat in protest to the sheriff's words.

"Did Sheriff Kirkman treat you well?" Pratt looked at Roman.

"Yes." Roman was quick to answer.

"Will you sign a letter to Judge Embree in Evansville verifying that he treated you well?"

"Certainly."

"Then hurry up and sign it," Pike said, "so I can put you in the dungeon."

"No," Pratt replied. "The dungeon is badly ventilated and poorly lit. It's unfit for any criminal, especially an innocent priest."

Pike glowered at Roman, his hand on the butt of his revolver. "He's a rake. In there he'll have to confess and atone for his lechery."

"Take him upstairs." Pratt took Roman's belongings from Pike, placing them in a large drawer.

"Why must you deprive me of my rosary and book?" Roman didn't move.

"You might use the chain to choke someone or hang yourself," Pike answered.

"Anything that can be used as a ligature is prohibited," Pratt explained. "It's the law, Father."

"But why my breviary?"

"You might tear out some of the pages and try to choke yourself to death," Pike laughed.

"I wouldn't do that!"

"The law's the law, Mister." Pike held the breviary away from Roman.

"But what of my religious freedom?"

"You've forfeited your freedom when you raped that woman," Pike replied.

Pratt intervened, taking Pike aside against his wishes. Mr. Pratt then returned to Roman taking him up the steps of the prison to the cell. Entering the upstairs cellblock, Roman was overwhelmed with the stench of urine and excrement. As he followed Pratt, the prisoners in each cell looked up. Some even rolled off their cots and came forward to stare at him through their bars.

Roman was placed in a six by nine foot cell and the iron door echoed closed behind him. He bent down, ran his right thumb through a mound of dust in a corner of the cell, and traced a cross upon the wall.

A feeling of abandonment seized him as he realized he could do nothing. *O Lord, am I even to be deprived of the solace of prayer?*

****

Within a fortnight, Deydier had written to tell him that Mother Theodore Guérin had made it back to the States, arriving in Evansville within the week of his trial. "She sends her prayers." In his letter he also wrote of how the bishop was calling for a synod in an attempt to get his priests to rally behind him. "There is one sure sign of unity among the priests, and that is their unanimous conviction of your innocence.

"And don't worry about Shadow. He's in good hands. The smithy, our bell ringer, Andrew Martin, is caring for him." Roman was relieved to know what had become of his horse.

Roman was soon leased out to a local wheelwright where he was felling trees and learning the craft of fashioning wagon wheels. The work helped him occupy his mind and his hands.

Chapter 25

Golgotha

All during April and May Roman taught Latin to Mr. Pratt's son. And though the prison authorities forbade Roman from praying the Divine Office, they could not prevent him from praying from memory the particular feasts, thus duly abiding by his ordination promise. Despite his continued prayer, it was a struggle, and he still resented the fact that his breviary had been confiscated.

Early in May, he received a letter from all the priests of the diocese. They were gathered in Vincennes, summoned there for the synod called by Bishop Hailandière in hopes of unifying his diocese.

We offer our deepest sympathy in your undeserved sufferings. Know that we can testify to your innocence and are convinced that every Catholic throughout the world, as well as every decent, intelligent, and unprejudiced Protestant, is equally convinced of your virtue. No man all at once falls from the height of sanctity into the chasm of corruption.

Your forbearance in surrendering to God's mysterious providential care, fills us with nothing but esteem for your faith. Your patience in suffering the insidious calumnies and the weight of chains and prison bars all in the cause of Holy Mother Church, gives us great confidence that your reward shall be great in heaven.

Bishop Hailandière and all the priests had signed it. *They must not know me very well*, he smiled. *It's a nice letter*, he said to himself, *but it won't release me from these bonds.*

By the end of May, Mr. Jones sent word to him that the Indiana Supreme Court had upheld the decision of the Gibson County Court.

Roman's world was disintegrating. And his despair only grew worse when the warden of the prison, Mr. Pratt, visited Roman in early June to tell him that he would be gone from June through December.

The day Pratt left, Roman heard him tell Calvin Pike, "Insofar as the law allows, treat Father Roman as you would my own son." Pike assured the warden that he would abide by his wishes.

Roman ate less and less and his headaches returned with severity as Calvin Pike took control of the prison. One of the first things he did was move Roman from his upstairs cell to the cell in the dungeon. The only window in his damp stone cell allowed no view of the outside save that of the wall of the new prison that was being built alongside the present structure.

His migraines became more and more frequent and with it the pain of stomach ulcers. Pike was perpetually taunting him, abusing his patience, tempting him to curse or fight, but he dare not respond lest he give Pike justification to shoot.

In the heat of June and July, Roman was reassigned to hard labor, sent out to work for various contractors. During the day he was made to fell trees for the corduroy road, or lay track for the railroad, or craft a wagon wheel well past the vesper hour, past the point of exhaustion, and by candlelight if necessary.

Yet he tried to take pride in the work of his hands knowing that all work is dignified when tempered with prayer. *Ora et labora.* The labor demanded his full attention much like the scribal task of a medieval monk illustrating opuses and transcribing ancient manuscripts.

Despite his best efforts at keeping his mind occupied with his labors, a deep sadness weighed on his heart, and blanketed his soul. Pike had even prohibited him from shaving, citing the threat a razor blade posed. By the middle of summer, Roman's mustache and beard was thick upon his face while his neck was scraggly with hair. Pike carried his revolver and often displayed it before Roman. Fingering the trigger, Pike refused to let Roman out of his sight, at times not even allowing him to speak to other prisoners.

At night, though exhausted with fatigue, he couldn't sleep contemplating the injustice perpetrated against him. And the extremely hot temperature of the cell, miserably hot from July's summer sun, exacerbated his outrage. His head throbbed thinking that he could do nothing to restore his honor. In the depths of his depression he tried to cry, but he was too angry, angry at the Schmolls, Old Man Long, the Chandlers, and the Whig presses.

Even the bishop.

As the season of summer wrinkled into autumn, he sank into deeper depression and grasped for the Latin words of the lament of the eighty-eighth psalm. *My soul is replete with evil, my life on the brink of hell...as the slain lying in their sepulchers...in the shadow of death. I am reckoned as one in a tomb. Imprisoned, I cannot escape. My one companion is darkness.*

Staring into the brick wall he plunged into a deep quagmire of silence, a wasteland, an abandoned abyss. His was a descent into the infernal regions, empty of grace and light, just as the psalmist had scribed. He was weary from grief, dumbfounded by such intense hatred, a pitiless struggle against the evil of calumny.

In this hell of lukewarm, tepid, tortured souls, there was no solace, not even the solace of death. Rather, it was the anguish of the throes of death stretched upon the strings of eternity, the state of the body in a perpetual condition of dying, death ravishing the body of its soul. His was the pain of fire and ice, grinding of teeth in a nightly dirge upon one's bed.

Passages of Judgment Day resounded in his mind and found their way to his lips. "Depart from me, ye accursed, into the eternal lake of fire prepared for the devil and his angels..." Infinite darkness, where there will be weeping and wailing and gnashing of teeth. Oh the tepid, torpid spirits and souls of the unredeemed, spewed forth like vomit from the mouth of God, devoured by Satan and digested only to be discharged excrement, black bile in the bowels of hell.

Days gave way to weeks and weeks to months, his time a journey on the River Styx into the depths of the earth approaching the fiery pit of hell itself. Even light itself was dimmed by the agony and lamentation while the malignant air of the prison was seared with hatred and fear and unrepentance. He slept upon his cot in an apathetic state of dejection and woe, the pungent smell of chamber pots and urine no longer distinguishable from the odors of the prison kitchen.

The summer heat of August carried over into September continually making sleep difficult in his sweltering cell. One afternoon, lying upon his cot, he looked up on the wall and saw a spider climbing his newly spun web. In the web was a fly, obviously trapped by the enemy. The spider approached to take his prey. Roman stood on the bed and took the fly by one of its wings, releasing it through the opened window at ground level. He wished it were that easy for him to be released from the prison. As he returned to his sleepless rest, a knock sounded from his door. It was his attorney, Benjamin Thomas.

"Bad news, Father. The U.S. Supreme Court has refused to hear your case."

American justice.

"Our last hope is the governor. I believe we might be able to get him to pardon you. You won't believe how many Protestants are petitioning him to do so."

"I'll believe it when these doors swing open. And if he does pardon me, there's likely to be an outcry."

"Yes, I suppose you're right. I'm sure you've heard all about the Protestant-Catholic riots in Philadelphia and New York."

"Unfortunately." Calvin Pike had informed Roman of the events and blamed the violence on him. Thomas showed Roman a copy of the *Louisville Catholic Advocate* newspaper.

Protestant-Catholic riots threaten nation's future.

On the sixth of May a drunken Protestant mob attacked the Irish Catholics in Philadelphia. The argument stemmed from a dispute whether the Catholic children should be required to read the King James Bible rather than the Catholic's Douay Version. Thirty-five Irish shanties were looted and burned. When the fire department arrived the Protestant firefighters refused to douse the flames. The mob then processed to St. Michael's church and subdued the Irish Catholics who were guarding the structure. The church and rectory both were torched and the priest barely escaped with his life.

The Protestant legion of torch-bearing horsemen next surrounded the Augustinian friary and church of St. Augustine. The mayor and a dozen constables stood on the front steps of the church and begged the horde of hooligans not to do such evil while a posse of decent Protestants guarded the church. However, the mob stormed the church property, trampling the mayor rendering him unconscious along with many others who were trying to protect the friars and the church. The drunken mob broke the doors down setting fire to all.

The barbaric mob, like good Vandals, plundered the friary's library, burning thousands of its books, many of them ancient hand-copied manuscripts. The entire church and friary is now nothing but rubble. The pack of wolves then attacked a convent of sisters and fired it as well.

Again, on the fourth of July, anti-Catholic hostilities were rekindled and a group of patriotic Americans set fire to fifty Irish Catholic homes. Subsequently, gunfire was exchanged between the two

groups, killing at least twenty, including several innocent citizens caught in the crossfire.

In the wake of such violence, angry Protestants in New York City prepared to burn St. Patrick's Cathedral. It is reported that the bishop of New York has asked that every Catholic Church should be guarded by as many Catholic men who are resolved to give their life for their Church.

"Who knows where all this unrest is going to end or how it will end?" Thomas asked. "If it can happen in Philadelphia and New York, then how long before something like it happens in Cincinnati or Louisville or even St. Louis or New Orleans? At least the good people in Evansville didn't burn the church or actually torch any Catholic homes."

"No, a drunken posse of angry Protestants just tried to lynch me."

"Father Roman, please recall that many of those men were just drunk and angry Americans. Christ never intended for Christians to be pitted against each other. As sure as the pope is Italian, very few Protestants actually hate you or the Church. Remember that my family in Pennsylvania is all Protestant."

Thomas then went on at length detailing what had been happening in Evansville since the March trial six months before. In July Martin Schmoll left Evansville and went to stay with some relatives in St Charles, Missouri. It was then that Anna Maria had filed for divorce. She claimed that her marriage to Schmoll had driven her to drunkenness and she also attributed the death of her baby girl to her husband's ill treatment.

"On the twenty-fifth of September the divorce case came before the court. Martin Schmoll had returned to Evansville and denied all the charges brought against him by Anna Maria. He claimed that Anna Maria was a habitual liar, an alcoholic, a thief, and a foul-mouthed lazy lout who only wanted to argue after they were married. The Court awarded her six hundred dollars and the divorce was granted."

Thomas continued, as Roman half-heartedly listened. "Before she left Evansville, she had become a regular fixture at the *Bull's Head Tavern*. Now the word is that she took her small fortune to New Orleans where she has become the madam of a bordello."

"Enough about her." Roman raised his hand. "How are you, Mr. Thomas?"

"I'm on my way to Indianapolis again for a second meeting with Governor Whitcomb to make a personal appeal on your behalf."

"It's no use, Ben. You ought to know that by now. I'm in here for the duration."

"Don't be so sure. Are you aware that even Lockhart, the prosecutor, who argued that the Indiana Supreme Court shouldn't even review your trial, is now advocating your pardon? Lockhart is convinced he was deceived from the beginning. He and the Chandlers aren't speaking. Lockhart and John Chandler got into fisticuffs at the *Bull's Head* two weeks ago.

"And now Will Chandler is trying to sell his newspaper. Right before Martin Schmoll left Evansville, he and Will got into an argument at *Wood's Tavern*. Later that same night, Schmoll, still in one of his drunken fits, went to Assumption cemetery at about midnight and like a ravenous hyena, dug open his innocent baby girl's tomb and removed the coffin of her remains. They say he was crying like a woman when he pried the coffin lid off and removed her body and cradled her in his arms. Sheriff Kirkman and Deputy Curl showed up as did a fairly good-sized crowd, but nobody quite knew what to do. Kirkman and Curl tried to subdue him, but he took out his pistol and threatened to shoot. Then he put the gun to his own head and threatened to kill himself. He put her corpse back in the coffin and carried it through the streets to the Lutheran churchyard between Sycamore and Vine. He found the sexton's shovel and proceeded to dig a fresh grave. All the while, he kept telling the baby that he didn't mean to hurt her, saying that it was her mother's fault. There are those who may say this is a fabrication, manufactured fiction told in order to gain sympathy for you, but the sheriff and his deputy can verify the reports for they attempted to subdue the fiend for desecrating the grave.

"Then in the midst of all this, Fräulein Caroline Long went to court. She was the Plaintiff in a bastardy case over her illegitimate boy. The defendant was able to provide a year long alibi, so the case was dismissed. Many people are convinced that the child is actually Martin Schmolls. Caroline stayed with him during February of 1843 to care for her sister's baby while Anna Maria was away in Cincinnati with the attorney Jay Davis.

"Now there's even talk that Martin Schmoll may have murdered Jay Davis. The body of a man was found in the weeds down river

325

from Evansville about five miles. It's badly decomposed, but Doc McDonald thinks it is Davis's body."

"Enough of this, Mr. Thomas. Any more and I shall be guilty of tittle-tattle myself."

"It's all a pitiful story—"

"Yes, one in which I unfortunately find myself stuck in the middle."

"By now you should know that the people of Evansville realize they've been had by a drunken husband, an unfaithful wife, a shyster lawyer, a libelous newspaper editor, and an economically distressed, xenophobic public."

Roman nodded, closing his eyes. "That won't change the verdict."

"Mr. Jones and I are in the process of petitioning the Governor of Indiana for a pardon. Until then, however, you're, as you say, stuck. In prison, that is. But don't forget, you've got a lot of Protestant friends—Remember, I was once a Protestant. There's still hope for you, Father. Several leading Protestant Whig attorneys are weighing in with letters to the Governor. Even Archibald Dixon is involved once again, this time with the support of many prominent Whigs. My friend, the Illinois attorney, Abraham Lincoln says it will only be a matter of time before the Whig party disintegrates. No matter what some of the Whig editors say, Catholic immigrants are here to stay and I'm sure there's a lot more on their way. Believe me, there are men of honor who attest to your innocence."

"Just as many believe I'm guilty from what they read in the papers. Sales of the book detailing my trial have been brisk from what I gather."

"True, but the tide is turning."

"I'm not so sure. Even my prayer is devoid of meaning anymore. The prison's guards won't let me have my breviary for fear I'll tear out a page and choke myself to death. I'm surprised the guard here, Mr. Pike, hasn't offered to feed the pages to me. He walks around massaging the handle of his revolver as if he can't wait for me to make a move justifying his shooting me in the head."

"I've written former President Van Buren in hopes he might help your cause," Thomas continued. "He remembers you from his visit to Evansville in 1840, but he can't help since he's so caught up in the abolitionist movement now—which is good, it's about time someone lay the axe to the root of that evil."

"Ben. Stop. It's no use. I'll be in here for the next four and a half years."

"I will not. The writer, Henry David Thoreau, wrote recently that, to secure the rights of one man is to secure the rights of all men. I believe that. If one member of the American Republic is deprived of justice, then the justice of the entire republic is threatened. As I've said, if you're innocent—of which I know you are—then America is guilty of a grave injustice.

****

15 October 1844

In the course of time, Roman learned that Mother Theodore Guérin had established a new school, Saint Anne's Academy, near St. Michael's parish in Madison, Indiana.

He was incredulous when he saw Mother Theodore enter the outer hallway with the guard, Calvin Pike.

"*Merci, Monsieur.*" She nodded to Pike, dismissing him.

"I can stand here if I like," Pike replied, glaring at her.

Mother Theodore addressed Roman in French, "*Bonjour, Père Roman.*"

He scrambled to his feet, addressing his visitor. "*Bonjour, Mere Theodore.*"

He thanked her for coming and he continued the conversation in French. "How did you get past the guard?"

"I have a letter of permission from Lieutenant Governor Bright. The guard had no choice."

"Hey, you're in America," yelled Pike, "so speak like it, not that Latin mumbo-jumbo, or else I'll make you leave."

"Sir," Mother turned to Pike, addressing him in perfect English, "I have already shown you my letter from the Lieutenant Governor. So if you would, please afford us the common decency of a little privacy or I may have to inform him of your behavior."

"I won't allow no woman to talk to me like that, and I don't take no orders from no woman either!" Pike fumed, moving toward the steps.

"I have learned that the higher courts have refused to overturn your conviction." She closed her eyes and returned her attention to Roman.

"Yes, there are times when I can't even pray, the cross is so heavy."

"We must never yield to discouragement, especially in prayer. Take courage. The Cross awaits us at every turn, but it is the way to heaven. You may have to wait longer than you would like, but persevere in your forbearance. Trust Him with all your heart."

"It's so difficult sometimes not to wish harm upon my enemies. Oh, the indignation I feel."

"Indeed, it is very difficult, and it requires an uncommon virtue, not to make others suffer when we suffer. I would suffer for you or at least alleviate your affliction, but be assured I do share it. Remember my father was murdered when I was but fifteen years old."

"Monseigneur Martin has reminded me that I must forgive my accusers. It isn't an easy task."

"Charity consists in sincerely loving persons whose inclinations are most opposed to ours, in pardoning those who injure us."

"'Seventy times seven,' but putting it into practice is another thing."

"Father, have confidence in Divine Providence, and if you lean upon Providence you will find yourself well supported. God will provide a way out for you, as the Lord told the prophet Jeremiah, 'I have plans for your future, full of hope, not woe. I know well the plans I have in mind for you, plans for your welfare, not for woe! I will bring you back to the place from which I have exiled you.'"

"Encouraging words, Mother, but none that will break through these bars."

"I understand your discouragement. Sometimes I have been so disheartened in this country. So much so that I feel that I am carrying on my shoulders the weight of its highest mountains, and in my heart all the thorns of its wilderness. There have been times where I have nearly lost all courage, but Divine Providence has never failed to break in upon the darkness and give me the strength to lift my soul and to lift up those around me who are faltering. None of us knows what the future holds in store for us, especially with what happened to you, and now is happening to our dear sisters in Madison."

"I am unaware, Mother."

"The Sisters have been hit with stones and eggs, insulted and spat upon. Just two nights ago the ruffians surrounded the convent and threw stones at us and verbally abused us. In September, some of the hoodlums climbed over our fence and were about to enter the cloister when some of the young Irish railroad laborers drove them away with pistol fire. Thank Providence no one was injured or killed. There is a story circulating that the sisters and I gained entry to the Protestant school and stole some books. We are also being blamed for the disappearance of a child in Madison. The claim is that we kidnaped the poor child and murdered her. These miseries weigh me down so much, but even more than these are the threats of future misfortunes."

"Mother, do they not see the good that you are doing?"

"I believe that to do any good in America, you must be entirely dependent upon the Spirit of God. To fulfill your vocation here, you must be a saint!

"And that is why I have suffered so. I am not a saint."

"Your humility is the first step to sanctity. You must trust God in these matters."

"Why must these Protestants continue their persecution of us here in America?"

"Oh, but even the poor little Protestant children who are enrolled in our school have been the victims of prejudice as well. Allow me to speak for the majority of Protestants. They are fine men and women. One such gentleman is the Lieutenant Governor, Jesse Bright. He's a Presbyterian, yet he has sent his three daughters to our Academy. We spoke about you, concerning your questionable trial and imprisonment. He is opposed to all bigotry and prejudice against Catholics. He assured me that he would speak to Governor Whitcomb regarding your case."

"Thank you. I have come close to despair within these prison walls. There have been days where I have prayed for death questioning whether all of what I have gone through was worth it."

"Father, when my own dear father was murdered it felt like I was in prison, the light of the sun did not shine for at least a year," she said, pausing containing emotion. "Of course, I was not in a dark cell like this. There have been times during my illnesses that I too prayed for death, but I have learned that the fruit of so many sufferings, physical and moral, borne for God, is profitable for our souls and account for great grace in eternity. For we know there is no glory without a cross. I know this to be true. The dear bishop of *Le Mans* in France told me before I first set sail for America, that there would be trials awaiting us here in the United States. How right he was. Nevertheless, he also said, everything concurs to the greater good of those who love God. God's chosen ones are molded in the winepress of affliction. So, Father Roman Weinzoepfel, I say to you, do not sink to despair, rather embrace this cross so as to rise again. In the cross is infusion of heavenly sweetness. Crosses are precious gifts from our Lord. He gives them to those he has chosen. We must offer our suffering to God. Prayer alone is our hope."

"Thank you, Mother." Roman knew that she was saying a lot without mentioning any of her own trials that she had experienced at the hands of His Lordship. "I will remember that some of Saint Paul's letters containing words of encouragement were written while he was imprisoned."

"Blessed be God. There is one thing of which I am certain: We must have confidence in Divine Providence."

"I will remember that Mother. Your visit has lifted my soul."

"Glory be to God."

Roman smiled at her. "How is Sister Mary Magdalene?"

"Wonderful. Sister Magdalene has brought our community great happiness."

"Mr. and Mrs. Linck must be very proud."

"Yes, they are. They send their blessings to you. I stayed in Evansville for a while this spring."

"How is Father Deydier?"

"He is doing well. He gave our Sisters their annual retreat this past August."

"And how is our Lordship, Bishop Hailandière?" Roman asked.

"He has a difficult task, managing such a large diocese. There are times when he spends weeks at a time at our Motherhouse in the Woods. Pray for him. He is so discouraged." She paused a moment before continuing. "We must not demand the same virtues and qualities from others that we demand of ourselves." She hesitated and looked out the window. "At times our harshest trials come to us from those closest to us.

"I do not think there is a man in the entire world so universally detested as the bishop of Vincennes. Our good sisters have often wondered if we should leave, but I am convinced that our Lord Jesus desires for us to be here. It is impossible to portray his Lordship's solicitude for me during my illnesses and all the attention he lavished on me. The tenderest father or the most affectionate mother could not have done more for an only child. Oh, to see this holy and venerable Prelate at my bedside offering me every consolation moves me to tears."

Roman knew that things had not changed. He knew what sorrows the community at Saint Mary-of-the-Woods had suffered at the hands of His Lordship, but he also knew that out of respect for the office of bishop and not to offend against charity, she would not speak ill against him.

Roman looked at Mother Theodore and said, "I pray that all shall go well for the Sisters of Providence."

"And I pray that Governor Whitcomb will pardon you." She paused, grasping the pectoral cross that hung about her neck. "Father Roman, with all your heart trust your affairs to God and put them under the protection of Mary and Joseph, and you will see that all shall be well. And know that here in prison you suffer vicariously for all those who suffer in our midst, none the least of which is the Negro and the American Indian. *Adieu.*"

Chapter 26

Poor Souls

31 October 1844

On All Hallow's Eve, Roman received a visit from Fr Durbin. Durbin told him that Benjamin Thomas was with the pastor of Jasper, Indiana, Fr Kundek, in St Charles, Missouri, taking depositions from some individuals who had heard Martin Schmoll boasting in a tavern that he and his wife had received money in perpetrating the tale that *that priest* had raped Mrs. Schmoll.

Mr. Thomas wanted to file a suit against Mr. Schmoll but Roman refused, asking that he put a halt to all further legal actions. He believed that his innocence was less important than the additional harm that might come as a result of more legal action. "My situation—indeed that of all Catholics in America—will be only be made worse if we continue to further exacerbate the public furor over my case. Regarding Mr. Schmoll's confession, any legal efforts could provoke more violence and only add fuel to the smoldering fires of Anti-Catholicism. I have resigned to serve my sentence. I fear it would also insult those decent Protestants who've had a change of heart."

The subject changed and Roman inquired of His Lordship Hailandière. "I have not received word from him since May."

"He has left the country," Durbin answered. "He set sail for Europe en route to Rome for his *ad limina* visit to the pope, but most believe he will formally submit his resignation as bishop."

"Resign?"

"Yes, Vicar General Martin is serving as temporary Administrator of the Diocese of Vincennes."

Roman was stunned, but not entirely surprised. He recalled his conversation with His Lordship in Vincennes two and a half years before.

On All Soul's Day, the second of November, a stranger entered the corridor outside his cell. "A distinguished visitor for you, Mr.

Weinzoepfel." Pike opened the cell door and let a man in gray overalls and a red flannel work shirt into the cell.

"I'm Governor Whitcomb," the man said.

"Please be seated," Roman said, straightening his shirt. The governor sat on a small chair at one end of the cell while Roman sat on his cot. "Sir, why are you dressed like a smithy?"

"There are a lot of people who wouldn't take too kindly to me paying you a visit."

"Then why are you here?" Roman sat down.

"I came to let you know I believe in your innocence."

"Then you've come to pardon me?"

"Uh, no, not at all, but my Lieutenant Governor *thinks* I should because some French nun in Terre Haute is pushing for it."

Roman's hopes sank as quickly as they had risen.

"Attorneys from all over have written me telling me the same. A leading Evansville attorney thought the charges against you were absurd from the beginning but didn't say anything. But now he's convinced of your innocence."

"Why tell me this if things are to remain as the same and I am to serve my full sentence?"

"I don't want you to think that I think you're guilty."

Roman said nothing but knew the governor was trying to balance politics with justice.

"I've read the transcript of the trial myself and it looks flimsy. I'm swimming in letters telling me that I should pardon you, but you must try and understand my dilemma. If I refuse to grant you a pardon, I'm liable to alienate the Catholic Democrat vote. If I do grant the pardon, then Protestant Democrats will vote for my Whig opponent in the Governor's race, and possibly the presidential race as well, costing Polk the election.

"The warden of the prison here, Mr. Pratt, has recommended I pardon you. He's never interceded on behalf of any of the prisoners, even prisoners that my predecessor pardoned. The Bishops of Vincennes, Cincinnati, St Louis, New Orleans, Detroit, Louisville—I can't remember the others—they've all written me about your sentence, asking me to grant you a pardon. I've never seen the likes.

"Even former President Van Buren has written me on your account wanting me to pardon you. Of course, he's embroiled in his own troubles. He up and quit the Democratic Party which he helped

333

form and took up the anti-slavery banner, becoming a regular statesman, I might say. Of course, he's lost most of the support from the Democrats, and the Whigs won't have him either.

"Then, like I said, my lieutenant governor, Mr. Bright, has been talking to that French Mother Superior from Terre Haute, Mother Theresa or Thomasina something or other."

"Theodore. Mother Theodore Guérin."

"Whatever, the woman seems to be everywhere—Evansville, Vincennes, Logansport, Madison—who knows where else. She's bold, she is. Anyway, her nuns teach my lieutenant governor's girls down at Madison and he's pressuring me to pardon you as well. What's the world coming to when men start listening to women?

"And speaking of women, just this past week I received a petition signed by nearly five hundred women of Vanderburgh County. They claim that the court was too quick to believe the word of the Schmoll woman, and in light of recent revelations concerning the Schmolls, they assure me that you're innocent. The women claim that though they have no political voice, they believe that in your case they must raise a united cry for your immediate pardon. Can you imagine what the press would do to me if I grant the pardon and then they get wind of this letter? They'll have a heyday accusing me of advocating women's suffrage and have something else to blame you for. It'd be political suicide!

"Of the letters and petitions I've received, there are about three thousand signatures. And the majority of the folks asking for your release are Protestant. And even if I did pardon you, who's to say that the political unrest between Catholics and Protestants that erupted in Philadelphia and New York after your trial won't spread to other cities? Before long the whole country would be embroiled in an Orange-Catholic war, whole cities being burnt by Protestants and Catholics. America could find itself at war from within. Banish the thought.

"These are strange times, Reverend. There have been preachers who've said your trial was prophesied in the book of the Apocalypse. Now they say the end of the world is imminent. Indeed, these are strange times. Try to understand my position. It's an election year, man. My hands are tied—"

"Mine *were*." Roman held out his hands, looking at his wrists where the cuffs had once rubbed him raw.

"It was a figure of speech, Father. But doesn't the scripture teach that it's better that one man suffer than for an entire nation to perish? I simply can't pardon you. It's an election year."

After the governor's visit, Roman slipped into a violet lachrymosity. He knew he could let the sorrow wash up from his heart and bathe his cheeks, but he kept his emotion in check for fear that once the floodgates were opened he wouldn't be able to stop. Barefoot in his cell, he scrawled a cross upon the damp stonewall of his cell and prayed.

By the Feast of Christ the King and the Advent Season, his cross had become nearly unbearable, with stomach pain and tremendously blinding headaches. *The accusation of profaning the sacrament of penance and violating my priestly vows is insufferable. O Lord, help me to see that it is for Thee that I have suffered and my suffering has not been in vain..*

From late November through December the snow fell deeply, preventing visitors and his usual weekly reception of the Eucharist. He did hear the news that Governor Whitcomb had been reelected and James Knox Polk of Tennessee had won the U.S. Presidency.

On Christmas Eve, Mr. Pratt finally returned from his long absence and entered Roman's cell. He returned Roman's breviary and the leather pouch containing his mass kit.

"A blessed Christmas Eve to you, Father Roman," Pratt said, handing Roman the mass kit.

"Mr. Pratt. Bless you."

"I know this is against the rules, but I thought you might want to celebrate Midnight Mass."

Roman opened the drawstring of the pouch, removing the altar stone, chalice, and paten placing them on his chair.

"Here's a small flask of wine and a piece of bread," Pratt said, holding the items out. "My wife made it without yeast. At least I think that's how you Catholics take it. I'll be back in the morning. Happy Christmas."

Roman blessed him and carefully removed the altar cards from the pouch and placed them on the seat. He then took out the tattered purple and white stole, reverently placed it around his neck, both ends draped over his shoulders and hanging down the front of his shirt, crossing the ends to form an X over his chest. Then kneeling upon the floor, he prepared to offer the sacred mysteries celebrating the

Solemnity of the Incarnation of Christ the Lord. He opened his breviary and sang the Latin Christmas hymns.

Holding the piece of bread in his hands over the small paten he whispered the words of consecration and lifting it up he beheld His Savior's humility in the frail morsel. Cupping his hands around the small dented silver chalice and breathing the benediction over the fermented fruit of the vine he raised the Precious Blood in awe.

He knelt in adoration as if he was in the lowly cattle stall to worship the babe in the manger on Bethlehem's plain.

He prayed the *Pater Noster* and the *Agnus Dei* and prepared to receive the Eucharist. *Lord I am not worthy Thou should enter under my roof, but only say the word and my soul shall be healed. Grant that I may be made one in union with Thee and Thy mystical body. Let my suffering be accepted as penance for lost souls.*

Roman placed the Bread of Life on his tongue, allowing it to dissolve into his being. Then taking the chalice of the Blood of Life he consumed it, the Savior's blood flowing into his own.

Though Mr. Pratt removed the mass kit from the cell the next day, he did allow Roman to keep his breviary. He prayed from it as never before, caressing the familiar colorful ribbons, looking upon the pages as if being reunited with a long absent friend returning from a forgotten war. Much of his free time he spent in prayer, chanting psalms and canticles, and uttering many recognizable passages from its pages.

No trial has come to you but what is human. God is faithful and will not let you be tried beyond your strength; but with the trial he will also provide a way out, so that you may be able to bear it.

He prayed that the scriptures might be fulfilled.

Chapter 27

Epiphany

6 January 1845

Roman's hope of one day committing himself to the demands of a thirty-day Ignatian retreat had oddly been granted yet this was no place to perform spiritual exercises. The silence of darkness, hour upon hour, was only periodically interrupted with cries of anguish from fellow inmates ruing their criminal behavior or bemoaning lost loves. In the loneliness of his sentence, he longed for an interruption, regretting the many times he had longed for solitude rather than fellowship, even more desirous for a companion in the abyss into which he had continued to descend. To simply have one visitor to draw him out of the cavernous gulf on the edge of hell where he was lost in a ravine of self-pity might shed light into the darkest crevices of his mind and the chaos of his soul.

How often had the question of a student seemed ridiculous? How often had he wanted to be alone to pray? Now he prayed for one meaningful question of creed, one student's question of faith, anyone's desire for prayers, or just two or three devout parishioners who longed to hear the words of the gospel.

How petty he had previously thought the penitents' confessions of venial sins and minor faults while they failed to name mortal sins. Yet now, he longed to hear one lost sinner's confession—though rife with imperfect contrition—just to know that he could still absolve the sinner.

Oh, to take the sacred vessels in his hands, pour the cruet of wine into the golden chalice, and let a drop from the water cruet disappear into the sanguine Burgundy. To behold the Sacred Host between his thumbs and index fingers lifted on high for the faithful to bow in worship. Such hallowed duties would surely assure him of his priesthood.

He thought of his accuser and her accomplices in the grave injustice that he now suffered.

****

Roman closed his eyes. He was eighteen. One of the village girls from the parish, a friend of his sisters was interested in him. The girl came to the Weinzoepfel farm one afternoon and in her love for him collapsed in his arms. Roman recalled the intoxicating smell of her hair in his face and the warmth of her body in his embrace. Wordlessly, he held her close communicating his care and concern to her. Was the priesthood or matrimony to have been his vocation and joy? It was only a fleeting thought at the time for his father had come out of the barn and startled him.

The girl, Colette, was shocked when Roman pushed her away ending the embrace.

"What are you doing, boy?" his father asked.

Wordlessly, Colette looked at Roman, pulled her hair back, and secured her headscarf.

"Every son of mine must pull his weight. I'm fifty years old. I can't have one of my sons courting a sweetheart on my time."

His older brothers, Jean and Valentin, had looked on in silence.

His father was easily agitated. Mother had suffered another miscarriage and was in bed recovering. His brother Franz could only ridicule. "Stay away from Colette. Some priest you'll be."

Roman's mother was fond of his desire to become a priest and had been the one to convince his father that he had a call to the priesthood. In the middle of second semester of his second year of minor seminary, on the sixth of March, his brothers Jean and Valentin sent word that his father was ill. Upon his arrival, he learned that his father had died. It was only after serving at his father's funeral Mass that he felt he could fully take up the mantle of the priestly life.

The thought of Colette returned. Had he only thought he had loved her? He wondered what had become of her.

His feelings toward his father were carefully denied until he found himself alone with them in the long night of prison silence.

When Roman was only six, the deaths of his newborn siblings, the twins, Joseph and Anne, changed his father. So had the failing crops and terrible seasons, not enough rain and the insufferable heat, not to mention the political unrest and the threat of military incursion or Protestant loyalists eager to control the Rhine Valley. His father had favored Franz among his sons, even over his eldest Jean and second born son Valentin. He always favored Franz. Franz resembled his side of the family. Roman and the other boys favored the Biehly's, their mother's side.

He could see how his father may have felt trapped for the demands he faced were daunting, providing for his wife, four girls and five sons. There was no question his father loved him and his family, yet for a young man, Roman was still hurt by his father's coldness. And his knowledge of the reasons his father was so stern didn't immediately ameliorate the grief he felt, then or now. It merely helped him to understand his father. Had he never been required by the prison bars to ponder his relationship with his father he may have never had the opportunity to forgive him.

What little sunlight penetrated his prison, the shadows slowly spilled down into the damp walls of his cell. During the days and nights of silence he thought of death. And if he hadn't had an opportunity to grieve his father at the time of his death, or grieve for his sister Catherine, brothers Jean and Valentin, or especially the death of his mother, he did now.

Never before and never more clearly was death before his eyes, especially his own. He believed it would have been enough to make the most austere Trappist or Carthusian monk cringe. Here in the silence of the penitentiary, Roman was face to face with the shadows of his past. As Ignatius had surrendered his sword upon the altar of the abbey church at Montserrat and made his retreat in the cave at Manresa where he crafted his spiritual exercises, Roman was forced to surrender himself to the will of God, though he had no sword, and Jeffersonville was certainly no Montserrat.

Take Lord, receive, my memory, my understanding, my entire will.

Working to recall where he was in his praying of the office, he considered the end of Christmas.

Epiphany, Greek for *manifestation*. What had this Christmas season manifested to him? There was no star hovering over Jeffersonville and no wise men bearing gold or frankincense humbling themselves to visit his lowly cell.

He resumed with his prayer, singing the words of a French Carol.

He discovered his eyes completely fogged as he looked at the barred and cracked windowpane frosted in January ice at the top of his cell wall.

As his cheeks became moist he questioned himself. Why such an emotional tumult? He tried to stop himself and swallowed hard the cry that would have sounded forth, echoing throughout the dank, horrid prison. Despite this, he still wasn't in control, either of himself or the situation. Something like this hadn't happened since Grandmother Weinzoepfel died. He couldn't understand. He had maintained his composure at the death of both his parents and three older siblings. But now such a display felt like a sin against not only his manhood, but at odds with his priesthood. The sleeves of his shirt were damp from wiping his eyes.

As he heaved sighs in a pathetic attempt at regaining measured breaths, a thought, or a voice, he wasn't certain, suggested that his effusive surge was not a sin at all, but rather a gift.

Had he heretofore been unmoved by God's grace and insensible to the urging of the Spirit? Was he only now seeing himself for who he truly was: poor in spirit, completely dependent upon God?

From his academic studies of spirituality, he knew that tears cleansed the soul by washing away evil desires. Gregory the Great explained that there were two types of tears: tears of compunction, which express sorrow for sin, and tears of joy which express an unfulfilled desire for God.

A passage from St. Paul's letter to the Romans came to mind. *I consider that the sufferings of this present time are as nothing compared with the glory to be revealed for us.*

Roman then understood his tears. It was his Epiphany, a true manifestation of God's Grace. The scriptures became clear. *We can endure the worst suffering imaginable because of Him who first loved us and loved us to the last upon the cross. No greater love is there than this. Beloved, do not be surprised that a trial by fire is occurring among you, as if something strange were happening to you. But rejoice to the extent that you share in the sufferings of Christ, so that when his glory is revealed you may also rejoice exultantly.*

He took heart in the Word of God.

In the middle of February, the snow began to melt and the first tokens of spring's new life broke through the surface of the wet earth. Roman knew that it was only by God's grace that he was surviving his imprisonment. He began to believe God might still have a mission for him once he was released.

O Lord, show me where in Thy vineyard where Thou would have me serve. Once released, am I to return to Europe? Or if I am somehow granted a way out and released before the appointed time I willingly accept it as a sign of your Divine favor and will to spend the rest of my days here serving you and building your Church in America. O Lord, I place my life in Thy hands. Grant me only Thy grace and charity in order to do Thy will.

Forgive my enemies, Lord. He paused. *And grant me the grace to forgive them as well.*

By the first weeks of Lent, he began the custom of praying the penitential psalms, prostrate with arms outstretched upon the floor in cruciform. Like the Apostles, Roman considered the things he had formerly regarded as all-important and reconsidered them in the light of Christ. Paul had considered all earthly treasure as dross compared to the knowledge of Christ, forfeiting everything for his sake, and accounted all else as rubbish in light of his faith in Christ. Roman prayed for the same grace so as to consider Christ his only wealth as he continually struggled each day to unite his own sufferings with the sufferings of Christ.

Chapter 28

Resurrexit

25 February 1845

Roman had nearly forgotten he was kneeling upon the stone floor in prayer before his scrawled chalk cross upon the damp stonewall when he heard the unmistakable voice of Monseigneur Abbé Augustin Martin.

"*Lazare, veni foras.*"

Lazarus, come forth? Roman turned and rose to see Monseigneur standing with Mr. Pratt. The warden's keys clanked against the iron cell door. The words of Christ to Lazarus from the eleventh chapter of the Gospel of St John returned to his memory: *And he that had been dead four days came forth, bound hand and feet.*

"Monseigneur Martin?"

Pratt began unlocking the door.

Roman stepped forward, his leg shackles clangoring against the stone floor. "What brings you here, Monseigneur?"

"Father Roman, your hopes have been realized," said the Monseigneur, appearing from the shadow of the adjoining cell. "This is the day of the Lord. Justice has spoken and set prisoners free!"

Was it just another dream?

Pratt entered the cell first. "What a glorious morning for the Resurrection."

Roman was incredulous at the words as Mr. Pratt worked at turning the key in its lock.

"It isn't Easter," Roman said aloud.

"It came early this year, Father," Monseigneur Martin smiled.

Mr. Pratt bent down and unlocked the shackles from his ankles. "You're a free man, Father Weinzoepfel. Here are the papers signed by the governor." He held out an official document for Roman to see.

"Is this true, Monseigneur?"

"Yes. I was on a visit to the Sisters of Providence at Madison when I received word of the unexpected news earlier today,"

"How did it happen?" Roman asked, excited.

"I think Mother Theodore Guérin pressuring Lieutenant Governor Bright had something to do with it, but Sarah Childress Polk, did it. She's a pistol they say. She's the wife of the newly elected President, James Knox Polk. She told the governor that if he didn't pardon you, her husband would.

"Think of it," Monseigneur Martin continued. "You were unjustly imprisoned at the word of a German Catholic woman and now you have been vindicated by the word of an American Protestant woman."

As they prepared to leave the prison, Monseigneur Abbé Martin told Roman the story of how President-Elect Polk and his wife, Sarah "Sally" Childress Polk, were en route to Washington, D.C. aboard the side-wheeler *The Clarksville* for the March presidential inauguration. The Governor of Indiana, and his Lieutenant Governor boarded the vessel in Louisville joining the president-elect's party.

When the boat passed Jeffersonville, the party observed a large tower. It was then that Mrs. Polk asked the governor about a large building and its tower. The governor told her it was the state penitentiary. "That wouldn't, by chance, be the same state penitentiary where the venerable Catholic priest, Roman Weinzoepfel, is incarcerated?" she asked. He affirmed that it was and she then asked him, "Well, Governor, what do you think?" she continued. "Do you think he is innocent or guilty?"

The governor explained how he had been inundated with requests for his release with nearly four thousand signatures on his desk. Mrs. Polk was astounded at the number and inquired further, asking if there was anyone else speaking on Roman's behalf. When the governor answered that about four hundred and eighty two women from the Evansville area signed a petition arguing for his innocence he maintained that their voice didn't count for anything. Indignantly, Mrs. Polk launched into the governor, retorting that someday women would have the right to vote and insisted that women have the right to voice their opinion in the face of injustice. She was ready to add her name to the petition to become the four hundred and eighty-third woman on the list.

"She told him, 'If everyone, including you yourself, knows that he is innocent, then why is he still in shackles? Pardon him. Set him at liberty. If you don't, I'll see to it that my husband does when we get to Washington.'" The governor must have seen his chance for a cabinet post in the Polk White House evaporate that very hour. The governor was true to his word and granted the pardon as soon as he returned to Indianapolis.

"Sally Polk is quite the formidable political figure," Abbé Martin laughed. "The story is that if it weren't for her name, *Childress*, James Knox Polk wouldn't have been elected lamplighter! She's old money."

****

Roman asked Monseigneur Abbé Martin where he would be sent now that he was freed. The Monseigneur informed him that he was to go to Bardstown to recuperate. "The Jesuit Fathers there at St. Thomas Seminary will offer you their hospitality."

"But I am vowed for Vincennes."

"Very well. I am the Vicar General of the Diocese of Vincennes and since the bishop is *in absentia,* I am the Diocesan Administrator *pro tempore*. I am sending you to Bardstown."

Calvin Pike suddenly showed outside the cell and handed Pratt a box.

Removing the lid, Pratt revealed Roman's priestly biretta and neatly folded soutane. "Your clothes, Reverend Father, freshly washed and neatly pressed. My wife wanted you to look your best. We heard last night that the governor was on his way to Indianapolis to sign your pardon." He paused briefly before continuing. "Oh, and I wouldn't want to forget this. Here." Pratt reached into his frock coat and produced Roman's rosary.

"*Deo gratias*." Roman took the sacramental object into his hands as if it were a recovered buried treasure, its chain pure silver and the beads solid gold.

Pike retreated up the stairs with nothing but a smirk.

Roman changed his prison garments for the soutane and placed his biretta down over his long uncut hair. It felt odd to be dressed as a priest once again.

He and the Monseigneur walked to the wharf, took a skiff across the Ohio River, and made it to the Louisville Cathedral in time for Vespers. Afterwards the elderly Bishop Flagét insisted upon taking Roman to dinner. Roman's bearded face and near shoulder length hair rendered his identity incognito.

"Monseigneur, Fr Roman, we will take dinner at the *Galt House Hotel*," Flagét said.

"Are you sure we can afford such luxury?" Roman protested.

"Not to worry, Fr Roman. As our beloved Fr Durbin says, 'shrouds have no pockets.'"

"Yes, the Irish have a way with wit," Martin smiled.

"And a way with shillelaghs," Roman said out of the side of his mouth.

Flagét and Martin laughed while Roman managed to keep a straight face thinking of the night in Evansville nearly three years before when Durbin's troops, as they came to be called, saved him from extinction.

Once at the *Galt House*, the *maitre d'* poured each man a glass of dark Burgundy, set the carafe in the center of the table, and told them the house specialties. The bishop and Monseigneur ordered *Kentucky Fried Passenger Pigeon*.

Roman ordered roasted pork with potatoes. He placed the crystal glass to his mouth, inhaled the bouquet, and enjoyed the smooth taste of the dry, dark red wine. There was to be no comparison between the *Galt House* dinner and prison gruel.

The bishop's conversation turned to the providential release of Roman. "I know Mother Theodore had a hand in it, but the best part of it all was the president's wife getting involved." They recounted again the story of what had happened aboard *The Clarksville* and how Sally Childress Polk had secured Roman's pardon from the Governor of Indiana.

The rest of the evening seemed unreal. After dinner, Roman accompanied Monseigneur Martin to Bishop Flagét's splendid home and retired to one of the guest rooms. He pulled back the covers and fresh linen of the featherbed, sat before the crackling fire in the hearth, and prayed *Compline*. Once his head nestled against the pillow sleep overtook his tired body and weary soul. He slept as he hadn't slept in several years.

The following morning Roman celebrated mass. He was still unsure he wasn't dreaming. After mass, Roman and Monseigneur Martin left Louisville for Bardstown. That afternoon they arrived at St. Joseph's Cathedral and made a visit to the Blessed Sacrament before announcing their arrival at the Seminary.

Much to Roman's chagrin, once his identity was discovered beneath the year's growth of hair and his mustache and beard, he was welcomed like a war hero. All he wanted to do was retire to the cloister and be at peace.

It took time for him to absorb the reality of his release. He prayed as never before in praises and psalms.

Thou hast loosened my bonds. Alleluia, Alleluia! From on high He reached down and seized me from the pit, snatching me from the grips of my foes, and rescuing me from the watery clay. Bringing me forth into freedom, He saved me because He loved me.

When the Lord delivered Zion from bondage, it seemed like a dream. Thou hast delivered me from my enemies, and from the hands of all who hated me. Alleluia, Alleluia!

****

7 March 1845

Within two weeks of arriving in Bardstown, Fr Durbin arrived at the seminary. Roman was just finishing dinner in the refectory when Durbin approached him. "Your pastor, Father Deydier, sends you his blessings, Fr Roman. He regrets not being able to visit, but he sends an old friend in his place. He motioned for Roman to join him outside.

Upon exiting the building, Roman looked on with great happiness. "Shadow." He hurried to his horse and patted him on his mane. "I've missed you."

The horse whinnied, nodded its head up and down, and stomped its right front hoof.

"He's happy to see his old friend." Durbin smiled.

For Roman, the feeling was mutual. Meanwhile, his Easter was a true resurrection from the dead.

****

Roman made Bardstown and the Catholic enclave of Nelson County and neighboring Washington and Marion Counties his temporary domicile as he adjusted to his reclaimed freedom. He fell in love with this part of Kentucky for it was so much like his native Alsatian homeland, hilly and populated by a large contingency of Catholics. Great joy was found in praying the rosary while riding Shadow. In a sense, he wished that he had known about Bardstown before Vincennes.

He spent Holy Week with the Jesuits at St. Mary's College in Marion County and stayed in the guesthouse of the Sisters of Loretto. Slowly, his life seemed to be getting back to normal.

He continued in Bardstown, preoccupied with the thought of where it was in the Church's vineyard God desired for him to spend the rest of his life. He discerned the call to religious life while living there at St. Thomas Seminary and envisioned a life of prayer and work where he would live his days in accord with the seven canonical hours of prayer, the rosary, holy mass, daily spiritual reading, and the measured steadiness of the devout life lived in fidelity to the teachings of the Church.

In a letter to Monseigneur Martin he told him his thoughts. Monseigneur replied that Fr Sorin of *Notre Dame* was looking for new members of his Congregation of the Holy Cross. The Monseigneur said he would consult with the bishops of Bardstown and Cincinnati about Roman's possible transfer to the religious life. And in a letter, Fr Sorin himself invited Roman to Notre Dame for a visit.

By late summer it seemed a shroud of gray mist concealed everything from May of 1842 to February of 1845. Not only could he not remember much, he questioned whether there was anything to remember at all. The depths of despair in his darkest hours was now nothing but a shadow of a forgotten time.

He prepared himself for a cloister somewhere. In fact, a hermit's life would serve both him and the church quite well, he thought. He thought of the Holy Cross Congregation again and again. Soon he had his answer. He would travel to Vincennes, meet with Monseigneur Martin, or the new bishop, whomever that may be, and explain his desire to become a religious.

After seven months in Catholic Kentucky, he prepared to leave for Vincennes. On the night before he was to leave, Fr Elisha Durbin and a couple of the Jesuit professors invited him to Talbot's Tavern for dinner. While they were there enjoying the house specialty of *Kentucky Fried Pigeon*, a group of Irish boys were drinking and singing their favorite songs. With a crowd gathered about his table, Roman told them that he was leaving for Vincennes in the morning where he was to receive his next assignment. Those in the tavern sang along while the pianist played *Auld Lang Syne*.

Roman thanked his well-wishers and returned to the seminary. Only there, in the solitude of his room, did he wipe away a tear.

The next day, the Seventh of October, the feast of the Holy Rosary, he saddled Shadow and trod away. There was a pang of regret and grief as the autumn sun burst upon the refulgent leaves of sunny yellow, golden brown, and apple red in the foothills of what had become his Kentucky home. Once again, he was leaving home. He told the *Ave* beads as he journeyed forward into an uncertain future.

Chapter 29

Lost at See

11 October 1845

Four days later, upon arriving at the chancery, Roman met with Monseigneur Augustin Martin concerning his transfer to the Congregation of the Holy Cross at *Notre Dame du Lac*.

"I consulted the Bishops of Cincinnati and New Orleans concerning your situation, Fr Roman," Martin explained, "however, an administrator of a diocese is not permitted to sign a letter of excardination unless the bishop has been absent for a year. However, since you had written me, and His Excellency Hailandière has been absent since last November, nearly a year—and who knows whether he has resigned or not, I will grant your excardination from Vincennes to Notre Dame. Nevertheless, always know that you will be considered a son of Vincennes."

"*Merci, beaucoup, Monseigneur.*"

The two went for a walk and recounted the events of the past few years. Standing on the steps of the cathedral, a swift breeze blew Roman's biretta off his head.

"It is good to see that some things never change," Monseigneur Martin chortled.

Roman smiled, chasing after the hat.

The following day he celebrated the Liturgy with the German-speaking congregation of the city before departing. He took one last walk around the cathedral grounds and along the river before climbing atop Shadow, bidding Vincennes adieu.

Once at Notre Dame Monseigneur Martin wrote Roman within two weeks to inform him that His Lordship Hailandière had returned on the sixteenth of October. The Pope had not accepted his resignation during his *ad limina* visit, but instead the pope had emboldened him to return and continue as bishop. "The bishop is also aware that you were granted a pardon and have incardinated with Fr Sorin's order. He regrets your decision to leave his diocese, but wishes you Godspeed."

Roman passed several months at *Notre Dame*. The Advent and Christmas Seasons were marked with three feet of snow and January and February offered more of the same with piercingly cold temperatures. In the meantime he had been appointed Novice Master for the Congregation. However, owing to the winter weather and the remote location there were no novices and there were few students to teach. Fr Sorin was doubtful that his school of Notre Dame would even survive, so remote was its location in Northern Indiana.

In the middle of February, Roman received an urgent letter from Monseigneur Martin.

Dear Father Roman, on behalf of His Excellency, Bishop Hailandière, you are hereby requested to return to the diocese. According to His Lordship, your excardination process was invalid. A priest ordained titulo missionis, specifically for the missions, may not enter a religious order without the permission of his Ordinary. I regret any misfortune this may bring upon you. And I regret my decision that impugned upon the bishop's authority. Out of obedience and under pain of suspension of your priestly faculties, you are expected to return within a fortnight.

Sincerely, Monseigneur Augustin Martin, Vicar General of the Diocese of Vincennes.

It was indeed apparent that there would be no resignation for the bishop. He had returned reinvigorated from his visit with the Supreme Pontiff.

Roman was stunned at first, then angry. "Why did he wait nearly four months to decide he didn't want me here?" He asked Sorin.

"It doesn't surprise me any," Sorin shook his head. "He claimed I was *non compos mentis*. Why the pope ever let him come back to Vincennes is beyond me. I feel for you, Fr Roman. Who knows, he probably ran the rest of his priests off. Now he's desperate and you're the nearest warm bodied priest that he can claim as his own. He certainly doesn't want me. I'm banished, you know.

"He's just a proud man who likes to lord his authority over his subjects. In my opinion the best bishop has always been the man who doesn't have to keep telling you that he's the bishop! Why do you think I abandoned our Black Oak location east of Vincennes? He wanted to run our Congregation of the Holy Cross like he's trying to run the Sisters of Providence! I should have expected something like this," Sorin lamented.

"I'm so sorry—" Roman started to speak.

"You have nothing to be sorry about, Fr Roman. There are no novices for you to master and I know the terrain here is flat, unlike your beloved Alsace and southern Indiana. I believe the Lord's hand is in all of this. His ways are not our ways nor are his thoughts our thoughts. Mother Theodore Guérin has convinced me that Bishop Hailandière was sent here to test our faith. I believe there will come a day when you will enter the vows of religious life, but not now. The time is not right. You still have churches to build and souls to save in the missions." Sorin put his hand on Roman's shoulder.

Roman was grateful. In the February thaw, he departed for Vincennes astride his steed in strict obedience to His Lordship's word. On the return trip he stopped at the Sisters of Providence at St. Mary-of-the-Woods. The sisters there informed him that Mother Theodore was in Vincennes at the bishop's request.

As he approached Vincennes from the north he thought about his calling as a missionary priest and questioned whether or not he might have been running away from his duties to the diocese by entering the cloister. Perhaps His Lordship's letter requiring him to return to the service of the diocese should be taken as the Word of God.

When he arrived in the See City it was very quiet. He stopped in the Cathedral to make a visit to Jesus in the Blessed Sacrament, and there were three Sisters of Providence praying in the front pews. After a few minutes of silent prayer in thanksgiving for his safe journey, he left the church for the chancery.

Roman rang the bell and patiently waited. He thought he heard His Lordship's voice from inside when Sister Angelique opened the door.

"*Abbé Roman.* Father Roman Weinzoepfel. *Bonjour, bonjour.*"

As she opened the door, Roman heard Bishop Hailandière through the slightly open door yelling at someone in his study. As he stood with Sister Angelique in the front foyer of the rectory, it was apparent to him that she didn't exactly know what to do.

"Your excess politeness is merely discontent badly disguised!" Bishop Hailandière barked. "Do you really wish to withdraw from our diocese? The gold that you see glittering down yonder in New Orleans, which will only prove to be brass! Does it tempt you? How many of your Sisters have been scized with this illusion? Remember you are bound to the Vincennes diocese and its bishop. If you oppose him, you violate your vows, and it would merit from your bishop a severe judgment and Canonical censure, not excluding excommunication! And that goes for all of your Sisters, not simply you!

"Oh, I have also received word from a mutual friend of ours, the bishop of *Le Mans*. You told him your conscience told you to obey me. Then why have you disobeyed your conscience? Why have you spoken ill of your bishop, to impress your sisters? To force me to expel you from the diocese, thereby blaming me for your troubles? I do not know whom else you have been consulting with, but they have given poor counsel and have rendered you a very bad service."

Angelique whispered in Roman's ear, "That nun has done it again."

"As for your alleged illness," Hailandière's voice bellowed, "you were not sick at New Orleans. No, it was a ruse so you could gather the necessary elements in order to have me removed. You have poisoned the mind of the Bishop of New Orleans against me. Sister St. Theodore, what you have written to France and New York concerning me, and knowing you, you have written the pope, but whatever you have written affects me but little," he cried out, his voice becoming hoarse, "but what touches me to the quick is that after having done so much for you and your rising community, which was my only hope, my only consolation, after setting all my priests against me for its advantages and covering myself in your debts...after doing all of this for you, Mother, what he would not have done for his own sister, he has received only ingratitude and continued complaints!

"I am heartbroken," the bishop's voice softened. "But it is without bitterness. Perhaps I have loved you—and your community—too much. I assure you, this is what causes me to suffer so, so much." The bishop stopped, his silence as deafening as his belligerent rage.

Sister Angelique poked her head through the crack in the doorway. Roman heard her whisper loudly, "My Lord, Father Roman Weinzoepfel is here."

"I am busy! Take him to the parlor," Hailandière said. Roman imagined his matching frown. "He will have to wait!"

"Yes, My Lord," Angelique replied in a whimper. Roman nodded to her. He saw that the door to the Vicar General's study across the hall was open. Looking in, the room was empty save for the desk and chair. The bookshelves were scraped bare and the walls were covered with nothing but a few nails where pictures once hung.

Roman stopped in the hall, concerned. "Is Monseigneur Martin...is he still with us?"

"No."

"He isn't dead, is he?" Roman thought the worst.

"Oh, my, no."

"Sister Angelique, what has happened to him?" Roman was relieved; yet still troubled.

"He and Reverend Shawe crossed His Lordship. They both left yesterday morning."

"Where did they go?"

"New Orleans? Baltimore? *Notre Dame*? Detroit? France? I have heard many rumors."

Roman took a seat in the plushly decorated parlor with a view to the school on Second Street. He heard the bishop's voice raise with wrath as the sound of slamming doors shook the floor. Roman took out his rosary beads and prayed for Mother Theodore and His Lordship.

A red-faced agitated Bishop Hailandière entered the room quickly.

"Father Weinzoepfel."

"Your Grace." Roman stood only to promptly kneel to kiss the bishop's ring.

"Why did you abandon me?"

"Abandon you?" Roman replied upon rising.

"Don't deny it. My traitorous Vicar General violated Canon Law and permitted you to leave the diocese without my authority. Only the bishop can grant excardination. He knew that and you should have as well. One cannot dispense with the Canons."

Roman could have reminded the bishop that in hastily ordaining him a priest certain Canons had been dispensed, but he held his thoughts bound.

"So, how is Fr Sorin?"

"Well, my Lord."

"I should place that whole institute under interdict! Sorin's been a thorn in my side ever since he arrived from France."

Roman stood motionless with his biretta in his hands.

"Well, your presence here shows that I have one obedient son in my diocese."

Roman gave a nod of his head to Hailandière and nervously fidgeted with the tassel atop the biretta.

"Walk with me, my son." Hailandière motioned to the dining room. "I was just about to sit down to my dinner. You will join me, won't you?"

"If it is no intrusion to your Lordship."

"Not in the least. I have few dinner guests these days. I welcome the company."

"*Merci beaucoup*, Your Lordship. I am quite famished." Roman noticed two place settings at the table. "Were you expecting someone else for dinner?"

"No." He looked down. "We will be dining alone." There was sharpness in his voice.

"I see that Monseigneur Martin is not in. Is he well?"

"Don't play me for a fool. Your *Abbé* betrayed my trust."

Roman made no reply as he stared at his bishop. Sisters Jeanne and Madeleine were standing in the doorway of the dining room with plates of food, waiting to serve them.

"Sisters, I believe you remember Father Roman Weinzoepfel. He is returning to our diocese. I am to reassign him today." Roman wondered where he would be sent.

"*Bonjour, Père*," both nuns replied as they removed the lids on the plates they carried, setting them before Roman and his bishop.

"Will your *other guest* be joining you for dinner?" Jeanne leaned over to the bishop.

"I have no guest but Fr Roman."

Suddenly Roman was startled by a loud knocking sound coming from the front of the house.

"I am always prepared to welcome a guest," replied the bishop, appearing to either not hear the knocking or else ignoring it.

"What was that?" Roman asked as the knocking continued.

"The rats are quite large here in Vincennes," the bishop said. "*Bon appetit!*"

The bishop began to cut his meat while Roman bowed his head. Keeping his hands on his lap, he nervously cleared his throat.

His Lordship looked up at Roman and dropped his knife and fork on his china plate. "I thought *you* could ask the blessing."

Once Roman had prayed a traditional meal prayer, Hailandière started speaking between bites of food.

"Imagine. I had an able vicar general, a superior of the seminary, and a rector of my Cathedral, but they have all failed me. I also have the order of the Sisters of Providence, but that rebellious Mother Superior, Sister Theodore Guérin, heads them so they have been no help to me at all. My friend and confidant, Monseigneur Augustin Martin, now has the heart of a woman because he spent too much time with that Mother Superior. And just today I hear that the chaplain to the Sisters of Providence is ready to depart for France.

"For myself, I am preparing to expel Father Sorin and all the members of his Holy Cross Order at *Notre Dame du Lac*. Your friend, the distinguished Englishman, Michael Edgar Evelyn Shawe, left me just yesterday to join Sorin at *Notre Dame*. It seems, again, that these men have allowed the weaker sex to influence their decisions.

"Monseigneur Martin is on his way to Baltimore to betray me. I believe his trip will end in Rome where he will inform the Holy Father of my incompetence. Oh, the Great Monseigneur Abbé Augustine Martin. Can you imagine that he believed those women's tales? They want me removed, you know. They are forever whispering that I have failed Bishop Brute. Father Roman, you may well be the only friend I have left in the diocese. You and my housekeepers, Sisters Angelique, Jeanne, and Madeleine." The three nuns appeared in the doorway as if summoned.

The noise in the house continued, but this time Roman heard a female voice. It was coming from one of the rooms down the hall from the dining room.

"Your Grace, is that a woman's voice?"

"*Pardon*?"

"That knocking appears to be coming from the next room. And I hear a voice."

"I hear nothing." He took another bite of potatoes. "How was your ride?"

"Long. I spent the night at the Woods in Terre Haute with the good Sisters of Providence at Saint Mary's." Roman dared not tell his Lordship what the sisters thought of their bishop.

Hailandière clanked his fork down on the china plate, glaring at him across the table, "Did you see their Mother Superior?"

"No. They said she was here in Vincennes."

"Well, yes, she is." He pushed away from the table, tossing his silk napkin onto his plate, as if he had lost all appetite.

355

The sound of the knocking turned to banging and the voice was now distinct.

"What is going on, My Lord? Is someone shut up in your study?

"*Oui*." He sulked in his chair.

"Monseigneur Celestin, let me out of here now!" The familiar voice of the Mother Superior, Theodore Guérin, thundered. "*Tout de suite! Maintenant*!"

Roman was shocked that Mother, locked behind the bolted door, called His Lordship by his first name. "The voice is familiar." Roman feigned ignorance.

"It should be. Come now, Father, you know it is the voice of Mother Theodore Guerin."

"What on earth? You must let her out!"

"No!" he growled, slamming his fist down on the table. "She is insubordinate. I have removed her faculties and taken from her the title of Superior. I have also a mind to excommunicate her. She was to have taken her dinner with me, but she became argumentative. So I locked her in my study. Perhaps this will teach her a lesson." The bishop stared at Roman's untouched food. "Go on and eat."

Roman hurried a piece of pork into his mouth and washed it down with a sip of wine.

"Who are these women who think they can tell a bishop what to do? Imagine her telling me that she has authority over her community. I am the bishop, and *all* religious orders in my diocesan see are under my jurisdiction! Christ did not call women to be priests or bishops! Listening to her you would think she was one of these American Utopians who think women should have the right to vote and the like. Well, what do you think? You were nearly buried alive by the word of a dame yourself!"

"Your Grace, it was the voice of a woman which secured my freedom as well." Roman could have reminded his bishop that it was also the word of a young Virgin from Nazareth which made possible the advent of the Savior, he who set free all souls, but he did not desire to provoke his bishop any further or else he may find himself locked in the cellar.

"Sister Theodore has betrayed me, you see. Proud little thing, she is. Writing letters to Europe, informing the Bishop of *Le Mans* with her lies about me. All of her letters defame me! She desires to leave the diocese. But where will a poor group of rebellious nuns go? I do not expect them to leave. I have threatened them all with excommunication and charged them thirty thousand francs for their property."

Roman recalled that Mother Theodore had mentioned the bishop of *Le Mans* to him before.

"Can you believe that her Superior in France told her that my mind has come unhinged? Who do these women think they are? Women have no rights! Christ chose men as his Apostles and no woman, especially that *Sister*, Theodore, is going to tell me what to do! I suppose the next thing she will desire is English in the liturgy and women to be allowed in the sanctuary! *Theologiae Americana.*

"Do you hear me, Sister Theodore?" He leaned away from the head of the table and shouted down the hall to the door of the east parlor. He straightened back up and looked at Roman. "She feigns her illnesses, you know. She had me believing her at one time. The way she carries on, you would think she had the dreaded Yellow Fever. No, she's an imposter masquerading as a saint." He leaned away from the table again, calling to the parlor. "You were not sick in New Orleans! No, it was a ruse. You and those Ursuline nuns were plotting against me." Hailandière turned back to Roman. "She is angry with me because I placed her postulant sisters in charge of the school here in Vincennes."

Roman kept his peace but found no logic in placing young, untrained and inexperienced sisters in front of a classroom full of students.

"Her congregation has agitated all of my priests in the diocese—but you. I wonder what will become of Vincennes. But then why am I telling *you* all this? Why *am* I telling you this? You were with her on occasion. You abandoned me when you became the novice master at Notre Dame."

"*Mea culpa*, your Excellency, but I had received permission from the Vicar-General, Monseigneur Martin, in your absence."

"Your beloved Abbé Augustine Martin should have never given you permission to leave the diocese while I was in Europe."

"My Lord, I had been in prison for over a year and with all the bigotry and violence against Catholics in Indiana, the twenty who died in Philadelphia during the summer of 1844, and with anti-Catholicism gaining momentum in Cincinnati and Louisville, I thought that I should retire to the cloister."

"Retire? You're too young to retire. You cannot run away from life's problems, my son! One must face them, head on. Besides, you are far, far too young to retire."

"*Oui*, my Lord."

"A monastery is no place for spiritual runaways."

"I agree, Your Excellency."

"Were you attempting to escape from the world and turn your back on your original mission?"

"Notre Dame isn't exactly a monastery, per se, and the members of the community aren't monks."

"Don't argue with me. They are Religious, no?"

"*Oui*."

"Believe me, the monastic life is most intense."

"I have lived in community before, Your Excellency. In Strasbourg."

"*Oui*. It is a demanding life. *Ora et labora—et labora et labora et labora*."

"*Oui*." Roman matched His Lordship's faint beginning of a smile.

"Father Roman, you will not fail me again, will you? Sister Theodore has violated her vows of obedience to me and in return she has spread the rumor that all of her sorrows have come through me."

By that time Roman had a mouthful of corn and could not reply.

His Lordship stared at him with his infamous frown. His nostrils flared, his brow furrowed, and his eyes glared. He did not wait for a reply. "Never mind that woman. You were friends with Abbé Martin and that priest, Shawe. They have both left us. Why in a short time, we will not have a single priest left in the parishes. What will become of a diocese without priests? I honestly do not know what I should have done to prevent what is happening."

Roman slowly nibbled at his food

"So, are you going to remain a missionary? Or have you decided to return to Europe and enter an abbey? The Benedictines are more respectable than the likes of these young upstart orders such as the Holy Cross Fathers."

"I will remain here as long as Your Lordship permits."

"What if your Lordship does not desire it?"

"I would be obedient to his wishes."

"He wishes you to remain."

"Your Grace—" Roman was confused.

"Father, I want you to remain here at the Cathedral for a time until I decide where I am going to send you. For the present you can assist in the seminary until the summer break."

"*Oui*, Your Grace."

"Honor me with a toast," Hailandière raised his glass. "To the diocese of Vincennes and all her priests...and to her next bishop."

Roman raised his wine glass and clanked it with His Lordship's, wondering if the man was still considering resigning his bishopric.

The bishop took a sip of wine from his glass. "Fr. Roman, I am thinking of sending you back to the missions."

Roman, confused, pulled the wineglass from his lips. "Which missions, Your Grace?"

"Evansville."

"*Evansville?*" He nearly choked on the wine.

"*Mais oui.*"

"Evansville? But you said—"

"Out of obedience, you will go. Besides, it is the last place that the Protestants are expecting me to send you."

"But my Lord—"

"Fr Roman. I have given my word to the people of Saint Joseph and Saint Wendel. Ever since you have been absent, they have continually petitioned me for a pastor of their own, so I think I should send you back to them. And I want you to dedicate another church to St. Philip just west of Evansville."

"Must it be me? Wouldn't it make more sense to send someone else?"

"Who are you to question me?!"

"I beg your pardon, Your Excellency. I simply thought—"

"I thought you vowed your obedience to me. Young man, you have become awfully headstrong, but you must remember that I am the bishop. Regardless of the rumors, I am still in control of this diocese. You promised obedience to me and my successors. So obey me. That is my final word."

"Evansville." Roman said again aloud, still more of a question than an affirmation.

"*Oui*. Evansville. Obedience." Hailandière wiped his lips with his napkin. "I want you to finish what you started, or rather, what the Lord started—you are merely his instrument, nothing more than a spade in His mighty hands as He plows the furrows in the fields of His Kingdom."

Roman considered his prayer that if he were freed from prison, he would remain in the states.

"Father Roman," the bishop continued, "I pray that in my voice you hear the voice of him who first called you to the priesthood and to the missions."

"Yes, Your Excellency."

The bishop looked tenderly at him. "Return to Evansville. Build the Church for my successor—*successors*. As St. Paul wrote his young priest, Timothy, stir into flame the grace of God which you received when I imposed the laying on of hands upon your head at your ordination. For the present you will remain here in Vincennes. I have arranged for you to stay at the seminary."

Suddenly there was the sound of a loud cry coming from the parlor. Roman took another sip of his wine.

They finished eating in silence though the doorknob down the hall occasionally turned accompanied with French phrases intended for the bishop.

The bishop offered Roman chocolates from an ornate china bonbonnière. "I brought them back from Switzerland."

Sisters Jeanne, Angela, and Madeleine came out and cleared the table and poured Roman and Hailandière freshly brewed coffee. Roman enjoyed the fresh roast of European coffee beans and the delicious Swiss chocolate.

Mother Theodore cried out from behind the door, "*Tout de suite*, Celestin! Let me out! This is childish! I am an adult! I thought you were one as well."

The bishop cleared his throat as if in an attempt to drown out her pleas. Roman wanted to open the door and release his friend, but alas, he had no key. With dinner at an end, the bishop rose as if in a hurry to see Roman to the door. Kneeling and embracing His Lordship's ring, Roman moved through the open door.

As he descended the steps of the chancery, three Sisters of Providence passed him on their way up.

"We've come for Mother Theodore," one of them said. "Where is she?"

"She is detained." Roman cleared his throat.

"Detained?"

"The Bishop can explain."
He quickly made his way to Shadow tied up at the hitching post.

****

Chapter 30

Compline

Once word got around that Roman had returned to Vincennes he was overcome with emotion as the priests and seminarians treated him like a would-be martyr who had out-witted the lions in the coliseum and survived the emperor's games. He celebrated the sacraments for the German Catholics of the place and nearly every evening he was invited to someone's home for dinner.

Roman stayed in Vincennes until May when Hailandière sent him back to Evansville to begin building and once again take up the cross of pioneer priest. He joined Deydier and went to the home of the Stahlhofers where before long it seemed the entire town was there to grant him a homecoming welcome, unlike the last time he left the Stahlhofer home. No, this was a joyful reunion of a shepherd with his flock and just as many Protestant neighbors assembled as if welcoming back the Prodigal Son.

He began the building of St. Philip's Church, and St. Wendel's rectory where he would live and tend to the Catholic communities including St Joseph's, Saint Matthew in Mount Vernon and Saint James in southern Gibson County.

****

The news from Vincennes was that Mother Theodore Guérin has been reinstated as the Superior. The bishop evidently realized he had no power. Deydier reported that he had nearly become his old self. "He has even joked about his resignation. '*Jetez Jonas a la mer et suavez le reste,*' Throw Jonah into the sea and save the rest, he says. I believe he wants to remain in Vincennes after the new bishop is named, but he will likely be asked to return to France."

****

Roman traveled to Evansville on the twenty-eighth of March, 1847, Holy Saturday, and on Easter Sunday many Protestants and Catholics gathered at Assumption Church. Evansville had just been incorporated as a city and the attorney James G. Jones had been elected the city's first mayor. The crowd sang Easter hymns, bringing about a unity of hearts, minds, and voices of Protestant and Catholic alike. *Christ the Lord is risen*, Roman thought. *Indeed. Resurrexit. Sicut dixit. As he said.*

In June 1848 Bishop Hailandière departed for France, his successor finally named.

From 1849 to 1851, work on another Catholic parish in Evansville took place. Many Protestants in the city had donated money for the building at the corner of Third and Vine and were on hand for the first mass. The church was named in honor of *The Holy Trinity* and was one of the most beautifully decorated Gothic churches in America, the pipe organ and much of the art donated by King Ludwig I of Bavaria.

Upon the church's completion on Holy Trinity Sunday of 1851, a parade down Main Street preceded the Pontifical High Mass celebrated by the new bishop. Many of the Protestants in the procession attended the mass irrespective of the foreign rituals and Latin language. In fact, more Protestants than Catholics were in attendance, the former hostilities between the two groups forgotten, having been replaced with friendship, forbearance, and curiosity. This was the New World, not the Old.

After mass, Mayor James Jones said to him, "John Chandler once told me I would never practice law again, saying that my defending you would ruin my career. I never doubted your innocence. And since those regrettable years when John Chandler and I were enemies we have become friends."

Jones had appointed him City Clerk. William Chandler had since sold his newspaper and had been named Postmaster. James 'Lockhorns' Lockhart was the City Attorney, Benjamin Thomas was Attorney General for the State of Indiana, Judge Embree was the Congressional Representative in Washington, rubbing elbows with the Kentucky Congressman, Archibald Dixon, and the Whig party was in disarray.

"You've received a hero's welcome in a town where you were once nearly lynched. Who would have ever thought?" Jones patted Roman on his back.

Roman smiled to think that just a few years before the evening streets glowed with torch lights threatening to fire his church and every Catholic home. He had been pursued down this very street with brickbats and sticks.

Today was a very different day.

"Miracles never cease, my friend." James Jones presented Roman with the key to the City of Evansville in the approving presence of over a thousand of its citizens.

Chapter 31

Requiem

November 1895

Like a holy and prolific marriage whose vows are fulfilled in familial obligations and the nurturing of children, well-lived day to month and months into years, so did Roman's priestly life steal away into eternity.

After more than thirty years of active ministry in the diocese and witnessing the influx of thousands of Catholic immigrants to southern Indiana and with the happy increase in the number of priests, he had turned his eyes to the contemplative life.

In 1852 Benedictine monks from Einsiedeln, Switzerland, had established a priory high atop a hill in Spencer County, Indiana, dedicated to Saint Meinrad. In 1870 the priory was raised to abbey status and in 1873 the brown sandstone monastery beckoned him to the monastic life.

In 1895, fifty-three years since Roman was first crushed in the winepress of American justice and made to drink of the opprobrious cup of suffering, he labored at gathering grapes from the abbey vineyard, squeezing the succulent scarlet juice from the fruit so that it might ferment into the intoxicating wine of worship and ritual and be placed upon the altar stone to become the Precious Blood of the Redeemer.

On a bright, cold, and windy November day, as the abbey's vesper bells tolled, eighty-two year old Father Roman glanced up from his prayer, out the window of his cloistered cell, observing the late changing season of southern Indiana. The wind breathed through the foliage dispersing the dying leaves like a mantle of crimson and auburn snow upon the gentle hills rimming the valley below the monastery while the afternoon sun filtered through a whirlwind of yellow and orange.

A cold draft of wind blew in around the window frame as Roman removed his thick glass spectacles from his face and laid them on his desk. A persistent fever had returned earlier in the week and with it a

365

pain in his stomach and left side that stretched to his heart. Not only were the autumn shadows lengthening, but the icy dagger of winter was closing in. Wistfulness gripped him to the depths, yet there was sweetness in it. He looked at his calloused, veiny, cracked hands and strained to see through his milky eyes. A myriad of illuminated dust particles swirled in a shaft of golden sun.

His meditation was interrupted when the figure of a fellow monk robed in the traditional black Benedictine habit stopped by for a visit.

"How are things in the vineyard?"

"Oh, lots of work," Roman replied, his hands searching his desk for his thick spectacles. "This summer it was so hot that there were many days I was forced to remain here at the monastery. The past two months I spent cutting and tying up the vines, but I am so old, and the vineyard has become so overgrown with wild grass, I fear my efforts were useless."

"You've done good work, Father Roman." The young monk assured.

Roman placed his glasses on his face again, looking out the window, content to simply quietly be in his brother monk's presence.

"Father Roman," the monk spoke, "please don't think me ill-mannered when I ask you about the circumstances of your trial and imprisonment, but I've been reading *The History of the Diocese of Vincennes*. You were called the *Martyr of the Confessional*."

"I understand. Believe me, there was a time when I was all that people talked about. I brought down great havoc upon the Church in my youth."

"*You* brought the havoc upon the Church?"

"Thankfully it is now all but forgotten," Roman said, reaching for his handkerchief.

"The librarian says there is a file of the trial in the archives."

"Oh, he did, did he?" He knew the file contained the court transcripts and the newspaper clippings of the trial. "Well, it will remain sealed as long as I am alive, *Deo gratias*. Only the abbot and the archivist have access to the archives."

"It happened over fifty years ago."

"Someday—after I'm dead—you may open it. But until then...." Roman coughed, causing his head to hurt. "Never underestimate God's grace. We are all marauders in one way or another. Mind you, Father Abbot's days *are* numbered—as are mine. All of us have a cross to bear." Roman had several crosses—headaches, stomach problems, failing eyesight, and now a persistent fever and cough. "My sight fails me and now I am suffering from the ague. And who among us does not know of Father Abbot's lung condition and throat illness. So, you see, we all have our crosses."

Their conversation was interrupted by a knock upon his cell door. Roman looked up. It was one of the young novices. "Father Roman?"

"Yes, Brother?"

"Father Abbot would like to see you in the church."

"Do you mean the chapel?"

"No, the church." The abbey church also served as the parish church. "There's someone here to see you."

"I'm expecting no one." Roman reached for his cane. "Is it one of my relatives?"

"He did not say." The novice vanished down the cloistered corridor.

"Very well. I suppose I should be on my way." Roman thumped his cane on the wooden floor. "Hand me my biretta, please."

The monk reached across the desk and handed him the hat.

Roman placed the biretta upon his head and stood.

"Allow me to help, Father Roman." The young monk assisted his elderly confrere from his chair and out of the cell into the dimly lit passageway as the vesper bells continued to peal, summoning all to prayer.

Accompanying Roman to the abbey church, the young monk held his senior's arm. Light filtered into the darkened halls from the transoms above and through the cracks at the bottom of the doors. The freshly polished wooden floor pungently smelled of kerosene, the scent stinging Roman's nostrils. They passed the library and went down the stairway and passed the chapel. A flood of light became visible at the end of the passageway.

"Careful," cautioned Father Roman, nearly stumbling, "I am not very steady on my feet. Any little jolt could very easily damage this frail, eighty-two year old skeleton of mine."

"Of course, Father. I apologize."

The light at the end of the long corridor opened into a small courtyard leading to the doors of the wooden frame church. A strong gust of the cold north wind howled between the buildings of the cloister and abbey church. The wind suddenly caught Roman's biretta, blowing it against the monastery's wall. The young monk ran to retrieve it.

"Thank you, my son," Roman smiled as the monk handed the biretta to him. "That always seems to happen."

The cold November air permeated the church, the warm mist of their breath still as visible as it was outside.

As they entered the church, Father Abbot met them. "Father Roman," he nodded to him.

"Thank you, my son," Roman said to the young monk before he turned and hastily reentered the monastery building.

Roman cleared his throat, adjusted his spectacles, and looked at his superior. "Father Abbot, I understand someone is here to see me?"

"Yes."

"Who is it?"

"We are unsure," the abbot spoke in his raspy voice. "She is an older woman and has been praying ever since she arrived."

"What does she want?"

"She desires to go to confession, but requests the Reverend Father Roman Weinzoepfel specifically."

"Why me? I'm an old man."

"She says she is an old acquaintance of yours. Wisdom comes with age, Father Roman."

He was not so certain he had such wisdom. "Well, where is she?"

"There, kneeling at the altar rail." The abbot took Roman by the arm, escorting him over near the front pews. The warped floor squeaked beneath their feet. "I'll have her meet you in the confessional."

She was dressed in black with her head completely covered.

Roman stepped into the small wooden box and reached for the violet priestly stole of embroidered silk that lay upon the chair. Placing the cloth about his neck and over both shoulders, signifying his priestly power to forgive sin, he slid open the wooden slat screen which separated priest from penitent. He could see the faint outline of a woman's face appear on the other side of the grill, but there was only a long, breathless silence.

Father Roman crossed himself and prayed.

"*In Nomine Patris, et Filii, et Spiritus Sancti. Amen.*"

The woman leaned toward the screen. Her voice crackled as she spoke the words of the *Confiteor* in Latin. It was a voice he knew, but he did not immediately recognize her. Her Bavarian German became clearer. "Bless me, Father, for I have sinned. It has been fifty three years since my last confession." He gripped the worn crucifix at the end of his rosary beads hanging from his belt beneath his scapular. He didn't know what to think. It was her. The memory of everything flooded his mind as spring rains swell streams. Before her next word, he remembered it all as if it were yesterday.

He recalled stepping out of the confessional at the sound of Anna Maria Schmoll's cry for help.

"Kiss me."

"Don't say these things, Mrs. Schmoll."

Her steps faltered as she placed her hand on his arm. "Father Roman." He was uncomfortable at her touch, fearing it was all a ruse on her part. He wanted to pull his arm away, but didn't, mindful of the child within her womb. Suddenly all her weight was on his arm and she began to collapse to the floor, dropping her prayer book. Reluctantly, he caught her in his arms and moved her to the nearest pew. As he did, her bonnet fell from her head.

Walking to the holy water font at the front of the church, he dipped his hand in and returned to her, daubing her face with the water.

She startled when he touched her. "O God! What happened?"

"You fainted.' He reached down and picked up her prayer book.

"Did I fall to the floor?"

"No, I caught you before you could drop." He handed her the book.

"You did?"

"Yes. Otherwise, you may have fractured your head upon the floor." He scooped up her bonnet and returned it to her.

"Kiss me."

"Mrs. Schmoll, please. The time for confessions is at an end." He brushed himself off. "I am locking the church." Pointing to the door, he avoided her direct gaze and focused upon the crucifix behind her upon the sanctuary wall. "I must ask you to leave."

"Grant me absolution!"

"Absolution can only be granted when one is truly contrite—"

"Don't you care the least about me?"

"I care for the state of your immortal soul."

"Then grant me absolution—or—or—"

369

"Or what?"

She angrily turned away.

"The sacraments are not Corinthian games."

She stepped back behind the curtain of the confessional and kneeling down, raised her voice, "My husband signed that marriage agreement, so grant me absolution so I can receive communion tomorrow! I must receive communion, or else!"

"You are subject to the laws of the Roman Catholic Church and so am I. Your unborn child had to be claimed for Christ and His Church." Roman remained standing in the aisle outside the confessional, looking at her feet dangling over the kneeler while the rest of her body was hidden by the curtain. "You're acting like a child, Mrs. Schmoll."

"I need absolution!"

"You lack contrition; therefore I am obliged to withhold absolution."

She rose quickly, batting the curtain away, and faced him in the aisle. With tears in her eyes, she said, "Forgive me."

He looked at her bonnet and continued to avoid eye contact. "If you confess with a sincere, humble, and contrite heart—"

"Never mind, frock! I don't need a priest to tell me how wretched or hopeless I am! And I don't need a priest to forgive my sins! Only God can forgive sin. No man—priest or pope!" She turned and ran for the door.

"Don't make a shipwreck of your faith, or else you'll reap a whirlwind of sorrows—"

"To hell with you!" She slammed the church door shut but it swung wide open.

Roman looked out into the warm May evening as a red sun shimmered on the virgin waters of the Ohio.

A frigid draft of damp air caused Roman to shiver bringing him forth into the present again. His attention refocused on the woman behind the slats of the grille who was beginning to speak.

She cleared her throat as Roman momentarily hesitated in acknowledging her, his mind still lingering upon the memory. "You may begin."

He studied his chapped, folded hands as he listened attentively.

"Fifty three years ago, I sent an innocent man to prison." She stopped and cleared her throat again. "The man was a priest. I had entered a bad marriage and I was with child at the time. I was in love with the priest. He was young. I didn't know what to do. My husband became jealous and threatened my life if I didn't admit that the priest had his way with me..." Her words broke off as she sniffled. "You do remember, don't you?"

Roman waited, but then spoke. "Yes. I remember." His heart hurt as he wiped sweat from his brow.

"I went to confession to fulfill my Easter Duty and I tried to seduce you. You wouldn't even kiss me. My husband was a jealous man, and when I returned home from church, he was waiting for me and said that I spent too much time with you. He wanted to know if you and I were in love and I said, 'what if we are?' Then I told him you were a much better man than he'd ever be. He was still angry over having to sign that marriage agreement, so he became convinced that we were lovers.

"I thought that if I gave him the impression that you and I were in love, then he would love me. It was stupid, I know, and it only made things worse. He accused me of deceiving him and said that I was with child before we married. He threatened that he had every reason to kill me, but that he would kill you instead.

"When he came back home later that night, he was drunk, and he woke me, only to force himself upon me. He began hitting me and said that the baby I was carrying was your bastard. After he was finished with me, he said that the talk at the taverns in town had it that the reason I'd been so quick to marry him was because I was pregnant with your child. He put his revolver to my stomach and said unless I told him the truth and admitted that I loved you and that the child was yours, he would kill me.

"Then I said that you had forced yourself upon me in the church during my confession. Later when I tried to convince him I had lied about it, he threatened to kill me if I were to ever recant the story. I tried to tell him a hundred times that I only admitted to his jealous ravings to keep him from killing me, but he wouldn't listen." She blew her nose in her handkerchief.

"He went in the kitchen where I heard him and some of his friends talking. Then he left the house again—" She stopped mid-sentence and wiped away tears.

Roman sat in incredulous silence and allowed her to collect herself.

"I was awake in bed the rest of that night crying. By morning he hadn't returned. My sister and brother came to our house and I joined them at the church for Ascension Mass. After mass, I invited my brother and sister to stay for breakfast. When we got home, Martin was at the kitchen table waiting for me. I saw the handle of his revolver under his coat. He had the look from the night before and threatened to kill me again, unless my brother and sister were out of his house as soon as they were finished eating.

"I'm so sorry, Father. You were young and handsome, but you were a priest. You were forbidden. And you were one of only a few men who refused my advances.

"I pleaded with my husband, but he beat me until I agreed to repeat the accusation against you. After I told the story enough times I began to believe it myself. After that, my husband began accepting money for my story.

"Once my father learned the truth, he forced me from his house and I moved to New Orleans where I became a harlot, living a life of debauchery. All the while I knew what I was doing was wrong. I pray God will forgive me. I pray you can forgive me, too."

"Mercy is at the heart of the gospel, which is why Christ gave us the sacraments." Roman was almost hesitant to speak, fearful that he wouldn't be able.

"Father Roman, I wanted you, but I knew that I could never have you. You were so devoted, so sure of yourself. I wanted someone like you in my life. The fact that I couldn't have you made my desire for you all the greater. So I decided that if I couldn't have you, then no one would—not even God! I was so unhappy in my marriage and I resented you so much for pointing out my sins…." Her voice crackled with emotion and sobs.

Roman's eyes burnt with his own emotion.

"I weep for all the years of suffering that I caused you. You must hate me."

"I do not hate you." He said, clenching his jaws, working to keep his emotion in check. "*All things work together for the good to those who love God*—even our sinfulness can serve to bring us closer to Christ."

She sat quietly before speaking again.

"After my divorce, I only saw my husband, Martin, a few times. He came to my sister Caroline's funeral, and the last time I saw him was at his funeral. He drank himself to death in Saint Louis, wandering up and down the streets, out of his mind, looking for our daughter, Maria Caroline, and mumbling about strangling the attorney Jay Davis to death."

"We must pray for your husband," Roman urged, perhaps admonishing himself more than the penitent. "Let us pray for him. He is still one of God's creatures. Perhaps he is in Purgatory."

She told of many other sins through tears and sobs, and in the midst of enumerating them she stopped, unable to continue.

"Through your tears of compunction," Roman paused, choking back a knot of emotion wedged in his throat. "You have made a good confession. The weight of your sins, after so many years of bondage, has been lifted from your soul. For your penance I ask that you pray..." A tear flowed down his ruddy right cheek. "I ask that you pray for all the poor souls in Purgatory and pray that you make a good death so as to enjoy eternal life." He stopped but spoke again. "And pray the same for me."

He extended his hand, absolving her of sin. *"Ego te absolvo..."*

At last she was free.

And so was he. Praying the words of absolution, he felt a sense of peace, a peace that he had not experienced in years. Looking up, through his mottled, irritated eyes, he saw that his penitent was gone, as if she had never been there.

A pain burst across his chest, reaching down into his abdomen, tightening his breath, and darkening his eyes. He heard the toll of the Vesper bells, which had been ringing throughout Anna Maria's confession, and opened the door of the confessional box and crept out into the quiet, empty church intending to pray the hour of eventide.

His abdominal pain lessened and his sight returned in the light, though now blurred with emotion, and he bumped his cane along the floorboards of the nave. As he made his way out of the church and back across the courtyard to the main buildings, he removed his biretta and covered his head with the cowl of his habit.

Entering the abbey chapel, the young monk reappeared at his side to help him on with the mantle of the pleated, wide-sleeved, hooded cuculla. The frost permeated the sandstone chapel and in his chill, even though the vesper sun surged through the western walls of the abbey's stained glass windows, he could still see his breath. As he ambled to his place, the wood floor squeaked, as did his knees as he maneuvered his way into his choir stall.

The toll of the vesper bell gave way to the chant of evensong as his fellow monks rose to begin chanting the office.

A swell of music ascended from the ranks of the pipe organ as the schola intoned a Gregorian chant.

Deus in adjutorium meum intende... O God, come to my assistance, make haste to deliver me.

Reaching for his Psalter, he crossed himself and prayed. *Gloria Patris, et Filii, et Spiritus Sancti...*

As he prayed, he reflected upon his experience in the confessional questioning whether it had been a dream or had Mrs. Schmoll in fact visited him?

Where sin abounds, God's grace more and more abounds.

Even darkness is not dark for Thee, O Lord.

Now dismiss Thy servant, O Lord, in peace, according to Thy word. For mine own eyes have seen Thy salvation, which Thou hast prepared in the sight of all peoples, a light of revelation to the nations, and the glory of Thy people Israel.

O Lord, grant me a peaceful night and a perfect end.

After kneeling in thanksgiving for the day, he crossed himself and stepped into the darkened hall, the psalms resounding in his heart, the scripture on his silent lips.

Even darkness is not dark for Thee, O Lord.

No sooner had the sacristan extinguished the candles did Roman pierce the Grand Silence and awaken to the First Light of Grace and the Divine Chant of Eternal Life.

****

On a dismal, dreary eleventh of November, the somber toll of the funeral bell knelled eighty-two times. Roman's earthly sojourn now complete, his body was placed in an unadorned pine box.

Three days later six of his Benedictine brothers replaced the lid of his pine coffin, hammered it shut, and carried his remains out of the sanctuary. The monastic community, following in procession, chanting the penitential psalms and carrying lit candles, suffered the elements of the wintry fog of sleet and rain as they solemnly conducted his coffin from the chapel down the pathway of the hill to a freshly dug grave in the cemetery that rested upon a gentle hill overlooking one of the abbey's lakes.

Once through the wrought iron cemetery gates, the monks placed the coffin down on three ropes upon the ground next to the earth's fresh wound. Upon the reassembling of the mourners among the ice-covered steel crosses that marked the graves of deceased monks, the abbot sprinkled holy water and intoned prayers. The six pallbearer monks took hold of the ropes and slowly lowered the coffin into the cold, wet grave.

The abbot then shoveled a scoop of dirt and let it drop on the coffin's lid, the loud thud a startling reminder to those gathered that death comes for all.

Requiem aeternum dona ei, Domine, et lux perpetua luceat ei. Requiescat in pace. Amen.

Eternal rest, grant unto him, O Lord, and let perpetual light shine upon him. May he rest in peace. Amen.

The abbot traced the sign of the cross over the grave as the sextons reverently returned the mound of earth atop the coffin. Filling in the grave they staked a simple cross made of two wooded slats into the muddy soil. Slowly the mourners departed in the freezing mist while the monks resumed their *ora et labora*. The sextons, once finished with their task, closed the iron gates of the cemetery behind them.

In the solitude of the cemetery a lone female figure draped in black emerged from the wood near the lake, opened the iron gate, and paused at Roman's grave.

The sleet became snow.

Afterword

In 1986, my cousin, Father John (David) McMullen, O.S.B., of Blue Cloud Abbey, South Dakota, celebrated his twenty-fifth anniversary of ordination to the priesthood. He had returned to Vincennes to his home parish of St. John the Baptist for the occasion to be with family and friends. Someone had taken the time to set up a table with old parish history books and other memorabilia that the parish had accumulated through the years. Perusing the material I picked up an old book covering the history of the parish. It described the beginnings of the parish as a haven for German speaking immigrants to the area around Vincennes, Indiana. The book mentioned a missionary priest named Roman Weinzapfel who had been accused of a horrendous crime in Evansville, Indiana, and had been removed to Vincennes. He was one of the first German-speaking priests to serve the Germans of the area. Being a college student at the time, I didn't give it much thought and forgot about it.

In 1993 while teaching theology at *Mater Dei* High School in Evansville, Indiana, I was given a paper written by Christan Stofleth for her Social Justice class. The paper was entitled *My Great Uncle Father Roman* and in it she gave a synopsis of the events in Roman's life and it intrigued me. At the time I considered the idea for an interesting research topic, but I shelved it for another day.

During the summer of 1997 I decided to begin work on *ROMAN*. In preparation, I began studying the history and politics and day-to-day life in America from 1830 to 1850. It is a most neglected period of American history, but a very important era. In 1999 I began writing the story of Father Roman and the final edited version was completed by Christmas 2002.

As for the spelling of the name Weinzoepfel, there are several spellings. For the sake of consistency I chose Weinzoepfel. Roman signed his name Weinzoepflen. There are numerous spellings of the name: Weinzaeplen, Weinzoepflein, Weinzopfeln, Weinzapfeln, Weinzopfel, Weinzapfel, Weinzäpfel, Weinzöpflen, Weinzöpfel, and Weinzäpflen, to list a few. I chose Weinzoepfel because it was the most common spelling associated with Roman and his trial, though the American version is usually rendered Weinzapfel.

When Roman first volunteered as a missionary, he came with three or four other clerics from Strasbourg, Alsace, and voyaged to America with nearly fifteen other missionary seminarians and priests from France.

When I began writing this story there were certain things that I wondered if the reader would think too incredulous, such as on the eve of Roman's first mass the Cathedral apse collapsed, or the fact that in order to grant him a safe exodus from Evansville he was dressed as a woman and traveled the underground route of fugitive slaves. Those events were true.

Roman did in fact know Mother Theodore Guérin, S.P., and he was in Terre Haute when the buildings at St. Mary-of-the-Woods burnt in October of 1842. The exact cause of the blaze was never determined. Mother Theodore, for her part, believed it was arson. The cause for Mother Theodore Guérin's canonization is underway and at this time she is *Blessed* Mother Theodore Guérin, one step from recognition as an official saint of the Catholic Church. St. Mary-of-the-Woods in Terre Haute is a testament to her faith and courage.

As for the court case, there were actually two trials. I merged the two into one trial for the sake of the story.

In February of 1843, prior to the March trial, the Attorney Jay Davis had gone with Anna Maria to Cincinnati to obtain testimonials to vouch for her character. On the way back to Evansville, the riverboat captain reportedly found the two in a compromising situation. This triggered a response from Martin Schmoll. Anna and the child were expelled from his house and Jay Davis mysteriously vanished from Evansville, never to be seen again. Whether Martin Scmoll actually murdered Davis is a valid question now as it was then.

In March of 1843 Benjamin Thomas and John Chandler squared off against each other in the Evansville trial. Roman's defense attempted to discredit Anna Maria's character. During deliberations, the jury could not come to a decision requiring the case to be retried. It was then venued to Princeton for September of 1843, but due to the death of the Schmoll child, the case was rescheduled for March 1844.

By the time for the March 1844 trial, Wilbur Jones had unexpectedly died and Benjamin Thomas did not actually argue any of the case. A Protestant attorney from Mount Vernon named John

Pitcher took his place. All six attorneys for both sides did give closing arguments that covered the better part of two days.

The unmarried Caroline Long did give birth to a son. Its paternity was never disclosed. The common opinion was that it was Martin Schmoll's child. There were others that accused Louis Long of incest with both of his daughters.

The governor of Indiana did visit Roman at the Jeffersonville prison incognito and expressed regret over his political predicament and inability to pardon Roman.

President Polk's wife, Sarah "Sally Childress, did facilitate Roman's release by her conversation aboard *The Clarksville*. Mother Theodore's Sister of Providence in Madison, Indiana, did teach the Lieutenant Governor's three children. She herself had traveled to Madison and did have contact with the man. When she returned from a trip to France in 1844 one of the first things she did was inquire as to Roman's fate.

After his release he did spend time in Bardstown, Kentucky, and then went to Notre Dame where he became the first Novice Master for the Fathers and the Brothers of the Holy Cross.

****

The bishop of Vincennes, Celestin De la Hailandière, eventually did resign. He had traveled to Rome for his *ad limina* visit in the fall of 1844 and made his request known to the pope. (Each bishop must give a report of his diocese to the pope every five years. It is an expectation that the prelate do this in person). Pope Gregory XVI would hear none of Hailandière's request to resign and instead encouraged him to return and maintain control. He also gave him the bodies of two early martyrs. Upon Hailandière's return to the diocese he gave the saints' bodies to Mother Theodore Guérin.

By June 1846 the situation in Vincennes with Bishop Hailandière had deteriorated so badly that he had once again submitted his Episcopal resignation to the Supreme Pontiff, this time at the behest of the Council of United States bishops. In addition, word reached Deydier that Monseigneur Augustin Martin had been sent to Rome by the Archbishop of Baltimore on behalf of all the U.S. bishops. The Monseigneur was to meet with the Holy Father personally concerning Hailandière who had unfortunately become a tyrant as bishop.

However, on the first of June, Pope Gregory XVI died and on the sixteenth of June Cardinal Ferretti was elected to the Chair of Peter, taking the name Pius IX. Hailandière let it be known publicly that his former Vicar General had indeed traveled to Rome to inform the Vicar of Christ that the bishops of the United States wanted him to be relieved of his see.

In November, the new pope accepted Hailandière's resignation, but refrained from immediately naming a replacement. Due to the death of Pope Gregory, and the subsequent process of electing Pius IX and his becoming familiar with the Papal Office, no new Episcopal appointments were made for a time.

Mother Theodore Guérin was reinstated as the Superior of her order when the bishop evidently realized he had no more power.

Finally in June 1847 Bishop Hailandière announced to the diocese that the pope had named a successor. John Steven Bazin, a distinguished French Monseigneur in Alabama, was destined to become the next bishop. Bazin was to be consecrated on the 24th of October.

On the 17th of October, the week before Bazin's scheduled consecration, Hailandière delivered his last homily as Bishop of Vincennes, maintaining his episcopal post to the last.

Bishop Hailandière, upon his resignation, said, "You will no doubt ask, 'why have we desired to withdraw from the diocese?' In all simplicity, the role of bishop is oppressive to all—and extremely so to us—on account of weakness. It was a responsibility— one of which I did not solicit for myself—and is a responsibility that terrifies even saints. We greatly love the diocese and yet believe that another prelate will serve more advantageously.

"Soon we will be gone. The twelve years of our life spent in your service—not without sacrifice and of which we regret not a single day of such sacrifice—will perhaps speak to you and prove that we loved you...

"We ask pardon for all offenses and from all those offended. Forgive us. Pray for us. Beseech the merciful God to pardon the numerous faults of our administration. And above all, let your prayers ascend to heaven when you learn that we have descended to the tomb."

Hailandière became known as the Bishop without a See, and he returned to his native home in France, but with explicit instructions that upon his death his remains were to be returned to Vincennes where he would be interred in the Cathedral crypt next to his predecessor, the Beloved Saint, Bishop Simon Gabriel Bruté.

The arguments that took place between Mother Theodore and the bishop were based upon the correspondence between the two and those eyewitness accounts of some of their meetings. As far as Mother Theodore visiting Fr Roman's cell, that was fabricated with literary license, though there is a possibility she did visit him since she did have a school and sisters in Madison at the time.

As for the attorneys in the case, James G. Jones did become the first mayor of Evansville in 1847 and John Chandler became the City Clerk. William Chandler sold his newspaper and became one of the city's first Postmasters. James Lockhart was the City Attorney. Benjamin Thomas became Attorney General for the State of Indiana. Judge Embree went on to serve congress in Washington. Archibald Dixon went on to be elected to congress representing Kentucky, and was instrumental in keeping Kentucky neutral during the Civil War.

By the spring of 1890 Roman had been a monk at Saint Meinrad's Abbey for eighteen years and had served fifty years as a priest. On the occasion he was honored as a Patriarch of the Catholic Church in the American west. He had outlived Bishops Flagét, Hailandière, Monseigneur Augustin Martin, Elisha Durbin, Antony Deydier, and Mother Theodore Guérin. Abbot Fintan Mundweiler of Saint Meinrad desired to vicariously honor all those who had gone before him by honoring Roman.

Here are some excerpts from the words the abbot gave at the abbey in April of 1890. "Father Roman we are honored by your presence here today. You are our honored confrere, our bond with the past and a symbol of the hope for our future. Our deepest regret is that during the lifetimes of our forebears in the faith they never received the honor or dignity that they so deserved. May we never forget those who have gone before us, bringing the faith of the Apostles to America."

Regarding the Schmolls, Martin Schmoll moved to St. Charles, Missouri, where some of his relatives lived. He disappears from the pages of history after Roman's return to the Evansville area.

As for Mrs. Schmoll, not much is known except that in the divorce settlement she received a portion of Martin Schmoll's savings and holdings. There are reports that she took the money and became a

Madame of a brothel in New Orleans. There are other stories that indicate she recanted her accusations later in life and perhaps was reconciled to the church. For the sake of the story I added the confessional scene at St. Meinrad Abbey to bring closure to the events. However, as always, "All things are possible with God."

John W. McMullen
Christmas Day 2002

Glossary

Aspergillum- A perforated container used for sprinkling holy water.

Biretta A stiff square cap with three or four ridges across the crown. Birettas are worn especially by Roman Catholic clergy and are black for priests, purple for bishops, and red for cardinals. Priestly birettas are three ridged while Episcopal and Abbatial birettas have four ridges.

Breviary A prayer book containing the hymns, offices, and prayers for the canonical hours.

Canonical Hours- The times of day that Canon Law prescribes certain prayers. (See list of hours below).

Canon Law-The body of official rules governing the faith and practice of the members of the Catholic Church.

Cassock An ankle-length garment with a close-fitting waist and sleeves, worn by the clergy as clerical dress and also worn by assistants in church services. It is usually black. It is also called a soutane.

Cope-A long vestment worn over an alb or surplice.

Crosier - A staff with a crook or cross at the end, carried by an abbot, a bishop, or an archbishop as a symbol of office.

Humeral Veil- A vestment resembling a shawl worn over the shoulders by a subdeacon during High Mass, and also worn by a priest when holding the monstrance.

Liturgy - A prescribed form for public worship, prayer, ceremonies, and rituals. Often word used for the celebration of the Mass or the Eucharist.

Miter - The liturgical headdress of a bishop. In the Western church it is a tall pointed hat with peaks in front and back, worn at all solemn functions. The shape of the miter symbolizes the tongues of fire which departed upon the Apostles at Pentecost.

Monstrance - A receptacle in which the Eucharistic Host is held. It is also called an *ostensorium.*

Mozzetta-A short, hooded cape worn over the rochet by the pope and by bishops.

Nativism-A political movement in the United States during the 19th century which sought to further the interests of the original immigrant peoples (Americans) over those of later immigrants.

Office- A ceremony, rite, or service, usually prescribed by the liturgy, especially the canonical hours, such as Morning or Evening prayer.

Passenger Pigeon- A migratory bird *(Ectopistes migratorius)* that was abundant in eastern North America until the latter part of the 19th century. It was hunted to extinction.

Pectoral Cross - A cross worn on the chest or breast, usually by a bishop, an abbot or a Mother Superior, to signify their office.

Prie-dieu-A narrow, desk like kneeling bench, for use by a person at prayer, often there is space for a book under the front of the bench.

Pyx- A small, pocket-sized container in which the Eucharist is kept when being carried to the sick.

Rochet-A white ceremonial vestment made of linen or lawn, worn by bishops.

Sacristy- A room in a church housing the sacred vessels and vestments, and where the priest vests for mass.

Soutane A cassock, especially one that buttons up and down the front.

Stole - A long, narrow cloth, usually of embroidered silk or linen, worn over the left shoulder by deacons and over both shoulders by priests and bishops while officiating at the administration of the Sacraments.

Thurible-A censer used in church ceremonies and liturgies.

Vicar General- A priest acting as deputy to a bishop to assist him in the administration of his diocese.

Xavier, Saint Francis-Spanish Jesuit missionary. Cofounder of the Jesuit Order (Society of Jesus, 1534) with Saint Ignatius of Loyola. Francis established missionaries in Japan and the East Indies. He is one of the patron saints of missionaries.

Canonical Hours

Matins - The office that formerly constituted the first of the seven canonical hours. The time of day appointed for this service, traditionally midnight or 2 A.M. but is often celebrated at sunrise.

Prime - The second of the seven canonical hours usually prayed around sunrise.

Terce -The third of the seven canonical hours usually prayed at the third hour after sunrise, or midmorning.

Sext - The fourth of the seven canonical hours usually prayed at noon.

Nones - The fifth of the seven canonical hours usually observed at the ninth hour after sunrise, or midafternoon.

Vespers - The sixth of the seven canonical hours, celebrated in the late afternoon or evening in many Western Christian churches. It is also called Evensong.

Compline-The last of the seven canonical hours recited or sung just before retiring which completes the cycle of prayer for the day.

Grand Silence- Following Compline, the monks of a monastery often refrain from any speaking until after morning prayers or even wait until after morning mass. Some monasteries observe perpetual silence in the cloister.

The Church in the Modern World

A word on Canon Law concerning Mixed Marriages between Catholics and baptized Christians of other denominations is in order. The 1917 Code of Canon Law maintained—provided there was a dispensation granted by the local bishop—the requirement that the non-Catholic had to sign an agreement promising not to interfere with the Catholic party's practice of the faith and to ensure that any and all children from their union to be baptized and reared as Catholics. In the revised Code of Canon Law promulgated in 1983, a marriage between a Catholic and a baptized member of another Christian faith can take place provided there is a dispensation granted by the local bishop and, as Canon 1125 states, *"The Catholic party* declares that he or she is prepared to remove dangers of falling away from the faith and makes a sincere promise to do all in his or her power to have all the children baptized and brought up in the Catholic Church. The non-Catholic party is to be informed at an appropriate time of these promises...so that it is clear that he or she is truly aware of the promise and obligation of the Catholic party." (Italics mine).

In the United States, as part of pre-nuptial instruction, the couple is to be informed of the Catholic party's promises and obligations. No formal written declaration is now required of the non-Catholic party, but knowledge of the Catholic party's responsibilities and a shared understanding of marriage is a prerequisite for reception of the sacrament.

Some Canon lawyers argue that the Catholic party's promise may be open for interpretation, such as in the case of a Catholic who is weak in his or her faith and the faith of the non-Catholic is deeper, or a situation where baptizing and raising the children Catholic will be disruptive to the marriage. In any given circumstance, the Catholic party is only obliged to do what is in his or her power to do; even if that means deferring the children's baptism and their being reared Catholic.

As for the Sacrament of Confession, today it is commonly referred to as *The Sacrament of Reconciliation* and is recognized as a sacrament of healing. Since Vatican II there is also the option of celebrating the mercy of God in a face-to-face encounter with the priest. Nevertheless, the seal of the confessional remains sacrosanct and the *Easter Duty* is still observed.

Regarding the priesthood, all of the faithful are called to be and are consecrated to be a priestly people. The common priesthood of the faithful is exercised by the unfolding of baptismal grace since the entire faithful share in the priesthood of Christ.

Those who receive the sacrament of Holy Orders are to serve in the name of and in the person of Christ in the midst of the community of the baptized. Only Christ is the true high priest, *the one mediator between God and men*. As Thomas Aquinas wrote in his *Summa*, "Christ is the source of all priesthood: the priest of the Old Law (Judaism) was a figure of Christ, and the priest of the New Law (Church) acts in the person of Christ."

Obviously many things have changed since the 1800s, both in the Church and in society. As the great theologian Henri du Lubac wrote in *Méditation sur l'Eglise*:

"We cannot run away whenever we feel like it to another age—not even if we don't actually intend a negative attitude in so doing. We cannot avoid the problems of our own day, any more than we can excuse ourselves from its tasks or run away from its battles. If we are to live in the Church, then we have to become involved with the problems she faces now...It would be a big mistake for us to think that we could ever rediscover the faith of the past in its exact tenor and all its richness.... For time cannot be reversed; even error and revolt, however complete their overthrow, impose a new lifestyle and a different emphasis on the life of faith, as on the expression of truth....

"Yet, in spite of all the obstacles we heap up, saints will spring up once more."

Timeline of Events

1839-Sub-deacon Roman Weinzoepflen leaves Strasbourg, Alsace, volunteering for the mission at Vincennes, Indiana. Celestin de la Hailandière named Bishop of Vincennes. In October Roman arrives in Vincennes, Indiana.

1840 In April, Roman ordained priest. Father Roman sent to Evansville, Indiana, as parochial vicar of Assumption Parish. 5 August cornerstone laid for Assumption Church. The incumbent, President Martin Van Buren was on hand for the event while campaigning against William Henry Harrison.

1841–St. Joseph and St Wendel parish churches erected.

1842–Reverend Roman Weinzoepfel is arrested on charges of assault, battery, and rape.

1843 –Evansville Trial ends in a hung jury.

1844-Second trial is held in Princeton, Indiana. Roman found guilty and sent to prison.

1845-February 25, Roman receives gubernatorial pardon. Roman joins Holy Cross Fathers at Notre Dame.

1846-Roman ordered to return to Diocese by Hailandière. He was then sent to serve the Evansville missions where he resided at St. Wendel rectory.

1847-Evansville incorporated as a city. James G. Jones elected first mayor. Roman's brother, Michael, immigrates to the United States and moves to St. Philip Indiana. St Philip's and St James Parishes dedicated.

1848- Hailandière's resignation accepted and he moves back to Brittany, France.

1849-Michael Weinzapfel marries Catherine Helfrich. Together they have twelve children, from whom most Weinzapfels in America trace their lineage.

1850-Monseigneur Abbé Augustine Martin named first bishop of the newly created Diocese of Natchitoches, Louisiana

1851-Holy Trinity, Evansville, completed.

1852 St. Meinrad Priory established by monks from Einsiedeln, Switzerland.

1856-Mother Theodore Guérin dies at St. Mary-of-the-Woods.

1858-Father Roman requests a new assignment from the bishop, thus leaving Southwestern Indiana and is reassigned to Southeastern Indiana. He serves as pastor of Saint Anthony parish in New Alsace, Ripley County, Indiana, and serves the mission parishes in both Ripley and Dearborn Counties.

1864-Father Anthony Deydier dies while in residence at St. Vincent's Parish in Vincennes.

1867-Knights of the Golden Circle formed in Tennessee (precursor to the Ku Klux Klan).

1873-Father Roman becomes a Benedictine monk at St. Meinrad Abbey in Spencer County, southern Indiana. Reverend Roman Weinzoepfel, O.S.B.

1875-Bishop Augustin Martin dies in Louisiana.

1881-Father Roman returns to Evansville to lay the cornerstone for St. Boniface Parish.

1882-In May, Bishop de la Hailandière died in France, but his will decreed that he be buried in the crypt of the Cathedral in Vincennes, Indiana. On 22 November his body was interred in the Cathedral crypt of Vincennes.

1890-Father Roman honored for fifty years of priesthood.

1895-11 November Roman Weinzoepfel, O.S.B., dies at Saint Meinrad Abbey.

About The Author

John William McMullen, a native of Vincennes, Indiana, holds a master's degree in Theological Studies from Saint Meinrad School of Theology. He is a Third Order Benedictine Oblate affiliated with Saint Meinrad Archabbey in Indiana and is a member of the Thomas More Society of Southwestern Indiana. He is a Theology Instructor at *Mater Dei* High School in Evansville, Indiana, and has authored various articles, assorted short stories, and is currently working on another novel. He resides in Evansville with his wife, Mary Grace, and their two sons, Andrew and Theodore.

Printed in the United States
16536LVS00001BB/3